Opposites Attract

"You're too good for me," he said, not even realizing he'd spoken the words out loud.

Jonni couldn't believe her ears. She didn't know much about men, but she didn't think this was standard procedure for Cameron.

She also didn't think talking would achieve much.

"Cameron," she whispered, lifting one hand to his cheek.

He made a deep sound in his throat, and she smiled.

His mouth found the smile and swallowed it, making it his. Jonni gasped and gave herself up to the sensation of his lips, hot and hungry on hers.

He broke away first, his breathing fast and shallow.

"Couldn't help myself," he said, a bit of a grin on his face. "I promise to behave."

Jonni almost pulled a pout. "You do?"

He laughed and pulled her close. "Yes, I do, because as you well know, I'm a notorious flirt and you are a lady who deserves to be treated as such."

"Of course," she said, starch in her voice, and then took his face in her hands.

Her kiss was wicked and naughty. Lifting her mouth from his, she said, "Now this is what I call being good."

Also by
Hailey North

TANGLED UP IN LOVE
DEAR LOVE DOCTOR
PERFECT MATCH
PILLOW TALK
BEDROOM EYES

HAILEY NORTH

Opposites
Attract

AVON BOOKS
An Imprint of HarperCollinsPublishers

This is a work of fiction. Names, characters, places, and incidents are products of the author's imagination or are used fictitiously and are not to be construed as real. Any resemblance to actual events, locales, organizations, or persons, living or dead, is entirely coincidental.

AVON BOOKS
An Imprint of HarperCollins*Publishers*
10 East 53rd Street
New York, New York 10022-5299

Copyright © 2003 by Nancy Wagner
ISBN: 0-380-82070-6
www.avonromance.com

First Avon Books paperback printing: June 2003

Avon Trademark Reg. U.S. Pat. Off. and in Other Countries, Marca Registrada, Hecho en U.S.A.
HarperCollins® is a registered trademark of HarperCollins Publishers Inc.

Printed in the U.S.A.

10 9 8 7 6 5 4 3 2

For David
"Quitting is not an option."

And for Snickers
October 15, 1992–November 21, 2002

Chapter One

Inside a New Orleans Garden District mansion

Jonquil "Jonni" DeVries had traveled on four continents, spent her Junior Year Abroad in Paris, and had not given a second thought to jetting to Manhattan for couture fashion shows.

She'd dined at chateaux in Provence and castles along the Rhine, and put in a dutiful appearance at her mother's Friday table at Galatoire's in her hometown of New Orleans.

Jonni had nibbled on Beluga's best, sampled the best satay Jakarta had to offer, and sipped the best champagnes France had ever corked.

But standing sock-footed in her kitchen, wrapped in a flannel bathrobe she'd found in a box set aside for the maid, Jonni knew she'd never ever tasted anything as delectable as the Cookie Dough Double Chocolate Chunk ice cream she spooned into her mouth at a pace that threatened to cramp her wrist.

She dipped her silver spoon crested with a scrolled

"D" into the softening butter-fat delight. The clock in her kitchen ticked loudly, and Jonni realized she hadn't been paying attention to anything save her need to eat. In the time she'd been standing there, sunlight had invited itself into the broad windows of the spacious kitchen. Soon, another day would be upon her. She sighed, and a hiccup followed.

Sugar, she knew, was good for putting a halt to hiccups. So she took another bite. And another.

"Mommy?"

Jonni froze. She shot a guilty glance into the almost empty ice cream carton and turned toward the sound of her daughter's voice.

"Morning, pumpkin. You're up with the mockingbirds." Jonni hated for Erika to see her when she wasn't at her best.

"I couldn't sleep." Erika rubbed one sturdy little hand across her forehead, looking far more world-weary than a five-year-old should.

Jonni slipped the carton onto the counter behind her. It tipped, and the spoon clattered onto the floor.

Erika jumped.

Jonni crossed the room quickly and gathered her into her arms. "Let's go back upstairs."

Erika shook her head and wrapped her arms around Jonni's hips. She tucked her head against Jonni's tummy, and Jonni knew there'd be no budging her. Once her daughter made up her mind, that was pretty much that.

So she stroked her tousled blond hair, long silky strands that mirrored Jonni's own equally disheveled mane, and balanced her weight against the edge of the doorframe. Soon Mrs. McLever, the no-nonsense nanny David had hired just before his death, would be downstairs, calling Erika to her morning duties. Mrs. McLever had impressed upon Jonni and David the importance of a disciplined routine in a child's life. David had wholeheartedly agreed, and of course Jonni concurred.

David was her husband, after all.

Still, Jonni had felt it was a shame for a child to miss out on the whims and joys of abandoned playfulness. She and her twin sister had pretty much enjoyed the run of their stately uptown home. Her mother had wanted to restrain them to the upper floor, but Daddy had always interceded. Children should be children, he'd said.

Jonni experienced a twinge of guilt as his words echoed in her head. She clasped her daughter's head to her tummy and wondered how in the world she was supposed to know enough to raise her child on her own.

A wave of anger at her dead husband swarmed up within her, and she almost blanched at the heat that flushed her body. Damn him, she thought, careful not to speak out loud. And then she caught control and said a quick prayer of repentance. Over a year had come and gone; surely she could learn to forgive and forget.

Erika twisted her head up toward Jonni's and then patted a hand against her hip. There was so much padding there now, fat that Jonni had never before carried in her life, that she felt the touch distantly. She closed her eyes.

"Mommy!"

"Yes?" She opened her eyes, wondering at Erika's excited tone.

Now she was tapping against the bulge below Jonni's waistline.

"Mommy, am I going to have a baby brother or sister?" Her face alight in a way Jonni hadn't seen it in quite some time, her little girl looked up at her, awaiting her answer.

For the second time that morning, Jonni froze. Glancing down at the rounded shape of her once perfect size six body, she swallowed. And for once, there wasn't food in her mouth.

There was pride, or what was left of her own ragged allotment.

"No, pumpkin," she said slowly, aiming for a cheerful tone and failing miserably. A tear had appeared in her eye, and she dabbed at it before it could splash onto Erika's eager, upturned face.

"There you are, Miss Erika," barked the voice of Mrs. McLever. "And why are you not upstairs brushing your teeth?"

Erika buried her head against Jonni again. "Good morning, Mrs. McLever," Jonni said. "Erika isn't there because she's here in the kitchen with me."

"That's not on her schedule, you know."

"What's wrong with a little bit of spontaneity?" Jonni was surprised to hear her voice saying those words. Her life—at least until her husband's sudden death—had been planned.

"That is not our arrangement," the nanny said, tucking her skinny arms across her chest and practically tapping the toe of her black lace-up shoes.

"Well, I don't like it," Jonni said, meeting Mrs. McLever's glower head on.

"It's what Mr. David and I agreed on, and I know he'd want his rules followed."

Jonni put her hands on Erika's shoulders and said, "Sweetie, why don't you go in the den and watch TV for a little bit. Mrs. McLever and I need to talk."

Erika glanced from her mother to her nanny.

"Do as your mother says," the older woman pronounced.

That did it for Jonni. As soon as Erika had cleared the room, she put her hands on her hips and said, "I am that child's mother. David is dead. And you, Mrs. McLever, are no longer her nanny."

"Whatever do you mean?" The woman had puffed up like the spiny fish Jonni used to poke at along the shorelines as a carefree child. Carefree—the way Erika should be.

"I'll pay you for the month but I want you to go upstairs and pack your things and leave." Jonni glanced around her kitchen. The sunlight brightened the room to a cheery glow, or perhaps it was lightened by the surge of strength she felt in firing the battle-ax.

"That child needs a firm hand. She's willful, and if you're not careful, you'll have a juvenile delinquent on your hands. Why, only yesterday I caught her in your room, and she'd broken off three of your lipsticks and was working on a fourth—"

"That's why she's avoiding you, isn't it?" Jonni advanced on the woman. "You did something you shouldn't have, didn't you? I told you I don't approve of spanking."

The woman sniffed. "I didn't lay a hand on your little darling. But I know what's good for that child better than you do. Why, you don't pay attention to anything that doesn't reach beyond the end of your fork or spoon."

"Get out!" Jonni jerked open the kitchen door.

Mrs. McLever shrugged and stalked to the door. "I wash my hands of the two of you. That child will turn out just like her mother."

"And what's wrong with that?!" Jonni was surprised how good it felt to yell. She never raised her voice. David had always liked how calm and quiet she was, and growing up, her sister had always been the rambunctious one.

The nanny raked her from head to toe with a true if-looks-could-kill expression, then swept from the room.

Jonni leaned against the counter, hands shaking. She took a few shallow breaths and spotted the carton of ice cream she'd abandoned earlier. Sunlight glinted off the silver spoon that lay on the kitchen floor. It sparkled and danced, and Jonni moved toward the cutlery drawer. She selected another spoon.

And stood there staring at it.

The ornate pattern had come down from David's family. The DeVries initials had been worked into the handles by a Parisian silversmith.

Jonni stretched out her arm and stared at the spoon, Mrs. McLever's harsh words echoing in her head, convicting her. The battle-ax was all wrong in her methods, but she had hit one emotional nail on a very sensitive head.

She studied the blurry reflection of her once-svelte body in the bowl of the spoon and stuck her tongue out at it. Before she could second-guess herself, Jonni swiveled, grabbed the ice cream carton, and dumped it into the trash compactor.

"And there you stay," she said, shaking the spoon at the trash.

Los Angeles International Airport

Cameron Scott signed an autograph for the first officer, accepted his carry-on suit bag with an appreciative smile from the one attendant who hadn't fawned over him during the flight, and headed into the terminal at LAX.

He blinked. Even from behind the dark shades he'd slipped on out of habit, the lights and noise of the massive space leaped out at him. No matter the time of day or night, there were people coming and going. It was like the tower of Babel, everybody speaking at once, in a flow of languages. Usually the energy excited him, but tonight he wished for a set of earplugs. He sure hoped Flynn showed up on time.

"Good buddy, over here!"

At the sound of Flynn's voice, Cameron swiveled his head. Just past the security doors, sure enough, there stood his friend and personal manager, his flaming red hair easily spotted even in the crowd. He waved with one arm. Cameron checked quickly to see if the other one was attached to one of Flynn's parade of bimbettes and was relieved to see his friend had taken seriously his request to show up alone. One never knew; Flynn was capable of appearing with a train of chicks in tow. Only thinking of his good buddy, of course.

Cameron smiled at that thought. Back in the days when he and Flynn had been penniless army private-first-class compatriots, Flynn had complained women never looked twice at him. Even without cash to flash, Cameron had never experienced a shortage of female companionship. And once he'd become Hollywood's hottest and sexiest box office bachelor . . . well, the rest was history.

Trouble was, Cameron had never found one he cared enough about to ask to stick around.

He was through the crowd now, standing beside Flynn, who tried to relieve him of his garment bag.

"I've got it," Cameron said.

Flynn shrugged. "I'm your man," he said, and clapped an arm around Cameron's shoulder briefly. "How was it?" The woeful expression on his friend's freckled face appeared to be that of a man inquiring about a funeral, even though the event in discussion was a wedding.

"Nice," Cameron said. "Is the car outside?"

"With your driver at the wheel, no doubt fending off the no-stopping-in-the-white-zone police," Flynn said.

Cameron grinned. "There are some benefits to being rich and famous."

"Some?" Flynn shook his head. "You're not coming down with something, are you? You're not yourself, man."

"True," Cameron said, halting in mid-stride just before he reached the exit doors. Looking around, he saw a couple with two kids dancing around them as they walked. He watched as a woman clung to the arm of a soldier in uniform as if she'd never let go. He noticed a white-haired woman hold out her arms to a baby being lifted toward her by a smiling man and woman.

"Let's go," he said, and walked on through the door, out toward the waiting limousine.

They were barely settled before Flynn had popped the cork on a bottle of Tattinger's best champagne.

Cameron accepted the glass his friend handed to him and watched as the bubbles drifted to the top and escaped into the air.

Flynn took a swig of his drink and scowled.

Cameron couldn't help but smile. Flynn hated champagne. "I don't know why you drink the stuff if you don't like it."

"Trying to cheer you up," he said. "Friends don't let friends get down in the dumps. You were fine when you left yesterday."

Leaning his head against the cool leather, Cameron said, "Ever wanted to be someone other than yourself?"

Flynn put his glass down on the limo's mini-bar. "Therapy costs extra, but no, the answer to that is no, but the most important question is why are *you* asking me that?"

Cameron shrugged. He wasn't sure he could put his feelings into words. "Maybe it was watching my baby sister get married. She had this look, I don't know how to describe it, but like she was walking on pillows stuffed with rose petals or some such nonsense." He took a drink. "But it wasn't just Melanie, it was her husband, too. Those two are nutty over each other."

"That's the way people who get married are supposed to be," Flynn said.

"So what's wrong with us?" There, Cameron had said it.

Flynn reached for his glass, a nervous grin on his face. "Good buddy, there's nothing wrong with you or me. We're different. Women are commodities. They give us what we want; we give them what they want. It's an exchange of needs."

"Hmm," Cameron said under his breath. "I guess you've never felt there was anything lacking in that formula?"

"And neither have you!" Flynn was looking pretty horrified. "At least not up until today. Did you meet someone special at the wedding?"

Cameron managed a laugh, though it was more of a sound of disgust. "I could have had any woman there I wanted. One of Melanie's bridesmaids went so far as to follow me into the men's room at the reception."

"How was she?" Flynn winked.

Cameron made a face. "Not worth talking about." And neither was this new feeling of missing out on something he wasn't sure he knew how to find. Flynn just didn't get it.

"Tell you what," his friend said, "if you really want to be someone other than who you are, I have a solution for you."

"Yeah?"

"You know that project I've been telling you about?"

"Oh, no," Cameron said. "I am an action hero. You're not going to get me into a cartoon."

"Quentin Grandy is directing. He says you're the man he wants for Mister Benjamin."

Cameron closed his eyes briefly and then reopened them. "N-O."

"N-O." Flynn refilled their glasses. "Funny you should say that. Principal photography is slated for New Orleans. N-O. Get it?" He laughed.

Cameron didn't. "Why do you want me to dress up like a butler and endure age makeup and some itchy wig and go to Louisiana in the hottest part of the year?"

Flynn pulled his wallet out of his pants and tapped it against his knees. "You've made me rich, good buddy," he said. "But I've made you even richer."

"True," Cameron said. No doubt he would have pissed all the millions away without Flynn, Mr. CPA-MBA, to manage his career and investments. But Cameron had always said yes or no to what films he did. So what they were all the same? The public loved him for it. Nobody expected a shoot-'em-up action hero to do anything but shoot 'em up, and get the girl, of course.

"So trust me on this one."

Cameron grinned. "You know what that means."

Flynn smiled. "Yeah, but this is me talking. You've had a string of box office successes. You're hot. But you've got to dig deeper. Show some range. And this film will create a whole new audience for you."

A knot of fear gripped his gut. "What's wrong with the one I've got?"

"They grow up. They have kids. This way their kids will be demanding to see Mister Benjamin. And the sequel potential is huge."

Cameron groaned. He carried his fear close to the chest. Nobody knew what he knew, not even Flynn. He wasn't an actor. He was a good-looking guy who'd gotten lucky.

"N-O spells ain't no way," he said.

"You said you wanted to be someone besides yourself," Flynn said, making it sound as if the entire discussion had been Cameron's idea.

"In life, not in the movies," Cameron said.

"Aha! Life imitates art."

"Don't you have that backward?"

Flynn stuck his wallet back into his pocket and leaned forward. "Know something?"

"What?"

"I think you're afraid."

Cameron lowered his glass. "What did you say?"

"I think you're afraid to play Mister Benjamin."

"I am not."

"Are too."

"Am not."

"Cameron Scott, chicken."

"Don't call me that," Cameron said.

The door to the limousine opened. His driver peered inside. "We're home, Mr. Scott."

Cameron hadn't even noticed that the car had stopped. "Give us a sec, Hoover." He waited till the car door shut, and then jabbed a finger toward his manager's smugly smiling face. "You think you can get me to say yes to this film by accusing me of being afraid to play something other than Cameron Scott, don't you?"

A look of understanding dawned on Flynn's face. Cameron realized, too late, that his friend had only been trying to push a button. He hadn't actually known Cameron feared his own lack of ability. Shit. He'd betrayed his own dirty secret. Now he'd have to do it.

"We start in less than a week," Flynn said, tipping his glass in a toast.

Cameron put his glass down on the bar, grabbed his garment bag, and reached for the handle of the door. "You were that sure I'd say yes?"

"Well, you always come through for your friends."

Cameron sat back down on the leather seat. "Are you telling me you already signed the contract even though I said no?"

"Yep."

"And what were you going to do if I didn't show up?"

Flynn grinned. "I think that's what lawyers call a moot point. Come on, Cameron, you'll end up thanking me before all is said and done."

"I ought to fire your ass," Cameron said, climbing out of the limo and looking up the façade of his Bel Air mansion. Lights burned softly in several windows, and the landscape illumination cast a warm glow all around. Inside, only his staff waited to attend to him. No wife waited. No children played. Well, hell, that's the way he'd always wanted it.

Flynn stepped out of the car. He clapped an arm around Cameron's shoulder and pointed toward the house. "Remember when we were so poor we dated girls who would feed us?"

Cameron nodded.

"And then I helped you get that first big break?"

He nodded again.

"Trust me on this one, too," Flynn said. "See you tomorrow. I'll bring over the script and the contracts."

The front door opened. His butler appeared, a silent silhouette.

Cameron tossed his garment bag over his shoulder. "New Orleans, you say?"

"Big Easy. Bourbon Street. Babes. Booze. Make you forget the funk you're in."

"Right." Cameron said. "It'll be good for me to get away." Perhaps a good dose of partying would cure what ailed him. He thanked his driver, waved good night to Flynn, and walked up the broad steps toward the front door of his house.

But as his butler said good evening and inquired about the wedding, Cameron reflected that what he needed was not another wild night, not another bevy of women, not another box office blow-out, not another Maserati, not even this mansion.

What he needed was a home.

Chapter Two

New Orleans
Audubon Park

"There's a line from a Chekhov play," Jonni said, pleased that she still had breath enough to speak after passing the half-mile point of the jogging trail, "that I keep meaning to look up."

"Chekhov? He's Russian, right?" Jonni's twin Daffodil James, better known as Daffy, moved easily, her gleaming blond hair pulled back into a ponytail that mirrored Jonni's. That was about the only thing still identical about them, Jonni thought, wondering for the zillionth time how she'd ever let herself fall into such sorry shape.

Jonni nodded, conserving her energy. Her running shoes were so new they glowed white in the dusky light. Her sister's, on the other hand—or perhaps she should say *foot*—were battered and dirty, supple from use.

"I recognize the name," Daffy said as they rounded the bend and began running parallel to Magazine Street.

"I think it starts with 'You can't go on weeping and wailing forever,' " Jonni got out, her delivery none too theatrical. And she couldn't continue putting one foot in front of the other at the pace her twin was setting. "Hold up," she said, drawing to a walk and grabbing her side with one hand.

Daffy slowed and said, "How do you keep all those lines in your head?"

Jonni shrugged. "It's only the opening line. I couldn't tell you whether it's from *The Cherry Orchard* or *Three Sisters* or *Uncle Vanya*."

"You've outdone me, just knowing those titles," her sister said, then added, "I take it you're rejoining the world?" Daffy, in her usual frank way, blurted out the obvious question, the question most of her friends and family had been tiptoeing around for the past year.

"I'm working on myself," Jonni said, unwilling to go further than that.

"Well, I have a great idea," Daffy said. "I heard at the paper this week that there's a production company looking for a New Orleans location, specifically, a Garden District historic mansion."

Jonni blew out another hard breath and wished for a fleeting moment that she hadn't brought her sister in on the secret of her renewal program plans. Daffy wasn't one to sit by in silence and watch. "What's that got to do with me joining Weight Watchers?"

Daffy paused and performed a hamstring stretch. "You've been so isolated. You'd have a house full of people, and besides, it's a children's film. Erika would love it."

"Oh," Jonni said. Since she'd given Mrs. McLever the

boot, Erika had seemed happier, but she'd not been the same carefree little girl she'd been before her father's death. "What would I have to do?"

"Sit back and collect a big fat check and watch people film a movie."

"I don't need money," Jonni said, somewhat wistfully. If she did, she might have some reason to get up in the morning and go to some job that would give her purpose.

"Well, at least David did one thing right," Daffy said, none too sweetly.

"You never liked him, did you?"

"Nope. But that doesn't matter now," Daffy said. "What I always want is your happiness, and if he made you happy, good. If not, well—" She made two fists and charged at the air in front of her.

"I wonder what people who aren't twins do?"

Daffy smiled and said, "So I can call the film people and set it up?"

"You said it's a children's movie?"

"*Mister Benjamin.*"

"Oh!" Jonni brightened. "Erika loves *Mister Benjamin.* She'll be dancing on her head."

"So what happens in that play?" Daffy asked, picking up their pace to a walk that had more in common with a jog than a stroll around the egret nesting grounds that ran alongside the Audubon Park trail.

"I don't remember," Jonni said. "But I don't think it matters. Just that one line is enough."

"You were always the smart one," Daffy said.

"Right." That's why she'd dropped out of college, too much in love with David, or possibly in awe of him, to wait to marry. But she'd planned her life, knowing she wanted more than anything to be a wife and mother. And she'd been perfect at the role.

For all the good it had done her.

She stumbled on a rock and caught herself. Seeing the concerned look her twin shot in her direction, she shook her head, not wanting her sister to hover too closely. If she was going to bring herself around, she'd make a plan and follow it, on her own. To Jonni's way of thinking, nothing good happened by accident.

"So I can have the production company people meet with you?" This time it was Daffy who slowed down, to tie a shoelace that had worked its way loose.

Something about the casual way she asked the question put Jonni on alert. She stopped and planted her hands on her hips, feeling far more cushioning there than she liked. "Have you already set this thing in motion?"

The innocent expression on Daffy's face might have fooled a hundred passersby, but it only confirmed Jonni's suspicions. "What's the date and time you've already arranged?"

"Now, why do you think I'd do that without checking with you first?" Daffy rose from tying her shoe. "Let's walk," she said, and veered from the paved path toward the water that lay to their left. A squirrel shot across the grass in front of them, and a few yards ahead a bevy of ducks gazed expectantly at them.

Jonni pulled a plastic bag of stale Ritz crackers from the fanny pack she wore. She tossed one toward the closest duck, and the rest of the clutch waddled toward her. She hated to admit it, but sometime over the past twelve months, she'd started to move in pretty much the same side-to-side fashion. Gosh, but it was a good thing that mean old Mrs. McLever had made fun of her or she'd still be building the girth she carried, rather than taking the first tentative steps toward melting it off.

"Always prepared, aren't you?" Daffy said, rather fondly.

Jonni shrugged and tossed a few more crackers toward the squawking birds. "It's one of those traits we share, isn't it?"

Daffy nodded, a smile on her face. "You're right, and yes, I did tell the production company people I was sure you'd love to talk to them. How's tomorrow morning at ten?"

"Let me check my Day-Timer," Jonni said, somewhat dryly. "So these people move in, take over my house, haul in cameras and lights and move my furniture hither and thither, and I'm supposed to be thrilled?"

"People are good for you," Daffy said, somewhat lightly.

"There's only so much I can take, even now," Jonni said, tossing the last cracker to the one duck who'd yet to fight its way to the front of the crowd. "A house full of people, I don't know, but for Erika, I'll do it."

"You'll be glad," Daffy said. "Just wait and see. And I'll come tomorrow, if you want me to."

Jonni folded the plastic bag she'd stuffed full of crackers and regarded it silently. Daffy, even though she was the younger twin by all of fifteen minutes, had always been blessed with a vibrance and resilience Jonni had never felt she herself possessed. But one thing had come clearer and clearer to her in the year since her husband had died. She needed to learn to stand on her own two feet, her own ten toes.

"Thanks," she said, poking the bag into her fanny pack. "I can handle it."

By Monday morning at ten o'clock, the last thing on Jonni's mind was some film company wanting to turn her house topsy-turvy. Besides, they'd have to take a number and stand in line to vie for that honor.

The pizza Erika had eaten for dinner the night before had definitely not agreed with her. Jonni had been up with her daughter most of the night, as had Mrs. McLever's replacement, Mrs. Betty, a more amiable version of the sort of old-fashioned nanny David had favored. By five A.M. Erika had fallen asleep and Mrs. Betty had succumbed to chest pains and been rushed to the hospital. Jonni notified Mrs. Betty's family and collapsed on the spare twin bed in Erika's room.

The incessant ringing interfered with her deep need for sleep. Jonni slapped at her alarm clock, only to realize she wasn't in her own bed. Tugging the pillow away from her face, she sat up and gazed around, blinking and rubbing her eyes.

The chiming continued. With a start, she realized it was her doorbell.

"Hold your horses," she muttered, wondering who wanted to talk to her so badly they'd make that much racket. Surely any wandering proselytizers or politicians canvassing the neighborhood would have simply tucked their literature into the door and sought more receptive territory.

Still dressed in the crumpled khaki capris and faded

Rock N Bowl T-shirt from the night before, Jonni tugged her hair away from her face and padded barefoot down the winding front staircase and across the cool cypress planking of the foyer.

She swung open the heavy door and blinked at the sunlight framing five men and women, all dressed in black and sporting dark glasses and sleek hair.

Her mouth fell open, and then her breeding came to her rescue. Holding her chin—no doubt specked from last night's disasters—high, she said in her best voice, "May I help you?"

The taller of the two men lifted his glasses from his nose and stepped forward. "We're here to meet with Mrs. DeVries."

"Oh."

"We're the advance scouting team from MegaFilms. I'm Boswell Crane."

Jonni motioned toward the house. "Won't you come in?"

Boswell gave a swift nod with his sharp-edged chin, and the troops behind him followed his signal. They swept into the foyer, and Jonni stood in the doorway for a long moment, contrasting her sorry appearance with this gaggle of polished professionals. And they were all so young.

"Is Mrs. DeVries expecting us?" Boswell asked, gazing around the foyer, no doubt calculating whatever it was location scouts calculated.

"Well, she was," Jonni said, "but a few things came up and the appointment slipped her mind."

"Oh, dear," Boswell said, tapping the onyx and silver watch that dominated his slender right wrist. "We are on such a schedule. I don't suppose you could just show us around and we could send the paperwork over by messenger?"

Jonni almost giggled. But the idea of pretending to be someone other than the lady of the manor appealed to her, especially when she looked such a mess that this clean team never once suspected she was Mrs. DeVries. "I'm sure she wouldn't mind. She pretty much lets me treat her house as my own."

"*Mi casa, su casa,*" Boswell said, rather archly, and snapped his fingers. One of the women produced a tape measure and another opened what looked like a clipboard but Jonni realized was a razor-thin computer.

"We'll need formal rooms," Boswell continued. "Parlor, dining room, oh, and butler's pantry." He swung round, one hand to his temple. "The house does have a butler's pantry?"

Jonni almost arched a brow in response, but restrained herself, stifling what might have been a giggle, only she hadn't laughed in so long she realized it must be only one more sign of sheer exhaustion. "Mrs. DeVries would never accept a house without one," she said.

"The parlor first," Boswell said.

Jonni wasn't sure what a location person should be like, but somehow Boswell was the antithesis of any image she could have conjured. He reminded her of the gaunt young men and women dressed in black she saw hanging out in front of the John Jay hair salon on upper St. Charles, inhaling a few quick puffs between clients. But he did seem to have his team well in control. He had only to nod or incline his pointy chin, and one of his assistants scrambled to take a measurement or photo on a very high-tech looking digital camera.

Boswell approved of the front parlor. He tch-tched over the dining room, complaining about the lack of natural light but giving credit where credit was due for the massive eighteenth-century chandelier that dominated the table that seated eighteen.

"We'll just need the downstairs," he said, "so should the family and staff wish to remain in residence, that shouldn't be a problem."

"*Should* they?" Jonni narrowed her eyes. Daffy hadn't said anything about her having to move out. As a matter of fact, she'd indicated it would be helpful for Jonni to have a swarm of people cluttering her quiet life.

Boswell shrugged. "Different strokes for different folks," he said. "Some people are star-struck and wouldn't budge. They are just dying to tell their friends all about their brush with Hollywood." He waved a languid hand and said in an awe-stricken aside to his male colleague, "Would you just look at that Egyptian piece. That must be from King Tut's tomb."

David had been fiercely proud of his antiquities collection. Jonni had dutifully admired the bits and pieces of pottery he called shards, appreciated the statuettes of cats and men with funny beards, and attempted to follow his convoluted descriptions of New Kingdom and Old Kingdom, but she'd never enjoyed the subject.

She had, however, been a diligent pupil. Tapping her bare foot against the crimson and gold carpet of the parlor, she said, "That piece predates Tutankhamen by approximately four hundred years."

Boswell turned his head. "My, my," he said, "you are full of surprises, aren't you?"

Jonni gave him a tight-lipped smile. "I'm not so sure Mrs. DeVries is chomping at the bit to have anything to do with Hollywood," she said.

"Now, dahling," Boswell said, approaching and putting a hand out to touch her forearm, "please don't go setting her up against us. This house is perfect. PERFECT. And if there's any hesitation on your employer's part and you can be helpful in persuading her, I'll be more than happy to reward you for your cooperation."

Jonni crossed her arms over a stain she'd spotted on her Rock N Bowl T-shirt. Dryly, she said, "I'll see what I can do."

"Oh, goodie," Boswell said. "It's not every day I get to work on a film with Cameron Scott, and when I see a setting that will so define him, I simply can't contain myself."

"And who is Cameron Scott?"

Boswell and his four assistants gasped in unison. One even held a hand over her heart.

Jonni glanced from one young, unlined face to the next.

The youngest-looking of the three women said, "Cameron is Elvis on velvet."

The woman next to her said, "Cameron is the gods' response to what's left unanswered within the feminine within."

The third woman said, "Cameron is the kind of man who'd make even a spinster want to snap open his Levi's 501s and bury her face."

"I see," Jonni said. "I thought this movie was about a children's cartoon character."

Boswell was studying her closely, and he seemed to re-alize his group of flunkies had traveled the wrong way down a one-way street. "Dahling," he said, "I may call you that, may I not—dahling, this film is a children's ca-per. Quite innocent, quite bright. Cameron Scott is grac-ing it with his star presence, but that in no way, despite what these silly girls have been saying, detracts from its innocence, its joie de vivre." He waved a hand in a spi-raling flip and gave her a sweet smile. "We've seen what we need to see. I'll have the office messenger over the contracts." He bent over her hand, only for a fleeting moment, and said, "Do let what I said about Cameron Scott be our little secret. That's hush-hush." He then backed his group toward the foyer. "We'll be in touch," he said.

Jonni flipped a hand toward their departing back-sides. "Do, dahling," she muttered, and locked the door behind them. She could care less about Boswell's fascina-tion with a man who must be quite stuck on himself if so many people idolized him. She had half a mind to tell them they could go find someplace else to film, but the diversion had entertained her.

"Better than wiping up puke," she said.

The ornate gold-framed mirror in the foyer glittered in the morning sunlight pouring through the glass in the front door. She turned and stared in horror at her reflec-tion. Every hair on her head stood on end or poked side-ways. She wore no makeup, unless you counted the smear of mascara beneath her left eye as such. Her lips were bloodless, her clothing a disgrace.

Her twin thought it would be healthy for her to have

other people around. Well, so it might be, if it didn't scare them all to death. She wondered, fleetingly, what type of woman the all-too-adored Cameron Scott preferred.

No doubt he had his pick of the litter.

Not that that had anything to do with her. She'd married and been widowed. Her life consisted of her daughter, and for that reason, she'd gotten a grip on her downward spiral.

Other men weren't in her plans.

And plans were something Jonni took seriously.

Chapter Three

Cameron's Bel Air estate

"... seven, eight, nine ... check your breath ... ten."

Cameron found the surge he needed within his legs and back and shoulders and completed the tenth rep of the power squat lift. Lowering the barbell to its resting position, he flashed a grin at Heather and Robby, his team of personal trainers. "Thought I'd gone soft on you?"

Heather flashed the sweet smile that had first brought her to Cameron's notice. No matter how cranky Cameron got, Heather never lost patience with him or raised her voice.

A woman like that, Cameron thought, could make a man happy. Hell, she did make a man happy. She and Robby had been married for five years. They'd been supervising Cameron's workouts for almost that long.

"Soft!" It was Robby, with his booming voice, who answered. "That's what you're supposed to be doing, according to what Mr. Lawrence has been telling us. He says you won't get it in your head to act like an old man as long as your body is in great shape. We're likely to get fired if he finds us here in your gym putting you through your paces."

Cameron wiped the sweat from his brow. He'd done an hour of weights and five miles on the treadmill and it wasn't even nine A.M. "You work for me," he said. "Besides, I'm an actor. A professional. Playing some old geezer is no challenge to Cameron Scott." Even as he said the words, he knew his bravado was phony. He was scared to death of the role.

"I'm sure that's true—as true as it is that it's Mr. Lawrence who writes the checks," Robby said, with a wink. "He told us yesterday we might as well plan a long vacation while you're in New Orleans."

"My good buddy Flynn can just butt out of my business," Cameron said. He faced one of the mirrored walls of the gym he'd had built into one of the guesthouses on his Bel Air estate. It wasn't the favored locale of the hot new stars, but Cameron liked it for its country feel. Sometimes he could almost pretend the rest of the city wasn't right outside those gates, pressing in on him, crowning him with fame that, along with its pluses, threatened his right to stroll the streets.

Besides, Cameron wasn't some star of the moment, some flash in the pan of the klieg lights. He'd proved himself, film after film. He was, as hard it was for him to realize even still, mainstream Hollywood. But you were only as good as your last film. His last movie had opened top of the money lists on Memorial Day weekend, and he had one in the can set to roll on Labor Day weekend.

Action flicks, sexy as Bond, with as many special fight scene effects as anything Wesley Snipes had ever seen or done, and brains, too, like the Terminator pics.

He had his choice of scripts, but he had to admit they were all starting to look the same. There were only so many times one could reinvent Macho Force Man.

"Cameron?" Heather's gentle voice intruded on his thoughts, and Cameron brought himself back to the moment. He flexed his pecs, aped a Jack LaLanne pose, and said, "You called, dear?"

Heather laughed. "Time to stretch."

Cameron groaned. "Hate that part."

"Because you spent too many years ignoring it," Robby said. "Anyway, are we supposed to take a long vacation?"

"Hell, no," Cameron roared, reacting as much to the question as Heather's motioned instructions that had him sympathizing with a pretzel.

"Well, well, what have we here?"

The gym door swung shut with a snap and Cameron lifted his head from where he lay on the floor, right knee to left. "Flynn, who the hell let you in?"

Flynn, spiffy as ever in a lightweight wool charcoal suit, flipped him the bird. "Stretching, I see. That's good, but don't get too supple. Mister Benjamin is an old man, very old. And he walks with a cane."

Robby stifled a grin, and Heather nodded, all seriousness. "Good morning, Mr. Lawrence. Are you coming for a session?"

"You talked me into that once," Flynn said. "You know I hate exercise. I could use a steam and a massage, though."

"Forget it," Cameron said. "I know you're up to something. Spill your guts now."

Flynn rolled his eyes. "The abuse I take."

Cameron tossed a hand towel in his friend's direction. All that abuse, which included 25 percent of Cameron's earned income, had made his friend not only wealthy, but a sought-after personal manager in the film world. "It's a damn good thing you saved my life."

Flynn shot his cuffs and flicked a hint of a dust speck from his sleeve. "I am here to ensure you make your plane to New Orleans."

"That's not till the day after tomorrow."

Flynn nodded. "As I said."

"You don't think I wouldn't go."

His manager remained silent, studying his reflection.

Heather made a rolling motion with her hand, and Cameron shifted onto his stomach. He lifted his legs and torso at the same time and held the lift till Heather tapped him on the back.

"You're supposed to have been minimizing your power workouts, shrinking into Mister Benjamin," Flynn said, "and judging by the level of cooperation I witness here, it's a good thing I did arrive ahead of time."

"Not all old people shrivel up and die," Cameron said, grunting between stretches. "I don't intend to. Besides, I have a different vision of this character."

"I'll let you and Quentin Grandy work out any vision issues," Flynn said, rather dryly.

"Yeah, right," Cameron said. He might be Mr. Box Office Star, but Grandy's directorial style never left an actor in doubt as to who was in charge. And it wasn't any member of the Screen Actors Guild.

"I think it's wonderful you're doing the *Mister Benjamin* film," Heather said.

"Why's that?" Cameron rolled onto his back. He respected Heather's opinions. She had a master's degree in physical therapy and a massage therapist license, and had run the New York marathon five times.

"Our daughter loves the cartoon. It teaches her that there are no limits to imagination, that good will triumph over evil, and that she should never give up in achieving that goal."

"Beautifully stated," Flynn said, applauding.

"Hmph," Cameron said. This paragon of virtue was the role he had to make believable? "That's touching. Are we done here?"

Heather nodded. Robby was busy stacking weights back onto the racks. Cameron leaped up, his nervous tension translating into hunger. "You guys make sure you're packed and in New Orleans by the day after tomorrow. You know I can't function without you."

They nodded, but Cameron noticed they glanced sideways at Flynn.

"Yeah, yeah, he has to stay flexible," his manager said. "Not to mention the benefits of massage. After all, you have to be on your best behavior during this production, and the Big Easy isn't exactly the best place to encourage that miracle."

"Best behavior?" Cameron grinned. "Oh, yeah, baby, bring on Bourbon Street!" He needed the distraction. Ever since Melanie's wedding, he'd not only been hit between the eyes with how empty his life was, but hadn't come up with any ideas on how to change things for the better.

Flynn grinned. "Now that's the Cameron I know. And speaking of which," he continued, "this might be the time to explain one peculiar clause in your contract that MegaFilms was most insistent on. I didn't think you'd mind, since this is a children's film, so I agreed to it. And we've also kept the lid on announcing you're playing the title role. 'All in good time,' Quentin says."

Cameron narrowed his eyes. Quentin Grandy was no fool. Frankly, Cameron wouldn't mind if no one ever knew whose face was behind all that age makeup. "You're my manager. I'm sure you wouldn't sign me to anything that was not in my best interests."

Flynn actually snorted. It might have been a chuckle, but it sure as hell turned into a snort of laughter.

"Something you're not telling me, buddy?" Cameron asked.

"It's a rather unusual morals clause," Flynn said.

"Morals clause!" Cameron spit out the words as if they were ants dancing on his tongue. "You've got to be kidding!"

Flynn screwed up his face, and Cameron wondered if his friend was thinking he was about to give him the boot.

Other jerks would have done exactly that.

But Cameron, no matter what his faults might be, was not a jerk. He tucked an arm around Flynn's scrawny neck and pulled him toward the door. "Catch you later," he said over his shoulder to Heather and Robby, and guided his personal manager out of the gym and along the path that ran back to the big house, all the time keeping him in a firm neck lock.

An hour later, Cameron still couldn't believe what Flynn had told him.

He poured them both another round of martinis and slumped back on the sofa overlooking the valley beneath his glassed-in deck. He hated the glass, but he hadn't settled on a contractor to remove it and open up the view to the cool evening air. "So you're telling me that if I fornicate with any member of the crew, cast, extras, or anyone in any way connected with the production of *Mister Benjamin* or land my butt in jail, I forfeit five hundred thousand dollars of my four-million-dollar deal?"

Flynn folded and refolded his cocktail napkin and nodded his head, not for the first time that morning. "Do you think I could have some bacon and eggs?"

Cameron crossed to the intercom and summoned the butler.

Flynn smiled, somewhat weakly.

Cameron grinned, but covered it with his hand. Flynn Lawrence had never been able to put one over on him, not during basic training, or through the rigors of their early days in Hollywood, when daily food intake had consisted of hot dogs or whatever food one or another of their girlfriends-of-the-moment produced for dinner.

Nah, Cameron was tougher. And he mixed a mean martini.

A silver-haired gentleman's gentleman appeared in the doorway. "You called, sir?"

Flynn grabbed his gut and laughed.

Cameron swung around. Well, he'd intended to get Flynn drunk, so he supposed he'd have to take him the way he'd made him.

"It's you," Flynn said, slapping his thigh and gasping for breath. "Mister Benjamin!"

Cameron looked from his clearly inebriated manager to his butler. "As you well know, Grimsley in no way resembles me," he said. "However, Grimsley, Mr. Lawrence desires a hearty breakfast of bacon and eggs." He paused, studied his still-guffawing friend, and added, "Over easy, with buttered toast."

"Quite so," Grimsley said. "And for you, sir?"

Cameron laughed and tipped his glass. "I'll be my own chef," he said, rising and lumbering toward the bar, where he emptied the martini shaker into his glass. Frowning, he turned to observe his buddy and realized that even though Flynn was laughing like an idiot, he didn't seem half as drunk as he should.

The rare orchid showcased in a Ming vase on a table next to where Flynn lolled on a Biedermeier chair, however, was drooping.

"Did you dump your drink into that plant?" Cameron advanced on Flynn, wielding his glass and the empty martini shaker.

Flynn hiccupped and smiled. "Nah," he said, "I didn't need to. I can hold my own better than you ever could."

"Is that so?" Cameron leaned backward, observing his friend. Unable to determine whether Flynn was simply baiting him, or sincerely desired to stick by his side to make sure he made it to New Orleans, he did the one thing he felt was safe. He drained his glass and sank to the sofa next to Flynn's chair. "Tell Grimsley," Cameron said sleepily, "that I'd like my eggs scrambled."

He could have sworn he heard Flynn laugh.

A hearty, chortling sort of laugh.

Cameron drew himself up and stood. With great dignity, he said, "Enjoy your breakfast. I am going to my room now."

"Yeah, right," Flynn said. "Tell you what. You sit down, and I'll quit trying to ride you and you can quit trying to outsmart me."

Cameron dropped to the sofa and pummeled his friend's leg. "Good buddy," he said. "You know I'm going to New Orleans. I gave my word."

Flynn nodded. "And nothing is more sacred."

"You got that right," Cameron said. "But I sure as hell wish you hadn't done something so stupid as to commit me to a morals clause."

"Think of it as eating nine helpings of vegetables a day," Flynn said, then went off in a peal of laughter. "I mean, it's good for you. New Orleans can be a dangerous place, and the last thing you want to do is go out partying and pick up the wrong person, not to mention the wrong microbes."

"Thanks for your advice, pops," Cameron said. "I'll be sure to be on my best behavior." He started to rise, then thought better of moving. "Am I really such an animal that the studio thought that clause was necessary?"

Flynn raised his brows. "I think we both know the answer to that one."

New Orleans, Garden District

Jonni closed the front door on the departing backside of the latest in a string of nanny applicants. Mrs. Betty, though recovering, had announced her retirement, repeating three times how exhausting she'd found that precious little Erika.

She climbed the wide front staircase, smoothing a hand over the banister and reminding herself to count her blessings. "You have a beautiful house," she said aloud, pausing to gaze toward the foyer below. Sunlight slanted through the glass inset of the front door. But rather than seeing the light, Jonni saw the small opening and felt more like a prisoner peering out of her cell.

"Idiot," she said, slapping her cheek lightly and continuing up the stairs. David's office overlooked the back of the second level. In the year since he'd been dead, she'd entered the room only once, to accompany the estate lawyers. Now she'd have to do so again, to search for a file he'd mentioned on nanny applicants.

She pushed open the door. The room should have been full of the cheery light filtered through the leafy trees of the back garden, but the heavy drapes blocked the wall of windows. David had preferred the room that way.

Jonni regarded the lifeless room. Without really thinking about the action, she strode across the room, past the mahogany partner's desk and leather chair and the wall of bookcases. She tugged on the curtain pull. A riffle of dust filled the air, and Jonni sneezed once, twice, three times. Evidently Sunny, her housekeeper, also avoided David's office.

Something jammed across the top of the drapery.

Jonni yanked but the curtains parted only a few inches. She'd intended to find the nanny file and slip out but now she was on a mission. Backing from the window, she lifted the bottom of the drape and angled it outward and then pulled.

"Darn it," she muttered, when the only result was more dust released into the air. Sneezing and dabbing at her nose, she backed from the room and headed downstairs and into the butler's pantry, where she kept a high step stool.

Armed with that, she approached the curtains again, mounted the stool, and reached for the hooks that held the drapes. Given the height of the windows and her own five-four frame, an impressive gap still existed between her fingertips and the top of the window.

"Leave it alone," she told herself. "Let someone else handle this."

That voice might as well have belonged to someone else. For whatever reason, those heavy drawn drapes stood between Jonni and satisfaction for the need to fill the room with sunlight and fresh air. She'd always hated the way David hunkered down in this dungeon of a room. He hadn't been that way at first, of course. But by the time they'd purchased this museum of a house, he spent at least ten hours a day at his law firm. Then he often retreated to this room after eating a late dinner, dinner Jonni kept warm and waiting for him until such time as he appeared, briefcase in hand, tie as tight and crisp as it had been when he'd left the house that morning.

This cloistered room represented the chasm that had grown between them. To the rest of the world, she and David had appeared the perfect couple. Inside the elegant walls of this house that was more mansion than home, Jonni had known the truth of that image, and she had conspired with David to ignore that truth.

A cry began building within Jonni, a shout that rumbled from deep within her abdomen, rising through her lungs, gathering strength and intensity.

"Eee-yiy-aye!" she yelled, heaving with all her might at the heavy curtains.

The drapes gave way, the weight of them tumbling her off the step stool and onto the carpet. She rolled, half buried and half cushioned by the velvet mass, laughing.

She was still giggling when someone knocked at the door. "Miz Jonni, you're hurt!"

It was her housekeeper, concern on her broad face.

"Oh, no, Sunny," Jonni said, wiping at her eyes and rising from the welter of fabric. She sneezed and then sneezed again and said, "I don't know when I've felt better."

The portly woman gave her a sideways look. "If you say so." She approached the mess, muttering under her breath. "I don't know how these could have fallen."

"It's what lawyers call an act of God," Jonni said. "Let's just get them hauled away."

"Yes, ma'am."

Jonni heard the disapproval in her housekeeper's voice. But as fond as she was of Sunny, Jonni didn't care. David was gone. Now David's drapery had been vanquished.

She marched to the desk and pulled open a file drawer. Just as she remembered from the time she'd looked through it with the estate lawyer, the files were neatly labeled, arranged alphabetically, with the precise plastic tabs cascading from left to right from front to back of the drawer. Jonni realized, with a start, that she didn't know whether David had done the work himself or had his secretary at the firm do it for him. He certainly had never asked Jonni for her assistance.

Not in his office, anyway. No, David's idea of the perfect wife was someone who kept herself fit and beautifully clothed, managed the staff, and hosted tasteful dinner parties. And graciously received the once-weekly sex he performed, almost to schedule. He'd been disappointed when Jonni presented him with a daughter, but he'd still gifted her with a diamond bracelet on the occasion.

A son, Jonni had thought before chasing the thought from her ungrateful mind, no doubt would have merited a tiara.

Snapping back to the moment, Jonni flipped past Household Accounts (including subfiles for Cable, Entergy, Sewerage & Water Board), past Resumes—David Current (had her husband been considering a job change and she'd not known it?), to Resumes—Nanny Applicants. Well, as things turned out, it was Jonni who should have been considering a job change all along. For all her efforts to please David, it had come to naught.

Ignoring Sunny, who was producing many heavy sighs as she removed the drapes, Jonni drew out the two manila folders from the Nanny file. They were labeled Interview and Reject.

An image of Mrs. McLever's dour face rose in her mind, and Jonni shoved the Interview folder back into the drawer.

The Reject folder she carried out of the room.

Chapter Four

New Orleans
Vincent's Restaurant
One interminable evening

Matthew Howell polished off his second glass of Chianti and winked at Jonni over the rims of his bifocals.

Ignoring the gesture, Jonni toyed with her salad, counting the minutes until she could escape this date from hell. What had her mother been thinking?

"I've known your father for years," Matthew was saying, speaking in a voice that sounded as if he were holding two fingers pinched against his nostrils. "I can't understand why we've never met. I've been handling the accounting projects for your father's firm and clients since I became managing partner of Howell and Associates."

"I see," Jonni said. "And how long have you known my mother?"

"I don't believe we've ever met." He waved an arm at

a waiter and lifted his glass. "Drink up there. You're falling behind."

"I'm fine," Jonni said, and almost choked on the expression. Well, at least she could forgive her mother. She'd probably assumed Matthew Howell was respectable.

Which he was, in terms of money and education. He had an MBA and was a CPA. He probably pulled in a hefty six-figure salary. She'd already heard all about his house in Lakeview and the boat he kept at the marina in Bucktown. He'd yet to ask her one question about herself.

"As I was saying," Matthew went on, but Jonni tuned him out. The waiter removed the salad plates, brought the bottle of wine Matthew had ordered to accompany their plates of blackened redfish and sides of pasta, and then returned with the entrees.

All the while he talked and Jonni nodded. She'd lost her appetite. At that thought she grinned, and Matthew spoke even more earnestly. Perhaps she'd discovered the secret to her weight-loss program.

Nah, she'd rather have her jaws wired shut than go out on another date with this guy.

"What the big eight firms did wrong was to let themselves believe in their own invincibility. They grew and grew and raced to gobble up the competition. Meanwhile, they weren't minding the store." Matthew finished the last bite of his fettuccine and mopped at the sauce with a chunk of bread. "My, but aren't you a dainty eater."

Jonni produced a faint smile. "Yes."

"You don't talk much, but you're mighty pretty," he said, brushing her knee under the table with his own.

Jonni jerked and hit the table leg with her knee. "Ouch," she said.

He patted her hand on the table and then rather than removing his hand, left it there. A smear of his pasta sauce dampened her skin. Jonni rose and said, "Excuse me. I have to go to the ladies' room."

He winked and she gathered her purse and walked as quickly as possible around the tables crowded together. She didn't know what she was going to do, but she wasn't going back to that table. She didn't want to embarrass her father with a professional colleague, but the guy worked for her father's firm. If he wanted their business, he'd get over the rejection.

Inside the rest room, she fished her cell phone from her purse and dialed her house. Thank God she'd hired that new nanny. Isolde, one of David's rejected applicants, would get a kick out of the assignment she was about to receive.

Jonni made a face, thinking what a fuss either Mrs. McLever or Mrs. Betty would have made. One would have refused; the other probably would have complained of shortness of breath.

Isolde answered on the first ring. Sure, she was more than happy to fire up her Jeep and haul butt to Jonni's rescue. Laughter in her voice, she assured Jonni that she and Erika would be right there.

Impending escape gave Jonni the strength to face her date once again. She applied fresh lipstick, studying her eyes as she did so. They stared back at her, so serious, so flat, so unlike the way she used to think she looked.

She'd planned her life so carefully, seeking even during college the refuge of a carefully selected husband. She'd found and married a man who formed a blanket around her world. Yet even within those safe confines, there had been moments when she'd envied her twin for her free-wheeling, independent, and frequently hair-raising ways. While Daffy had played the madcap, Jonni had taken on the cloak of the matron.

But what role was she to play now? Skulking in the ladies' room, avoiding dates provided by well-intentioned family and friends? Jonni sighed and snapped her lipstick case shut. Tonight all she wanted to do was retreat to her kitchen and indulge in Cookie Dough Double Chocolate Chunk ice cream.

"There you are," Matthew said as she approached. He half rose from the table, but that gesture made him look even shorter than he was. At five feet four, Jonni rarely found herself looking down at a man, but the view the accountant afforded her at the moment gave her more than she wanted to see of the top of his thinning black hair. "Funny, but I was starting to wonder if you were coming back."

"Now why would you think that?" Jonni took her seat, counting silently the moments it would be until Isolde appeared with her five-year-old charge.

He pushed his spectacles up on his squat nose. "You do seem a little on the shy side," he said, once again producing one of his annoying winks.

"I am quiet," Jonni said.

"There, you did it," he said, flashing a grin. "Managed an entire sentence." He shook his head and once again reached for her hand. This time she was quicker and dropped it into her lap before he could touch her. "Of course, after burying one husband, I guess a girl can get kind of spooked."

"Excuse me?"

"It's statistical," he said. "Kill off one man, might happen again."

Now Jonni truly was speechless. "I did not kill my husband," she said.

"Of course not," Matthew said, in the sort of voice a nursing assistant might use in speaking to an unruly patient in a convalescent home. "But men like David De-Vries don't just drive off the Causeway without some compelling reason."

"My husband did not drive off the bridge," Jonni said, eyeing the glass of water the waiter had left and wondering whether she should fling it at this insufferable man. "He had an auto accident."

Matthew sighed. "Take my advice and put it from your mind. If men like me are willing to overlook your situation, then hey"—he winked and Jonni almost screamed—"what's to worry about?"

Jonni pushed back her chair. It tilted and hit the floor. The diners at the next table, an older man and woman who looked as if Jonni and Matthew's conversation was the most interesting thing they'd listened to in a month of Sundays, abruptly bent their heads to their plates.

A waiter sidled over.

"Mommy!! Mommy!!" Jonni turned to see her daughter skipping between the tables.

"Erika, sweetheart, what a nice surprise!" Jonni moved eagerly toward her and lifted her high above her head.

Isolde, her hair a fascinating array of purply-black spikes, walked up behind Erika. "I hope you don't mind, Mrs. J., but we were driving by and I mentioned this was where you were having dinner and she wanted to come in and see you."

Jonni smiled. "I don't mind at all." Then she turned to where Matthew was sitting, his face a study in consternation. Whether he was more dismayed at the sight of the family interruption or the bill the waiter had laid before him, Jonni didn't know. And didn't care.

"Meet my daughter, Erika, and her nanny, Isolde," Jonni said.

Matthew performed his half-rise from the chair again. "Pleased, I'm sure," he mumbled and returned to the check.

"Mommy, can we go home and play Barbie?"

Jonni brushed the hair back from Erika's face. Blue eyes so like her own shone up at her. Erika had the same straw-blond hair that Jonni had been born with. Try as she had when her daughter was first born, Jonni had never been able to see any of David's family features in her daughter. David's none-too-welcoming mother had had the same difficulty, a source of tension at family occasions.

But Jonni knew she had never strayed. Fidelity was one of her strongest virtues.

But as she'd asked herself over and over again, had her husband shared that value?

"Barbie sounds like fun," Jonni said, turning toward Matthew Howell. "Thank you for dinner," she said, "but my family commitments are calling me."

"Oh, what's that?" Matthew looked sincerely surprised. "Why hire a nanny if you have to run home at your daughter's every whim? Seems like an expense you could do without. Salary, room, and board, just think of what you could do with those funds."

Jonni held her hand out. She could manage to shake hands, yes, she could, if only it allowed her an end to this dinner date disaster.

Matthew ignored her hand. Tapping the bill, he said, "Your share is $42.50."

Jonni stared at the man. "I don't believe I understand," she said slowly.

"Dating," Matthew said, "in the modern world, is a quid pro quo encounter. You're leaving with your daughter rather than coming back to my place, so ante up."

Jonni narrowed her eyes and studied the accountant. "I do believe you're serious," she said.

"I'm always serious about finances," Matthew said.

"Good," Jonni said, taking Erika's hand in her own. "You can send the bill to my father." With those words, she turned on her heel and marched to the door of the restaurant, daring him to pursue her and make a scene. She'd choke before she'd pay for that meal.

She settled Erika in the back seat of Isolde's Jeep and leaned back with a sigh.

The nanny glanced at her, gunned the engine, and pulled a U-turn, crossing the streetcar tracks to head back down St. Charles Avenue. "What a Spleen," Isolde said.

Jonni smiled at the expression, even though she wasn't sure exactly what Isolde meant by it. "I take it you're referring to my date?"

The girl nodded and tapped with one finger on a spot between the center of her collarbones. "A Spleen is a Body Part," she said, speaking in capitals. In the several days Isolde had worked for her, Jonni had become familiar with Isolde's penchant for emphasizing words and expression.

"I have a theory," Isolde said, which set Jonni to smiling.

"You have a lot of theories," Jonni said, appreciating the young woman's intensity.

"But of course," Isolde said, stopping at the light at Napoleon. A streetcar rumbled up beside them, and one age-worn black woman garbed in a white uniform stepped off and then made her way over to the drugstore on the corner. "My old nurse used to take the streetcar to work at our house every day."

The light changed and they surged forward. Jonni was relieved that Erika was playing quietly in the back, her two dolls conversing with each other in relatively quiet tones. "Mine, too," Jonni said.

"Hey, and now I'm the nanny," Isolde said. "The times, they are a-changing. So anyway, I have this theory about men. They can be categorized by Body Part."

"What's cat-gorzized?" Erika piped up from the backseat.

Jonni shifted around in her seat, appreciative of the reminder that little ears never turned off their antenna.

"Cat-e-gor-ized," Jonni said, sounding out the syllables. "A category is a group, sorted by type."

Erika's sweet face was a study in concentration as she repeated the word under her breath.

"We can group your toys by type," Jonni said. "One category would be dolls, another sports, such as your roller skates."

"And cars," Erika said. "And teddy bears."

Jonni smiled and nodded. She turned back toward Isolde. "And the categories of your theory are?"

"Every day brings a new one," Isolde said, shaking her head and looking far too worldly-wise for someone her age. "Take Spleen, for instance. That just popped into my head when that goofball tried to make you pay. Some guys are Feet, you know, they walk all over you. There's the Gut, too."

Jonni was amused, and impressed with the concept. From now on she'd avoid the Spleens, and she was coming to see she'd been married to a Foot. "How about Heart?" She said it somewhat wistfully, thinking of what a good marriage her sister and Hunter enjoyed. They were at the gate to her driveway, and Jonni reached in her purse for the automatic opener. She had to remember to find the spare one for Isolde.

"Heart is of course a wonderful one," Isolde said, "but not so easy to find. Funny, but the bad outweigh the good."

"I suppose men say that about women, too," Jonni said, unfastening her seat belt as Isolde brought her Jeep to a halt in the drive.

"Only the Tongues, the ones who don't know truth from lies," Isolde said, jumping out and reaching in the back for Erika.

Jonni watched as her daughter leaped into the nanny's arms. Isolde swung her around to Erika's delight. She thought of the stiff-rumped Mrs. McLever and how subdued her daughter had been over the past year, and nodded in satisfaction.

Isolde's purply-black spiked hair bounced with her circling movements. The security light mounted on the garage glinted off the girl's silver nose ring. Jonni wondered if she would have considered the applicant or had the insight to see past the unorthodox exterior of the twenty-year-old if she hadn't had the advantage of knowing Isolde's family. She didn't mean to be a conservative snob, but she had to admit it ran in her blood.

"Mrs. J.," Isolde said, bringing the game of whirling dervish to a halt, "want to make some popcorn and watch a movie?"

"Sure," Jonni said, moving toward the house. "It's our last night of peace and quiet because the film crew is set to invade in the morning."

"That will be interesting," Isolde said. "Too bad I have to go to class in the morning. But it's the last week of the short summer session, so as I said when you interviewed me, I'll be able to work full-time between now and September first."

"We'll work around your schedule," Jonni said. She hadn't said anything to anyone else yet, but she, too, planned to return to college in the fall. She might be the oldest junior in the classroom at Newcomb, but she'd finish the degree she'd interrupted to marry David no matter what it took. "Let's get in our pajamas and watch the movie in the den."

Erika skipped off happily up the stairs. Over her shoulder, she called down, "I want to watch *Babe*."

Negotiations would definitely be in order.

A short time later, the three of them were in the den,

sitting on the floor in a welter of pillows enthusiastically collected by Erika and Isolde. Jonni was thumbing through a stack of DVDs and inhaling the aroma of the freshly made popcorn.

"What's the movie your house is going to be in?" Isolde asked.

"*Mister Benjamin*!" Erika shrieked the answer, bouncing on a pillow. "Mister Benjamin's coming to my house!"

Jonni made a wry face. "It's a film version of the children's cartoon *Mister Benjamin*. I didn't really want the disruption but when I realized how excited Erika would be, I gave in and said yes."

"Whose idea was it?"

"My sister Daffy's."

"Ooh, she's the one who used to write that Love Doctor column."

"That's the one."

"It must be nice to have a famous sister."

"Of course," Jonni said, one hand poised between *Independence Day* and *Scooby Doo*, wondering why that innocent comment rankled so. Though younger by fifteen minutes, Daffy had always led the way. Jonni had shadowed her. What would it be like to be the woman in the spotlight?

She sighed, knowing that she was not only likely never to find out, but that if she did, she'd have no idea what to do. Jonni performed best behind the scenes.

"Who are the stars?" Isolde helped herself to a handful of popcorn from the overflowing bowl.

Jonni selected *Babe*, one of Erika's favorites, if not

one of Jonni's, and slipped the disc into the player. After her daughter fell asleep, she and Isolde could indulge in something more to their tastes. Over her shoulder, she said, "I don't know. It never occurred to me to ask. I like old movies but I'm not much of a modern film buff. There's some information on the desk over there if you'd like to look. It's in a glossy black folder."

Isolde jumped up and padded across the floor, the floppy ears of her rather endearing bunny slippers waving as she moved. "My cousin Keenan is stage crazy. He wants to be an actor but of course my aunt won't hear of it. Would you mind if he dropped by?"

"Not at all," Jonni said, settling onto the floor, remote in hand. Over the next few weeks, her house was going to be full of friends and acquaintances "just dropping by." Since the word had leaked out that her Garden District manse was to be the sight of a movie shoot, she'd heard from more people than she had since the week David had been killed. Everyone, it seemed, was stage-struck. She gathered a handful of popcorn, and inhaling the salty buttery joy, she smiled and gobbled it down. She followed the first gulp with a second handful and leaned back against the leather sofa with a contented sigh. How much better this was than spending an evening with the Matthew Howells of the world. "Oh, someone named Cameron Scott is in the film."

"Cameron Scott!" The expression in Isolde's voice was something between awe and shock. "He's coming here, to this house?"

"So Boswell said, though please don't spread that news," Jonni said around a mouthful of popcorn, amused by Isolde's reaction but much more concerned about her own starving state.

"You really don't have any idea who he is, do you?" Isolde approached from where she'd been standing beside the desk.

Erika bounced up and down on the pillows. "Babe! Babe!"

"He's a seriously famous actor."

"I like old movies best," Jonni said. "Is he in Cary Grant's league? Or Alec Guinness?"

Isolde snorted, a most unladylike noise of which her socially prominent mother would have disapproved. "Cameron Scott isn't old. Well, he's old compared to me, but not ancient. My cousin must own every one of his films. They're all action thrillers. He's like a young Sean Connery crossed with Bruce Willis." She folded her lanky body onto the floor. "He's seriously sexy. He's been paired with just about every starlet in Hollywood."

Jonni finished another handful of popcorn, already regretting saying yes to the film crew. "Just what I need underfoot, a womanizing actor." She dusted her hands and dabbed her mouth with a napkin. "I wonder why he's in *Mister Benjamin*. It doesn't sound like his cup of tea."

"It's probably a cameo," Isolde said.

"Hmm, maybe he plays one of the characters Mister Benjamin morphs into," Jonni said.

Erika clapped her hands. "Morph!" She leaped up and danced around singing, "Poof! Shazashabam!"

Dutifully, having been through the routine during countless Saturday morning cartoons, Jonni repeated Erika's motions and magic words.

At Isolde's puzzled look, Jonni said, "It's the magic incantation Mister Benjamin utters to invoke a morph, or a change in state."

"He changes into bears and buildings and cars and spiders!" Erika waved her hands as if that would help her speak even more rapidly. "Then when the evil Mister Snooks is back in his cave, he turns back into Mister Benjamin."

Covering her eyes, Jonni intoned, "Mabahsazahs! Foop!"

Erika mimicked her, then fell back on the floor, giggling.

"Clever," Isolde said. "He says the phrase backward and turns into his regular self again."

"The show has a lot of elements kids like," Jonni said. "Ritual, word play, lots of costumes, good versus evil, and everything always turns out all right."

"Mister Snooks always has to go back in his cave," Erika said.

Jonni smoothed Erika's silky blond hair back from her forehead and bent down and kissed her lightly on top of her head. "That's right, sweetheart," she said, wondering somewhat wistfully where to find Mister Benjamin's sort of magic for grown-ups.

"Maybe I can do my paper for child psychology on the show," Isolde said. "But even more intriguing than that is what part Cameron Scott is going to play."

Jonni shrugged. "From the way you describe him, I'd say it's probably Mister Snooks."

Isolde looked shocked. "He never plays the bad guy."

"Well, as long as he doesn't disturb my house or my family, it really doesn't matter to me," Jonni said, reaching for the remote.

Isolde leaned against the couch, Erika between them. She eyed Jonni with a curious glance. "Do you miss being married?"

Jonni aimed the remote control at the DVD player. She enjoyed Isolde's company, but there were some topics she found too sensitive to discuss with anyone.

So she merely shook her head and settled back to enjoy Erika's anticipation as her favorite pig took on the challenges of the outside world.

Chapter Five

❧◦❧

Cameron told himself he'd behave.

He'd been repeating that mantra to himself throughout the flight from LAX to New Orleans. Even if he didn't care about his own reputation, he owed it to his buddy Flynn. But now, on the ground, in the pulsing crowd, doing his best not to be noticed, despite the attendant entourage of managers, production assistants, personal trainers, and a few other people whose identities or purpose Cameron had no idea of, Cameron wasn't sure he'd fixed the resolution firmly enough in his mind.

He'd divided his time on the flight between reading the latest version of the shooting script and responding to the none-too-subtle attentions of one of the flight attendants. She was pretty, but something about the way she smiled bothered Cameron. Either he was getting old or jaded, or maybe he was just plain spoiled rotten, but when a guy could have any woman he came across, the thrill of the chase just fizzled.

So he paid her enough attention to allow her to go out with her girlfriends and boast how Cameron Scott had come on to her, while with most of his mind, he concentrated on the work that lay before him.

That reality in and of itself would have had most of his friends slapping their thighs and chortling. Cameron Scott never pretended; he was the first and the last to say he never worked at anything, let alone acting. Cameron Scott played Cameron Scott. And it worked.

But leafing through the changes in the shooting script, he faced the knowledge that the making of *Mister Benjamin* was likely to be the undoing of Cameron Scott.

Last-minute rewrites were more the norm than the exception. But this particular version varied considerably from the prior one. Flynn had mentioned that Quentin Grandy had never felt the script delivered the emotional impact he wanted. Magic without depth, the director had said in his quiet yet emphatic way, would take the viewer only so far.

Well, Quentin ought to be happy now. Cameron had sensed the difference, and it was a difference that had him moving restlessly in his cushy first-class seat. He wasn't worthy of the role. Mister Benjamin, elderly old goat, was a far better man than Cameron Scott would ever be. He rose to the occasion, rescued the innocent from harm, and slayed evil.

Cameron knew in his heart he could not do justice to the character.

A hubbub broke out near the outside of the baggage claim area. Naturally someone else took care of collecting and hauling Cameron's luggage, so he had the opportunity to investigate the scene between a very young woman clad in a scanty silver minidress and a man wearing what Cameron could only describe as a pimp suit. The man had his arm on the woman's wrist, shaking it and speaking in a low-pitched shout.

She didn't look to be more than twenty. Mascara dribbled over one cheek. Long black hair flowed over her shoulders and rose and fell with the heaving of her breasts. Cameron moved closer, the image of his baby sister filling his mind, a protective anger surging through him.

"I want to go home," she was saying. "I have a ticket and I'm leaving."

"Baby, you ain't going anywhere." He shook her wrist again, and then tucked it into the front of his waistband. "You don't go anywhere I don't tell you to go." He withdrew her hand but didn't let go of her wrist. "Now dry your snot and let's get you back where you belong."

Cameron glanced around. Other travelers rushed for cabs and talked with friends and family. His bevy of attendants appeared engrossed in the management of all they had to load into the fleet of limousines. He cocked an eye and saw Flynn engrossed in a conversation on his cell phone. No doubt his good buddy was making even more money for him.

Well, one thing was for sure, Cameron thought, moving up behind the pimp, he might be acting out but at least this time it was in a good cause.

The girl hadn't quit crying. The pimp lifted his hand. Cameron caught it and squeezed.

"Shit!" The man tried to turn to see who had him in

the vise, but Cameron hadn't done his own stunts for years without learning a whole bag of tricks. He was tempted to throw the man over his head and into a trash can, but calling attention to himself wouldn't serve any purpose. The last thing this poor girl needed was a photo of herself and a pimp in the tabloids. She probably had three or four baby sisters and two doting parents back home in Whereversville. They didn't need to know what she'd been doing in her time in the Big Easy.

"Keep your mouth shut and I won't kill you," Cameron said, shoving the man in the back with one knee. "No one ever teach you how to treat a lady?"

The man laughed. "You must need glasses. That bitch is no lady."

The girl stopped crying. "Oh, yeah, well whose fault is that?" She wiped a hand across her face and stared at Cameron, recognition clearly dawning on her impressed features. "Oh, my," she said.

Cameron shook his head, warning her to keep quiet. The snake didn't need to know who it was who was about to toss him into a cab. Shoving the pimp forward toward the line of waiting cabs, Cameron said, "You're never going to see this girl again, you pitiful punk. Picking on women is a crime."

The man struggled, attempting to turn his head around. Cameron clamped down on the arm he held against the man's back. The cabdriver didn't even glance in the rearview mirror as Cameron shoved the pimp into the backseat of the cab and slammed the door.

Then before the few curious types who were looking in his direction could come close and satisfy their own curiosity, he dusted his hands and cocked a brow at the now-smiling girl.

"That was so cool," she said. "And you look just like Cameron Scott, and that's exactly the sort of thing he'd do."

Cameron nodded. It was the sort of thing his character would do. But damn if he hadn't done it, and in real life, too. Reading about the sensitive and courtly Mister Benjamin must have gone to his head. But now what was he supposed to do with the girl?

Flynn was approaching, cell phone back in its leather hip holster. Cameron felt the glare of his disapproval even from several yards away. Well, the girl in the slip of a silver dress did look like Flynn's vision of just the sort of hussy Cameron would pick up and misbehave with.

Something about the way his buddy was shaking his head pushed Cameron over the edge.

"Want a ride?" he asked the girl, turning to the next cab in line.

"Might as well," she said, "I already missed my plane."

"Run," Cameron said, hustling as Flynn shouted and gave chase.

They leaped into the cab, and Cameron slapped the door locked as Flynn grabbed the handle.

Cameron rolled the window down and said, "Don't worry. I'll be there for the call."

"You promised!"

"Yeah, I know," Cameron said. "I'm only going to see the lady home and I'll meet you at the hotel."

"Where to?" the cabdriver asked.

Cameron looked from Flynn to the rescued prostitute. "What's your pleasure?"

"Now that's nice to be asked," she said with a giggle.

"You don't even know the hotel," Flynn said.

"Tell me."

"Get out. Come with me in the limo like a good boy."

The girl's eyes widened. "You have a limousine?"

Cameron nodded. The girl couldn't have been in the business long. She was so wide-eyed. "Would you like to ride in it?"

"Oh, yes, please!"

"You guys going somewhere or not?" The driver had pushed his glasses up on his head and half turned to watch the discussion.

"It appears we have made other plans," Cameron said. "Good buddy, pay the driver," he said to Flynn.

With a sigh, Flynn peeled off a twenty from a roll of bills and handed it to the driver.

"Don't be cheap," Cameron said. "We've cost this guy a fare."

The cabdriver grinned and gladly provided the requested receipt as Flynn doubled the pay.

"I know what you're thinking," the girl said, as Cameron prepared to hand her into the back of the limousine.

"You do?"

She nodded.

"Want to bet on that?"

Flynn groaned.

The girl stuck her hand out. "What are you offering?"

Cameron indicated she should get in, and she obliged. Really, someone should have taught this child to be less trusting. No wonder she'd ended up with that creep. Where were her parents?

"You guess wrong and I send you home, all expenses paid."

Her eyes widened. "Maybe I don't know what you're thinking."

"Miss," Flynn said, "I would take that bet. By the way, I don't think we've been introduced. I'm Flynn Lawrence."

She leaned forward and shook his hand rather than Cameron's. As she did she glanced shyly up at him. "Cosey. Cosey Parks."

"That's your real name?" Cameron lounged against the seat opposite the girl, joined by Flynn.

"No, that's my stage name." She stuck her tongue out at Cameron, rather impishly, and added, "So if I guess what you were thinking, what do I win?"

"I don't know, Flynn, what should she get?"

"A plane ticket home."

"But that's the same prize either way."

"Smart, too," Cameron said. "Look, Cosey, you seem like a nice girl, too nice to be working the streets."

"You were thinking I'm a prostitute!" Her mouth formed a circle of shock, and a tear welled inside the corner of one eye.

Cameron glanced from Flynn and back to the girl. The limousine had surged forward into traffic. Already, Cameron was tired of playing Prince Valiant. But he didn't regret rescuing her from that creep.

"My pal wasn't thinking that at all," Flynn said, quite gently. "As a matter of fact, he wasn't thinking."

A hesitant smile reappeared on her face. "Thank you

for taking up for me, Mr. Lawrence, but I guess I shouldn't be too offended." She smoothed the silver lamé that covered just the tops of her thighs. "I mean, just look at me!"

Cameron nodded. She could have been Julia Roberts's understudy in *Pretty Woman*. As a matter of fact, Cosey reminded him of Julia. She had that same slow-to-appear smile that once it did, beamed out of a face both too old and too young for her willowy body. "Are you twenty-one, Cosey?"

She nodded.

He figured he should have made her prove it, but what the hell. Live dangerously. Yeah, that had always been his motto. He reached over to the bar and lifted one of the two magnums of Tattingers kept stocked in any limousine he might happen to occupy. "Would you like some champagne?"

Again she smiled and her whole body lit up. "Oh, yes, thank you. At least, I think I would. You see," she said, confidingly, "I've never had champagne before."

Cameron almost dropped the crystal flute he'd just picked up. He shot a look toward Flynn, checking to see whether his pal was sending warning glances his way, but rather than fussing as he usually did whenever Cameron was going down some road he deplored, Flynn was leaning against the leather seat and smiling somewhat bemusedly at Cosey. When Flynn accepted a flute of bubbly, Cameron realized that for once he was the grown-up, and if anyone was going to be doing any caretaking, it would be him steering his manager clear of trouble.

Go figure. Who knew what surprises a day would bring. Time to bring some reality into this tableau.

"So, Cosey, you want to be in the movies and that's what you were doing with that creep at the airport," Cameron said.

"A toast to your future stardom," Flynn said.

Cameron joined them in the toast.

"Ooh, this tastes good," Cosey said, settling for the first time comfortably against her seat. As she did, what little dress covered her legs rose an alarming degree.

Flynn took a very long swallow of his champagne.

"So tell us about the creep," Cameron said, refusing to be put off track.

"His name is Billy. I met him on my waitressing job. I was telling him about how I was studying to be an actress, and he told me he was a producer and he could get me an audition."

Cameron shook his head. Of course the girl had believed the jerk. What young starlets wouldn't do in Hollywood to get even a foot in the door could fill a book. A thought passed over his mind and he shook it away. No, he hadn't misused any woman, ever. If any of the ingenues he'd romped with had chosen him because he was Cameron Scott, well, that was on their heads, not his own. Not completely true, his self whispered back.

"That's why I went with him last night," Cosey said, her shoulders drooping. "But instead of a studio we went to this ugly warehouse and there were a lot of men and women. The men were all old and the girls looked like they were my age, maybe younger. There were lots of tents and a man and woman would disappear into the draped-off area and then come back. Billy told me there was one man in particular I was supposed to be nice to because he was the one who was going to finance my movie. So I did what he said and spent hours and hours with him, though he was old enough to be my grandfather."

Cameron wasn't sure he wanted to hear any more. His mind was wandering to how many times this young innocent had been debauched when she said, "I guess it's a good thing he was so ancient because it didn't take me long to figure out that if he hadn't been, I wouldn't still be a virgin."

Cameron choked on a mouthful of champagne and just kept from spitting it out.

"He said he'd paid extra for a virgin 'cause he figured it would act on his li-libido"—she stumbled over the word—"better than Viagra 'cause the doctor wouldn't give that to him anymore, but once he started talking to me I reminded him too much of his granddaughter Suzee so he lost all lustful desire."

"Is that so?" Cameron didn't know what to say, but he hoped she'd learned a lesson. Yet here she was in the car with them.

"He gave me five hundred dollars and told me not to tell Billy about it, but to use the money and go home where I belonged. I was going to the airport when Billy saw me. He followed my cab and made me miss my plane. I thought he'd leave me alone if I gave him the five hundred dollars, but he just laughed and said if I brought in that kind of tips he wasn't giving me up." She shivered, and her voice caught on a sob.

"It's okay, honey," Flynn said. "You're safely away."

"Flynn's right," Cameron said. "Now look, Cosey, we should turn around and take you back to the airport and send you home to—"

"Poplar Bluff," she supplied. "That's in Missouri."

Cameron did a double take. He, too, hailed originally from the same boot heel of the Show Me state, but he'd never been this naïve. "Yes, Missouri. But I think you deserve a shot at being in the movies."

Her face clouded over.

"What's the matter?" Cameron asked. "I thought you wanted to be an actress."

Cosey rubbed one hand on her knee and didn't lift her head. "You're both very nice and handsome, too, but I don't want to have sex with anyone but my husband. When I get a husband, I mean."

Cameron leaned forward and patted her on the shoulder. "Sweet child, I don't want to have sex with you. No legitimate producer would do what those turds did last night. I'm offering to help you get a job. On my new film. Here in New Orleans."

She dashed at her eyes. "Can you really do that?"

Cameron turned to Flynn. "What's the answer to that question?"

"Yeah, buddy," he said.

"Then you really are Cameron Scott," she said. "I thought you looked like him, but couldn't believe it was true." She pinched her arm. "I am riding in a limousine with Cameron Scott and drinking champagne. And Mr. Lawrence, too," she added, sending him a smile that would have melted even the hardest of hearts.

Anyone but Cameron's, that was. Other than being glad in a philosophical sense that he'd saved her from the wolves, he was already bored. He wondered if he'd ever meet a woman who could hold his interest long enough to capture his heart. Deciding there was little chance of that, he polished off his glass of champagne and poured himself another round.

He spent the next several hours on a detour to a mall, as Flynn and Cosey decided she must have decent clothes to wear and didn't dare return to the apartment she shared with three other young women. Flynn was happy to escort her, so Cameron remained in the limo, watching a DVD of Quentin Grandy's Oscar-winning *Dino-Daddy* and sipping Tattinger's best.

By the time they drove into the circular sweep of the Windsor Court's main entrance, Cameron had ceased to care about much of anything. He was grinning like a fool, afraid of working with someone of Grandy's genius, yet determined not to back down. Cosey's problems seemed resolved, the only danger being Flynn's apparent infatuation. But as she continued to refer to him as Mr. Lawrence, Cameron didn't think there was much to fear. She clearly regarded the two of them in an avuncular light.

The one relief of his jaunt to New Orleans so far was that the typical trail of paparazzi hadn't discovered their whereabouts. The ones who had known of their arrival had no doubt followed the entourage into town, but because of the rescue of Cosey, Cameron had evaded the herd.

When the attendant opened the door of the limousine, Cameron hoisted the second magnum and handed

Cosey out of the car. A flash of bulbs erupted, and he instinctively caught her and drew her close, covering her face as best he could with his own. Her hair fell forward, draping the two of them in what he knew would appear to be their very own private world.

Chapter Six

Interior
Jonni's breakfast room

"Well, would you look at that?"

Isolde, her backpack slung over one shoulder, stood by the table, tossing back a handful of shredded wheat squares. She pointed at the newspaper that lay open. "It's Cameron Scott. How does the guy do it? He's been in town less than twenty-four hours and he already has some girl hanging on him." She shook her head.

Jonni glanced up from where she sat, nursing a cup of coffee and dreaming over a volume of Yeats. She was determined to be up to speed when she returned to college in September to finish her degree in English. "Maybe he brought her with him," she said, guessing she was wrong even as she said the words.

Isolde finished her shredded wheat and said, "You are an idealist, Mrs. J., and I respect that. But I am going to be a clinical psychologist and I must learn to look deep into people's psyches and face whatever it is I find there."

"Even if the person is a Butt," Jonni said.

"Especially then," Isolde said. "Well, with that, I'd best be off to class. Thanks again for working around my schedule. You are an angel. If you knew how much it means to me to be living here rather than with my parents, well, you'd make *me* pay *you*!"

Jonni smiled. "You've done wonders for Erika, and I enjoy having you here. The house seems so much more full of life."

"Speaking of which," Isolde said, pointing out the window toward the street, "here come the troops!"

Sure enough, the gate bell rang. Isolde waved and skipped out. Rising slowly, Jonni walked to the gate control panel and pressed the button that would usher the movie crew into her hitherto quiet retreat.

"Mommy, they're here," Erika cried, racing from the front window where she'd been watching. "Mister Benjamin's coming."

"Honey, you do remember I explained that Mister Benjamin himself might not be here every day?" Jonni didn't want Erika to be too disappointed. Even though Jonni paid scant attention to the film world, she didn't suppose the main character had to be in every shot, or that he showed up on the first day to pull cameras and cables into place.

A firm knock sounded at the side door that opened from the drive. Jonni moved toward the door, pausing for a moment beside where Isolde had left the newspaper spread open. She garnered the impression of a man of power and grace, but also one who cared little for the value of his own reputation. The girl he was clutching was probably Isolde's age, and the way he held the wine bottle proclaimed him an intimate friend of the grape. The brief story that ran alongside the picture informed the readers that Cameron Scott had hit New Orleans running in his well-known hard-living style and that residents of the staid Garden District neighborhood where he was going to be filming should brace themselves for hordes of hormone-driven fans.

The knock sounded again, peremptory. Jonni could picture Boswell or a dozen clones checking their watches and tch-tching over their clipboards. Great. Impatient crew. And she'd never thought she'd have to deal with starstruck fans when she agreed to this deal.

"Mommy, aren't you going to answer the door?" Erika danced from foot to foot, clutching one of her Mister Benjamin rag dolls.

"Yes, sweetie," Jonni said. "For better or worse, Mommy's going to answer the door."

"What could be worse about Mister Benjamin?" Her daughter's wide-eyed gaze was so full of innocence that Jonni almost ignored the door. She had a sudden urge to barricade the two of them inside the house, to hide from a world that so often delivered disruption and pain. On the other hand, it was her daughter's own sweetness that prevented her from doing just that. She couldn't let her down, not after all the anticipation. Whoever the actor was portraying Mister Benjamin had better not disappoint Erika, either. She'd have to speak to Boswell about arranging a meeting. Unless warned, the actor would no doubt not appreciate being pestered by a five-year-old.

Rather than supplying an answer she didn't have, Jonni opened the door. In flew Boswell, his black-clad munchkins shadowing him as they had the other day. "Oh, hullo," he said. "Charmed to be here. That color is much better on you than what you had on the other day. The missus still not home?"

Jonni realized he still mistook her for the maid or housekeeper. At least today she wasn't bedraggled. She had actually thought that morning as she slipped into her new black and aqua Danskin workout top and yoga pants that she was beginning to notice some results from her dieting. But Jonni didn't see that it made any difference what Boswell thought, so she nodded and waved one hand vaguely toward the door. "Always out and about."

"Oh, yes." He sighed dramatically. "To be one of the pampered rich, now that would be the life. But, in the meantime, we have a movie to make. Chop, chop," he said briskly to his crew. "You each have your teams to direct. Do make sure no one harms any of those wonderful pieces in the parlor. The rich do buy the best, don't they?"

With that, Boswell flitted toward the front of the house. Jonni knew that inside the house, they would be using the front parlor, the entry level and grand staircase, and the garden room at the back of the first level. The rest of the scenes were, as Boswell had termed them, "exteriors."

"That's not Mister Benjamin," Erika said, sounding on the verge of a display of temper.

"I told you he might not come the first day," Jonni said. "But it's just after nine. Why don't you play with your dolls for a while?"

Erika stamped her foot. "If I wanted to play with my dolls, I would have stayed in my room."

"Don't be ugly," Jonni said, holding one hand to the side of her head. All she wanted was her peaceful, quiet, predictable life back. But it was like a bunch of snakes let out of the basket. She heard the tromp of feet on her gleaming cypress floors, and outside a truck rumbled onto her brick drive.

"I'm not ugly. I just want what I want."

Jonni started laughing. She couldn't help herself. Scooping her daughter into her arms, she gave her a hug and a kiss. "Baby, that's what we all want. Now be a good girl and I'll go ask Boswell when Mister Benjamin is coming to the house."

"Okay," she said, much to Jonni's relief.

But she insisted on following Jonni through the house. And the look of skepticism on Boswell's face did nothing to reassure Jonni that she'd get any peace from Erika any time soon.

"Mister Benjamin?" Boswell put one bony finger to the side of his nose and tapped it, as if doing so could produce the answer. "I haven't seen the final shooting script, so I really couldn't say. But I shouldn't think it would be today," he said, and laughed, rather nastily, Jonni thought.

"Why not?" Erika asked, her doll thrust across her chest within crossed arms.

"Oh, my little precious, you're much too young to understand these things, but let's just say he's otherwise occupied."

One of Boswell's flunkies grinned, and Jonni wondered what the joke was. Well, what some actor chose to do was none of her business. Take that Cameron Scott, for instance. If he chose to pick up every young thing in the French Quarter and bed them all at once, what was it to her? Just more proof of how hard it was to find a man who could be trusted.

"When he is going to be here, would you arrange for him to meet with my daughter?"

Boswell lifted his finely arched brows. "I'll see what I can do."

"I would think it wouldn't be any trouble," Jonni said, in her very uptown voice, forgetting that Boswell regarded her as the hired help.

"Of course," he said, eyeing her with far less favor than he had earlier. "If it were up to me, there'd be no problem. It's just that stars are so very peculiar. Why, I've worked on films where you wouldn't believe the abuse heaped on me. Me! Let alone some member of the public."

Erika stamped her foot. "I'm no public. I'm Erika Livaudais DeVries and I want to talk to Mister Benjamin!"

Boswell's eyes popped.

So did Jonni's. She couldn't believe her daughter could be so ill-mannered. "You apologize right now for speaking so rudely," she said in a firm voice.

Erika stubbed the toe of her shoe against the edge of Aubusson carpet.

"I take it you're not the housekeeper," Boswell said, sotto voce.

Jonni shook her head. "Erika, apologize. It is rude to throw one's weight around."

"Sorry," she said in a low voice. "But I am Erika Livaudais DeVries. Even if I don't have a daddy anymore."

"Oh, sweetheart, your daddy's with you in his heart," Jonni said, dropping to the floor and gathering her little girl to her. "He's in heaven now."

Erika made a face. "What good is heaven? I want Mister Benjamin."

Oh, no, Jonni thought, understanding way too late why Erika had been so excited over the movie company. She thought the magical character could bring her father back to her.

One of Boswell's flunkies cleared his voice, rapidly and loudly. Boswell glanced around but Jonni continued to hold her daughter, who was now working herself up to a prolonged set of tears.

"I think there's someone here to see you," Boswell said.

Jonni glanced up and around Boswell, toward the back of her front hall. Just at the foot of the grand staircase stood an old man, his face bronzed and lined, his hair a toss of silver mane. In his prime he must have been a good six feet four. Now he hunched a bit, and leaned on a cane. He wore a black suit, the sort the headwaiters at most of New Orleans' better restaurants affected. Instead of a bow tie, he wore a red silk scarf tied in a bow.

Jonni rose, and before her brain could parse the identity of the man, Erika turned and spotted him.

"Mister Benjamin!" She shrieked his name and ran forward, throwing herself against his knees.

Jonni held her breath. Surely any man playing the character of Mister Benjamin would be sensitive enough to the role and to the impact it had on children that he wouldn't brush her daughter aside. And perhaps he truly was a kindly sort of man. On the other hand, Anthony

Hopkins had nothing in common with Hannibal Lecter. She'd seen that movie, watching portions from eyes shielded behind her fingers, because it had fascinated her deceased husband.

She waited for him to say something, anything, but rather than speaking, he leaned down and tipped Erika's chin upward. He studied her face, the tears still staining her cheeks, the doll clutched around his legs. Even Boswell kept silent.

"I've been waiting for you," Erika said.

He nodded and lifted one hand. He placed it over his chest, as if about to say the Pledge of Allegiance. "I feel that here," he said in a raspy voice.

"Oh, it's really you," Erika breathed, letting go of the man's knees and placing her right hand over her heart.

Darn the man. Jonni didn't know whether to thank him or bless him out. Now Erika would have the hardest time separating reality from playacting. But she still believed in Santa Claus, and if that was okay, she supposed she could deal with her faith in Mister Benjamin, too.

There were plenty of days Jonni wished she still believed in Santa.

Boswell turned back to his crew. To him, the older man was just another actor, his presence in the house heralding simply another day of work.

Jonni stepped forward, thinking she'd welcome the man, but stopped at the scowl on Erika's face. Oops, she'd forgotten there were no adults in Mister Benjamin's cartoon world. There were children, and Mister Snooks, and of course Mister B. himself. But even Mister B.'s employer, in his cover role as butler, was a child.

So she hung back, respectful of Erika's desire to keep the imaginary character all to herself, yet careful, as any mother would be, of this unknown male.

"Would you like some Cheerios?" Erika asked her hero.

Jonni bit back a smile. Now here was a test. Would the actor oblige her daughter or excuse himself and hurry off to whichever of the oversize trailers that had appeared along Prytania Avenue a day earlier belonged to him?

He cocked his head to one side, obviously pretending to consider the request. Then, again in that deep, rough-edged voice, said, "If you please."

Erika held out a hand, carefully staying on his left side, avoiding the cane on his right. "The kitchen's this way."

He accepted her hand, and as he did so, he lifted his gaze to Jonni's face. In that weathered face, his blue eyes shone dark and brilliant, the fire in them unlike anything she would have expected to see in an old man. It was disconcerting, actually. Jonni hitched her chin up a notch and fixed him with her best no-nonsense look, not allowing him to see she was in any way affected by the magnetism in those dark eyes.

He gave her a slight nod, and tipped his cane. Then a ghost of a smile lighting his weathered face, he turned and limped down the hall, Erika chattering at his side.

Boswell recalled her to the moment with his harsh tittering. "Well, well, one never knows who will waltz in the door."

"As long as my daughter's happy, I'm happy," Jonni said, keeping an eye on them. "Now I'll let you and your crew get to work."

"Of course, Mrs. DeVries," Boswell said.

"And don't call me that," Jonni said, somewhat snappishly.

"Are you or are you not the lady of the house?" Boswell had one hand on his hip. "Was I right the first time?"

"Maybe I'll just let you wonder about that," Jonni said, heading to the breakfast room to keep an eye on Erika.

"Women," Boswell said under his breath.

Women, if Boswell only realized it, were much easier to deal with than men. Jonni recovered her book of poetry and poured herself another cup of coffee. Sunny would arrive soon, and once she was bustling about the kitchen, Jonni would coax Erika away from her hero. Unless the man managed to shake himself free first.

He was being remarkably kind, accepting the bowl of Cheerios Erika shook out for him, and offering to pour milk for both. Every few minutes Jonni felt his eyes leave her daughter's and seek her own across the room. After the first time or so, she allowed herself to respond with a small smile. He was, after all, some Hollywood star, taking the time to be kind to her child.

He didn't talk much, and when he did, it was almost as if his throat bothered him. Instead of concentrating on the volume open on her lap, Jonni wondered whether the voice was an affectation for the role of Mister Benjamin or for natural reasons his voice carried that much of a burr to it. His inclination to silence didn't much matter; Erika chattered enough for three Mister Benjamins.

Cameron observed the mother while listening to the child. He hadn't known what to expect when he arrived at the site of the location filming, but if he'd had to bet, he wouldn't have come up with anything close to sharing Cheerios with the most talkative little girl he'd ever met.

A talkative child with an almost silent mother.

Pretty, though, in an understated way Cameron found himself appreciating. Certainly not a babe by Hollywood standards. Her lush body filled out the top and pants of the outfit she wore, in a way that most of the women Cameron had known would have decried.

It wasn't until that moment, shoveling cereal into his mouth and glancing yet again at the blond-haired woman, that he realized every single woman he'd ever dated in L.A. had no flesh on her bones.

How had he held on to any of them? Hell, he hadn't, had he? Nor had he wanted to. His thoughts caused him to frown.

"Don't you like my doll?"

Cameron cleared his expression. The makeup caked on his face made that task difficult, but the last thing he wanted to do was frighten this child, especially after he'd overheard her grieving her dead father. What a terrible loss to suffer at that age. Cameron still had difficulty accepting that his own dad had passed away at only age sixty-five. Maybe it was that stirring of empathy that had caused him to step forward.

He'd like to think it was his own courage, this dry run of the role of Mister Benjamin, but he doubted that very much. Why, only last night, after seeing Cosey safely installed in a room the sold-out Windsor Court arranged for her at the nearby Wyndham, he'd retreated to his room. After more champagne, he'd worked up the inebriated bravery to track down Quentin Grandy by telephone.

He still cringed at the conversation, but even as he played it over in his mind, he kept his expression kindly. He reached for the doll, clearly intended to be a replica of his own character's cartoon self, and gravely shook hands with it, much to Erika's delight.

"Quentin, my man, Cameron Scott here." He'd played it very jolly.

"Yes, Cameron, what can I do for you?" Businesslike, that was Quentin Grandy. He'd been described many times as boyish and childishly enthusiastic but Cameron had yet to see that side of him. He seemed to hold Cameron at arm's length, rather like a teacher inspecting a pupil and finding him not up to snuff. Well, if he hadn't wanted him to take the role, he could have turned him down. His stupid slip with Flynn didn't commit Grandy to anything.

"It's about this film." Now that was articulate, and he hadn't slurred one word of the short sentence.

"I would assume so," Quentin answered. In a muffled voice, he said, "It's Cameron Scott. Go on to bed. I'll be there in a minute."

He'd be with his wife. At that moment, he hadn't re-called her name, or even her existence, but all of Hollywood knew of their sweetheart marriage and the films the two of them made together. Quentin directed; Mia produced. Cameron wondered if it was a bad omen that this movie was the first in a string of successes Mia wasn't producing. She was pregnant and needed a lot of rest. She must have come along to New Orleans, pregnant or not. Cameron didn't think, from what he'd heard of the director, that Grandy would be in bed with anyone else.

That thought both cheered and saddened him. He took another swig from his champagne bottle and wondered why that sort of relationship always passed him by.

"I assume you called for a reason," Quentin said, more gently than the words might have been stated.

"It's this last rewrite," Cameron said. "I'm not the man for this film. You might as well know it now. I'll get my manager to work out the details with you, but I'm pulling out."

"My, my," Quentin said, whistling under his breath. In a weird way, he sounded happy. "Isn't that interesting."

"I don't know how interesting it is," Cameron said, sounding belligerent, something he hadn't intended to do. "But if there's ever been a role I'm not cut out to play, it's this old geezer."

"And that bothers you?"

"Why, hell, yes."

"Why?"

"What do you mean why? You want to go on a PGA tour and swing a golf club for all the world to see when you've never even had one in your hand before?"

"Interesting point," Quentin said.

"Say that word one more time and I'm coming over to your room."

"Good idea," Quentin said. "I'm in 913."

And that's how Cameron had found himself in Quentin Grandy' suite until the wee hours of the night. His wife, Mia, bundled in a purple silk kimono, had joined them, her bare toes peeking out from beneath the gown from where she'd curled up on the sofa next to Quentin. Cameron accepted the mug of tea she had sent up from room service, and settled down in a Queen Anne chair.

And when all was said and done and Cameron sobered completely, Quentin Grandy had gotten it all from him. His fear of failure, his desperate desire not to fall on his face, and also his boredom with the roles he'd been doing for so long they brought no challenge, if indeed they ever had.

Now, sitting there in the kitchen with Erika Livaudais DeVries, Cameron said a silent thank you to the director-and-producer couple. They had challenged him to try out living within the skin of the character, and had sent makeup and wardrobe around to his suite early that morning. Nothing like leaping into the water, especially when it's icy, Mia had said.

So feeling both foolish and more alive than he could remember feeling of late, he'd donned the persona and traveled by streetcar to the Garden District. Mister Benjamin wouldn't have arrived in a taxi; he was, after all, the kindly old butler who occupied the house at the corner of Prytania and Third.

"Erika, why don't you ask Mister Benjamin if he'd also like some coffee?"

The mother's voice was low-pitched, gentle. She rinsed her own cup in the sink and lifted the thermal carafe from the coffeemaker's base.

"Okay," she said.

"If you please," he said, staying in character, though, watching the mother's graceful movements, he wished he could be himself. As Mister Benjamin, he couldn't exactly come on to the woman.

But this test had convinced him he could pull off the role. And that meant he'd be back. And once he'd finished filming each day, and scrubbed off the goop on his face, he'd be right here, not just on her doorstep, but inside her house. Cameron grinned and quickly covered the expression by accepting the coffee cup and executing a half-bow.

"Now go away, Mommy," Erika said.

"She can stay," Cameron said.

"But she's a grown-up!"

"Is she your mother?"

Erika nodded.

"That makes her more than a grown-up."

Erika wrinkled her little face, apparently considering why this should be so. "That's not the way it works on the cartoon."

"Ah," Cameron said. What in the hell was he supposed to use as a comeback to that line? He'd studied the script, not the animated version, though he remembered Flynn telling him he'd had videos of that version delivered to Cameron's Bel Air estate. Water under the bridge now. A quick glance at the mother told him she, too, was waiting to see how he'd get out of this conundrum.

She'd paused, one hand on the back of her daughter's chair. This close, he could tell her eyes were blue, but no ordinary blue; they brought to mind water that ran pure and clean and warm in the sun off tropical beaches. He'd like to swim in those eyes, he thought, the image hitting him out of left field. Somehow, he sensed he'd better come up with a darn good answer right now, or she'd be ordered by the somewhat bossy child to the other side of the room.

He stretched out his arm alongside the cereal bowl. The makeup people had done a good job of turning his hands and wrists into those of a withered old guy, and the sleeves of his black jacket covered the rest. "Pinch me," he said in the raspy voice he'd decided to give Mister Benjamin after Quentin's advice to make the magical butler into his own image of the character and not worry about what everyone else expected. Except him, of course, he'd said with a grin and a shared look of understanding with his wife.

"Are you serious?" Erika asked.

The mother, Cameron noted, stayed put, curiosity in her compelling eyes.

He patted his upper arm. "Here."

She reached out and gave a hearty tweak to his biceps.

"Ouch," he said. "Now pinch your doll."

Erika was looking pretty puzzled, but she did what he said, on the upper arm of the rag doll.

The mother smiled, and Cameron knew in that moment that she understood what he was doing. His eyes met hers, and even though he said nothing, he knew the two of them had connected.

The feeling threw him. It was almost as dizzying as his fears of the earlier evening. Cameron didn't connect; he conquered. He didn't empathize; he blew into town, scored with the ladies, and wiped the dust of the town, along with any tears or recriminations, off the soles of his hand-tooled boots.

"I didn't hear your doll say anything," Cameron said, dipping his ear toward the tabletop.

Erika giggled. "This Mister Benjamin doesn't talk."

"Ah," Cameron said. "So there are differences."

The mother covered a smile with her hand.

"I get it," Erika said. "Cartoons are one way and movies are another. Okay, Mommy, you can stay."

"Thank you, Erika," her mother said, very seriously, and pulled a chair out from the table.

"You're a bright child," Cameron said, impressed in spite of himself she'd made the leap that quickly. He hadn't exactly been sure of his own point when he'd started talking.

"Yes, thank you," the girl said. "Mommy says that, too."

"And does Mommy have a name?"

"Mommy."

Again, Cameron glanced at the mother and exchanged another smile that caused that weird feeling to go off inside his head again. Not that the rest of him was immune to the woman's appeal.

"Jonquil DeVries," the mother said. "My friends call me Jonni."

Every inch Mister Benjamin, Cameron half rose from his seat and bent over her hand. "Then I hope that I may come to call you Jonni."

Erika giggled, but it was her mother's reaction that held his attention. He could have sworn she blushed, ever so slightly, as she gently removed her hand from his.

Chapter Seven

Jonni's breakfast room (cont'd)

The side door banged to and then Jonni heard Isolde call out, "Oops, sorry."

Jonni smothered a smile, something she seemed to be doing a lot this morning. Only yesterday she'd asked the nanny to be a little less hard on the doors. Her energy, so much like a puppy pent up in a kennel and then loosed to romp, could be a little hard on the nerves of someone used to a restrained household.

She hadn't expected Isolde back from her morning class quite so soon, but the interruption was probably a good thing. The presence of the Mister Benjamin actor had Jonni feeling quite unlike the withdrawn and half-alive self she'd come to recognize as her own.

"Hullo," Isolde said, framed in the doorway that led from the side entryway. "What a scene it is outside. I'm glad our teacher blew off the class after the exam."

"Look who came to visit," Erika said, patting the man possessively on the arm.

"Ooh," Isolde said, dropping her book bag on the floor. "I'm impressed. You conjured Mister Benjamin."

"Con-jured?" Erika sounded out the word

"Made to appear by using a magic spell," Jonni supplied, at which point the old man smiled at her with those brilliant dark-blue eyes. He must have been quite the knockout as a younger man. She blushed slightly as the thought that he was still quite the knockout crossed her mind. What would her family say if they knew she was sitting at her kitchen table fantasizing over a man no doubt old enough to be her father, if not her grandfather? Surely not even in the movies did they match up such old characters with young actors? Maybe she'd have Isolde ask her cousin, the one who knew so much about Cameron Scott.

"I hate to disappoint," the actor said, "but I arrived by airplane."

"Truth is good," Isolde said. "Especially with children."

Jonni nodded, her mind occupied with other thoughts. What was this man's attraction? She hadn't taken her eyes off him since his arrival.

Truth, Jonni had always believed and then come to hold sacred, was always best. The torment she'd undergone after concluding that her husband had lied repeatedly to her was made so much worse because of the ongoing nature of the falsehood. Had David strayed, then confessed, she would have granted him forgiveness. She'd married him, after all, for better or for worse.

Several years before he died, when she'd suspected him of cheating on her, she'd forced herself to deny the reality that, later, too late to matter, had returned to haunt her. She had no proof; only the fact that he'd lied about where he'd been the night he died in a traffic accident.

Isolde dropped into a chair, joining the trio around the breakfast table. "There appear to be two groups outside," she said, filling a handful with Cheerios. "One loves Cameron Scott and one thinks he's the scourge of the male gender."

"Don't tell me they're protesting," Jonni said. "Whatever will the neighbors say? They gave me a hard enough time as it was when I mentioned the film company was using my house."

"It's time for me to go," Mister Benjamin said, his voice not at all raspy. Instead, it was like whiskey flowing over velvet.

Jonni looked at him in surprise, intrigued that his voice matched his eyes. But as suddenly as the vision of him as a younger more energetic person flashed in her mind, he seemed to huddle over his cane, shrinking before her eyes.

"Doctor's orders," he said, voice all rough again.

"You will come back," Erika ordered. "Tomorrow."

"That would be cool," Isolde said. "Would you mind if I interview you for a paper I'm writing? It's for child psych."

Mister Benjamin inclined his head, the king granting an audience to his subjects. "Tomorrow it is then."

For once, Cameron was ready when the production assistant tapped at his door to collect him for the chauffeured ride to the location scene. As he stepped down the front stairs of the hotel's main doors, he paused for a moment. A liveried valet and bellman snapped to attention, but Cameron waved them off. The car waited in the sweep of the drive. At this early hour, few other vehicles were moving in or out of the courtyard. He breathed in the morning air, tasting the coffee-scented humidity almost as he would a fine cigar.

It was the darnedest thing, but Cameron Scott felt better than he had in a long time.

"Morning, Mr. Scott," the PA said, hustling up beside him, juggling an armful of papers, but keeping pace alongside Cameron so that he reached the car first and opened the door.

Cameron nodded. "Good morning," he added. He was famous for not talking to anyone first thing in the morning, but for once he felt wide awake before noon. "How's life treating you today?"

He was amused, and possibly a little surprised that the assistant's jaw dropped, but the young man made a quick recovery. "New Orleans in the summer, nothing like it."

Cameron had slipped out of character. Or perhaps his own was blending with that of Mister Benjamin. He'd have to watch that. He swung a foot into the limousine and as he did he heard his name called out by an excited female voice.

"Oh, Mr. Scott, don't go without me!"

He hesitated. Cosey. He'd managed to forget all about her. Too bad she hadn't done the same.

"Ooh, thank you!" She landed at his side, flung her arms around him, and smiled angelically. "Do you like my new look? Flynn, I mean Mr. Lawrence, says it's me."

Cameron blinked and pulled back to study the girl. In the silver lamé miniskirt she'd been somehow innocent despite the tarty outfit. Now, dolled in what he recognized as trendy and skintight Nicole Miller top and greased-on capris, she looked the role he'd assumed she'd been playing for real. Her hair was pulled up in a topknot of sorts, more suitable for a competitor at the Westminster Kennel Club than for what should have been a fresh-faced girl more at home on a farm than navigating the shoals of the acting world.

The PA gawked, making no attempt to hide his staring appraisal of what he no doubt assumed to be Cameron's fling of the day. For a moment, Cameron considered telling the guy if he liked what he saw he could have her. But surely someone had to keep this child from ending up back on the streets. And even though he didn't relish the role of hero, he did have a few twinges of conscience to his credit.

"Cosey, honey," he said, freeing himself from her eager arms, "I'm sure Mr. Lawrence wouldn't lead you astray, but there's no doubt who has got a better sense of style. And it's not him, if you know what I mean."

Her lips doubled into a pout. "You mean you don't like it? Which? My hair? I'll change it. Here!" She tugged at whatever held the hair atop her head and it fell, cascading over her shoulders.

"Well, that's a start," he said.

She moved as if to lift her top from her body. "This can go, too. All I want is a chance to be a star."

Cameron caught her hands before she could bare her breasts. He had no illusions about her having had the sense to put on a bra under that Saran wrap top. "Cosey, how about we have this conversation another day? I'm late for work."

"But I want to work. You said you'd get me a job."

The PA shuffled his stack of papers. "I could use an assistant, Mr. Scott."

Cameron turned on him.

"Sir." The youngster swallowed, but didn't flinch.

Cameron regarded him. He was probably Cosey's age. Not a bad idea to get her away from Flynn, especially as his good buddy appeared in danger of diving into the deep end without there being any water in the pool. At least, if he'd been the one to dress Cosey in this getup, he was close to cruising the danger zone. Flynn had never had any sense when it came to women.

"What does she have to do?" Cameron asked the PA.

"Follow me around. Run errands. Get coffee and bottled water when I need it for someone. Make phone calls. Get show tickets. Call girls."

Cameron narrowed his eyes.

"Just kidding, Mr. Scott," the young man said, tripping over the words.

"Act your age," he said. "Cosey, go upstairs and change. You've got ten minutes."

Her eyes widened. "What's wrong with what I'm wearing?"

"With all respect, Mr. Scott, we're way late now."

"The show starts when the star arrives," Cameron said, leaning against the limo and folding his arms across his chest. "Now, scram and wipe some of that makeup off your eyelids and put on a bra and a T-shirt and jeans. I know Flynn bought some normal clothes for you."

"He did, but I don't want to look normal. I want to look like a star." Cosey's words reminded him of the little girl who'd told her mother yesterday she wanted what she wanted when she wanted it.

Cameron smiled, remembering not so much the child but the mother's sweet, honest, and heartfelt reaction to that statement. "I'll be waiting," he said, more gently this time.

She hung on for another minute or so, stabbing at the flagstones with her pointy toe topping a three-inch heel, and then turned and stormed back to her hotel. Cameron wasn't positive, but he thought he spotted a flash or two from behind a bush beside the drive. "Damn photographers," he muttered, and climbed into the limo to wait for Cosey's return. He popped his head out to request the latest rewrite from the PA and to inform him that he, Cosey, and the driver were to share the front seat. And that she wasn't to come near him on the set or they would both lose their jobs.

Jonni took refuge in her kitchen. She didn't pretend to understand any of the commotion occurring in the front rooms of her house. She'd intended to vacate the premises, maybe go shopping or visit her sister. But after delivering Erika, against her wishes, to her weekly etiquette class, she'd returned to her house.

The protestors who had been there yesterday had dwindled down to one white-haired woman carrying a hand-lettered sign that read, "Repent for the end is near."

Jonni had driven past her and made her way along the street crowded with recreational vehicles that she assumed were for the use of cast members. She had wondered which one housed Mister Benjamin, and as she sat curled in a white wicker chair near her breakfast area, she found herself returning to that question.

Not that she'd seek him out. But when she saw him she would like to thank him for being considerate of Erika. David, though he prided himself on being the role model of fatherhood, had had little patience for Erika, other than ensuring that she learned to read earlier than their friends' children and that she was accepted for the exclusive McGehee School for Girls. Nothing less would do for a DeVries.

With a flash of irritation, Jonni wondered whether her two-timing, supercilious husband had repented when the end was near, or whether he'd had even a moment's notice that he was about to be rear ended and plummeted over the railing of the Causeway Bridge into the choppy waters of Lake Pontchartrain.

"Forget it," she muttered out loud, cross with herself for even going back to that useless train of thought. She rose and crossed the room toward the refrigerator-freezer. Maybe, just maybe, she hadn't tossed all her favorite ice creams out when she'd started this starvation diet.

Surely she'd saved something, if not for herself, then for Erika. Jonni yanked open the door of the freezer and studied the shelves. The housekeeper had them neatly organized. And thanks to Jonni's own instructions, frozen vegetables and low-fat waffles and no-sugar-added fruit juice bars stared at her from the shelves where her favorite indulgences used to lie in wait for her.

A feeling akin to panic began to itch around the edges of her scalp. She wanted something to eat. No, face it, she corrected herself, she wanted to dig into a quart of

Ben & Jerry's, drop down to the floor, and lick the carton clean. It was stupid of her to feel this desperate. All she had to do was get in her car and drive a few blocks and she could buy anything she wanted.

Laughter and mingled voices, male and female, drifted from the front of the house. Jonni got down on her knees and tugged on a package of plastic-wrapped butcher paper. And that's when she spotted it, the crunched-in pint of long-ago abandoned Swiss Almond Vanilla.

Standing, she pried the top off. Ice crystals cracked and dropped onto the crisp tile of her kitchen floor. She paid them no heed. The carton didn't feel very full, but it was a start. She kicked the freezer door closed with the back of her tennis shoe and reached for a spoon.

Something about that connection made her pause. Blinking, she looked down at her shoes. Running shoes. She could see the mound of her tummy, but it was less visible than it had been only a few weeks ago.

Desire warred within her. She glanced from the now-open carton of vanilla to the laces of her shoes, still white and fresh.

Jonni licked her lips, spoon wavering over the carton.

She'd been diligent. But something about the hustle and bustle and so many people moving with so much purpose here in her huge house made her feel lonelier than usual. She'd been so good, the perfect wife and mother. Surely she deserved a reward.

Closing her eyes to all but the carton she cradled in one hand, she stabbed at the frozen vanilla concoction. A flicker of ice shards flew upward as the spoon hit the rigid surface.

She was beyond reason now. She craved the cool slide of fat and sugar over her lips and tongue, both cooling and heating her mouth, and then the satisfaction of the treat easing down her throat. But frozen this solid it wouldn't be the right consistency. Out of long practice, she knew what to do. She popped the carton into the microwave and set it on defrost for twenty seconds.

The beep-beep signaled the crawl of time and Jonni, one eye observing her pathetic behavior, yanked the door open. The softened ice cream greeted her, a long-lost friend arrived in the nick of time.

She let out her breath and lifted the carton, spoon at the ready.

"Good morning."

At the sound of that deep, raspy voice, Jonni whirled, almost dropping the carton. She caught it close, smearing vanilla ice cream on her top as she did. Humiliated to have been caught in the act of bingeing, she colored up and hid her embarrassment as well as she could. Almost choking on the words, she managed to say, "Hello. What a surprise."

The Mister Benjamin actor wagged a bushy white brow. "Is it now?"

Jonni nodded. Should she set the ice cream carton down? Dump it in the sink? Pretend she wasn't standing there holding on to the weeping cardboard with the same ferocious intensity she'd seen tourists grasp trinkets thrown by Rex maskers?

"I did say I'd come today."

"Oh, right." She edged toward the island table that stood between the microwave, refrigerator, and sink and the rest of the airy kitchen and breakfast room.

"If this is a bad time . . ." He let the rest of his offer to scram trail off.

"I was just having my. . . . um, lunch," she said. "I'm afraid I don't have enough for two, but I can offer you something else."

Instead of taking gracious leave of her, he limped closer. Today he wore a pair of rhinestone-studded reading glasses perched low on his nose. He made her feel as short as she was. Even leaning on his cane he towered over her five feet four inches. "Vanilla," he said, peering at the carton. "That's my favorite, too."

"Yes," Jonni said, blushing. Why oh why had she succumbed to the craving to eat until all other sensation was blotted from her mind? Of all things, with a house full of strangers. She had been raised better than that. Why, she could almost hear her mother's socially correct voice lecturing her on how a lady behaved. Not, Jonni thought, easing the carton onto the countertop, that her mother had practiced what she'd preached. No wonder she'd gotten along so well with her son-in-law.

She sighed and said, "I think I've lost my appetite."

"Don't let me stop you," the actor said, something like a twinkle in his eye. "It's a treat to see someone eat real food."

"Oh. Well, then," Jonni said, deciding for the sake of convention to spoon the melting vanilla into a bowl, "far be it from me to deny you that pleasure." With the bowl in hand, she gestured to the table where they had sat the day before. He limped alongside her and pulled back a chair for her.

"Thank you," she said, sinking down and dipping a spoon into the ice cream.

After the first sensuous bite had melted down her throat, she smiled and said, "I hope you don't think I'm rude, but this ice cream was exactly what I had to have."

"And sometimes we want what we want right when we want it," he added with a gentle smile that she found rather endearing.

"You do understand," Jonni said. "It's nice to have someone accept what I say instead of critiquing it or challenging me as to my logic."

He nodded.

She spooned another delicious bite. "Take this, for instance." She waved her spoon. "I know I shouldn't be sitting here eating this, but I want it. I never got what I wanted when David, that was my husband, was alive. Everything I did was rationed or inspected or criticized. As a result, I was the best-looking matron in the Orleans Club, but I was miserable."

She dipped again, swallowed. He nodded and smiled. "And now you're happy?"

"I don't know that I'd go that far, because I really did let down my own standards, but I've been regaining my composure." Jonni blinked and looked down at the bottom of the bowl. The blue and gold of the china pattern stared up at her through all that remained of the ice cream, a smear of milky white. "Or at least I thought I was."

"Don't tell me you're on some wacky diet."

Jonni was surprised at his energized, not to mention opinionated, comment. "Isn't everyone? Especially in Hollywood."

He dropped into a chair. "Someone done told me

wrong. I thought I was in New Orleans where people know how to live."

"I bet you've done some living," Jonni said.

"Oh, yessirree," he said, letting out a sigh and tapping the side of his head with one wrinkled hand. "There's not much this old face hasn't seen."

Jonni crumpled the carton and fed it into the trash compactor. "I wish I could say that."

"And why is that?"

He was so easy to talk to. Joining him at the table, Jonni propped her chin on her hands and considered her answer to that question. "I've traveled. Lots. My family and I have been all over Europe, and when my husband was alive, we traveled quite a bit on business. We spent several weeks in Jakarta not too long before he died." She knit her brow. "But it was always so sanitary. Sheltered behind tour buses or limo drivers. And David hated mingling with what he called the local element." She dropped her hands into her lap. "But why visit another country and ignore that?"

He was nodding his head. "Exactly, my dear."

One of the many wraiths who wore black and ran around busily with clipboard at the ready peered around the doorway. "Back in five," she called, then whipped back toward the front of the house.

"Slave drivers," he said, wagging his brows.

Jonni smiled. "Erika will be sorry she missed you."

"And I her," he said, rising from his chair and performing a courtly bow.

Jonni rose, too, and felt like sketching a curtsy. Something of the idea must have flitted across her face, or at least her hesitation.

"I always act on impulse," he said. "I recommend it."

She colored, but only slightly, and laughed. Feeling as much a five-year-old as her daughter, she dropped him a graceful curtsy.

He lifted her hand to his lips and brushed the back of her hand ever so lightly.

She could have sworn his eyes were even darker blue than they'd been the day before.

"Make-believe," he said, "is so much nicer than real life."

And then, before she could respond, he lowered her hand, turned, and limped from the room.

With one fingertip, Jonni touched the back of her hand where his lips had grazed her skin.

And then reality returned, one slow ticking of the kitchen clock at a time. Did she have some sort of father complex? How could this old man loosen her tongue, her emotions, and even that deadened part of her that used to be described as feminine and sensual? She had to know who this man was, not just in costume, but behind the face and body of Mister Benjamin.

Chapter Eight

❦─❦

"Aw, shit, why can't I be somebody besides me?" Cameron sat on the edge of his rumpled king-size hotel bed, holding his head in his hands, wishing Flynn a million miles away.

"Then what would I do?" Flynn held out a proper dark dinner jacket. "Be a pal and slip into this thing."

Cameron lifted his head and glared. "I hate this show-and-tell crap. I make movies. I'm not a politician."

"It's part of the package. You make this film, you play along. And wherever Quentin Grandy makes a movie, he makes sure he's a good citizen. Some of the movers and shakers in this city invited you to this party, and it's my job to get you there."

Cameron rubbed a hand along the stubble that framed his jaw. "It's been a long time since this morning."

"Go shave." Flynn jerked a thumb over his shoulder

toward one of the suite's three bathrooms. "But be quick about it."

"All right." He rose, throwing one glance back toward the bed. He'd dined in his room, polishing off a rare New York steak with a bottle of vintage Mouton Cadet. He'd hoped his absence at one of the dinners he'd been expected to grace with his presence would have dissuaded Flynn from collecting him for a reception he had no intention of attending.

He'd made it through the first day of shooting without falling on his face. Grandy had had a few words of direction that morning, but otherwise had stepped back and let him feel his way through the scene. When he'd finished, rather than rolling into his car and hightailing it, he'd wandered back toward the kitchen, telling himself he didn't want to disappoint the child.

Knowing he'd really been seeking the blond widow.

Widow.

Cameron threw water on his face and leaned over the sink. He had no business messing with either children or widows. He smeared lather on his face and stared at the reflection meeting his critical look in the mirror.

She was too good for him.

Innocent and sweet and cuddly, yet he could tell her heart had been broken, and broken bad. The blend of soft and tough appealed to him, in a way none of the flashy chicks did.

He scraped the right side of his cheek, dashed the spreckles of beard into the sink, and watched as the mess bobbed then sank into the drain.

What was he doing, thinking of this mom?

Hell, she didn't even know who she'd been talking to.

Would she have been as friendly if she had known?

Of course. He was Cameron Scott. Why doubt his appeal?

Jeez, was he losing his touch or what?

He'd make it through this ordeal, and then he'd high-tail it back to Hollywood and make damn sure the next project Flynn signed him to was a shoot-'em-up, knock-'em-dead Cameron Scott action flick. This touchy-feely stuff had him acting out of sorts. No, it was more than that. He hadn't been himself since his sister's wedding. Yeah, when he began to get a clue as to how empty his famous life was.

He attacked the right side, and then tipped his chin forward.

What kind of name was Jonquil? He squinted, considering that the exotic sound matched her personality. Moving the razor carefully around the dimple that got him such raves from the female sector, he played some other choices in his mind.

Elizabeth?

Nah.

Mary?

Too virginal.

He grinned, and then swore as he nicked his chin. Jonquil. It was perfect for her.

"Need some help in there?" Flynn called.

"The day I need help shaving is the day I throw in the towel," Cameron said, blotting his chin.

Flynn's ever-cheerful face appeared in the doorway, followed by the rest of him. "Yeah, well, it shouldn't take half so long. Get with it or I'm going to turn into Sergeant Hash."

"Screw you," Cameron said, jabbing a friendly punch at his friend's rib cage. "Ever wonder what the old guy is up to?"

Flynn grinned. "No."

Cameron splashed water on his face. "That surprises me. I thought you'd kept in touch with him ever since basic training."

"That's why I don't wonder." He feinted back at Cameron. "He's retired and living in Jacksonville, rocking his grandbabies on his knee."

"Now I know you're making that up," Cameron said. "Ogres don't go soft."

Flynn tossed the dinner jacket at him. "Love can do that to you."

Cameron groaned. "You're not thinking you're in love with Cosey, are you?" He shrugged into a crisp shirt and his evening wear, hoping his pal hadn't fallen for the half-wit half-child half-woman. If he had, it would be up to Cameron to rescue him. Years ago, in their army days, they'd sworn a blood oath to pull each other from the fire if the coals ever got too hot. Sometimes Cameron wondered whether Flynn even remembered it. But Cameron sure did. They were bachelors, and bachelors they would stay.

Checking his reflection in a mirror, Flynn said, "What's not to love?"

Cameron thrust his cuff links into place. "It was Cosey I was questioning." He dragged one shoe on and said, "At your age, you should start looking for quality over quantity."

Flynn hooted. "My age!"

"Speaking of quality, you should see the lady of the house where we're filming."

"Oh?"

"She's got this sweet lost-soul thing going on that does something to me."

Flynn was watching him the way he did when Cameron had been out drinking and tossed back one too many. "What do you mean by that?"

Cameron shrugged. "It's hard to describe, but come meet her, and you'll understand."

"Oh, yeah, so, tell me, what's she look like?" He drew a 36–24–36 figure in the air with his hands and winked.

"Blond, not too tall, a little on the plump side but in a nice way. Her eyes are—"

Flynn was waving his arms. "Stop. Stop. Plump? Cameron Scott has the hots over someone he describes as 'plump'? I'm calling the *Enquirer*."

Cameron gave his friend the classic gesture of the raised third finger, and tied his shoes.

Laughing, Flynn said, "So tell me what this Louisiana baby doll thinks about Cameron Scott paying attention to her?"

He straightened up and slowly adjusted his tie before answering, "Well, she doesn't exactly know I am Cameron Scott."

"She's not only plump, she's been living in a monastery the past twelve years?"

Cameron headed toward the door of his suite, his friend falling into step with him. "Something like that. She's been widowed recently. And I've been rigged out as

Mister Benjamin the two times we've met. I think she feels safe with me, me being so old and all."

Flynn clapped him on the shoulder. "Good buddy, let me give you one piece of advice."

"I hate it when I hear that tone in your voice," Cameron said, though he added a smile. He did hate it when Flynn was right and he was wrong, but he was usually thankful—much later—for the advice. "But lay it on me."

"You'd better make sure you're the one who reveals the truth of who she's been talking to and not someone else—or you'll never get into her panties."

With all the grace and dignity Cameron could muster, he swung open the door. "That was the last thing on my mind," he said.

Flynn laughed. "Even God loves a liar."

New Orleans' exclusive and gated Audubon Place

"I can't go in there," Jonni said, clutching her twin's arm as they sat in the valet parking line in front of No. 2 Audubon Place.

"And why is that?" Daffy asked the question in what was a fairly low-key way, at least for Daffy.

"Look at me." Jonni tugged at the jacket of her cream-colored linen suit and smoothed the skirt where it hugged her rounded thighs. "It was all I could do to squeeze into this, and if I eat anything the skirt will pop open, even with the safety pins I used!"

Daffy inched the Volvo forward. "Forgive me for sounding like Mother, but keep your chin up and remember that you are Jonquil Livaudais Landry DeVries. These are a bunch of film people, and your friends and neighbors and some politicians. They'll be so busy being in awe of you, they're not going to check your waistband."

Jonni laughed, despite herself. "It's funny to hear *you* quoting Mother. And it's even funnier because Erika pulled that name thing just the other day, trying to throw her weight around."

"See, when you laugh you forget to be self-conscious. Anyway, thanks for coming with me. When Hunter told me he had to fly to San Diego, he suggested I invite you to come with me."

The valets were opening their doors. Jonni waited till they were walking up the broad sidewalk to the spacious house and said, "I confess I had an invitation but I wasn't going to use it."

Daffy tucked Jonni's arm into hers. "Then I'm glad Hunter couldn't make it. You need to get out more."

Jonni started smiling. "Did I tell you about the last time I got out? Daddy's accountant?" She rolled her eyes. "You're a far better date."

"Thanks, I think," Daffy said. "Hunter was teasing me that the reason I wanted to come was to meet Cameron Scott in the flesh."

"Your husband knows full well he's the only guy you ever look at," Jonni said.

"Yes, I know," her sister said, sounding supremely satisfied. "That's why he can tease me."

Jonni felt a slight ache at what she had never known. Her sister and Hunter had the kind of marriage she wished she and David could have had. Instead of dwelling on that regret, she said, "So what's so great about this Cameron Scott guy?"

"You mean you haven't met him yet?" Daffy nodded at a couple strolling by.

"No."

"He's was *People*'s Sexiest Hollywood Bachelor last year. And the year before," Daffy added. "It's big news that he's doing this film and that they kept his role under wraps until it hit the papers yesterday. I'm sure he'll be at your house soon."

A thought crossed Jonni's mind, and she stopped and withdrew her arm from her twin's. "You wouldn't have matchmaking on your mind, would you?"

Daffy's eyes glowed and her brilliant smile widened. "You and Cameron Scott?" She tipped her head, obviously pretending to consider the idea. "No, sweetie, I don't think even heaven could make that match."

For whatever pigheaded reason, that statement made Jonni bristle. "Why not, I'm too fat?"

Daffy caught her sister's hand. "I did not mean that in any way. It's just that he's supposedly a real ladies' man."

"You mean a liar and a cheat?" Jonni heard the bitter edge in her voice.

"If you can trust the press," Daffy said, somewhat lightly.

"Well, you ought to know." Her sister was a card-carrying member of that sorority.

"Jonni, you deserve a man who is so good to you, the world stops for him when you enter the room. You deserve a man who will sit up all night with you when you have a tummy ache, and do the same for Erika. You deserve a man who—"

"Oh, Daffy, please stop." Jonni couldn't take any more of her sister's well-intentioned sentiments. Her words caused her to feel all mixed up and lonesome inside, emotions she didn't want to acknowledge. "I'm here to have a night out, not to find a husband. I've had one, thank you very much, and one was more than enough. Now, let's go inside and sip champagne and kiss cheeks and call everyone dahling." She tried and succeeded fairly well, she thought, in achieving a light note.

Daffy made a zipping motion across her lips. "Okay, dahling," she said and winked.

Both smiling, they moved up the sidewalk toward the broad porch of the house. Clusters of men and women dotted the area, light spilled from the floor-to-ceiling windows, and the sounds of a jazz ensemble fed the festive atmosphere. Several people nodded at Daffy, not surprisingly, as she'd been the society columnist for the local paper for several years before her marriage to Hunter.

They entered the house and found a reception line inside the foyer. Daffy seemed to know everyone, introducing her to the president of the university and his wife, the head of the film commission, the state representative from the area, two female city council members, and the mayor's wife. Jonni shook hands and murmured greetings, wondering why she'd been hiding inside an ice cream carton feeling sorry for herself while all these people were out living their lives, building careers.

They made it to the end of the line, and Jonni

glanced around at the formal, rather somberly deco-
rated home. With 99.99 percent of the guests decked
out in black, some in silk, some in satin, and even one
or two in leather despite the late summer heat, she
could as well be at a wake as a party. Even the lively
music didn't differentiate.

"I shouldn't have worn this outfit," she said to Daffy.

"Shh," her sister said. "It's Cameron Scott, just inside
the next parlor."

"If I didn't know better," Jonni said, "I'd suspect you
of having a crush on him."

"Don't be silly. I'm thinking of doing an article on the
bad boys of Hollywood."

"You've been doing a lot of freelance work lately,
haven't you?"

Daffy nodded and said hello to a passing couple.
"Aren't you at least going to check him out?"

Jonni's foot was tapping to the music. Feeling cheerier
than she had in a while, she said, "Sure. He can't be as
drippy as that Matthew Howell."

"There's quite a crowd around him," Daffy said.

Jonni half turned, letting her gaze move around the
large front parlor toward the double doorway leading to
the room beyond. A cluster about three deep buzzed
there, apparently fans eager for a taste of the star's
honey. She smiled at the silly simile just as the center of
the attention lifted his head and looked straight at her
across the room.

He smiled, not at what the woman in front of him
was saying, Jonni was sure in that split second of knowing, but at her.

She stood there, gazing back at him. One or two

heads in the cluster swiveled in her direction. The man was gorgeous. Glossy black hair, cut short but not enough to hide the wave, a chiseled face, with the hint of a dimple in the middle of his chin, a strong nose, and eyes that even across the room she could see were a brilliant dark blue.

"My, my," Daffy murmured under her breath. "I think he likes you."

And then Jonni realized what—or rather who—the actor was looking at.

She smiled, ever so slightly, back at him, the way a chaperone would at a young man gawking at her charge, and turned back to Daffy as if nothing out of the ordinary had taken place.

"No, he likes you," Jonni said, somewhat wistfully.

"Are you nuts?" Daffy sounded almost angry.

Jonni pointed at her sister. "You're the same size six we both used to be. You're wearing Valentino. Your hair isn't overgrown and twisted in a knot on the back of your head like some granny. At least I'm coming down from the twelve I'd reached, but barely." She placed her hands on her too-ample hips and stuck her chin up, defying her sister to contradict her.

Instead, Daffy just laughed softly. "Pairing you with a man with Cameron Scott's reputation is the last thing on my mind, but I think you have a few things to learn about the man-woman game."

"I was married far longer than you have been." She sounded obstinate and hated that tone. But as close as she was to her twin, she disliked it when Daffy took the superior role. Jonni was, after all, the elder by fifteen minutes.

"Being married has nothing to do with it," Daffy said, somewhat dryly. "There's Mrs. Smithers-Price. I need to speak with her about the, um, the upcoming opera ball." And with that, her sister deserted her.

"Opera ball, my foot," Jonni said under her breath. Anyone who knew anything about New Orleans society knew that event was not held in August. Clearly her twin had decided it would be good to let Jonni get used to fending for herself at social events.

She had grown used to the role of David's shadow. Parties with him had been so easy. She drifted through at his side, pretty, agreeable, present on the surface yet disengaged internally.

"Champagne, miss?"

Jonni looked up. A waiter held forth a tray. Jonni calculated the calories in the crystal goblet, dismissed the thought, and accepted a glass. Just one wouldn't edge her back up to a size twelve.

She sipped the drink and let the chatter and hum and music wash over her. She felt no urge to mingle but was content to stand there, slightly sheltered by a large palm near the parlor wall. The jazz trio was at the far end of the double parlor, beyond the cluster surrounding the sexy movie star.

And he was sexy. Jonni couldn't help but notice. She might be a widow but it was her husband who was dead, not her. She wouldn't mind taking a closer look, but she had her pride. Besides, she didn't have to gawk at him here. He'd be filming at her house and she'd peek then.

"Now if that's not a sight that breaks my heart—a pretty lady drinking alone." A robust male voice broke into her thoughts, and Jonni almost groaned aloud. Being married so young had spared her a lot of social encounters she'd yet to learn how to handle.

"Name's Harrison," he said, extending a hand clammy from the glass he transferred to his left.

Jonni let his hand touch hers and almost made a face at the sensation. "Hello."

"Ooh, just hello. I knew it. I said to myself, 'Self, that lady standing over there all by herself is one of those Hollywood stars.'"

That line brought a flicker of a smile to her face. "I take it you're a local?"

He had a card out from his suit pocket in a flash. "Harrison G. DePaul. You need insurance—I've got it all." He laughed and swigged at his drink.

Jonni offered a silent prayer for someone to save her from this man, along with the faint chuckle she granted his jingle.

"That's why I'm here tonight." He ran a finger around a collar too tight against reddening flesh. "Make a movie in this town, I'm your man." He leaned a little too close for Jonni's comfort and said, "I bet you'd like me to be your man, too."

"No, she wouldn't," a deep voice said from behind Jonni's right ear. "She's taken."

Harrison's eyes bulged and he fell back a step.

A strong, pleasantly warm hand touched her shoulder, and Jonni tilted her head, to find none other than Cameron Scott had come to her rescue.

Chapter Nine

Audubon Place reception (cont'd)

Cameron checked his TAG Heuer chronograph for the tenth time in under ten minutes. He'd long ago learned to do this with a discreet shift of the hand with which he held his martini glass or champagne flute. That way he kept from overtly signaling his enormous desire to be anywhere other than where he stood at that moment.

He'd deepened his dimple and posed for a few photos, signed autographs, chatted with the mayor's wife, or was she the mayor? Then a group of women beseiged him in the doorway of a room done up like a set from *Gone With the Wind*. He'd been trapped and forced to endure a discussion of the state of the film industry in Louisiana as well as an onslaught of flirtatious glances and giggles.

Had he asked to become a star?

And then he'd seen her, the lady of the manor, across

the room, standing next to a woman who had to be either a sister or a cousin.

He'd kept an eye on her even while chatting up the women who swarmed around him. Once, when he'd had his eyes fixed intently on her, he could have sworn she'd realized she was under observation. But she'd been ever-so-cool.

Cool? Dammit, she'd ignored him.

After the conversations they'd already had, she acted as if he were a bug on the wallpaper.

Which, he reflected rather ruefully, an almost unknown reaction for Cameron Scott, he was.

The lady of the manor had shared her problems and secrets not with Cameron Scott, but with the kindly, grizzly, and graying Mister Benjamin.

Shit.

Flynn was right. He'd better win her over fast, or find some real smooth way to ease her into the truth of his character's identity. Because she didn't seem too impressed with his actual card-carrying movie star self.

The other blond, good-looking in her own right, but to Cameron a mere shadow of the one who held his interest, drifted off. Cameron was sure she'd glance over then, but she remained where she was, an island of contemplation in a sea of babbling.

And that's when the doofus had moved in on her.

Cameron could tell just by the lady's body language that the guy had his approach all wrong. What was it with some men anyway? It wasn't hard to pick up women. As a matter of fact, Cameron found it all too easy. But he'd known since he was fourteen never to try too hard. Women interpreted that—correctly—as a sign of a product with inferior workmanship and shied away.

"Oh, Mr. Scott, thank you so much for the auto-graph," cooed a helmet-faced woman who ought to know better than to try to dress like her granddaughter, but apparently didn't. Her miniskirt barely covered thighs that bulged beneath the skimpy black fabric, and her false eyelashes could have served as pennants on a sailboat.

"What do you do professionally, ma'am?" Cameron couldn't decide whether she looked more like a madam or an unhappy housewife.

She clutched her autographed cocktail napkin. "Oh, you don't want to hear about that. I'm an epidemiologist."

He blinked. He had no idea what it was but it sounded like it took a lot of brains and schooling. Hell, what was she doing fawning over Cameron Scott, high school dropout whose diploma was a GED?

What were any of them doing going ga-ga over him? The young babes he understood. He assumed they wanted to score. But some of these women were his mother's age.

Almost without realizing it, he shifted his gaze across the room, back toward the one woman who'd coolly turned away from his attention. The overeager guy had been busy moving in on her. Her expression, had the guy taken the time to notice, was one of boredom bordering on irritation. Yet she didn't just walk away.

She was probably too nice to hurt the man's feelings.

The epidemiologist tapped him on the forearm with a

bony finger. "So what's your favorite New Orleans restaurant?"

Across the room the lady of the manor was clutching her glass. If someone didn't rescue her from that jerk, she was likely to snap it in two.

"Oh, do tell," someone else added. "We'll look for you there."

Cameron glanced around at the gaggle surrounding him. "Burger King," he said. "Gotta run, babes." He turned and they made way for him.

"Free at last," he muttered, careful not to meet the eye of any of the people milling about the large room. He beckoned a waiter carrying a tray of champagne glasses to follow him and crossed the room, arriving in time to hear one of the stupidest lines of all time. If it had been in a script he would have refused to say the words.

"I bet you'd like me to be your man, too," Mr. None-Too-Swift was saying, even as his quarry inched backward.

The man saw Cameron looming, coming up behind the woman, raising an arm. Sounding as possessive as he suddenly felt, Cameron said, "No, she wouldn't."

The man had the good sense to put some space between him and the lady.

Cameron slipped a hand onto the lady's shoulder. The gesture was a gentle one, the lightest of touches, meant to reassure, certainly not to cause fright.

She tipped her head around. Vivid blue eyes met his. Her expression was calm and assessing, though he liked to think he caught a hint of relief in there, too. His liked the feel of the smooth fabric under his touch, and liked even better the warmth of her rounded shoulder. The neckline of her evening suit wasn't at all low, but by the way the fabric hugged her breasts and one button strained against its button loop, Cameron knew that this lady would be rounded and lush and hot, hot all over.

She was still watching him, and so was the guy. So he said the second stupidest line he'd heard that evening. "The lady's with me."

"Oh, well, gosh, if that's the case," the man said, his words tripping over one another. "I knew you were one of the movie stars, as pretty as you are." He held out a hand to Cameron and said, "Well, I'll be moving on then. No harm, no foul. Harrison G. DePaul. You need insurance—I've got it all."

Cameron shook hands with the guy. "No problem, buddy. I can see why you'd park your car right here." He could be one of the boys; hell, if he hadn't stumbled into Hollywood, he'd probably be selling insurance or repairing tractors, for that matter.

"Excuse me," the lady said, firmly removing his hand from her shoulder. She spoke in the same sweet voice he knew from his two conversations with her, but the light of battle now sparked those beautiful blue eyes.

Oh, oh. Cameron beckoned to the waiter. "Drink, everyone?"

He reached out a hand for her empty champagne flute but she passed it directly to the waiter. Harrison G. DePaul looked both confused and amused at the same time. Cameron lifted one from the tray and held it out to her.

It was pretty juvenile of him, but Cameron wanted that sensation of flesh against flesh as his fingers touched hers. Given the way her shoulder felt beneath his palm, he wanted more contact, wanted to explore this impact she had on him.

He'd seen scripts with dumb lines like "jolt of electricity" and laughed at them. With all the women he'd chased and bedded, he'd never once had the feeling that if their fingers met, some force would shake his world. The only thing close that had ever happened to him was the shock he'd suffered the time he was fifteen and dropped his electric razor with the frayed cord into the bathtub.

Meeting his look, she accepted the glass from him.

It was a good thing she had a grip on it, because he almost dropped it. It was the merest brushing of fingertips, but he felt the desire rocket straight to his brain, execute a somersault, then take aim on his BVDs.

Amazed at the strength of his reaction, Cameron grabbed a glass for himself from the waiter and noticed in a bit of a blur that Mr. Got-It-All had done the same.

Jonni stood completely still, her eyes fixed on the bubbles rising from her fluted glass. Her heart beat more quickly than she willed it to, and all because some movie star was paying attention to her. Even that briefest of brushes of his fingers against hers as he handed her the drink had caused a sizzle that started in her fingertips and raced crazily throughout her body. When she had politely shaken hands with Harrison G. DePaul, all she'd felt was moisture.

Every woman in the room, including her own happily married twin, seemed to have a crush on this man. And she could see why, too. From across the room he'd been handsome; up close he was breathtaking. His dinner

jacket fit smoothly across broad shoulders and narrowed to what had to be the perfect male butt. His jet-
black hair was just tousled enough to beckon female
fingers to want to slip their way through, on their way to
an exploration of his face, with its strong jaw, appealing
dimple, lush yet rugged mouth, and eyes that burned
with the intensity of midnight-blue coal. Jonni had to
smile at her own fanciful description, but she couldn't
deny how darn sexy the guy was.

But it was something more than that. Jonni watched
him watching her, and realized that Cameron Scott had
the power to make her feel as if she were the only
woman in the room—no, the city—no, the entire world.

How did he do it?

She sipped her champagne. DePaul was exclaiming
how much he liked Scott's last movie but he might as
well have been talking to the large palm he stood beside.

Cameron Scott had eyes only for her.

She felt like such a silly Sue to be so flattered, especially with the things she'd heard about his reputation as
a ladies' man. Why, he'd probably never been faithful to
a woman in his star-studded life. Well, that was a chill-
ing thought. Finding her tongue at last, she said, "I don't
believe we've met."

"You might be right," the actor said, his voice deep
and lazy, "but somehow I feel as if we've known each
other a long time."

Before Jonni could respond, Harrison laughed and
slapped his knee. "Boy, is that a line to chase off a girl!"

Jonni smothered a smile. If the insurance agent had
said those words to her, she would have felt sorry for
the guy and done her best to fend off his advances.

Coming from Cameron Scott, the words sparked the opposite reaction, but also the determination to show him that not every woman in the world would swoon at his feet. His voice was rich and sexy and somehow familiar. For a moment, she thought of the actor who played Mister Benjamin. There was a similarity there, sometimes when his voice changed from the raspy tone, and the eyes reminded her of him. But the resemblance stopped there.

This walking ego was no Mister Benjamin, the kindly old guy she'd opened up to and discussed her overeating with.

"Wait a minute," Harrison said, "are you all telling me you've never met before?"

Cameron shook his head. "Sad to say, that's what the lady seems to think. I must be mistaken, but I could have sworn you were my date."

"If she's your date, what's her name?" Harrison had that gotcha gleam in his eyes, which Jonni found amusing because she'd managed not to tell him her name when he'd introduced himself.

"You tell me," Cameron said.

Harrison drained his glass and scratched his head. Both men looked at Jonni. The two of them were far more entertaining than dinner with Matthew Howell. She smiled, enjoying herself in a silly, lighthearted way she couldn't remember experiencing in a long, long time.

"Hey, sis, what's happening?"

Jonni turned at the sound of her sister's oh-so-casual greeting, amused at Daffy presenting herself for Jonni to introduce her to Cameron Scott. It was also the first time she could remember being the one with the upper hand, so to speak. Daffy, the social columnist and journalist, not to mention wife of the world-famous technology guru Hunter James, was usually the one introducing her stay-at-home twin to the rich and famous.

"Twins," Harrison G. DePaul pronounced, in the voice of one discovering gold in a mining pan. "Would you look at that?" He winked. "Talk about double your pleasure."

Daffy didn't have any trouble squashing pretension. She looked the insurance man up and down and, in a measured way Jonni wished she could have imitated, said, "I'm Mrs. James. And I don't believe we've been introduced." To Harrison, it was a brush-off, but as she finished the sentence, she turned toward Cameron Scott and her eyes widened, inviting the introduction.

Before Harrison could introduce himself and launch into his jingle, Jonni said, "Daffy, this is Mr. DePaul and this is Cameron Scott."

Harrison's mouth opened and closed several times, like a redfish that couldn't quite believe the hook had found its quarry.

Cameron turned the full strength of his smile on Daffy. "Mrs. James, you are just the woman I need to talk to."

"She is?"

"I am?"

Jonni laughed as she and Daffy spoke at exactly the same time.

"Twins. Just like I said," Harrison said. "Except you're a little on the underfed side, Mrs. James, if you don't mind me noticing. Though actuarially speaking, that makes you a better risk for life insurance. Yessirree, it's a proven fact." He patted his belly double-parked over the belt of his suit pants. "Can't speak to the quality of those extra years, but those who eat fewer calories extend their lives."

"Is that so?" Daffy murmured the words, but Jonni could tell she was wishing Harrison would take himself off.

"You see," Cameron said, ignoring the insurance man, "I've yet to be introduced to your sister. I am correct in assuming the two of you are sisters?"

"True, she's shy about saying her name," Harrison said, helping himself to another glass of champagne. "Maybe it's Gertrude or something else she can't stand to be stuck with."

Cameron shook his head. "I'm sure these two spring flowers aren't named any such thing."

Jonni exchanged a glance with Daffy. They both started smiling.

"Gertrude is a perfectly respectable name," Jonni said.

Cameron looked at her as if she'd said something brilliant. Or stupid?

"That's a nice comment," he said, looking into her eyes so directly she could swear he could see inside of her.

"I went to school with a Gertrude. Remember, Sis?"

Her twin nodded, eyeing Cameron in a way that signaled to her twin that some shift had occurred in her thinking regarding the famous Cameron Scott. Somewhat absently, she said, "Yes, she was nice. But she hated her name. Don't you remember, she made us call her Trudie?"

"Did she? I don't remember that."

"Well, there's really no mystery about my sister's identity," Daffy said. "And you did hit it on the head when you suggested we were two spring flowers."

"Iris and April," Harrison said, with that aha gleam in his eye again.

Jonni shook her head.

"April's not a flower," Daffy said.

"Liriope and Zinnia," Harrison said.

Cameron was starting to look annoyed. Jonni couldn't blame him. She sneaked a quick peek at him and caught him looking right back at her. When their eyes met, they both smiled, as if sharing a private joke.

"Jasmine and Lavender," Harrison said.

Jonni couldn't help but giggle. "Daffodil and Jonquil," she said.

Harrison shook his head. "Too obvious."

At that both Daffy and Jonni started laughing. They laughed so hard they couldn't stop. Finally, Jonni dabbed at her eyes with the back of her hand. Dimly she was aware of a few flashes popping as a photographer circled.

Cameron handed her the handkerchief from his breast pocket. She patted at her cheeks with it.

"Let me guess," he said, studying her and then her sister. "You're Daffodil," he said, correctly, "and you," he said, smiling into her eyes once again, "are Jonquil."

If there'd been even the teeniest of breezes moving in the room, Jonni was one spring flower that would have swooned then and there. The man knew how to work a room, or in this case, weave his spell.

"Good guess," Daffy said, suddenly sounding brisk and businesslike. Something in the tone of her voice sounded dimly as a warning in Jonni's brain, and she realized just how comfortable she'd become with Cameron Scott.

That wouldn't do. She'd heard too much what a scoundrel he was. And seen for herself that he was a walking ego. Why, just think of the way he'd approached her, pretending to be her escort when the two of them had never even met each other. He'd probably used that technique countless times. If he'd tried it on any of that bevy of chattering women who were now looking enviously at them from across the parlor, no doubt he could have had a carload of women driving off with him.

But he hadn't.

He'd saved it for her.

Why, she had no idea. She couldn't begin to guess why he'd waste the effort on an overweight matron in a cream-colored suit that made her look like a tub of the ice cream she so loved to devour.

Whatever the reason, Jonni was smart enough to know that if she responded too much to his attentions, he'd get bored and go on to his next challenge. That was probably what had happened to her husband. The dutiful wife, she'd always been there for him. He hadn't had to put out one ounce of effort to keep her happy; she'd taken all that responsibility on herself.

And off he'd gone, to find his pleasure elsewhere.

She didn't believe in her heart Cameron Scott was really interested in her, but just in case he was, the last thing she was going to do was make it easy for him.

Chapter Ten

Audubon Place reception (still under way)

Cameron knew this woman was too good for him. Taking up for a girl when everyone else was making fun of her name! The only other person in his life who would do such a kindhearted thing was his baby sister.

The women he hung out with knew how to drape their pencil-thin bodies in the latest fashions, were experts at Pilates or Tai Chi, kept up with the latest gallery openings, and thought nothing of jetting to Vail for a ski date. A few of them were pretty good actresses, too.

But their lives, Cameron realized, revolved around them and nobody but. Dating Cameron Scott was probably just another way to show their friends or agents how important they were.

Now that was a humbling thought. Surely that last part couldn't be true.

All the while he'd stood there lost in his thoughts, Harrison G. DePaul kept on talking. Jeez he could spout, but at least he covered Cameron's silence.

From the wide-eyed way Jonquil was watching him, he could tell she was listening to his brain, not to the insurance guy. It was a funny feeling, standing there all silent in a room of babbling people next to a woman he scarcely knew, believing she could hear inside his head.

Cameron broke eye contact. "Ladies," he said, "this party is winding down. What do you say about joining me on a jaunt to the French Quarter?"

The married twin looked sideways at Jonquil. Cameron could tell they were telegraphing each other; he just couldn't interpret the code. Dammit, there wasn't another female in that big house who would hesitate for even a second at an invitation from Cameron Scott.

Jonquil shook her head. "Thank you, but I have other plans."

"And I have a phone date with my husband," Daffy said. "We always have a phone date when one of us is out of town on business."

"Now ain't that sweet," Harrison said. "Your husband is one lucky man."

"We'd better not make you late for that date," Jonquil said, turning toward her sister. "And I have to be up early in the morning. The film crew shows up at the crack of dawn."

A thought seemed to occur to her. "Mr. Scott, will you be working on the film soon?"

Flynn's words of warning flitted in his head. He could tell her right this moment, he'd been there working. He'd been sitting at her kitchen table talking to her. He moved his tongue against the back of his teeth, but he couldn't force the sentence out. She didn't seem to like him too much; yet she clearly enjoyed Mister Benjamin's company, and those two times in the kitchen with her he'd felt more at peace than he had in a long time. Cameron wasn't ready to give that up.

"Oh, soon, yes, but not immediately."

"But—" Harrison said, and before he could say another word, Cameron smoothly and almost invisibly eased his elbow into the guy's champagne glass.

"Now how did I go and drop that?" Harrison stared at the wine dripping onto the carpet. "Well, that's what insurance is for." He laughed. "You know what I always say: Harrison G. DePaul. You need insurance—I've got it all."

Cameron could have sworn Jonquil groaned. He flicked her a grin and she smiled back at him.

Aha! So she wasn't immune to him after all. That thought cheered him. And emboldened him to try again.

"Sure you won't come for a spin with me?" he asked in a low voice, while her sister and Harrison were summoning a waiter and dealing with the mess Cameron had caused. "It's a full moon tonight."

"You remind me a little bit of my daughter," she said.

Whoa, that was a line no one had ever used on him! "How's that?"

"She's five and when she wants something, she keeps on asking. No matter how many times I say no she just comes back and asks again. She's smart, too, and will rephrase the question each time, slightly different from the wording she used before."

Cameron grinned. He'd been treated to some of little Erika's mental jousting already. Then he remembered he wasn't supposed to know Erika, or that she even had a child. "And your point, ma'am?"

She smiled. "That was my point."

"You can't knock a guy for trying to ask out the prettiest woman in the room," Cameron said, this time his voice low enough so the words were only for her ears.

She blushed ever so slightly. Cameron lifted a finger and brushed it lightly against her cheek. As he did, the flash of a camera caught his attention. He dropped his hand and swung around. A skinny little guy in an olive-green suit was removing a roll of film from a camera and preparing to reload.

Cameron barreled over to him and held out his hand. "I'll take that last roll," he said.

The photographer barely glanced up. "No you won't."

Cameron bent down, his hands on his thighs. One word spit out at a time, he said, "Give me that roll of film or I'll break your scrawny chickenshit neck."

That got his attention. The guy looked up, his eyes widened, and he said, "I've got my rights. I'm here to take pictures. You can't interfere with my making a living."

"Go get a job at McDonald's," Cameron said, and reached down and palmed the roll of film.

The photographer jumped up, his fists clenched. Cameron had a good foot on him. "I don't think you want to do that," he said softly. The noise level in the room had dropped and he was sure that meant people had stopped jabbering and were now staring at his back. Cameron hated the fact that he had had to check his privacy at the door of stardom. But that didn't mean Jonquil had to have her picture spread across tabloids. He'd traced the line of the soft pink tinge on her cheek from some unbidden need to connect. And no photographer was going to flaunt that to the world.

"I'll see you in court," the guy finally said, and turned to collect his camera.

Yeah, right. Cameron thrust the film into his pocket. Sure enough, most of the people in the room were watching the stupid scene. He lifted a hand and smiled. "Drink up, everybody," he called. The waiters hustled and the conversational volume rose sharply.

Cameron returned to Jonquil's side. She was watching him with a very curious expression.

"Thank you," she said softly. "I saw him take that picture, too. That was a heroic thing to do."

"Hell, I'm no hero," Cameron said.

"Shouldn't contradict a lady," Harrison said.

Cameron laughed, somewhat ruefully. But surely now she'd go out with him. "Guess I have a thing or two to learn."

"Oh, you're doing all right," Daffodil said.

Jonni regarded Cameron, her head tipped slightly to one side. She couldn't figure him out. One minute he was the walking ego she'd expected him to be; then she'd catch sight of some gentler aspect of him. And then, poof, that image would dissolve, and it was as if she'd only imagined the nicer side. He was, she decided, a confusing man.

"Ready to call it a night?" Daffy asked.

"Why don't we drop you off?" Cameron said, his voice smooth, his smile ready.

Jonni couldn't believe her ears. Did the man not understand the word no? "Daffy and I came together and we're leaving together."

His lips pouted and his dimple deepened even more. "Don't break my heart."

Walking ego. Her first instincts were right. "I'm sure you and Harrison can find lots to entertain you in the Quarter," she said. "It was nice meeting both of you." She shook hands with Harrison, fighting the urge to wipe her palm afterward.

She hesitated then, but good manners required she also shake Cameron's hand. "Good night, Mr. Scott," she said, extending her hand.

He clasped her hand lightly but rather than responding with a sensible handshake, he lifted it to his lips. The brush of his mouth across her knuckles sent skitters of excitement through her flesh. His breath, warm and sweet, ignited her blood. Confused at her own reaction, she snatched her hand free.

He stood there, his dark eyes all-too-knowing, the satisfied tilt of his lips communicating that he knew the effect he had on her.

"Ready, Daffy?" Jonni walked quickly toward the door, unable to meet her sister's curious gaze or the eyes of the many envious women who watched her leave.

No doubt they'd move in on the hunk now. Well, he was welcome to any of the women foolish enough to fall for his blarney. He had the power to break any woman's heart, and Jonni had had enough heartache to last her two lifetimes.

The next morning, Jonni rose early after spending the night tossing in a bed that seemed far too big and empty.

She'd tormented herself with visions of herself, back to her former size six and draped in a sophisticated black gown, sitting beside Cameron at the Oscars.

What an idiot.

She'd definitely spent too much time alone, living inside her head. It was a good thing she was starting college again within the month. She'd wasted enough of her life; now it was time to make something of herself.

Making her way down the back stairs to the cozy kitchen, she put on the coffee, then trailed through the house to collect the newspaper from the front walk. At least today the delivery guy had managed not to get it tangled in the rose bushes, as he'd done the past five days out of seven. Outside on the porch, she paused and breathed deeply.

Jonni loved the way the air smelled early in the morning. It was as if the night purified it, and sent it back recharged. Those who woke up early experienced the best of it, Jonni believed. Dew spilled off the leaves of her roses and onto the carpet of lawn surrounding them. Tinges of pink edged the bluing sky. Jonni frowned slightly, recalling the sailor's jingle, "Red sky in morning, sailor take warning."

Summer rain in New Orleans could come down so fast and heavy streets and houses flooded in less time than it took to say "rain, rain, go away." She hoped that didn't happen today. Erika had her play group coming over, and with six lively five-year-olds around, Jonni wanted them to be able to occupy themselves outside. Actually, she'd tried to hold it elsewhere, due to the filming, but the other mothers had insisted none of their houses was available this week.

No doubt because they all wanted an excuse to "drop by."

Jonni reentered her house and shut the door after her. She opened the paper. The usual headlines of overnight murders and promises to clean up city hall led the news. She flipped the paper to check below the fold and her jaw dropped when she read:

"ACTOR CAMERON SCOTT ARRESTED
IN FRENCH QUARTER BRAWL."

Inside Flynn's rental car

"What in the name of Jesus, Mary, and Joseph were you thinking?" Flynn, normally a pretty quiet type, was yelling at him.

Cameron held his throbbing head in his hands, wincing at the noise, the sunlight pouring into the car window, and the bruises on his grazed knuckles. "Would you mind whispering?"

"Whisper?" Flynn was shouting now, full volume. He pointed out the window, toward the city jail where Cameron and Harrison had spent the wee hours of the night. "I should haul your sorry ass back in there."

Cameron held up his hands in surrender. "Okay. I screwed up. It's not the first time."

"No, and I daresay it won't be the last," his disgusted manager said before turning to the semi-lifeless form slumped in the back seat of the rented SUV. "What got into you two? Last time I checked at the reception you were conversing with two respectable, not to mention very pretty, ladies. How'd you get from there to slugging the bouncer at Gentlemen's Paradise?"

"Re-shection," Harrison said, with only the faintest of slur remaining in his speech.

Cameron groaned. Then he sniffed. "Harrison, you stink. Open the window." Then he started laughing.

Flynn frowned and jerked the car into gear. "Go ahead and laugh. Quentin Grandy and the studio lawyers aren't going to be sharing that joke."

Cameron sobered slightly. "I was s'posed to stay out of trouble."

Snores erupted from the backseat. Cameron closed his eyes. "I'll make it up to you, Flynn. I can't even remember why I decided to get drunk."

"Not just drunk, Cameron. You got in a fight. In a titty bar."

Cameron considered that picture. "Not pretty."

"Who rejected you? One of the dancers? Tell me no." Flynn was shaking his head. "There's not one female dancer on Bourbon Street who wouldn't do it with you for half-price."

"Gee, thanks." Cameron marshaled his hungover thoughts. "One did offer herself for free." He frowned. "That may have been what got that bouncer all riled up. Anyway, he insulted the chick, and I bopped him. No rejection there. That was from the lady of the manor. She wouldn't go out with me. Smart. She's too good for me anyway. So Harrison here says, who needs her anyway? I can set you up with some real babes. So off we went in his Corvette."

"Really? A 'Vette? What year is it?"

Cameron frowned. "How can you think of cars at a time like this?"

Flynn shrugged and eased through an intersection where the light showed green, yellow, and red all at the same time. "Am I drunk?" Cameron asked, blinking.

"Don't ask," Flynn said. "So the lady wouldn't go out with you—wait a minute, you're talking about the pretty blond who owns the house where we're filming and thinks you're some kindly old geezer playing Mister B.?"

"She's the only lady I know," Cameron said.

Flynn whistled. "She's not going to be too impressed with you now."

"Aw come on, you don't have to tell anybody. This can be our little secret."

"How long have you been in this business, Cameron?" Flynn pulled over and stopped the SUV right next to a "No Parking" sign.

Cameron knew his buddy had to be pretty upset to do that. Flynn liked rules. "You know the answer to that." He ran his tongue over his lips. "I could use a bottle of water," he said.

Flynn reached into the seat behind him, but instead of a chilled, sweating bottle of Dasani, he had a newspaper in his hand, which he proceeded to use to bash Cameron across the shoulders.

"Have some pity," Cameron said, snatching the paper.

"Forget pity," Flynn said. "How do you think I knew where to find you?"

"I didn't call you?"

Flynn pointed to the paper. The sick feeling in his gut

grew as Cameron unfolded the paper and attempted to focus. As the image came into view, he wished he hadn't made the effort.

Box office superstar Cameron Scott, in town to play the title role in the children's film Mister Benjamin, spent an anything but well-behaved night out on the town. In the company of local businessman Harrison G. DePaul . . .

Cameron looked up. "Harrison, you made the paper," he said. "That ought to help business," he said, chuckling weakly. He rubbed his bruised hand. "I wonder if this story gives me credit for doing my own stunts last night?"

He flipped to where the story continued. What met his eyes was a picture of two half-clad women hanging on him, two more on Harrison, and a muscled beefcake hitting the floor. Cameron stared at the image. He felt even sicker as he envisioned Jonquil opening her morning paper and seeing the story. That was no way to impress a lady! "You know, I wasn't trying to screw up. Not this time."

"I'll have to take your word on that one," Flynn said dryly. "We're two blocks from the Windsor Court and I've got to figure out how to sneak you inside. The press was all over the lobby when I left."

"I hate the stinking press."

"Yeah, well, you brought this one on yourself. I guess we could skip the hotel and go straight to the wardrobe trailer."

"I can't work today."

Flynn snorted. "Fake it. You're an actor." He pulled into the traffic.

Cameron leaned back against the headrest. "What are the chances she's seen this story?"

"Does it matter to you?" Flynn asked the question in a quiet voice, quieter than he'd been since picking Cameron up at the jail.

Cameron, eyes closed, nodded his head. "Yes, it does."

Flynn sighed. "You think she's the understanding type? Some women take offense when you ask them out and they say no and then you go off and pick up some other chick. Makes them feel not so special."

"Thank you for that advice, Dear Abby," Cameron said. He opened his eyes and looked over at his friend. "Maybe you ought to stop someplace where I can buy a shovel so I can start digging myself out of this hole."

"Better make it stainless steel with an unbreakable shaft," Flynn said.

Chapter Eleven

Back in Jonni's kitchen

Jonni was rereading the article on Cameron Scott's foray into a French Quarter gentleman's club, an expression she regarded with disdain, when Isolde bounced into the room.

"Mrs. J., you'll never guess what I learned last night!"

Jonni glanced up, thinking that what she'd learned last night was to listen to her inner warning voice. To think she'd almost let this scoundrel charm her. Why, all along he must have been laughing at how stupid she was that she couldn't figure out the sexy actor and the grizzly old character were one and the same.

"Are you okay, Mrs. J.?" Isolde crossed the room and dragged out a chair from the table.

"Yes, thanks," Jonni said. "Now what news were you going to share?"

"After you left for the party, my cousin called. He's the one who's mad about becoming an actor. Anyway, he told me that Cameron Scott is playing Mister Benjamin, which means that cool old guy who's been—"

"Yes, I know." Jonni said, cutting off Isolde's enthusiastic stream of words. "Did you learn anything useful?"

Isolde's eyes widened.

Jonni regretted her sharp words immediately. "I'm sorry," she said, pushing the newspaper over to show Isolde the headline. "It's just that I met Mr. Scott at the reception last night and there were a few minutes when he seemed like quite a nice man."

"Oh, I see," Isolde said, in a voice that sounded far too knowledgeable for someone not yet of legal drinking age.

Jonni rubbed the back of her neck with her fingers. As she did, the memory of Cameron brushing the curve of her cheek filled her mind. "And what exactly do you see?"

"He's complicated, isn't he? I mean, it makes sense. Actors aren't going to be one-dimensional personalities, at least not good ones. I wonder if he's a Brain? Hmm." She shoved the paper away without even glancing at the story. "By the way, Erika's up. She's planning a surprise for her play group friends."

"That's nice," Jonni said, thinking she should go see if Erika wanted any help. But her independent child would no doubt order her from her room.

"Do you think you can tell whether someone is basically nice versus basically rotten?" Isolde had gotten up and was shaking Cheerios into a cereal bowl.

Jonni considered the question. She'd lived a fairly sheltered life, punctuated by two strong exceptions: as a teenager, she'd found her mother in bed with a friend's father, and then she'd lost her husband and discovered he'd lied about his whereabouts, adding to her doubts about his fidelity. Her mother wasn't a bad person, and had been forgiven by her father. "That's a tough question," she said slowly. "I think I can, but as I mull it over, was my husband basically nice or basically rotten?"

Isolde dumped milk over her cereal. "Want some?"

Jonni shook her head. "I guess I feel he was rotten but since he's Erika's father, I argue for the good in him."

"Ergo," Isolde said, "it's not a black-and-white answer."

"I'm not sure I'm following your logic," she said.

"You think you can sense goodness and badness, but consider the range. Take my Aunt Teensy. She does all kinds of charity work but she pays her household help almost nothing and treats them like slaves. Literally," Isolde said, rolling her eyes. "She doted on my cousin Jules and he was such a loser. I mean, what I'm trying to say is, none of this is simple. Maybe Cameron Scott has a lot of good and some bad all mixed up inside of him."

"Maybe," Jonni said.

"Sometimes people just need someone to reach out to them to help them get rid of the bad. I was like that."

"You?" Jonni knew she sounded surprised. "You're the most together young lady I've ever met."

Isolde munched on a mouthful of cereal. After a moment, she said, "You didn't know me when I was fifteen. If it hadn't been for Aunt Meg, Parker's wife, I'd probably be living on the streets somewhere, totally tuned out to the world."

Jonni did have a vague memory of some family scandal hushed up by the Ponthier clan. Her parents moved in Teensy Ponthier's social set, so of course they'd known about it and no doubt discussed it.

"They were all so messed up, every single one of my family, except Parker, maybe, but he was running the business, so he was hardly ever around. Jules taught me how to buy drugs—"

"What a creep!" Jonni was shocked. She thought of her own innocent five-year-old. "How could he do such a thing?"

Isolde shrugged. "He's dead now, but he lived in a world that was altered by his addiction, so maybe looking from the outside in, we can't understand that. Anyway, when he first told me about it, I wasn't interested but by my last year in high school, I was pretty miserable. My mother hated me, my father had remarried and moved to New York, all my friends cared about were boys and what colleges they were going to. And then Meg asked me to come and live with them and help with their children."

"And your mother didn't mind you moving out while you were still in high school?"

Isolde laughed. "Well, she told Meg that she was nuts to trust me around innocent, impressionable children but she was welcome to me if she thought she could put up with me."

"That's terrible!"

Isolde shrugged. "I was fairly unbearable. I wore my Walkman twenty-four hours a day, well, except to shower, and refused to speak to my mother. I never got into the drugs Jules told me about, because they only made me feel sad. But I drank. A lot."

No wonder David had filed Isolde's resume in his Reject folder. He no doubt had followed the scandal, as he always had an opinion on everything that went on in town.

Erika's voice sounded in the distance, singing happily, growing louder.

"Anyway," Isolde said, "Meg and Parker welcomed me into their family, and they gave me a gift no one else had ever given me." She looked off across the room, a smile forming at the corners of her mouth. She turned back to Jonni. "They believed in me," she said. "They believed in the good in me, not the bad. They helped me find sobriety, a precious gift."

Jonni reached across the table and gave Isolde a hug. "That is so beautiful," she said.

"It can make all the difference," Isolde said. Then she spooned the last bite of cereal into her mouth, looking for all the world like a young woman who'd never known a sorrowful moment.

"Mommy!" Erika cried, launching herself across the room and into Jonni's lap. "This is going to be such a fun day!"

Among the army of film professionals who worked behind the camera, Cameron Scott was regarded as a regular guy. He said "please" and "thank you" and didn't throw tantrums or expect the impossible. On the other hand, he was a notorious flirt, which some of the females loved and others were neutral to and accepted him for the way he was, especially as Cameron never pressed his attentions where they weren't welcomed.

Not that he had to worry about that. He was Cameron Scott, his decade's answer to Sean Connery.

It was a good thing the crew liked him, Cameron was thinking as he slipped from Flynn's SUV and hustled into the wardrobe trailer. They'd passed up his personal one with the stupid oversize star, as it had been staked out by a motley crew of press and paparazzi, along with one solo protestor warning of the end of the devil's reign on earth.

The wardrobe mistress, a nasty old woman who wore her red hair tied up in a pink velvet ribbon atop her head, regarded him through rhinestone-studded black-rimmed glasses. "Well, look what the cat done drug in," she said, her voice ripe with an Arkansas twang.

Cameron had never worked on a film with Queenie Gilmore before, but he and the rest of Hollywood had heard of her. Quentin Grandy and his producer wife Mia Tortelli had discovered the seamstress-designer in the hills of Arkansas several years back, and now it was common knowledge that the Grandy-Tortelli team never made a movie without her at the helm of wardrobe.

"Yeah, yeah," Cameron said, not in the mood for either casual conversation or any more lectures.

She fixed him with a gimlet eye and suddenly he was gangly C. Walter Scott, back in the principal's office. He scuffed one soiled leather toe against the floor of the trailer.

She crossed her arms over her chest. "You smell bad," she said. "Kind of reminds me of a brewery suffering a poison gas leak." She barked a laugh and said, "Well, don't just stand there. The crew's been sitting around for a good three hours now. Quentin's ready to hang you from that old statue of Robert E. Lee just down the road a bit."

Cameron ran a hand through his hair and it came out flecked with bits of goo he didn't dare identify. He grimaced.

"Get yourself back there to the bathroom," she said, "and don't come out till you don't stink." She rummaged in a closet and tossed a washcloth and towel in his direction. "I'll let makeup know to get ready for you."

"Thank you, Mrs. Gilmore," Cameron said, feeling rather humbled.

She glared at him. "The name's Queenie," and then she laughed and slapped him on the butt.

Cameron jumped and took off to the back of the trailer. He couldn't wait to get out of his clothes. Inside the small bathroom, he kicked off his shoes. He should have left them behind at the jail; he'd met a few guys who would appreciate them. He knew he'd never wear them again. They practically stuck to the floor when he walked.

He had left his suit jacket behind, using it to cover a skinny old man shivering where he lay on the holding tank floor. That was actually how he'd ended up busting his knuckles, proving the point to some dimwitted bully that no one was to steal the coat from the helpless old dude. He'd barely popped the obnoxious bouncer.

Cameron turned on the taps and splashed water on his face. Bending his head forward sent a pain richocheting through his head like a pinball gone wild. He groaned out loud and promised himself he'd never drink too much again, as long as he lived.

"Feeling pretty bad in there, ain't you?"

Cameron started and hit his knee on the sink. "Shit!" He shot a glance toward the door, but it remained shut. "Can a guy get some privacy around here?"

He could hear Queenie chuckling on the other side of the door. "Yeah, about now you're probably swearing liquor won't ever touch your pretty lips again."

Standing there naked, looming over the sink, Cameron faced the three-way mirror. Three images of a face known around the world stared back at him. Yeah, a face everyone recognized, but not even Cameron understood what lay beneath its surface. So how did this Queenie get so smart? Was the wardrobe woman some sort of witch? "What are you, one of those telephone psychics?" he said, aiming at making a joke of her comment rather than admitting to its truth.

"Oh, it takes one to know one," she said. "This is your first time working with Quentin, ain't it?"

Cameron dunked the washcloth into a sinkful of soapy water and started to wash his grimy body. "Yes, but I expect you know that," he said.

She cackled. "Bright guy. He saved my life, did Quentin Grandy."

Cameron's ears perked up. He'd always felt the Oscar-winning director possessed a depth few others in the business would ever reach, and despite his disgust at having been tricked into the role of Mister Benjamin, he'd been looking forward to working with the highly regarded director. Of course, today was only the second day of filming, and he'd screwed up royally. "How's that?" he asked, sounding as casual as a guy could while taking a spit bath and conversing through a flimsy door.

"He helped me see there was more to life than the bottom of a bottle," Queenie said. "But more importantly, he helped me believe I deserved better."

In the midst of wringing out the washcloth, Cameron halted. The woman was clearly sending him a message, a message he wasn't sure he was open to receiving. Still, he could appreciate she meant well.

"And then he gave you a job?"

He could have sworn he felt her sigh all the way to the tips of his bare toes.

"You're not ready, are you?" she said.

He glanced down at his naked body. "I'm still washing up."

"Don't be dense, boy," she said.

"Yes, ma'am," he said, meekly enough. She was right. He wasn't ready to listen to what she was trying to tell him, but he was Cameron Scott, and as long as he kept on being Cameron Scott, he didn't have to be ready for anything else, especially not facing his own insecurities.

"So you let me know when you're ready for makeup," she said.

He heard her steps trailing off as she moved away from the door.

He toweled off, dunked his head and scrubbed it clean, then looked around for a blow dryer. Not finding one, he rubbed his hair with the towel, left it standing on end, and considered his clothing.

Or rather, the lack of clothing.

He wasn't about to step into the filthy clothes that had lived a night in jail.

That left him either his birthday suit or the towel Queenie had given him.

"Serve her right if I parade out there buck-naked," he muttered, still somewhat irritated at how right-on some of her comments had been. But then common sense won out and he wrapped the large towel around his waist and tied it in a knot. Once he was decked out in Mister Benjamin's butler suit, he'd be able to head out of the trailer, stop in makeup, and hightail it into the house.

His hand on the doorknob of the bathroom, he stopped.

Jonquil would be in the house.

Shit.

He'd wanted her to respond to him, to like him, to want to go out with him. And she'd rebuffed him. He butted his head against the door and decided that only a wimp backed away when the chips were down.

By the time Cameron got rigged out as Mister Benjamin and allowed the makeup artists to turn his strong hands into the gnarled vestiges of the character's aged years, big drops of rain were plopping onto the sidewalk and grass of the shooting scene.

Quentin had declared they were filming outside that day, rather than continuing with interiors, for some reason only he knew. But when Cameron glanced up toward the angry sky and was hit by a handful of fat drops smack in the eye, he considered protesting the conditions.

But some grain of self-preservation caused him to hold his tongue. If he had been on time, they'd be done for the day.

Hunched over Mister Benjamin's cane, Cameron worked on emptying his mind of Cameron Scott and his behavior-related problems and filling it with the clever kindness of his character. He'd done this the other two days before taking his mark and before wandering into the kitchen of the house and meeting Jonquil and Erika and the nanny.

No wonder the lady of the manor had liked him, then.

He hadn't acted like himself.

Cameron laughed softly, mocking his thoughts.

"Ready?"

At the sound of Quentin Grandy's voice, Cameron stopped laughing. The two of them were about the same age, but something about the way Quentin walked and talked made him appear both much older and much younger, all at the same time. Cameron had seen him only yesterday give brilliant guidance to the villain on how evil wasn't interesting if it was all bad without some particle of good, and then he'd turned and started a game of drop the handkerchief with three of the child actors.

"Sure," Cameron said, in the raspy voice of Mister Benjamin, his cane bearing his weight.

Quentin pushed his glasses up on his nose. "What was it like in jail?"

Cameron shrugged. "One of life's adventures."

"I used to party a lot," Quentin said, in a conversational voice. "You've probably heard some of the stories."

"Yeah, I have," Cameron said, grinning and straightening from his Mister Benjamin pose. "They say there wasn't a female on the MegaFilms lot you didn't poke."

Quentin shook his head. "Not quite accurate."

"Not for lack of trying," Cameron said, laughing,

buddy to buddy, glad to be doing guy talk. He didn't want any more lectures, a là Queenie, about his behavior. Then he thought of how Quentin and Mia had stayed up late with him in their hotel, easing him through his prefilming jitters. "I take it Mrs. Grandy wasn't around in those days?"

Quentin's face grew serious. "Oh, she was there, right by my side. Every film I've done she's produced."

Cameron looked at the director sideways. He'd assumed the Grandy-Tortelli union was one of Hollywood's most solid.

Quentin must have caught his look, because he said, "Don't get the wrong idea there. We worked together but I was too stupid to see the gem right under my nose. But once I did"—he smiled and an expression of awe came over his face—"there's never been anyone but Mia."

He slapped Cameron on the back, all of a sudden, and said, "Maybe you'll get lucky, too, and find the woman who turns your life around, but until you do, let's get to work on time, okay?"

Chapter Twelve

Jonni kept herself occupied upstairs in the back of the house, taking on the task of sorting out David's office. With the heavy curtains gone and the cheerful music from the golden oldies radio station to keep her company, the room had lost some of its power to dampen her spirits, even on a day when the rain drummed steadily against the windows.

Plus, she admitted as she dumped another set of files from the cabinet onto the floor, her exasperation with Cameron Scott fueled her engine. Just knowing he was outside her house, decked out in his Mister Benjamin disguise, annoyed her. Part of her wanted to know if he'd wandered into the house looking for her, another part wanted to march outside and confront him. The upstairs was off-limits to the cast and crew and she'd made sure to remain there, except when she'd run down to welcome Erika's play group friends, all of whom had arrived by the entrance at the back of the house.

In the midst of what appeared to be tax receipt files, she spotted one labeled Horton v. ICU. Had David misplaced one of his law firm's client's files? For someone as meticulous as her husband had been, she thought that unlikely. Humming along with the Everly Brothers as they urged little Susie to wake up, Jonni opened the file.

From Erika's room down the hall toward the front of the house came a shout of laughter followed by little-girl giggles. Erika and her friends were indulging in a game of dress-up. Jonni had promised them a tea party after they were finished decking themselves out in the old clothes she and Erika had collected from secondhand shops.

The file did appear to belong to a client. It was arranged as all of David's legal files had been, the contents held down on the left and right side of the folder with a two-hole bracket. The top sheet on the left was a brief letter on firm letterhead, confirming a meeting. Jonni felt a pang of loss as she noted the date of the letter, signed with David's lawyerly scrawl, was two days before his death. On the right was a thick sheaf of what appeared to be billing records.

Jonni closed it and set it aside. She'd call the office tomorrow and they could have their messenger collect it. The other files in that section were receipts of expenses. She stashed them in a box and labeled them with her accountant's name. That made her think of her date from hell with Matthew Howell, and she grinned. At least she'd escaped that!

Thanks to Isolde, who had the afternoon off. Thank

goodness David had kept his Reject file. Something about that memory gave her pause. Her dead husband had been an incredibly organized man. His ties were laid out in special drawers by color and style; his shirts always faced button side to the left in his closet. He had his car detailed once a month.

Yet he'd died in a car accident on the Causeway bridge miles from where he had told her he was. Jonni had suspected he'd been with another woman, but other than her own fears and the subtle indications of his own waning interest in her, she'd never found proof.

She eyed the legal file, so out of place in his meticulous office. Had Pandora doubted her own actions before flipping open the lid of her mythical magic box?

Drumming her fingertips on the top of the file, she listened to the radio announcer warn of tropical moisture dumping in excess of several inches on the city that afternoon. She glanced out the wall of windows and noted the steady rain.

What meeting had that letter arranged? Was it the one where David had been the night he died? He'd called that evening and said he'd had a dinner meeting with clients that was running late. That was the last time she'd heard his voice.

Jonni picked up the file and walked over to the windows. Drops pelted the glass as she read the letter. It had been sent to another attorney, a woman.

Well, about half of the lawyers in America were women. There was nothing unusual in that.

Jonni flipped to the second document in the stack. Her breath halted somewhere between her lungs and her heart when she saw it was a copy of a handwritten note

to the same addressee. Only this one carried the saluta-
tion, "My dearest Vivienne."

Jonni blinked and flipped through the sheaf. Sure
enough, they were the same, photocopies of letters
David had written. She peeked under the top bill on the
right, sure she'd find the answering letters from the vixen
Vivienne. And sure enough, they were there, originals,
prettily penned on pink-edged stationery.

She thought she'd be sick. Forcing herself to take several deep breaths, she laid her forehead against the glass,
wishing the rain would penetrate and wash her away.

No such luck. She sighed and pushed away from the
window, staring at the open file, wondering whether it
was worse to read them or to be tortured by not knowing what the two of them had said to each other.

Squinting, the way she did when she watched scary
movies so she could squeeze her eyes closed quickly at
the sight of a monster too horrible to bear, Jonni flipped
to a letter in the middle of the right-hand stack.

*There I was in Judge ____'s courtroom, and all I
could think about was yesterday. My panties were
damp! The judge asked me a question and for the first
time in my life, I didn't get an answer right. But with the
feel of you still inside me—*

Jonni threw the file across the room. "That fucking
bastard," she said out loud. She would have screamed
the words, but she was mindful of the children down the
hall. And what kind of ego did this woman have? She'd
never gotten anything wrong? That was a joke! Well,
she'd earned an A in Adultery.

Jonni dashed at her eyes and found she no longer had
any tears.

She heard a noise in the doorway and whirled around. She didn't want Erika or the other girls to see her in this state of fury. But when she looked, no one was there. Satisfied she was alone, she stalked across the floor and quite childishly jumped up and down on the file.

Horton. What kind of code name was that? And then she realized what it meant. Vivienne Horton.

She'd heard the name countless times in casual conversation when David talked about his work. She was co-counsel on numerous cases. Jonni had met her, along with her husband, on several occasions. A retching built up in her throat as she considered the knowledge she now possessed and wondered whether Vivienne's husband would want to see the contents of Horton v. ICU.

She dropped to the floor, cross-legged, and held her head in her hands, reflecting on the man to whom she'd pledged and delivered unceasing devotion. If he were alive and she discovered the truth, then she would have gone to Mr. Horton, but now with David dead, perhaps it was best to let it all die with him.

Perhaps Mrs. Horton had learned her lesson.

Jonni certainly had.

Cameron didn't know what had gotten under his skin. As bad as he felt, with those damn hammers knocking on his skull from the inside out and the heavy makeup coating his face and hands on a day with 110 percent humidity, he ought to just go into his trailer and close his eyes until they called him for the next scene.

Instead, here he was, scouting the inside of the house for the lady of the manor.

He passed down the long entry hall, heading for the

kitchen in the back. A television played and he picked up his step. He didn't understand it, but being around Jonquil made him feel better. It didn't make sense; she hadn't flirted or come on to him. She'd actually turned him down flat last night.

Yeah, she turned down the real Cameron Scott, he said under his breath and then pushed open the door to the kitchen.

Some afternoon soap played on the counter television. Cameron gave a quick prayer to the gods of Hollywood that he'd been spared that route to the big time and glanced around. Empty.

He frowned and then noticed a door ajar at the far side of the room. Crossing that way, he stopped when a woman he'd never seen before turned, broom in hand.

The maid.

Well, naturally the lady of the manor didn't sweep her own floors. "Good afternoon," Cameron said.

Her eyes widened. "Good afternoon to you," she said. "Can I get you something?"

Yeah, Jonquil. "No, thanks," he said.

"You're the movie star, aren't you?"

Cameron nodded.

She nodded, too, staring at him. "I studied acting once," she said.

Oh, no. Cameron thought of Cosey. Did every female want to be in the movies? "Really." He never knew what to say in these situations. He'd had it so easy in his path to the top that he found it hard to snub those who wanted what he'd stumbled upon.

She moved into the room, attacking the edge of the floor along the baseboards with vigor. Cameron retreated a few steps. Maybe she'd tell him where Jonquil was, or if he hung out, perhaps she'd appear. The crew was on a union-mandated break so he had a bit of time before they'd be looking for him.

"Starred in my high school play," she said. "Got it into my head I could make it on Broadway so off I went on the Greyhound with my things in a carry bag." She sighed and shook her head. "That was a long time ago."

"I see," Cameron said. Would he have believed in himself enough to do such a thing? "How long were you in New York?"

The maid stopped sweeping and rested her chin and hands on the top of the broom. A dreamy look came over her brown eyes. "Twelve months and two days. I'd just gotten my first bit part in a small production when my mama called. Daddy had died and she needed help with the little ones." She faced Cameron. "I was the oldest, you see."

He nodded. "So you went home."

"Yessirree, came home, got a job in a hotel, and helped my mama. Then I met the mister and married and raised my own brood. And do you know, until Miz Jonni signed on to this filming thing, I'd forgotten all about that year."

"And two days," Cameron said softly.

She flashed a smile at him. "And two days."

Cameron made a mental note to see about getting her a spot as an extra. Then he shook his head. Heck, he was starting to act like Mister Benjamin, going around helping people.

"Anything wrong?" She'd gone back to sweeping the floor.

"No. I was wondering, is Mrs. DeVries at home?"

The maid looked sideways at him. "The missus don't like to be called Mrs. DeVries," she said.

That was intriguing. Cameron leaned forward, all ears.

"No, since Mr. David died last year, she's just been plain Jonni DeVries. I wouldn't be surprised if she didn't take her own name back. Except for little Erika's sake, she probably would have done it before the funeral came and went."

"Is that right?" Now this was interesting news.

"I've been with this family since before Miz Jonni was married. It like to broke my heart when I saw how Mr. David treated her."

"And how was that?"

She was back to leaning on the broom. Cameron supposed he should feel guilty about pumping the maid, but he didn't feel one ounce of regret. He wanted to know everything he could about the lady of the manor.

"Oh, all pretty in front of the world, and then when no one else was around, he'd pick at everything. And then he started staying at work all day and night. And traveling on business, if you know what I mean." Her look spoke volumes. "Mr. David never met a fact he didn't know better than," she said. "He was a rich, successful lawyer, but every time he came into the room, my toes curled under."

Cameron smiled at the description.

"Go ahead and laugh, but I can tell who's good and

who's not. And I don't have to hold it to my nose, like a carton of milk, to tell what's rotten."

"Are your toes curling now?" Silly, but he felt a little nervous waiting for her answer.

She laughed and reached under the table with the broom. "Just by you asking that question should tell you the answer."

He wasn't sure what she meant by that puzzle but since she was smiling at him, he took it to mean he fell into the "good" side of her checklist. "Thank you," he said.

"Some folks say as you shouldn't care what other people think, but that's really not true," the maid said. "You just have to learn who matters and who doesn't. If you take the back stairs," she said, without looking up from the floor, "you'll find Miz Jonni in the room to the right."

"Thank you, Mrs.—?"

"Oh, you can call me Sunny," she said, "everyone does."

"Thank you, Sunny," he said, and headed for the stairs. He'd gained an ally in that exchange. The stairs opened to a wide expanse of gleaming wood floor that stretched ahead. To the right, through an open door, came the sound of the Beach Boys. Cameron smiled. Their music never failed to cheer him.

He approached the door, unsure of what he should say, a most unusual state of affairs for Cameron Scott. He still didn't know whether she realized the old face he wore was that of his character, but with Flynn's warning in his head and the newspaper no doubt somewhere in the house, he figured he ought to confess the truth.

He'd heard somewhere that women would rather be told the truth than a lie, but he'd always doubted that. No one wanted to hear that her new dress was a rag or her hair looked better before the two-hundred-dollar haircut than after.

At the doorway, he paused. He poked his head into the large masculine-looking room, no doubt "Mr. David's" office, and at first he didn't see her.

Jonquil stood all the way across the room, her back to him, leaning against windows that ran from the floor to the ceiling. He started to speak, then he realized her shoulders were shaking.

She was crying.

Down by her side, she held what looked like a file folder. Over the sounds of "California Dreamin'," he thought he heard sobs alternating with sniffles.

Jeez.

Should he go to her or leave her alone?

Women were funny that way. Some of them hated to be found with their nose all red and eyes puffy and swollen and tearstains wrecking their eye makeup.

Others wanted nothing more than a strong pair of arms wrapped around them.

He backed out of the doorway, weighing the decision.

And then he heard a splat and her voice, in a low, furious tone. When the words "that fucking bastard" registered in his brain, his decision was made for him. Approaching a woman while she was in the throes of man hating was a lose-lose proposition.

Cameron edged down the hall and onto the top stair. From the front of the house came girlish laughter and chatter. Despite his miserable hangover and not getting to speak to Erika's mother, he smiled at the sounds. He didn't spend much time around kids, other than the child actors he worked with, but he liked their energy and innocence. With his sister settling into marriage, no doubt she'd make him an uncle soon.

He'd like that, Cameron realized, making his way down the stairs. Having a niece or nephew would be nice. And so would having his own.

Cameron halted in his tracks, one foot suspended above the next-to-the-bottom stair. Where in the hell had that thought come from?

"You are a confirmed bachelor," he said aloud. "And don't forget it."

Chapter Thirteen

On the porch of Jonni's Garden District house

Instead of finding the cast and crew ready to return to work, Cameron returned to a group huddled on the front porch around the director. Quentin Grandy was talking on a cell phone and tugging his free hand through his hair. If he kept that up, Cameron thought, he'd be bald by the time the sun went down.

Not that there was any sun. While he'd been inside the rain had gone from trickle to downpour. Protective coverings had been thrown over the equipment, lighting, and props. The other actors had retreated to their trailers.

Quentin snapped his phone closed. "That was Mia. She says the weather people are taking this seriously. They call it training, meaning the storm is sitting over the city and not moving away." He slipped his phone onto a leather holster. "It seems it takes nothing more than a few bucketsful of water to flood this town."

The second assistant director said, "New Orleans is under sea level."

Grandy glared at the guy. Then he said, "Sorry, but we'll be almost a full day behind if we shut down now."

"If we'd started on time . . ." the same guy said, and then trailed off.

Cameron stepped onto the porch, and all eyes turned in his direction. "You mean if I hadn't landed my sorry ass in jail, don't you?"

Someone giggled nervously.

Grandy was watching him. Cameron took a deep breath and said, "I owe you all an apology. It won't happen again."

A couple of the guys looked stunned. One of the women was looking at him as if she'd like to devour him for dessert.

"Thank you, Cameron," Grandy said. "Apology accepted. Okay, everybody, that's it for today."

A gust of wind slammed its way across the porch, blowing water with it. Everyone jumped. Cameron wiped at his face and came away with a handful of Mister Benjamin's wrinkled complexion.

"I'll take care of that, Mr. Scott," the makeup man said. He opened his case and reached for some toweling and cold cream. The rest of the group dashed for the street and the various vehicles parked there.

"Mister Benjamin, oh where are you, Mister Benjamin?" Erika's voice carried out to the porch.

"Hang on a sec," Cameron said to the makeup man.

Erika's impish face, framed in a hat that could have held its own at Ascot, peeked around the front door, quickly followed by the rest of her, swathed in a long red dress and a feather boa, and four other girls, all of whom looked as if they'd raided a costume shop.

Or perhaps their mother's closets, Cameron reflected, grinning at the sight of them dripping in costume pearls and feathers and lace and silk. "What lovely hats," he said, bowing to each of them.

"Mister Benjamin, I *knew* you'd play with us," Erika said. She turned to the others. "See, I told you he was my friend. He's not like regular grown-ups."

The makeup guy was trying hard not to laugh. Cameron shot him a glance guaranteed to stifle any outburst. "And what are regular grown-ups like?" Cameron asked, squatting so that he was on their eye level.

The only redhead in the group lifted an imaginary glass and shook her hair back over her shoulder. "Dahling, if I have told you once, I have told you a hundred times, only a drop of vermouth." She giggled and then said in a sad voice, "Grown-ups are always fussing."

"My mom's not like that," Erika said. "She's giving us a tea party, and you, too, Mister Benjamin."

"Oh, I'm invited, am I?" Cameron pretended to consider the invitation. What he wanted to ask was whether her mother knew of his inclusion in the party.

"Grown-ups are always working," said the other blond-haired child. She glared at Cameron. "And they're always too busy to play with us."

"Yeah, that's why we have nannies," the redhead said. "They have to be nice to us or they get fired."

"Nice life," the makeup guy said.

"Oh, yeah," Cameron replied, wondering what these

girls would think of the way he'd grown up in a cramped house built onto the back of his father's machine shop business.

The rain continued to beat down. Water was now standing along the sidewalk and the yard and splashing over the curb from the street. The few cars that moved down the street did so slowly, windshield wipers beating furiously. Cameron ought to leave now. Quentin might have been surprised, but Cameron knew how quickly the water could overwhelm the city. He'd been in New Orleans once before when some poor guy had drowned in his car beneath an interstate overpass. The rain that day had been no worse than what was coming down now.

"How are you getting back to the hotel?" he asked in an aside to the makeup guy.

He looked surprised. "I figured you had a car coming for you and I'd hop a ride."

"Oh, well, of course you'd be welcome but I didn't order a car." Flynn had planned to swing back by but there'd been no sign of him since he left on his mission to deliver the snoring Harrison G. DePaul to his loved ones.

The guy scratched his head. "I guess I'll wait in the trailer till it slacks off and call a cab."

Erika tugged on Cameron's jacket. "Is he a friend of yours?"

Cameron nodded. He didn't even know the man's name, come to think of it.

"Then he can come to tea, too."

"Thanks," he said before Cameron could scowl at him and signal him to say no. These girls' mothers were probably particular about the adults they hung out with.

"Maybe we'd better ask your mother what she wants us to do," Cameron said.

"Erika's mother is cool," the redhead said. "What do you do on the movie?" she asked the makeup guy, staring at the open case on the porch beside him.

"My name's Luther," he said, "and I'm a makeup artist."

"Ooh," all five girls said in one voice. "Makeup!" Shouts of delight erupted and Cameron knew what it felt like to be upstaged as the children crowded around Luther and his magic case.

"Erika!"

Cameron cocked an ear. Jonquil's voice sounded again, calling her daughter's name.

"Inside, now," she called, her voice growing louder.

Erika put her fingers to her lips.

Jonquil appeared in the doorway, wearing a twenties flapper dress that hugged her curves. At the reception Cameron had admired her fresh appearance, the glamorous yet demure cut of her creamy linen suit. He thought it suited her perfectly, but now, taking in the shimmering red beaded dress and the lush fullness of her breasts and hips set off by what on some women would look like a sack of a dress, he realized there was a heck of a lot of hidden fire in this woman who wore the airs of a matron.

Jonquil was hot.

She just didn't realize it.

Cameron knew, then and there, he'd found the role he'd been waiting for. He grinned.

She glared at him. "Oh, it's you."

He smiled back, not put off at all. "Mister Benjamin, at your service," he said, adding one of the character's courtly bows.

The girls giggled.

Jonquil gave him the evil eye. So she knew the bad boy Cameron Scott lurked beneath the stage makeup. She was no doubt reluctant to reveal that in front of the children. Well, that could work to his advantage. As soon as the two of them were alone, he'd bravely confess, before she could accuse him of gaining her confidence by false means.

Which is of course what he'd done. Oh, well, generals couldn't balk at facts when it came to strategy.

"Girls, you know you're not to interrupt the film crew," Jonquil said.

"They left," Erika said. "Look, it's only Mister Benjamin and Luther. He does makeup."

Jonni shifted her attention from the porch to the yard beyond. Sure enough, all the equipment was covered and some that had been there the day before had been packed away. The two guys on the porch were the only other people in sight.

Not that she could see far, with the way the rain was coating the air, thick and furious. She sniffed the heavy fresh air and relaxed slightly, despite Cameron's too-near presence. Something about him made her feel on edge, but not in a bad way, just strangely alive in a way she wasn't sure she knew how to handle.

Besides that, he was on her bad list for pretending to be a kindly old uncle.

"Can Luther do our faces? He said he would if it was okay with you, please Mrs. DeVries?" That was Read

McCall, the redhead whom Jonni felt was already far too adult-acting for a five-year-old.

"I don't know," she said.

Read rolled her eyes. "When a grown-up says that," she said to the group in general, "it means they're stalling for time so they can think of a way to say no."

Two of the other girls clapped their hands over Read's mouth. "Shh!"

"It's no problem," Luther said. "I have two little sisters and I know how much they like having their makeup done."

Just then a gust of wind blew the rain straight onto the porch. Everyone jumped and stampeded into the house. They stood in the entry, shaking droplets of rain.

Sunny was heading their way from the back of the house. "You all ought to use the sense God gave you and come in out of that storm. Bob Breck says this storm is just sitting on the city this afternoon. I know I'm not going to get home 'cause my street's already flooded."

"You know you can stay over," Jonni said.

She caught Cameron looking at her, felt his piercing look as much as spotted it out of the corner of her eye. She turned to him, and sure enough, he was looking like a cat left alone with a flock of canaries. She just didn't understand the man. He could have, and apparently did help himself to, any woman he came across.

So what was his interest in her? Or was she just so starved for male attention that she was imagining it? But he had asked her out last night.

She sighed. Erika took her hand and said in her sweetest voice, "I invited Mister Benjamin and Luther to stay to tea. We can't put them out in the rain."

Jonni looked at her daughter's angelic expression and knew she'd lost this round. To Luther she said, "Don't overdo the makeup. They're only five."

"Yeah!" The girls danced around Luther and his magic case, even Read, who seemed to remember she was a child and not a subdeb.

"Let me watch 'em," Sunny said.

"Oh, I can do that," Jonni said.

"You'll need your strength for the tea party," Sunny said, with a wink and a smile. "Why don't you and the mister here take a break in the parlor?"

Jonni had the funniest sensation she was being railroaded, but why her maid would have any ulterior motive in throwing her together with someone who by all appearances could be her grandfather, she couldn't fathom. And she wouldn't mind a break from the five girls. The choosing of clothes and costumes and then their convincing her she had to join them in high style, too, had quite exhausted her patience. As long as the girls were supervised by Sunny she needn't have any qualms at leaving them in the other room with the makeup guy. Sunny hadn't raised five boys of her own without knowing how to invoke law and order.

"All right," Jonni said. "We'll be in the dining room arranging things for the tea party. Why don't you do the makeup in the breakfast room?"

Read removed her hat. "I'll go first," she said.

"Ya'll march yourselves into the kitchen," Sunny said. "I'll decide who goes first."

Jonni smothered a smile. Read was a pill. Jonni was blessed that Erika was such a sweet-natured child.

They traipsed toward the back of the house. Left

alone in the foyer with Cameron Scott disguised as Mister Benjamin, Jonni crossed her arms over her chest, unsure of what to say to him. Perhaps she'd pretend she didn't know he was the same man who'd asked her out last night.

She smiled slightly. Let him wonder. Serve him right. "The dining room is through here," she said, indicating the formal parlor to the right of the entryway. "That is, if you feel up to helping set the table."

"I feel fine," he said.

"Well, I noticed you didn't have your cane," she said, ever so sweetly. Cane, schmane. He needed a cane as much as she needed a walker.

"Oh," he said, looking around as if he hadn't even noticed its absence. "Must have lost it in the storm."

"And your sore throat," she said. "You lost that raspy voice, too."

"So I did." He was looking amused. "There's nothing like a good storm to clear the air."

Jonni was leading them through the formal parlor, a room David and the decorator had loved, and one she seldom paused in now that both her husband and the decorator were out of the picture. Jonni had wanted to do the house herself, but David had insisted that they hire the woman who'd done several of their friends' historic houses. David, as always, had won out, and as a result, Jonni lived in an architecturally and artistically accurate period house that did nothing to lift her spirits. She despised the crimson and gold so prevalent in the antebellum years of the house's origin. The production people had loved it for the same reasons she hated it; perhaps when the filming was over, she'd rip it all out and start over. To Cameron, she said, "Or a good renovation."

"Ah, yes, a makeover." He was glancing around the room. She gave him points for not uttering platitudes about the room's appearance. The filming was being done in the matching double parlors that ran along the other side of the front entrance hall.

"Where do you live?" There, see if he'd answer as Cameron Scott. Not that she knew anything about the man, except what she'd read in the morning paper and what she'd observed last night. But she could check it out and see if he told the truth.

"I have a place in Bel Air," he said. "It doesn't have the same sense of history, but it's comfortable."

"Bel Air," she said. She was pretty sure that was fabulously expensive territory. But money, she well knew, didn't buy happiness.

He shrugged. "I have a little home at the beach, too." He was watching her, and suddenly Jonni didn't feel like playing games with identities anymore. She flicked on the lights of the massive chandelier that ruled over the dining table that sat eighteen guests in spacious ease. Crossing to the china armoire, she opened it and lifted out a stack of fragile Meissen plates. "Oh, in Malibu?"

When she turned around from the cabinet, she almost bumped into him. He was standing there, far too close for comfort.

"Let me take those," he said, reaching for the plates.

His fingers brushed hers, and her reaction was just as electric as it had been last night when he'd handed her the champagne glass. She stood there, not letting go of the plates, not moving, not breathing.

He watched her, those dark eyes gazing down into her face, no doubt able to see through to her very nerves to observe the sensations he stirred within her.

She wet her lips with the tip of her tongue. Annoying man, he knew he had this effect on women and took great advantage of it! But try as she might to force her brain to break the spell, she could not.

"Pretty," he murmured, stroking her fingertips.

"They're Meissen," she said, forcing some sense into her head.

"Mine," he said, "they're mine."

She shoved the plates against his chest and let go of them. He'd either catch them or she'd be cleaning up chunks of china. He clutched them in his hands, grinning.

"You are the most provoking creature," she said.

"My business manager says the same thing about me," he said. He turned and put the plates down on the table. "Before we go any further in playing house, there's something I need to tell you."

Oh, so he was going to confess. Jonni couldn't wait to see what he'd have to say. One thing was for sure; she wasn't going to make it easy for him.

Chapter Fourteen

Once again in Jonni's dining room

She was so darn cute. Cameron knew she knew his identity and she was just playing him along like a kite string. He held his tongue, watching how avidly she looked up at him, no doubt awaiting his earnest confession that he'd played her for some sort of fool.

Only he hadn't.

He'd met a woman he enjoyed talking to, sitting comfortably with at her kitchen table. When was the last time that had happened to him? Cameron ran a hand along his jaw. Maybe his mother's table back home in Missouri?

She had reached into the cabinet again and was now handing him two cups. He noticed she held them by their fragile handles and extended the bowl of the cup toward him. So she'd felt the same surge of sensation when they touched, had she?

He cradled a cup in each hand, and as he did, the image of her lush curves filling his hands shot through his brain. He almost dropped the cups.

"Nice," he said, his eyes fixed on hers.

"They were my husband's grandmother's," she said, in a rather matter-of-fact voice. But the warmth in her eyes encouraged him.

Cameron transported ten cups and saucers to the table. He counted, and said, "Your daughter, her four friends, you, me, Sunny, Luther—that's nine."

"Isolde may come in," she said. "Or the rain may trap her on campus. But I like to be prepared."

"That doesn't surprise me," he said.

She colored slightly. "It's the way I am."

"Hey, that's meant as a compliment, not an insult," Cameron said. "I'm a real spur-of-the-moment kind of guy."

"Always operate on impulse?"

He nodded, then pulled out two chairs from the table. He guided her to one, noting the silky heat of her arm. "Always," he said, taking a seat facing her. "For instance, the other day, I wandered into your kitchen and what did I find but one of the most intriguing women I've had the pleasure of meeting in I can't tell you how long."

Her eyes were shining and that delightful pale rose color tinged her cheeks. As he'd done last night, he traced the plane of her cheek with a brush of his finger.

"And there I was, decked out in costume, makeup, the whole nine yards. It did occur to me at some point you regarded me as a kindly old uncle sort of guy, but when I saw you the next day and you welcomed me, I couldn't just interrupt and say, Hey, guess what, I'm not Uncle Joe."

"And this isn't *Petticoat Junction*," Jonquil said, a half-smile hovering on her sensuous mouth.

"You like those old TV shows, too?"

She nodded. "So does Erika, though I'm not sure she understands a lot of the references."

"And oldies music?" Cameron thought of the music he'd heard her playing when he'd slipped up the back staircase. "I bet you love the sixties stuff."

"How did you know that?" Her eyes were smiling at him.

He shrugged. "Good guess?"

"And old movies."

"You don't watch much of the recent crop of films, I gather," Cameron said, checking her reaction to his words.

Jonni shook her head. She was having much too good of a time talking to this man. But then, he was clearly in his character's persona. Or was he? Before she could ask him the answer to that question, he leaned toward her, his hands on his knees.

"What I'm trying to tell you is that when I met you the other day, I didn't intend to pretend to be someone I wasn't." He lifted one hand, displaying the gnarled skin of an elderly man. "At first I assumed you would have heard the news that Cameron Scott was playing Mister Benjamin, and then when I started to realize you didn't know, well, heck, it was easier just to keep on talking to you without worrying about who was who."

Jonni looked from the weathered hand to the wrinkled face. She looked into Cameron's eyes. In those dark depths she saw only good. "So you weren't laughing at me for being the only woman in New Orleans who had no clue?"

He captured her hands in his, pressed them lightly, and let go at once. It was the merest of touches, really, but he might as well have still been holding them. Staring at her lap, Jonni tucked her hands under the sides of her red flapper dress. When she did, she was reminded of how silly she must look in the getup the girls had insisted she wear. Of course someone as world-wise as Cameron Scott would laugh at her.

"Hey," he said softly, tipping her chin up. "Just out of curiosity, when did you know?"

"The morning paper," she said, pushing her chair back and rising to tend to the task of setting the table.

He slapped a hand against his forehead. "My terrible reputation precedes me!" He reached for the saucers and started laying them beside the plates. "Wait a minute. You knew I'd spent the night in jail and you still invited me to stay for tea?"

Jonni paused, one fragile cup in each hand. "Technically, Erika invited you."

"Oh, ho! So with you I'm in the doghouse?"

He smiled in such a charming way as he asked the question that Jonni found she couldn't say, Yes, of course, what do you expect? "Well, it is raining cats and dogs," she said.

"And I'm a very lucky dog that you let me stay," he said. "You have a forgiving heart."

Jonni looked into one of the cups, remembering the letters she'd found earlier. More grimly than she intended, she said, "I'm not so sure that's true."

"You're thinking of someone else?"

She nodded. She started to speak, then remembered this man coaxing secrets out of her wasn't Mister Benjamin. "You don't want to hear that sob story," she said lightly. "Let's do the silver."

He patted his shoulder. "You have to admit these are pretty broad."

Jonni smiled. "That's sweet, but I prefer to keep my troubles to myself."

"Now that's something I can recommend against," he said, accepting the teaspoons she handed him from the armoire's silver drawer. "Repression is very bad for your health. That's why I let everything out."

"And isn't that how you ended up in Orleans' most exclusive overnight accommodation?" Jonni enjoyed teasing him. It was easy to keep thinking of Cameron as Mister Benjamin. And compared to the proof of David's betrayal she'd uncovered, Cameron's game of make-believe didn't seem so terrible, especially since he had confessed.

"I believe, ma'am," he said with a twinkle in his eye, "I have that the wrong way around. It's them as let me out."

She laughed and then quickly caught herself. "Being arrested is no joke," she said, disliking how prim she sounded. Cameron Scott, Mr. Playboy, was used to women making up to him, not delivering lectures.

"You can say that again," he said. "Last night's diversion is going to cost me a bundle."

"Lawyers are expensive," Jonni said. Again, she felt that twist of a knife as she thought of David. "And not to be trusted," she added.

He finished laying the forks to the right of the plates. "The lawyer is the cheap part. It's the stupid deal my manager agreed to that's going to bite me."

"Oh?"

He shrugged. "Yeah, I have to behave myself the entire time I'm here in the Big Easy or I get hit with fines. It's a morals clause, believe it or not."

"Oh," Jonni said, her voice trailing off. Was that why he was paying attention to her? Because he figured she was the one woman he wouldn't get in trouble with? The thought rankled. And then it inspired the almost buried imp that she'd long ago lost touch with. "So what types of things will get you in hot water?"

"Let's not talk about me," he said. "Very boring topic."

She glanced over at him, wondering if that was a line he used to disarm his audience or whether he believed it. A million females would probably pay to change places with Jonquil Landry DeVries at that very moment, and every last one of them would want to hear all about Cameron Scott.

Or would they? She wrinkled her brow, reflecting. Perhaps they'd see his presence as some sign of their own value and want only to focus on self.

"Well, Mr. Scott," Jonni said, "if we can't talk about me and we can't talk about you, then we may have arrived at an impasse."

"Impasse?" He grinned, and said, "Impassable!"

She smiled back at him and decided to leave the forks on the wrong side of the plates. If the girls noticed, which she doubted that they would, she'd tell them it was done California-style.

"I do need your advice on something," Cameron said, tapping the side of his cheek. "Shall I remain Mister Benjamin for the tea party or may I shim-sham myself into the humble Mr. Scott?"

"Shim-sham?" Jonni stalled, realizing she preferred him to stay safely behind his mask.

"You know, whatever those magic words are the old guy mutters when he changes shape."

"Oh, you want to morph?"

"Yeah, that's it. Morph."

Erika ran into the room as Cameron repeated the term. "Mommy—" She stopped and stared from her to Cameron. "You're really going to morph?"

"I may," he said, his voice low and raspy, his shoulders suddenly slumped forward, his head held to one side.

Jonni was amazed at the instantaneous transformation. No wonder she'd been fooled! Cameron Scott acted the role with his entire self.

"Is the evil Mister Snooks up to no good?" Erika glanced around.

"Never fear, he can do no harm while I am near," Cameron said.

Erika giggled. "You're a poet."

He gave her a formal bow. "If you'll escort me to your friends," he said, "I'll take my leave of them."

"Can't we watch you morph?"

He looked from Erika to Jonni and back. "This may be a particularly difficult transition. Tell you what, you can help me with the magic words, but sometimes I need to be alone to, um, to . . ." His look was so beseeching, Jonni took pity on him.

"Morph meditation," she said. "You have to put your mind into the proper state," she said, keeping a straight face and wondering if this was any different than letting Erika believe her Christmas presents came on a sleigh from the North Pole.

"Ah, yes, the word escaped me," he said, tapping on the side of his head. "One gets rusty after so many years," he said with a sigh.

"If you're tired, you can take a nap," Erika said. "Mommy always says I'm much nicer after I've napped."

Something lit in Cameron's eyes in a most un–Mister Benjamin–like way. "That is good advice. Does Mommy follow it herself?"

"Oh, yes," Erika said. "Sometimes—"

"Sweetheart," Jonni said, cutting her off before she could make any undue revelations, "why don't you take Cam—Mister Benjamin into the parlor and let the girls say good-bye?"

She didn't know why, but the image of taking a nap with Cameron Scott lying beside her filled her mind. She could scarcely glance at him as he passed by, the jacket of his coat brushing the side of her arm. He smiled at her, a wicked gleam in his eyes, and she knew he was thinking exactly the same thing.

Impossible.

He was Cameron Scott.

She was matronly Jonquil DeVries, squeezed into a sausage of a dress picked up at Bloomin' Deals for twenty dollars while shopping with the girls for dress-up costumes.

"We'll be right back," Erika said. She took Mister

Benjamin by the hand, and chattering away, led him from the room.

In the doorway, Cameron turned, and to Jonni's chagrin, he caught her fanning her flushed cheeks with one hand.

He winked.

His mind squarely on the mother, Cameron walked with the daughter, checked Luther's handiwork, nabbed a tub of cold cream from him, and performed, with the girls, the incantation required to morph.

A nap with Jonquil, now that was the best idea he'd heard all day. He'd forgotten all about his hangover and sleepless night. Not that he'd waste any time sleeping when he was alone with a woman like Jonquil. Her body cried out to be caressed, stroked, laved with his tongue. He wanted to march back into the dining room and spread her open on the table. Forget tea and cookies.

He wanted to taste Jonquil.

"Mister Benjamin, you got the words wrong," Erika said, tapping the toe of her dress up heel.

"I did?" Darn. He'd better pay attention. Besides, his body was going to betray him if he didn't get control of his mind.

"Yes, you did," she said, sounding very much like her mother.

The redhead was whispering something to another one of the girls. She lifted her head and said, "You can't really morph because you're an actor. We know that. Erika, you're too grown up to play this kind of pretend."

"It's not pretend," Erika said, sounding pretty darn stubborn. Cameron wondered if she got that from her mother, too. He grinned. No doubt she did. Jonquil had certainly stuck to her guns last night. "Now, say it right this time," she commanded.

"Poof! Shazashabam!" Cameron intoned.

"See, nothing happened," the redhead said.

Cameron was holding the container of cold cream behind his back. "I need some of that meditation time," he said. "Might I use your bathroom?"

"Certainly," Erika said. "The closest one is behind the kitchen." Then she stuck her tongue out at her friend.

"It's at the foot of the back stairs," Sunny said. "And Miss Erika, let's mind our manners."

Cameron backed from the room, then made his way quickly through the kitchen. Once inside the bathroom, he eased the jacket over his hands, rolled up his sleeves, and slathered the cream over his hands and face. It took the makeup guys a long time to turn him into Mister Benjamin but he'd figured out it didn't take too long to get back to plain old Cameron Scott.

He grinned, thinking of Jonquil. Then his good feeling vanished as he considered how she'd reacted to him last night. Would she give him the cold shoulder? He peered into the mirror, studying the face that had made him a fortune many times over. What was not to like?

He shrugged and whistled a few bars of "California Dreamin'." The blood still throbbed in his groin but he realized he was more concerned about whether she'd continue to accept him once the makeup was gone than he was about scoring with her.

He paused, and then wiped the cream and muck off with wads of toilet paper. Strange. Normally all he considered were the ins and outs. He met a woman; he wanted something she had; she wanted something he had; they gave and they got. And life moved on.

He shook his head and then doused his face and hands with water. He tried to shake off the unfamiliar feeling of being concerned about what a woman thought of him as a person, but it clung to him the way the water drops did to the patches of his skin that gleamed with remnants of the cold cream.

The towels were monogrammed with an elegant "DV." He grabbed the thick white hand towel and scrubbed at his face and hands. Muttering Mister Benjamin's morph trance words under his breath, he removed the bow tie, loosened the collar of his shirt, left his sleeves rolled up, and tossed the jacket over one shoulder.

The best solution to all this thinking was action. He'd charm the woman, bed her, maybe even a few times, and that would be that. She'd end up screaming at him like all the other women he'd known. Selfish. Egotistical. Unreliable. A great lover, of course, but once out of the sack it seemed women found him full of fault. Though if that was the case, he'd never understood why the biggest complaint against him was that he'd never settle down, get serious, whip out an overpriced ring, and stick his neck into the noose of wedded bliss.

But, as Flynn could tell anyone who asked, that's just who Cameron Scott was. This time would be no different from any other. He'd finish filming, split town, and she could tell her girlfriends what it was like to screw Cameron Scott.

He'd been there, done that so many times he could write the script. One hand on the crystal doorknob,

Cameron paused, his shoulders slumping even though he'd left the Mister Benjamin persona behind. He ought to be feeling pretty darn good. He knew Jonquil was hot for him. If they weren't stranded with a house full of kids, he'd have her naked and quivering beneath him in, oh, a minimum of an hour.

And here he was making a movie that would in turn earn him another small fortune, provided of course he stayed out of trouble. So why did he feel so empty?

Looking over his shoulder into the mirror, he said, "Shape up, Scott. I mean, what more can a guy ask for?"

Chapter Fifteen

Inside Jonni's kitchen

Jonni was on the phone with Isolde when Cameron walked into the room. The transformation was so startling she stopped speaking in mid-sentence to stare at him.

He'd said he had broad shoulders, and the sleek-fitting white shirt confirmed that fact even more so than had the dinner jacket he'd worn last night. She liked the way he'd turned up the sleeves of his shirt. The open collar revealed that he was blessed with the perfect amount of chest hair—not too much and not too little.

Of course, the pants were the same baggy trousers the character wore, but even the folds of fabric couldn't hide the long legs and narrow hips. His hands, one so casually holding the coat over his shoulder, showed lean, strong fingers. The other hand rested on his hip. Jonni stared at that powerful hand, now so different from the wrinkled and puffy one that had traced the line of her cheek not so long ago.

This powerful beautiful hand was the same one that had made that same gesture last night.

And set off that same delightful, yet troubling sensation within her.

Jonni swallowed and dared a glance at his face, steeling herself for that cocky come-and-get-me attitude he'd no doubt be sporting now that he was out of Mister Benjamin mode.

"Mrs. J." Isolde's voice sounded from the receiver.

Jonni ignored her nanny.

Cameron Scott actually looked insecure. He stood there in the pose of a cover model, yet the way he scanned her face, apparently seeking her reaction, her approval even, amazed her. Or was she imagining that? Or even more likely, he was playing a role designed to win her over?

She'd seen how he'd transformed himself into Mister Benjamin's character in front of her eyes. She shook her head, clearing her thoughts. She was letting her mind run away with her. He was an actor stuck in her house due to inclement weather. He was amusing himself dallying with her.

"What was that, Isolde?" Jonni turned her attention to the phone. "You're stranded on campus?"

He had walked over and was standing behind her, way too close for comfort. She could swear he was inhaling the scent of her hair.

"Do you mind?" Jonni said.

"I hope you're not upset with me," her nanny said, sounding surprised. "It's the weather. I can't do anything about it."

"Neither can we," Cameron murmured in her ear.

"Stop it." Jonni said the words but she wasn't sure she meant them, a wishy-washiness she despised. She lived a steady life, not one fraught with disruption, especially not the type of turbulence this man represented.

"Mrs. J., there's nothing I can do. When the water goes down on Freret, I'll be able to get out."

"That could take hours," Jonni said.

"Exactly the way I like it," Cameron said.

"Keep that up and you're going to be in trouble," Jonni said, holding her hand over the mouthpiece.

"Please don't fire me," Isolde said. "I love my job."

"Why would I fire you?" Jonni said. "You can't help it that it's flooding."

"And you can't deny the fire inside of us," Cameron said, running the back of his thumb over the hand that held the receiver. "A little bit of rain can't put that out."

"I'm not upset with you, Isolde. I am, uh, distracted at the moment. Everything's fine here. Don't worry about us and make sure you stay there until it's completely safe to drive."

"Sure thing," Isolde said, sounding more like her usual cheerful self.

Jonni hung up the phone and swung around. Hands on her hips, she said, "You are an impossible man. Why you think you can come in here and proposition me, I can't imagine. I haven't given you one ounce of encouragement—"

Cameron placed one finger lightly against her lips. "Shh," he said, cocking an ear toward the front of the house. "As much as I'd enjoy describing each and every look you've given me, each and every reaction to my touch, I think we have company."

"Ooh," Jonni said, but as she heard the clumping footsteps of Erika in the oversize high heels of her tea party costume, she held her tongue. Still, it was hard to be upset with a man so sensitive as not to disturb her daughter or the other children.

He stepped a few feet away and draped his jacket over one of the breakfast room chairs.

"Mommy, did he morph?" Erika clomped into the room, followed by her girlfriends, Sunny, and Luther the makeup man. He'd obviously been busy as each of the girls had been transformed from five-year-old playmates to candidates for a beauty queen contest.

"Yes, and so did you," Jonni said, studying the amazing yet subtle differences.

"I tried not to overdo the look," Luther said. "Just some skin smoother, prep for the foundation, crème foundation, powder, three shades of blush to heighten the cheekbones . . . uh, maybe I'll step out front on the porch for a bit." He patted the pack of cigarettes in his shirt pocket.

"Yes, I see," Jonni said, not sure she approved, but as the girls seemed ecstatic, primping in front of the mirror near the back door, she saw no reason to dampen their enthusiasm. "Go ahead. We'll call you when tea is ready."

"Hello," the redhead said, leaving the mirror in favor of Cameron. "I don't believe we've met."

Jonni rolled her eyes. The child's mother and father had a lot to answer for, leaving Read alone to her own devices far too often. Why, she acted like an adult, or rather, like her mother.

"This is Mr. Scott," Jonni said. "He's visiting me."

"Hello," Cameron said, waving all around.

Read glanced over at Jonni, her oh-right expression probably the same one her mother would produce if Jonni mentioned that Cameron Scott had actually been coming on to her. Even her friends thought she'd buried herself along with David.

She'd show them. She'd already started working on her overeating and weight gain. Just let them catch sight of her with Cameron Scott. She experienced a blip of guilt as she considered how dishonorable that motive was. Well, she was sure Cameron Scott's intentions were anything but honorable.

For once, she was going to live dangerously.

"Girls," Jonni said, "let's make the tea. We've gotten off schedule and you'll want to have the tea party before your mothers arrive."

"It's raining way hard," Pepper, the quietest of the girls, said, pointing out the window. "It's like it's trying to get into the house."

"As if," Jonni said, automatically.

Pepper nodded, rather solemnly, and repeated her sentence, substituting "as if" for the offending "like."

"Let me guess," Cameron said, "You're really a teacher?"

"She's just my mom," Erika said.

Just my mom. Jonni smiled at her daughter, but the words clanged in her head like an alarm bell. She loved Erika, but somehow the phrase reminded her of all she'd not accomplished, all she'd put ahead of her own interests.

"I'll put the kettle on," Sunny said, shooing the girls

toward the dining room. "You can carry the sandwiches out," she said, pointing to Cameron.

Jonni smiled at her, grateful that she'd jumped into her own silence.

"Penny for your thoughts, Teach," he said as soon as the girls had cleared the doorway.

Sunny was bustling back and forth between the stove and refrigerator, loading the serving island with platters of finger sandwiches and tea cakes.

Jonni looked into his face and saw sincere interest. "I can't figure you out," she said, speaking softly.

"Me, either," he said, with a smile. "Try not thinking so much."

"Then my thoughts wouldn't be worth that penny," she said, smiling back at him.

"I'm not smart like my manager, Flynn Lawrence," he said, "but I do remember one thing he taught me early on in my acting career, if you can call it that."

"Why wouldn't you call it a career?"

He waved a hand. "That's a subject for some other time. The first time Flynn brokered a multimillion-dollar deal for me, I almost fainted. And that's when he explained the concept of what the market will bear." He tapped lightly on the side of her head. "Whatever someone is willing to pay determines the value of the object or service."

Sunny made a harrumphing noise. "Well, then get yourself over here and act like the highest-paid butler this household's ever seen," she said, holding out two platters.

"Sure thing, Sunny," he said, tossing her a wink.

"You two have met?" Jonni didn't think she'd introduced them or said her housekeeper's name in front of Cameron.

Cameron and Sunny exchanged glances and nodded together. Cameron took the food and headed out of the room.

"Now that's a nice young man," Sunny said.

"When did you get to know each other?"

The Le Creuset teakettle whistled, the shrill cry drowning out even the wind that was now throwing itself against the window, driving the rain exactly as Pepper had described.

Sunny lifted the kettle and filled the earthenware teapot with boiling water. "Oh, he was decked out in his old-man costume when we were talking earlier. You were working upstairs in Mr. David's room."

"My room," Jonni said, surprising herself. "It's not his anymore."

Sunny pursed her lips and looked Jonni up and down. "Bless the Lord, this is a happy day."

"I gather you think I should have gotten over my husband's death a long time ago," Jonni said, feeling her way through the observation. She was fond of Sunny, had known her for years, but had always assumed she regarded David in the same high esteem Jonni had felt for him during the years of their courtship and up until the last year or so of their marriage.

"There's a time to weep and a time to rejoice," Sunny said. "It's fine to see you making time for something other than moping." She tipped her head toward the dining room. "And that man has a good heart, no matter what the press prints about him. There's always stories to be told about rich and famous people. You know that from what your mama went through, and you know sometimes there's truth behind it and sometimes there's not. Learning to tell the difference, now that's better than knowing how to knit and purl."

"Back for more," Cameron said, striding into the room. He announced himself, no doubt as a sop to his underactive conscience. He'd been listening at the door to the last bit of Sunny and Jonquil's conversation. He was touched that Sunny was taking up for him, and also curious about the reference to Jonquil's mother. Something had hurt her, and hurt her bad. His own life had been so carefree that when he saw someone carrying pain, he wanted to make the injuries disappear. And when that someone was a beautiful woman, well, that carried its own reward.

He didn't have to be a do-gooder of any sort to step up to the bat for that kind of duty.

Sunny handed him a tray loaded with milk and sugar and sugar substitute. He pointed to the colored packets. "This stuff is bad for you," he said.

Jonquil wrinkled her nose. "So is being overweight."

"And who in this gathering is overweight?"

"One minute I dislike you intensely," Jonquil said, "and the next, I could hug you."

"Just let me put down this tray," Cameron said.

"Get on with you," Sunny said, "and come right back for the teapot. It needs a man's strong arms."

"Will do," Cameron said, heading for the dining room.

There he found the girls engaged in an argument over what had happened to Mister Benjamin.

"Real people don't morph," Read was saying. "Erika, you are such a baby."

"If I'm a baby, then you're a brat," Erika said.

"My little brother's a brat," Pepper said. "He sneaks up behind me and bites me on the ankle."

One of the other girls giggled. "Maybe you can get Mister Benjamin to make him behave."

"He's gone and he's not coming back," Read said. "He ran out the door to get away from your boring tea party."

"You know," Cameron said, setting the milk and sugar platter on the dining table, "I think someone in this room is a brat."

"Who's a brat?" All five girls spoke at once.

Funny, but Cameron had never found himself in the role of the adult. He played hard, goofed off, did whatever he felt like whenever he felt like it. If he wanted to buy a new pair of cowboy boots or a dozen of the bikini briefs he favored, any number of shops opened up after hours just for his convenience.

Every so often he'd stop a fight, when he wasn't busy starting one. And last night in jail he'd defended the old guy he'd given the coat to. And he'd do anything to protect his baby sister, including blacking both eyes of her new husband if he even once treated her wrong.

But this talking to kids when they were acting out, well, he probably should have just kept his mouth shut and let the girls carry on until Jonquil got there.

Only he'd opened his mouth. They were all staring at him.

He remembered the judge who'd sentenced him as a

juvenile delinquent, the man who'd offered him the choice between going to jail and joining the army the day he turned eighteen. The wise old man had said, "Good will out and so will bad. You make the choice, every day, in every way." Not quite getting what the guy was yammering about, Cameron had laughed and flipped a coin. Heads, he'd go to jail; tails, he was off to boot camp.

That casually he'd chosen the path of his life.

He pulled out a chair and said, "Good will out and so will bad. Now who in this room wants to be called a brat?"

They all shook their heads. The way Luther had done their makeup, all grown up and smooth and elegant, they looked like wax dolls more than they did children. He felt like suggesting they go wipe it all off, and then decided he must be getting old and grouchy. They were kids, having fun.

"I pertickly don't want to be a brat," Pepper said, "because then I'd be as bad as my brother."

"Part-ic-u-lar-ly," Erika said, enunciating each syllable.

Cameron hid a smile. Jonquil might not be a teacher by profession, but she'd done a good job initiating her daughter in speech, pronunciation, and vocabulary, along with other subtleties of grammar Cameron had never bothered to master.

Read was tossing her hair. "This is so boring. Where's the maid with the tea?"

"Sunny is a guest at this tea party, too," Erika said, jumping up from her chair. "Let's go help her."

"Now that's a nice suggestion," Cameron said.

"But first you need to tell Read that she's a brat," Erika said, taking her seat again.

"Yes, good idea," one of the other blond girls said. "Maybe she'll listen to you."

Cameron was in too deep to know how to back out. So much for playing older and wiser. It wasn't his place to tell the girl how or how not to behave. He heard a noise in the doorway and glanced over to see Jonquil standing there. How long had she been watching him? He wiggled his brows, trying to signal he could use some help.

Instead of coming to his rescue, she leaned against the doorframe and crossed her arms, and smiled at him in such a deliciously wicked way that he sat there, wishing the girls had picked someone else's house for their tea party.

"Just say it," Erika prompted.

He frowned. "These things make more sense when they come from your friends," he said, grasping at some way to explain himself. "Look at it this way, I'm Mr. Nobody. If I say someone is a brat, what does that mean? You'll never see me again. But if you, and you, and you, and you"—he pointed his way around the circle at everyone except Read, who had her nose stuck in the air—"say shape up or ship out or behave or you can't play with my Barbie doll, then that means something."

They were all looking at him. One girl scratched her head. "It's like democracy then. My dad's always talking about how the people rule in a democracy."

Had he even heard the term when he was five? Cameron stared at the child in amazement. He glanced over and saw Jonquil watching him, amusement in her eyes. "Yeah, that's right," he said. Just wait till he got that minx Jonquil alone to himself.

"So I vote Read is a brat," one of the other girls said. "And for punishment she gets only one tea cake."

"That's not fair," Read said, her face a study in pouting. "I can't help the way I am."

"Okay," Jonquil said, advancing into the room. "Enough's enough. Erika, go open the door for Sunny. She's bringing in the tea."

She walked up beside him, and Cameron exchanged glances with her. Funny how intimate it felt, being here in this formal room with the old-fashioned china, with Jonquil wearing a dress from another era and him in his Mister Benjamin's butler's togs and the overdressed little girls arrayed around the table like colorful players in a Japanese opera.

Jonquil was close enough to touch. Cameron smiled as he realized that even if the children were on another planet and Luther long gone and the maid off for the day, he was having just as good a time, if not better, than if the only thought on his mind was getting Jonquil into the sack.

"I must be getting old," he muttered, just as a huge clap of thunder exploded over the house and the lights went out.

Chapter Sixteen

❦

Jonni's dining room

The girls screamed in unison. Stunned by how utterly dark the blackness was, Jonni reached out blindly.

And found Cameron's chest.

She held on. The connection calmed her, especially when his strong arms came around her shoulders and he said, "Okay, everybody, let's be cool here. Last one to stop screaming is a rotten egg."

The challenge worked like magic. Jonni heard Sunny start chuckling, when a moment earlier she'd been moaning.

"Only babies are afraid of the dark." That naturally was Read.

"There are candles on the table," Jonni said.

"Got a lighter?" His breath ruffled her hair when he spoke. Jonni continued to hold on to him, even though she knew it was childish. Her eyes were beginning to grow accustomed to the darkness, and she made out the shapes of the girls, still in their seats around the table.

She was the capable one, the one prepared for any emergency. But without letting go, she said, "There's a fireplace lighter in the front parlor."

"I'll get it," he said, slowly removing his arms from her shoulders.

Funny, but she felt naked without his touch. He took a step forward, feeling for furniture in his path. A flickering light appeared in the other room, heading in their direction.

"Lights went out," Luther said, holding a cigarette lighter. "Everything is pitch black as far as you can see up and down the street. Good thing I haven't given up this vice yet."

Jonni had actually forgotten the makeup man had stepped outside. "Well, it does come in handy, but I'm sure you know cigarettes are very bad for you."

"That's right, Luther," Cameron said. "But as long as you have the lighter, get your butt over here and fire up these candles."

"Sure thing, Mr. Scott," he said, ambling over and applying the flame to the six tapers in the silver candelabra.

"Now isn't this fun," Jonni said, pulling out her seat. "We'll have our tea party by candlelight."

The other adults joined her at the table. The expanse of polished wood was so long that Jonni had clustered the group of nine at the end closer to the kitchen. Erika, as official hostess, sat at the head of the table, with her friends on either side. Sunny and Luther took seats on the opposite side from Jonni, rather obviously leaving the spot next to Jonni open for Cameron.

Thunder crashed again, followed by a jagged bolt of lightning that looked as if it had struck right outside the window. The girls shrieked again. Cameron crossed quickly back to the seat beside Jonni's. He laid a hand on her shoulder and said, "New Orleans knows how to throw not only parties, but storms, too."

He sat down and the children quieted. Light and shadow met in patches around the flickering candles. Jonni glanced toward the head of the table, where Erika sat. She wasn't screaming but Jonni could tell by the puckered state of her mouth she was bothered by something, and she didn't think it was the storm. Erika was used to the weather fury that broke over the city on a regular basis.

"Please pass your cup," Jonni said, "and I'll pour the tea. Erika, penny for your thoughts?" Then she remembered Cameron asking her the same thing earlier. She turned her head to the right and saw him watching her with a hungry expression. Not quite sure what to make of that look, she whipped her head back toward her daughter.

"I was hoping Mister Benjamin's okay," she said. "And Isolde. The storm is pretty bad."

"Isolde is safe at school," Jonni said, filling the first cup and passing it back.

"What if Mister Benjamin morphed into a squirrel or a dog and he's out in the storm?" Erika was worrying the question the way she did each time one of her baby teeth loosened.

Cameron cleared his throat and leaned forward. "Allow me to answer this question," he said, his voice a low, conspiratorial stage whisper.

"Like you could," Read said.

"As if," Pepper said. "Can't you get anything right?"

"Shh," Jonni said. "Listen to what Mr. Scott has to say." She wanted to know just how he was going to answer Erika's fears. Somehow, he'd do exactly that, she had no doubt. His presence was so darn reassuring. His leg brushed hers as he shifted in his seat a bit more. Jonni didn't move away. She reasoned she didn't want to distract him while he was comforting Erika. She continued pouring tea.

"There's something I didn't tell you earlier, but I'm not who I seem to be."

Was he going to tell them he was the actor playing Mister Benjamin? Well, it might be for the best. She'd appreciated the truth, but then she wasn't a five-year-old who believed in cartoon characters. Nor was she a woman with too much faith in the opposite sex, but as much as she distrusted Cameron as a womanizer, she couldn't fault the sensible manners he displayed in dealing with the children.

Erika clapped her hand to her forehead. "I get it! Mister Benjamin morphed into you. He can do that, you know, become a different person."

"That's one way to describe it," Cameron said. "Does that make you feel better?"

"Oh, yes," Erika said, picking up the platter of finger sandwiches and offering them to Read.

"Then let's leave it at that," Cameron said, shooting a stern glance at Read, who appeared about to object, no doubt to the simplistic explanation.

Even though Cameron leaned back in his seat, he didn't scoot his leg away from Jonni's. She glanced, somewhat shyly, over at him. He saluted her with his teacup, then complimented Sunny on the brew.

The housekeeper smiled at him, definitely a victim of his considerable charm. That reminded Jonni that she was dealing with a consummate actor, and to let down her guard with him was to be left standing in the rain without an umbrella. But even that warning thought couldn't make her leg obey her brain when she ordered it to scoot free of Cameron's touch.

"Maybe we should turn on the radio," Luther said out of the blue.

"Hot date tonight, Luther?" Cameron said in a lazy drawl. He had settled back in his chair, hands folded across his lap, looking relaxed enough that he might doze off any moment.

The young man colored up. "As a matter of fact, I do have plans."

"If the rain slacks off you might be able to get a cab to the Quarter," Sunny said. "I'd take you, but my neighborhood always gets cut off in a storm like this so I'll probably be putting up here for the night."

"Of course you will," Jonni said. "You're not going out in this mess. Everyone can stay here."

"Sleepover!" The girls were back to talking in unison.

"Sounds nice," Cameron said, his eyes half closed.

"Mr. Scott is falling asleep at the table," Pepper announced. "May he be excused?"

Jonni grinned. "That's up to Mr. Scott," she said. So only he could hear, she said, "Rough night last night, Mr. Scott?"

He rubbed a hand over his eyes and straightened his posture. "Not exactly the Windsor Court."

"I love that hotel," Jonni said. "Is that where you

stay, when you're not in the hoosegow, I mean?" She didn't think the girls would pick up on the reference.

Leave it to Erika, though.

"Mommy, what's that word?"

Jonni cast about for an explanation. "Well, it's, uh, it means, um . . ."

"It means time out," Cameron said. "Like when you're naughty and have to have to go to your room."

"As if," Read corrected, looking around the table for approval.

The other girls giggled at her and she tossed her napkin down. Jonni knew she should explain that grammar wasn't always logical, but for once she felt too mellow to worry about rules.

"I do have a suite at the Windsor Court," Cameron said. "Maybe you'd like to see it? The etchings are originals, I'm told." He winked at her, and Jonni figured he was just kidding around. The last woman Cameron Scott was going to lure to his hotel room was Jonquil DeVries. Today didn't count; he was trapped by the storm and making the best of it by amusing himself.

"Oh, can we?" Erika clearly listened far too well.

"Drink your tea," Sunny said.

The lights burst on. Jonni blinked, disappointed at the rude return of power, so in contrast to the intimacy of the candlelit table. She moved her leg, as abruptly as the energy had shot into the house, recalled to her sense of reality.

"May we leave the candles burning?" That was Pepper, the quietest of the girls. Jonni smiled and nodded, in sympathy with the sentiment.

"We can always turn the lights off," Cameron said.

"Let's go watch TV," Read said.

"If you're finished, go ahead," Jonni said. "I'm going to call your mothers and see when they'll be able to pick you up. Why don't you all go upstairs and change clothes?"

Luther jumped up. "I'll go look outside," he said and headed out of the room. The children rose from the table and scrambled toward the stairs.

"Must be one really hot date," Cameron said again. "Don't know why anyone wants to rush around. It feels good right here."

"Why don't you go into the parlor and lie down?" Jonni placed a hand over his brow, then quickly removed it. Touching him even in the slightest made her want to keep on touching him.

He gave her one of those slow, wicked, delicious glances and said, "If you can do without me for a few minutes."

"Oh, you go on, Mr. Scott," Sunny said. "You need your rest."

"Especially after that time out," Jonni added, impishly sticking her tongue out.

He imitated her gesture.

Something hot and wicked uncurled deep within her. She had to resist the impulse to lean over and plant her mouth on his.

Shocked, she pushed her chair back from the table. He caught her hand and stroked her fingers. "Don't fight it," he whispered.

"I'll just take these things into the kitchen," Sunny said, grabbing a platter and bustling off.

"Ah, now that's better," Cameron said, her hand still captive in his.

She tugged, but barely. "It shouldn't feel this good," she said, aware that the fire he'd started within her was licking its way into a full-fledged dance of flames.

"Why not?" He turned her hand over and traced the lines of her palm. "What's wrong with pleasure? Tell me one thing," he said, lifting her hand to his lips.

She held her breath. He was going to kiss her hand. The romantic gesture would prove her undoing. But still she didn't snatch it back.

But he didn't kiss her fingers, or her palm, or the back of her hand. Instead, he lifted her middle finger to his lips and gently sucked the tip into his mouth. Then he danced it in a bit more, moving it more quickly.

She felt the rhythm in the deepest center of her desire. Forget feeling as if she were on fire.

She was fire itself.

Jonni gasped. He swallowed her whole finger, moaning. His eyes were open, watching her, daring her to let the feelings explode within her. She read the message in his eyes and tried to resist.

Useless as that was.

"Stop it." She finally managed to breathe the words.

He eased her finger from his lips, but didn't let go of her hand. "And here I thought you were enjoying this," he said, in an aw-shucks kind of voice.

"Too much, and you know it," she said, somewhat more gruffly than she intended.

"Something's made you afraid of pleasure," Cameron said, pulling her down to the seat beside him. He leaned over and smoothed a lock of hair that had fallen over her cheek. "You're too pretty not to savor all there is to taste and feel."

"I don't even know you," she said, sounding to her own ears like some uptight spinster.

"That's probably a good thing," he said, with a somewhat rueful laugh. "People generally like me better before they get to know me."

"I don't know why that is," Jonni said, then immediately slapped her lips together.

"Taking up for me, weren't you?" He grinned and continued tracing circles on her hand. "Tell you what. Spend a few days, maybe even a week, getting to know me and then you can be the judge."

"Judge of what?" If he kept on stroking her hand like that, she'd lose all reason.

"Why people like me better before. But if you like me better afterward, it will prove you're smarter than the average bear."

"Oh, I see," Jonni said. But she didn't see at all.

Neither did Cameron. He sat there, holding this woman's hand, asking her to spend time with him, not understanding his own motives. He was pretty darn sure she wouldn't just jump in the sack for a quickie. Actually, he'd be willing to bet a cool thousand that wasn't going to happen. So why waste his time in New Orleans pursuing a woman who wasn't his type, a woman who no doubt would despise him once she learned that behind the famous face there was just another insecure, underachieving man who wore his hormones on his jeans zipper?

"Have dinner with me tomorrow night?" There went his mouth, operating without benefit of his brain.

She stared at their hands. He wished he could see inside that pretty head of hers.

"Please?" Cameron Scott couldn't remember begging a woman for a date. Not even when he was fifteen and wanted the senior prom queen to go out with him instead of the captain of the basketball team. He'd made his interest known and she'd danced in his arms all that night, both at the dance and afterward in his souped-up Chevy Malibu.

He also couldn't remember the answer meaning so much to him.

She lifted her eyes to his and he read in them a struggle. She wanted to say yes but for whatever reason she also wanted to say no. Perhaps she feared the media splashing her picture all over the tabloids? Nah, it was something else, something inside herself. Cameron sensed the battle between self-control and desire. And he wanted to be there when desire won out.

"We'll go somewhere quiet," he said. "I'll pick you up in a limo around seven. Very private."

"No one will notice that," she said, with a smile.

"Okay, I'll take a cab," he said. "You name it, you got it." There he went again, groveling. Damn. What was she doing to him? He'd be down on one knee if he didn't get a grip.

"Look what the cat drug in!" Luther walked in, Flynn and Cosey in his wake.

"Shit," Cameron said.

Jonni tugged her hand free.

Talk about lousy timing.

Cosey came running over and flung her arms around him, planting a big smooch of lipstick on the side of his cheek. "We were so worried about you! But then Flynn thought of checking here for you."

"I don't know why anyone would be the least bit concerned about me," Cameron said, getting up and in the process freeing himself from Cosey's grasp.

"Might have been back in jail or drowned, for all we knew," Flynn said. "Hope we're not interrupting, ma'am," he said.

"Jonquil, this is Flynn Lawrence, my business manager, and Cosey, his um . . . friend. Meet Jonquil De-Vries, gracious hostess of the location site."

They murmured greetings all around. They all stood there, each one sizing up the other. Cameron could feel the wheels turning in Jonquil's brain as she gazed at Cosey in her tight spandex pants and top that did a fine job of squeezing her cleavage out like toothpaste from a tube of Close Up.

"Hello, anyone else home?" The nanny's voice hailed from the back of the house.

"I didn't even notice that the rain had stopped," Jonquil said.

"It's awful," Cosey said enthusiastically. She clutched Flynn's arm and rubbed her chin against his chest, for which Cameron figured he owed her big-time. Surely Jonquil would see Cameron wasn't at all interested in the giddy and misdirected young doxie.

"I like rain," Jonquil said.

"Well, we were almost flooded out, and if Flynn hadn't been so smart we would have ended up like the other people we saw stranded everywhere."

"All it takes is slowing down so the water doesn't splash up into the brakes and engine," Flynn said.

The nanny appeared in the doorway. Cameron couldn't help but compare her to Cosey. The two looked to be about the same age, but the contrast was remarkable. Instead of an outfit that looked as if it had been painted on, the nanny wore a long, flowing skirt topped by a Tulane University T-shirt. Her spikey, purple-black hair bounced when she walked. She carried a book bag.

Cameron thought of Cosey and the lousy jerk who'd been taking advantage of her when he had rescued her. No one should have to live such a rough life. A strange stirring to do something to help kids not end up in trouble buzzed in the back of his mind. Maybe he'd talk it over with Jonquil. That thought cheered him and he looked over at her. She had to say she'd go out with him. Even if it meant he had to get down on two knees and beg.

Chapter Seventeen

Interior
Jonni's den (that evening)

Three hours later, Jonni collapsed on the couch in the den. Isolde was overseeing Erika's bath. The flooding had gone down sufficiently that Sunny had been able to make it to her house. All the kids' mothers had retrieved their children, all of whom had been promised a sleepover at another date.

Relief didn't begin to describe what she felt about Cameron having gone back to his hotel along with Luther, the business manager, and that outrageously garbed bit of jailbait who'd greeted Cameron as if he'd been her long-lost lover. To add to the tension, Isolde and the girl, Cosey if that was really her name, had gone after each other like two cats. The usually well-mannered Isolde had reacted very badly when Cosey had snickered at how unfashionable her outfit was, especially dissing the Birkenstocks Isolde wore, who then took the opportunity to say she was glad she'd learned better than to use her body instead of her brain to get by in the world.

The young woman did seem to share her favors liberally, including hanging all over the other man, Jonni thought, punching the fringed jacquard pillow she'd plucked from one of the chairs before dropping prone. She liked to clutch a pillow when she was in need of comfort, or when she was trying to think straight. But thinking about Cameron Scott led her more to violence than to peace.

"Irritating man," she said aloud. What did he mean, asking her out like that? As if she'd go to dinner with a man with his reputation?

But you don't really know what he's like, her mind argued.

The phone rang. She flattened the pillow over her face, willing it to stop.

It kept on ringing.

Grumpily, she reached for the portable phone perched on the coffee table. "Yes?"

"Good evening, Mrs. DeVries," said a man's voice that sounded familiar but she couldn't quite place. Her heart had leaped at the first masculine tone, then crept properly back into place as she quickly realized it wasn't Cameron.

Traitor, she thought, wondering who was trying to sell her yet another long distance service or cable fast access account she didn't need or want.

"Your mother gave me your number," the man went on. "Allow me to introduce myself. I am Stephen Propper."

"Yes?" Jonni wished the caller would get to the point so she could return to her ruminations. With everyone descending on the house all at once, she'd never gotten a chance to say yes or no to Cameron's dinner invitation.

Or more honestly, she'd avoided any situation in which he might press the question.

Chicken, she chided herself silently.

"So I thought dinner would be a nice opportunity for us to meet," the man said.

"Excuse me?"

"I realize it may seem I'm speaking out of turn but your mother assured me that although you honored your deceased husband's memory, you were beginning to accept social invitations."

Jonni held the phone away from her ear and stared at it. The man sounded like a throwback to the former century, and the very early years at that. "Are you asking me out?"

"Yes, Mrs. DeVries, I am."

"Please don't call me that," she said. "It's no longer my name."

"May I call you Jonquil?"

May I hang up on you now? Jonni stifled a groan. Dating was sheer torture. What had possessed her mother to give this stranger her home number? But then, look at the geek she'd set her up with the other night. She knew her mother meant well, but Jonni needed to call off the assistance.

"How is it you know my mother?"

"As I said, Mrs. De—Jonquil, my mother and your mother were sorority sisters. I've recently transferred here as a consultant to a major brokerage firm and through that contact, I spoke with your mother. She suggested you would be delighted to introduce me to our peers and show me the sights of the city."

"Naturally," Jonni said. "I mean, if my mother thinks that's a good idea, I'm happy to help."

"Very good," he said, his formal voice lightening a bit. "How about tomorrow evening at seven?"

Tomorrow evening at seven? Why was it that when Cameron Scott had said those very same words her heart had knocked about in her chest like a ping pong ball?

"I'm sorry, but I'm busy tomorrow," she said, deciding at that very instant she would accept Cameron's invitation.

"The next evening, then?"

Now how did she get out of it? Darn her quick response, one that sprang from her thinking more about Cameron than paying attention to this conversation.

"All right," she said, hoping her reluctance didn't border on rudeness.

"May I know the address where I may pick you up?"

She pictured him, his hand poised over a PDA, his date with her merely one more entry in his electronic calendar, and she made a face. "Oh, don't worry, I'll meet you," she said, thinking of the nightmare dinner with Matthew Howell. "That's my dating policy."

"I really would prefer to call for you with my car," he said.

Wait till she got her mother on the phone! "Well, I prefer to meet you. What restaurant do you suggest?"

"Your mother thought Commander's Palace would be appropriate," he said.

She started to back out then and there. Couldn't he

pick a restaurant on his own? Then she relented. He was new to town, after all. It was natural for him to ask a native for a recommendation.

"Okay. I'll see you there at seven, night after tomorrow. I have to go now. My daughter's calling me."

"You have a daughter?" She wasn't sure but she thought she heard a note of panic in the man's voice.

"Yes, and she's quite a handful," Jonni said, ever so sweetly. "But I have a live-in nanny and that helps."

"That must be quite costly," he said.

Jonni sighed, somewhat theatrically. "It's the least I can do for the poor fatherless child," she said.

"Oh, yes, of course," he said. "That's quite commendable."

"See you day after tomorrow," she said, and hung up before he could say anything else.

Jerk. Just hearing she had a daughter had scared him off. Why hadn't her mother mentioned that piece of information?

Then she thought of Cameron and how great he'd been with Erika and the other kids. *Last one to stop screaming is a rotten egg.* A smile tugged at her mouth.

She still held the phone in her hand. She took a deep breath, and punched in the number for information.

When the front desk clerk answered at the Windsor Court, she asked for Cameron Scott and was told he wasn't taking calls but that she could leave a voice message for him.

Of course he wasn't taking calls. Every female in the city must be after him.

But he'd invited *her* to dinner.

When the voice mail instructed her to leave a message, Jonni said, "I'll be ready at seven tomorrow. And go ahead and bring that limo you promised."

She hung up, letting out her breath in a giggle worthy of a schoolgirl.

Somehow she didn't mind being picked up at her house when her date was Cameron Scott.

Cameron didn't get the message until the next morning and then only by accident. He was allergic to checking voice mail. He hated the electronic system and knew from long experience most of the calls would be people chasing him only for their own good.

But he woke up earlier than usual, having fallen into bed the moment Flynn had delivered him to the hotel from Jonquil's house. He hadn't even eaten dinner, so exhausted had he been.

And he'd slept better than he had in ages.

So after breakfast in his room, he was ready ahead of schedule. He thought of phoning his sister and seeing how she was doing now that they were back from their honeymoon. Or maybe she had called him. So he dialed into the phone system.

He almost dropped the phone when he heard her voice, sandwiched in between interview requests and breathy messages from female fans.

He made a mental note to call his sister later. If it hadn't been for thinking of her, he wouldn't have known Jonquil had said yes. Jeez, talk about lucking out! He needed a car, a dinner reservation. He started to summon one of the production assistants who stood at his beck and call, but caught himself.

Jonni deserved privacy. Any word of his whereabouts

getting out meant that some photographer, maybe even the jerk he'd wrested the film from the other night, might track them.

What a pain in the butt being famous was. Cameron caught sight of his face in the large mirror over the sitting room's fireplace. It was a face that stared out from dozens of movie posters, from screens around the world. But it was just a face; he was just another guy.

Another guy who needed a plan. But he never sorted things out in advance. Cameron leaned against the arm of a sofa and considered the irony in his situation. His style was to arrive and do whatever came to mind. Generally on dates he'd end up at one or two of the hot clubs, mingle with a few other celebrity pals, and check out whatever private parties were happening. So many of the people he knew had to live behind security forces and high walls and cameras that much of the entertaining was by invitation only.

And it was wild. He'd been to many a wild bash in Holmby Hills, danced naked in the surf at Malibu once or twice, and maybe more times that he couldn't recall. Anything and everything was laid out for the appetites of the top dogs of Tinseltown.

And most of it, Cameron reflected in surprise, bored him. He'd enjoyed himself more at yesterday's tea party than at any mad rip he'd attended in the past year. But then, maybe he was getting old. When he'd first hit the big time all that carousing had put him over the top, the troublemaking kid from Missouri thrilled to be chugging Heinekens with rock stars and film idols.

"Right," Cameron said. None of this thinking action

was getting him any closer to a solution to where to take Jonquil for dinner. He eyed the phone, then he lifted it and punched in the code for the concierge.

In his best British accent, he said, "Good morning, sir. Where do you recommend I take a lovely lady for dinner this evening?"

"Good morning, Mr. Scott," the polished female voice answered.

Shit. He'd forgotten they knew the guests by caller ID. He dropped the phony voice and said, "Can you give me a couple of names where privacy is respected and make a reservation for two?"

"Certainly, sir," she said. "I can call Commander's, or would you prefer Emeril's?"

"Which one is more on the quiet side? I need to conduct some business."

"I'd say Commander's. The acoustics are probably better."

Cameron had been around the block enough times to know enough to throw off the concierge. "Emeril's at eight," he said. "And put a tip on my bill for yourself. Say a hundred dollars if you get me in there at eight."

"Why, thank you, Mr. Scott," she said, her voice much warmer. "I will do everything that is necessary."

"Great," he said. He hung up, hunted till he found the yellow pages, and thumbed through for the restaurant section. He dialed Commander's and was told there were no dinner reservations available for the next two weeks. Would he like something for the first available date?

He considered the question. In his best administrative assistant's voice, he said, "Oh, dear." He'd certainly gotten the impression that Jonquil was from one of the old New Orleans families. Crossing his fingers, he hoped his ruse would work.

"Excuse me?"

"Mrs. DeVries is going to be very upset with me."

"Mrs. DeVries? This reservation is for her?"

"Yes, sir. And one guest."

"Which one? Mrs. Ernest or Mrs. David?"

Trick question. Cameron closed his eyes and pictured Jonquil. Had she mentioned her deceased husband's name? He couldn't remember but surely she hadn't been married to someone named Ernest. Best not to blow this one, though.

"She instructs me to call her Jonquil," he said, very primly.

"Mrs. David," the man said. "Well, we do seem to have one table open, say around eight, downstairs."

"Perfect," he said.

"But she does prefer the Garden Room."

"Beggars can't be choosers," Cameron said, pleased with himself. Beggars—he could no doubt buy the restaurant several times over. He ought to have Flynn look into that. Owning a piece of a New Orleans restaurant might be something he could sink his teeth into.

He laughed. The man on the other end of the phone said, "I'm glad you're pleased. We'll see Mrs. DeVries and her guest at eight."

After that, Cameron decided not to press his luck. During the day's filming, he remained outside the main house. They were still shooting out of doors, catching up on the time they had lost during the storm the day before. Midday, when he disappeared to his trailer, he was tempted to go in search of her. Instead, he sent one of the production assistants into the house with an envelope for Jonquil.

Inside on a sheet of hotel stationery, he'd written, "Dinner at 8. C."

He figured he'd be better off not giving her any excuse to cancel on him. Also during the break, he took a walk and visited the florist he'd spotted nearby during the drive from the hotel to the location site. He ordered a bouquet of spring flowers to be delivered the next morning. No point in rushing his fences and sending flowers ahead of the date. Several times he'd sensed the push-pull of emotions in Jonquil, and he figured he ought to go slow.

Go slow?

He ought to run in the opposite direction, go find himself some young starlet starved for attention, and get himself laid.

Maybe he was coming down with something. That image held no attraction for him.

All afternoon he rushed his lines. Quentin finally pulled him aside.

Walking to the edge of the spacious yard, one arm thrown over Cameron's shoulder, the director said, "You were more on after spending the night in jail. What's going on in your head today?"

"Nothing," Cameron said, shrugging off the idea that thinking about a woman could interfere with his acting concentration. He might not be a classically trained actor, or trained in any way for that matter, but that loss of focus had never happened to him.

At the end of the pathway that led through a rose garden, the two men turned around and strolled back toward the house. Cameron spotted a flash of blond hair in an upstairs window.

Quentin followed the direction of his gaze. "Ah," he said.

"Ah, what?" Annoyed at having betrayed his distraction, Cameron growled out the words.

"Mrs. DeVries is an attractive lady."

"Yeah, you got that part right," Cameron said, feeling protective of Jonquil. "And the emphasis is on lady."

"I understand you stayed here at the house yesterday with Luther after the rest of us hightailed it back to the hotel?"

Cameron nodded. Again, Quentin made him feel like the boy speaking to a wise father.

"You like to bet, don't you?" Quentin asked, his hands in his pockets.

"Sure."

"Make something of a thing out of it, don't you?"

"I think of it as a tradition," he said, giving his voice a dignified resonance.

"Traditions, now those are good things," Quentin said. "Mia and I have some of our own. Private ones only we share."

"Which means the two of you live in your own special zone even when you're in a crowd, doesn't it?" Cameron's sister had tried to explain this phenomenon to him the evening of the rehearsal dinner. But he hadn't gotten it.

Glancing up to the window where Jonquil had just appeared, he understood. He wasn't sure he'd experienced that sensation, but at least now he'd smartened up enough to know it was worth finding.

Quentin nodded. "Here's the bet."

"Hit me with it," Cameron said, feeling invincible and vulnerable all at the same time.

"When you meet the lady you can't live without, you'll have to propose at least three times before she accepts."

Cameron looked sideways at the director. "What kind of bet is that? Everyone knows I'm not a marrying man."

Quentin laughed. "Okay, you want to throw away your money, that's good by me. How about this? I bet you a thousand dollars you'll have to ask three times *and* that you're married within the year."

Cameron stuck his hand out. "I'll make it two grand," he said. "Just because I'm hot on a babe doesn't mean I'm going to the altar."

Quentin rocked back on the heels of his tennis shoes. "Oh, Cameron, sooner or later it happens to all of us, if we're lucky. Just a few minutes ago you were barking at me to refer to Mrs. DeVries as a lady. Now she's just a babe? Methinks you protest awful loudly." He shook his head and started toward the house. "When the pain gets too bad, you're welcome to come have a long talk with my wife. She'll give you tea and sympathy, then a good swift kick in the butt."

Chapter Eighteen

❦

Interior
Jonni's house (later that day)

Jonni changed clothes three times, running down-stairs to the den to model each choice for Isolde, who finally took her to task for exhibiting symptoms of low self-esteem.

"If you were more self-actualized," Isolde said, glancing up from where she lay on the floor of the den, text-book spread open in front of her nose, "you wouldn't allow the way a man perceives your outfit to matter so much."

Erika was sprawled in a position mimicking her nanny, carefully coloring in a Scooby Doo coloring book. "Mommy, you're pretty all the time," she said.

Jonni swooped down and planted a kiss on her daughter's head. "Thank you, sweetie." To Isolde she said, "So the black skirt or these pants?"

Isolde tipped her head, considering. "If you like the guy, the skirt's a signal that you're open to his advances, to one degree or the other. The pants are much more closed."

"Now why didn't I learn that when I went to Newcomb?" Jonni planted her hands on her hips. "I guess I should major in psych when I go back to school."

"Only if that's what you want to do," Isolde said. "Following someone else's dreams won't work for you."

"Isolde is very smart, isn't she, Mommy?" Erika paused in the act of choosing a new color from her set of sixty-four Crayolas.

"Yes, dear, she is."

"Not really," the nanny said. "But I'm learning to utilize both theory and practice."

"Is that how you came up with your body part theory?" Jonni asked, studying her reflection in the mirror. She liked this linen outfit because it hid the plumpness at her waist and hips. But Cameron had liked the way the red flapper dress clung to her body; that reaction had been quite obvious yesterday.

Even if he had avoided the house all day today. Darn him. If he hadn't sent that note, she would have assumed he'd gone on to his next flirt.

"I guess so," Isolde said. "I haven't been able to decide where Cameron Scott falls in the anatomy and physiology scheme, though. But after tonight, I bet you'll be able to tell that for yourself."

"We're simply going to dinner," Jonni said, directing a warning glance toward Erika.

"Hmm," Isolde said, flipping pages in her textbook. "I bet it's not McDonald's."

Erika sat up at the mention of the fast-food chain. "I'm hungry, too," she announced. "Can I go with you?"

"No, sweetie," Jonnie said, deciding she'd stick with the black linen pants and top. No point in signaling anything to Cameron Scott she was in no way prepared to deliver. "Remember how Daddy and I used to go out for business dinners? This is the same sort of thing. And remember I promised to bring you dessert."

Isolde rolled her eyes, but fortunately Erika couldn't see her face.

"Does that mean Mr. Scott is going to be my new daddy?" She was sitting back on her ankles, her face suddenly anxious.

"No, Erika, it does not." Jonni crossed the room and took her daughter in her arms. She gave her a hug and said, "I went to dinner a few days ago with Mr. Howell and he's not going to be your new daddy, either. Mommys go out to dinner. It's just one of the things we do."

"Like taking me to the doctor?"

"Or having your play group over," Jonni added.

The doorbell sounded, the chimes ringing through the house. Jonni looked down at her bare feet and shrieked. "That can't be him already!"

Isolde put a pen between the pages of her book. "Run on upstairs. I'll get the door."

"I don't know what I'd do without you," Jonni said. "Want to come with, Erika?"

Her daughter looked from the front of the house back to her. "No," she said. "I want to ask Mister Benjamin if he's okay in there."

"Oh," Jonni said. Well, she hoped Cameron was prepared to deal with the question because she had no idea how to explain to her daughter the reality between the actor and the character. She had moments when she couldn't even keep it straight in her own head.

Isolde was striding toward the front of the house. Jonni scooted for the back stairs, taking them two at a time. "Low self-esteem, indeed," she muttered, thinking of Isolde's pronouncement. "I simply want to look good. It's not every middle-aged matron who gets to go to dinner with Cameron Scott."

And then she actually laughed at herself. She was thirty-two years young, very much alive, and on her way to regaining the body she'd known most of her life. Today when she'd done her aerobics class she'd made it through without one stitch in her side.

She recalled Read's mother's disbelief when Jonni had mentioned in passing on the phone earlier that she and Cameron were having dinner. She'd practically called Jonni a liar. Jonni dashed into her bedroom, gazed at the welter of garments decorating her four-poster bed, and chuckled. And all of a sudden, she stripped the black linen pants and top from her body, threw them on top of the collection, and wiggled into the black sheath she'd first modeled. It hugged her body exactly the same way the red flapper costume had done, and as she drew on a pair of sheer black thigh-high stockings, slipped her favorite diamond and emerald earrings into her earlobes, spritzed with Opium, and stepped into a pair of three-inch heels she'd forgotten she owned, Jonni experienced the thrill of transformation.

She sure hadn't felt like this when she'd gotten ready for dinner with Matthew Howell.

She grabbed her purse and a silky black shawl, pirouetted in front of her full-length mirror, and headed down the front stairs.

"Now that's what I call a grand entrance," Cameron said, watching her descend.

The warmth in his expression was reward enough. He followed her every move. Feeling quite delectable, Jonni added a bit of a swivel to her step as she reached the entryway where Cameron stood along with Erika and Isolde.

"Hi," she said. Gosh, he looked good. Dark hair tousled, eyes dark yet brilliant, his powerful shoulders at ease in an exquisite black jacket shot with silver threads.

And she was his dinner date?

Jonni almost fled to the safety of her room.

"Ready?" he said, his silky voice asking far more than that one word alone represented.

She'd accepted his invitation. She could turn tail and run from life, stay buried under the protective layers she'd piled on over the past year, or she could go forward with her head held high.

And it was only dinner.

She'd dined with senators and governors, for Pete's sake! And she'd survived Matthew Howell. That made her grin, and she met his expectant gaze. "Quite," she said.

Cameron let out a breath he hadn't realized he'd been holding. Jeez, but this lady was a challenge. He could have sworn that for a moment or two, she'd been having second thoughts.

"Can I really have anything I want for dessert?" Erika asked her mother.

Cameron glanced down at Erika. "If your mother said so, I'm sure the answer is yes."

She nodded her head, rather vigorously. He hadn't known the child long, but he had a sinking feeling she was up to something. He exchanged glances with Jonquil, noting the way her eyes smiled as she regarded her daughter and caught his look at the same time.

"I did say that," Jonni said.

Cameron reached his hand out and she slipped hers into it. The gesture of acceptance rocked him to his toes. "So what would you like?" At the moment, he'd promise her anything, even if he had to send a crew to rouse the owners of an ice cream parlor at midnight.

She'd screwed her little face into quite a study of heavy thought. Cameron tapped her lightly on the tip of her nose. "Your wish is granted," he said.

He felt Jonquil's hand tighten in his, realizing all too late the warning she was attempting to signal. But what could be so difficult that he couldn't find it in New Orleans?

"I'd like to see Mister Benjamin," she said.

"He'll be here tomorrow," Cameron said.

She shook her head. "Tonight, with you and Mommy."

This time Jonquil definitely scrunched his hand good. But she didn't let go. He cast a glance at her, desperately seeking direction. "You'd rather have that than your favorite dessert?"

She nodded. "Dessert's no good when you're worried about someone."

He could have slapped himself straight into next week. Still holding Jonquil's hand, he hunkered down,

Jonquil moving as one with him. "You're worried he went out in the rain? But you saw him here today, didn't you?" And then he remembered he'd been so busy avoiding Jonquil so she wouldn't nix the date, he hadn't seen Erika, either.

"Nope."

"So you want to make sure Mister Benjamin's okay."

"Yes, please."

Cameron looked into the serious eyes of the child. He wasn't one to dwell on deep thinking or the mysteries of the subconscious, but he was willing to bet her concern was all wrapped up in her daddy having gone away and never come back.

"Sweetheart, Cameron can't just snap his fingers and have Mister Benjamin appear," Jonquil said.

Erika's answer was a silent pout, which Cameron read as a direct appeal to his ability to do exactly what Jonquil said he couldn't do. Well, if he'd ever seen a surer way to win a woman, it had to have been written on a wall somewhere. Produce Mister B., make the daughter happy, win the mom.

That was a formula even Cameron could decipher.

"What time do you go to bed?" he asked.

"Nine-thirty," she answered.

"Well, your mother and I have dinner reservations and we won't be back before bedtime, but if it's okay with your mom, we can wake you up when we get home and you can tiptoe downstairs, just like Christmas, and see who's come to visit."

She clapped her hands together. "Shazashabam!"

Jonquil was practically tugging his hand out of the

wrist socket. He rose lightly to his feet, sliding her up with him, as naturally as if they'd always moved as one. Before she could say anything to counter his insane offer, he said, "Catch you later. We don't want to miss our reservation."

He scooted the two of them through the front door. She stopped on the porch. Grinning at her, he said, "Last one into the limo is a rotten egg."

"You are crazy," she said, but she kept her hand in his as they ran to the car waiting outside her front gate.

The driver hopped out, opened the door, his face a blank. Cameron hoped the man wasn't on the take from any tabloids, but at the moment he wasn't even going to worry about that.

He had a far bigger problem on his hands.

And not much time to solve it.

Jonquil slid into the seat, her hands on her lap. The skirt of her dress had edged up, and Cameron caught sight of the lacy top of her stockings. Nice. Very nice. He tugged his gaze from her thighs to her face to find her watching him, eyes wide, lips slightly parted.

Maybe they could skip the dinner thing and spend the next two hours in the limousine. He had everything he wanted right here.

"Nice car," she said. "But I don't see Mister Benjamin."

He groaned. So much for a night of unrestrained passion. Him and his moment of compassion.

"Are you okay?"

He leaned back and draped his arm across the back of the seat, close but not touching her. He knew better than to scare her off. "I'm on my way to dinner at Commander's Palace with the most beautiful woman in New Orleans. What's not to be okay?"

He could have sworn she blushed. He stroked a tendril of her hair. "Don't underestimate yourself, Jonquil," he said.

She sighed.

"That's the first time I've called you by your name," he said.

"I like the way you say my name," she said. "Everyone calls me Jonni. Not even my parents ever called me Jonquil."

"But they named you." Her hair felt better against his fingers than whiskey on his tongue.

"They named a pair of twins born in the spring after two seasonal flowers," she said, sounding practical, though he thought her voice was a little breathy. He wondered what she'd do if he kissed her. Now.

She tipped her face up toward his. Darn if she wasn't thinking about him kissing her, too, Cameron thought. Her lips were parted now, and there was no mistaking the soft welcome of that lush mouth. He lifted his little finger and traced the curve of her chin toward her ear. Her body softened and shifted on the seat, a sure signal she was offering herself to him.

One kiss.

He looked into her brilliant blue eyes, and saw more than he deserved to see. Welcome, yes, but doubt.

Something in his gut twisted. He had no right to play his usual games with this woman.

"You're too good for me," he said, not even realizing he said the words out loud.

Jonni couldn't believe her ears. Cameron Scott was about to kiss her. She didn't know much about men, but she didn't think this self-doubt was standard procedure for Cameron.

She also didn't think talking would achieve much.

She sighed softly and dropped her head back on his arm. Her hair draped over his sleeve, and he lowered his head toward her mouth. She'd been prepared to distrust him, figured she should still feel that way, but darn it, when he wasn't trying to be a hotshot, he was such a nice person.

And tonight was one evening out of time.

"Cameron," she whispered, the sound of his name an invitation as she lifted one hand to his cheek and let her hand discover the texture of his skin, the plane of his jaw.

He made a sound deep in his throat, and she smiled.

His mouth found the smile and swallowed it, making it his. Jonni gasped and gave herself up to the sensation of his lips hot and hungry on hers. She moved her hand from his cheek to the back of his neck, caressing the warm flesh there with circles that danced faster as his tongue found hers and teased it with a promise of so much more.

He broke away first, his breathing fast and shallow.

Jonni leaned against the seat, shaken. She'd only wanted to know what it would feel like, kissing this man who made her afraid and brave all at the same time.

Now she wanted to do it again.

And again.

"Couldn't help myself," he said, a bit of a grin on his face. "I promise to behave."

Jonni almost pulled a pout worthy of her five-year-old. "You do?"

He laughed and pulled her close. She leaned into his solid strength. "Yes, I do, because as you well know, I'm a notorious flirt and you are a lady who deserves to be treated as such."

"Of course," she said, starch in her voice, and then took his face in her hands.

Her kiss was wicked and naughty, a choreographed dance of all the kisses she'd always dreamed of experiencing but never had. She nibbled on his lip, parted his mouth, and drew his tongue deep inside, opening her throat as if she'd swallow him whole.

Part of her brain sounded a warning; the rest of her body squelched such scaredy-cat thoughts. For once in her life, Jonni wanted to be the wildly desirable siren she'd never let herself be.

Cameron had his arms around her, one strong hand pulling her fanny onto his lap, burying her thighs against the front of his body, against the heat and need of his erection that burned through their clothing.

Jonni lowered one hand to his lap and felt him strain against her hand. Lifting her mouth from his, she said, "Now this is what I call being good."

He groaned again, and said, "I knew you'd be this hot, beneath that proper surface."

Jonni looked down at her dress that now revealed the tops of her stockings, at her breasts pushing against the low neckline, her nipples threatening to burst with the need to break free from the silky fabric of her bra, and her hand on Cameron's crotch.

Slowly, her senses started to function. Not the out-of-control erotic ones, but the common ones.

"I don't look very proper right now, do I?"

"Oh, yeah," Cameron said, "you look exactly proper."

And then he kissed her again.

Which is when the driver opened the door.

And the flash of the photographer's bulbs popped, one after the other, after the other.

Jonni lifted her head and looked up.

"Don't do that," Cameron said, reaching up and covering her face with his arm, then grabbing the door and slamming it shut and hitting the lock button. He pushed the intercom button and swore at the driver to get the car moving.

"F—ing idiots," he said. "Are you okay?"

"I think so," she said. She'd scooted over on the seat, tugged her dress down to a proper length, and was busy restoring some order to her hair. "It's just as well that happened," she said, "I think I was forgetting myself there." She tried to laugh, as if making a joke of it all.

"There's nothing wrong with that, in the right place at the right time," Cameron said. "Especially when you're with the right person."

"Hmm," Jonni said. She was afraid any woman he happened to be with at the moment qualified as the right person for Cameron. "Why did you say I was too good for you?"

He ran a hand over his face. "Can we talk about that later?"

"Sure," she said.

"We need to think about what to do about dinner. And making Mister Benjamin appear."

He slapped the intercom button. "How much did they pay you to do that?"

"Excuse me, sir?"

"You know what I mean," Cameron said. "Someone paid you to open the door without warning."

"Two hundred," the driver said.

"Tell you what," Cameron said. "You lose the bums following us and we won't mention this side work to your management."

"Management gets paid, too," the driver said.

"Now ain't that democratic," Cameron said. He looked disgusted. "Go back to the hotel," he said.

Cameron flung himself back against the seat, upset with the ruin of his dinner plans, furious that Jonquil's privacy had been so rudely trampled, angry at himself for not taking more precautions.

But the taste of her lips had chased all reason from his mind.

"Does this happen to you all the time?" Jonni asked.

"Hell, no," he said. No woman had ever had this impact on him. Sex was sex, he'd always figured. All he'd done was kiss her, and he wanted to beat on his chest and shout and fall on his knees at her feet and whisk her away to an island where they could make love day and night and night and day.

"Oh," she said, clearly not understanding.

"The photographers, yes," he said, reaching for her hand. "Finding someone like you, no."

Chapter Nineteen

Inside the limousine

"Right," Jonni said. The shock of the photographer's intrusion had snapped her back to her senses. Experiencing a walk on the wild side was one thing; falling for a playboy's charm quite another.

"I'm ser—" Whatever he was going to say, he kept to himself. His face unreadable, he stretched out an arm and lifted a bottle of champagne from an ice bucket Jonni hadn't even noticed earlier.

Well, that wasn't surprising; her gaze had been pretty much stuck on Cameron's face. Eyes. Lips. Warmth stole over her cheeks as she cast a quick glance lower on his muscular frame. Had she really put a hand around his . . . his . . . private parts? Jonni pressed her hands to her cheeks, rattled at how swept away she'd been.

"Since we're not going to Commander's, we may as well have a before-dinner drink here," he said, wrapping a cloth around the top of the bottle and working on the cork.

Thankful his attention was focused on the wine, Jonni returned her hands to her lap. She cast about for some safe topic of conversation, but everything that came to mind seemed either inane or dangerous. Funny, but when he'd been Mister Benjamin, words had tripped off her tongue. Tripped? Why, she'd rattled on like her daughter when she was excited over an upcoming treat.

His strong fingers caressed the cork, easing it from the bottle with a hearty pop. Jonni swallowed at the image, unable to keep her mind from straying to the image of those hands on her own body, slipping her dress from her shoulder, teasing her breasts as he freed her from her bra.

The fizz of the champagne and the sweet yet yeasty smell filled the air. Cameron poured two glasses, put the bottle back on the ice, and handed one flute to her. "To our night out," he said, toasting her.

"To our night out," she echoed. Night. Singular. Jonni manufactured a smile and sipped the bubbly liquid. Now that she was back on planet Earth, it was time to be practical. Time to plan.

"I may have to stop at the ATM," Cameron said.

"Oh," she said. "Which bank do you need? I know the main ones."

He grinned and leaned against the seat. "Just kidding, Jonquil. I meant I'd need more than a penny to pry those busy thoughts out of your head."

He said the words gently. "Oh," she said again, feeling both foolish and liking him all over again for being so sensitive. "I do live inside my mind a lot."

He nodded. "When a mind is inside a head as pretty as yours, I can see why."

She looked at him, pleased but confused. "I'm not sure that's logical."

He laughed. "Call Flynn and ask him if I've ever been logical."

"Is he your best friend?"

"Yep."

"Did you all grow up together?" Jonni turned half-sideways on the deep seat, tucking one foot under her leg. She liked Cameron when he was like this, relaxed and talkative. Just like when he'd been Mister Benjamin. She forgot about being tongue-tied.

Cameron took a big swallow of champagne. "We met in the army."

"You were in the army?" She didn't know why, but that surprised her. Other than Elvis and the World War II–era actors, she didn't think of too many movie stars as having been in the service. But then, as she'd told Daffy, she knew less than nothing about the film industry.

"It's a long story," he said.

"Traffic isn't moving too fast," she said, curious.

He smiled at her. "You might not believe it from the events of the other day, but I'm a reformed character compared to my bad old days."

In the middle of a sip of her drink, Jonni choked. He patted her on the back, and she caught her breath. "Sorry," she said. "It just went down wrong."

Cameron grinned. "The same can be said of a lot of the things I've done in my life. Anyway, the short version. I goofed off in high school, drove my parents crazy, ran with the wrong crowd, broke a bunch of windows in a housing development under construction, and ended up in front of a judge who I thought was a real hard-ass."

"Just out of curiosity, why were you breaking windows?"

He shrugged. "It's a vice of mine. When someone challenges me, I can't resist proving my point. Offer me a bet"—he lifted his free hand and dropped it to his lap in a gesture of surrender—"and I'm lost."

"So someone bet you you wouldn't break the windows and you did it anyway and went to jail?"

"Not exactly." He shifted a bit in his seat. "This was a long time ago."

"Of course," Jonni said. She reached over and touched his arm, realizing he was embarrassed by the story. "You don't have to go any further if you don't want to."

"I've been told confession is good for the soul," he said lightly. "My buddy bet me I couldn't shoot the windows of each house out at five hundred feet with a .22 in less than a minute. So, you see, for a seventeen-year-old hothead, it was a challenge not to be passed on. Oh, and just so you realize I wasn't a complete reprobate, you should know the houses weren't occupied."

"I see," Jonni said. "Did you win?"

"Oh, yeah." He reached over for the bottle, topped off her glass and refilled his. "I've always been a fair shot."

"And if you knew that, then you also knew you didn't have to prove it to any of your buddies." Jonni felt her way through the thought.

"Naturally. Anyway, the judge told me I could either go to jail for malicious destruction of property, trespassing, blah blah blah, or I could swear I'd join the army the day I turned eighteen. He even had a recruiter there in the courtroom."

"Well, I'd certainly choose the army over jail."

He laughed and ruffled the top of her hair with one hand. "You are a sweet and innocent soul."

She stared at him. "You didn't go to jail, did you?"

"No, but I could have. I flipped a coin." He grinned. "The recruiter won."

"Is that what you mean by living your life by impulse?"

He nodded.

"I could never do something like that."

"That's reassuring," he said, stretching his legs out and leaning his head against the back of the seat. When he moved, his thigh nestled against her leg.

"You didn't explain how you met Flynn."

"That's right." He sat upright all of a sudden. "Speaking of Flynn, I'd better get him on the phone before we pull up at the hotel." He reached for the limo phone beside the bar and exchanged his glass for it. When he shifted away, his leg moved from hers. It was all Jonni could do to keep from scooting over to regain the connection. Thankfully, he returned at once.

Cameron punched in a number, waited briefly, then said, "Buddy, need some help."

Jonni heard a shout carom out of the receiver. "If you're in jail again you can damn well stay there."

Cameron pointed to the phone and drew his lips into a downward smiley. Jonni laughed quietly at the mock-hurt expression on Cameron's face.

"Been there, done that," Cameron said. "This is an SOS."

Jonni couldn't hear the response. She tipped her head against the leather, took another sip of champagne, and reveled in the unbelievable intimacy of the two of them in the darkened car, Cameron's thigh warming her leg. It was the oddest sensation. For a split second Jonni realized the strangest thing of all was that she felt as if the two of them had sat this way time and time again and tonight was simply one more evening in a blur of nights past and so many to come.

"And find Luther."

Jonni glanced over at the sound of the makeup man's name.

"Make sure he brings his heavy-duty makeup."

The manager must have been making quite a long speech. Cameron nodded, then rolled his eyes. He winked at her, and then suddenly, none too happy, said, "If you must, but, buddy, she could be your daughter." He put his arm around her again, and Jonni relaxed her neck into his touch. She could do that, surely, without forgetting herself again.

"We're at the hotel," the driver's voice sounded over the intercom. "Do you want me to pull into the circle?"

"Go around the block," Cameron said. Into the phone, he said, "Ten minutes. Pick you up in front of the casino."

He cradled the receiver. When he leaned forward his arm brushed along her shoulders and then he pulled it free and jammed his hands into his lap,

"When we were in the army, Flynn saved my life," he said. "And he's been doing it ever since."

"Ooh, what happened?" She wanted him to put his arm back around her.

He flashed one of his breath-stopping grins. "Want the story I always tell or the truth?"

"You mean they're not one and the same?"

"Don't kid a kidder," he said. Then he did slide his arm back around her shoulders. Pulling her against his side, he said, "There's something about you that makes me want to stumble my way into the light of becoming a better person, and I can't for the life of me figure that out."

"Oh," Jonni said, because she had no idea what else to say.

"We're in the grenade pits, learning how to toss those suckers. Well, there's always at least one dumbass, excuse my fancy language, but the word fits, who pulls the pin and freaks."

"Then what happens?" Jonni had never thought much about how soldiers learned to do things like toss grenades or shoot weapons or drive tanks. The men in her world were lawyers and doctors and accountants.

"The guy pulls his arm back, drops it behind him. Someone shouts 'live,' and there's a sergeant whose job it is to kick the grenade into a reinforced hole before it goes off."

"And someone did that when you were close and Flynn saved you by hiding the grenade?"

Cameron looked down at the one hand that rested on top of his thigh. "That's what I tell the press. But the truth is I was in this crummy bar near Fort Polk drunk as a skunk and I got in a fight with this guy who said I was flirting with his wife and when the guy was about to punch both my lights out, Flynn showed up."

"The guy must have been pretty big to beat you up," Jonni said.

Cameron laughed. "He was. But it's not all about bulk," he said. "Flynn uses his brains. He yanked some soccer referee's whistle off his neck and blew it, yelling 'MP, MP'—that's the military police—and the guy freaked and ran out the door."

"Oh," Jonni said again. "The other story is a lot more dramatic."

He laughed. "I've never told any woman I've dated the truth of that stupid story." Leaning over, he brushed the tip of her nose with his thumb. "I'd better be careful, hanging around with you."

Hanging around with you. The words echoed in Jonni's mind, the tantalizing promise of more to come. But it was a promise as empty as his made-up tale of heroism. He'd amuse himself during the filming and jet off to his world.

And here she'd be, in New Orleans, alone with her memories.

Cameron sensed her shift, both physically and in her attitude. He stroked the curve of her shoulder, and decided he'd gotten far too dramatic and heavy. "You must be starving," he said. "I know I am."

"Oh, yes," she answered, her full mouth curving in one of those delectable smiles.

Cameron knew what he wanted for dinner. And it wasn't served on a plate. He shifted his legs, hiding his reaction as well as he could. He was on the brink of frightening her off, and that wouldn't do.

Not at all.

If there was one thing Cameron knew how to do, it was how to lure a woman. Hell, he should have had the lead in *What Women Want*. Mel was great, of course, one of the best, but he'd been married and settled for so long. What did he remember about the lurk and pounce of the male/female game?

Women liked men who listened to them. And here he'd been running off at the mouth and building a hard-on that was making it difficult to think straight.

"So what's your favorite food?" Weak, but it was a start. And talking about food would help him back off the surge of physical desire that kept overtaking him.

"You don't remember?" She looked a little bit disappointed.

Shit. He'd done that all wrong. "Oh, you're referring to the ice cream."

She nodded. "Though talk about spilling secrets! I can't believe you caught me microwaving my ice cream and then made it feel completely natural to confess to bingeing. There, I said the word out loud."

"But you already told me."

Jonni shook her head and flicked him gently on the tip of his nose. "No, silly, I told Mister Benjamin."

"Who happens to be a lot easier to talk to than the scary Cameron Scott?" He gentled his voice as he asked the question.

"You're not so scary anymore," she said, and the way she looked deep into his eyes made more than his groin leap. Disturbed by how good those simple words made him feel, Cameron cleared his throat and looked out the window.

"Flynn should be here any minute."

"I like shrimp," Jonni said. "Especially shrimp cocktail with the large white shrimp. They're just so delicious when they first cross my lips"—she tipped her head back and mimed lowering a bite past her lips—"and the taste and texture explode in my mouth. Oh, yes, I really like shrimp."

Cameron swallowed. Hard. "Are you doing that on purpose?"

"You did ask me about my favorite foods," she said in a sweetly innocent voice.

He caught her by the shoulders and crushed her mouth to his. She gasped, stiffened for a sliver of a second, and then responded, as hungrily as he had taken her. Tasting her tongue and her lips and the sensuous smoothness of the top of her mouth, he plundered until he heard her moaning.

Sweet, panting, breathy moans that were asking him for more.

He yanked free, his chest rising and falling, his hard-on about to open the zipper from the inside of his pants and climb out. Her mouth was puffy and red and beautiful, her eyes wide and shining. "You're incredible," he said, his voice almost as rough as the make-believe one he'd invented for Mister Benjamin.

But there was nothing make-believe about his reaction to Jonquil.

She touched her fingertips to her lips. "I'm so—"

He didn't get to hear what she was about to say. Someone pounded on the window and then he heard Flynn call, "Let me in, you doofus."

"Go away," Cameron said, but not loud enough for Flynn to hear him.

Jonni smiled, somewhat shakily. "You can't very well send him away when you told him to show up, can you?"

Cameron leaned over and smoothed a long strand of hair away from her face. "If I hadn't promised your daughter that Mister Benjamin would make an appearance, I'd keep that door locked for a long, long time."

Her eyes grew even wider.

"Open the door or you can rescue yourself this time."

Cameron flicked the lock switch. The door swung open. And in climbed not only Flynn, but Cosey, Luther, and another young man he'd never seen before.

"I do love a party," the stranger said.

Cameron looked a question at Flynn. Busy settling himself close to Cosey, his manager said, "Luther's dinner date. You want makeup, it's a two-for-one special."

"And I'm on overtime," Luther said. "Not that I'm not happy to help you, Mrs. DeVries."

"Why, thank you, Luther," Jonquil said. "I'm Jonni, and your friend is?"

"P.J." the young man answered, straightening the leather vest he wore over a striped dress shirt.

"Pleased to meet you," Jonquil said.

Cameron had to admire her good manners. She didn't even look rattled, and all it took was one quick glance at her face and any man could tell she'd just been thoroughly, deliciously kissed.

"I'm hungry," Cosey said.

P.J. giggled. "And people say my name is odd."

Cosey stuck her tongue out at him.

Jonni glanced around the menagerie that filled the limo's luxurious space. "Perhaps you could serve champagne," she said to Cameron in a low voice.

"We were waiting for room service when your SOS came through," Flynn said, his voice rather dry.

"Great. We're all starving," Cameron said. "We never made it to Commander's, thanks to the money-grubbing driver and a photographer I'm going to beat to a pulp the next time I see him."

"Ooh," P.J. said.

"He's just talking," Luther said. "All movie stars talk like that."

"Is that so?" Cameron leaned forward.

Jonni grabbed the second bottle of champagne from the ice and plopped it into Cameron's hands. He opened it, and she handed him glasses to fill as the members of the group each sized one another up.

"Maybe we can go to Camellia Grill," P.J. said. "It stays open late."

"What do they have?" Cosey asked.

"Omelets and hamburgers are the main items."

"Lot of tourists there?" Cameron asked.

"Yeah, that's the only drawback," P.J. said. "We used to have this cool dive called the Hummingbird and no matter how late it was or how drunk you were, you could go there. But now some money types have turned it into a fancy-schmancy place."

"I make a pretty good omelet," Jonni said, surprising herself. "Why don't we go back to my house?"

"That's too much trouble for you," Flynn said.

"I'm supposed to be taking you out for dinner," Cameron said.

"But we're going there anyway," Jonni said. "I mean, isn't that why Luther is here?"

"Flynn, too," Cameron said.

"Why exactly am I here?" the manager asked.

"I need you to play Mister Benjamin," Cameron said.

Flynn choked on his champagne. Cosey patted him on the back, none too gently. "I'd rather haul your carcass out of jail," he said.

"It's not for me," Cameron said. "It's for Erika."

"If that's true," Flynn said, glancing from Cameron over to Jonni in a way that showed her he saw more than he let on, "It'll be the first time you've ever done something just for somebody else."

Jonni couldn't really believe that was true. Or maybe she just didn't want to. She'd slipped up and started to like Cameron Scott. Darn it, not a little, but a lot.

Chapter Twenty

Inside the limousine (cont'd)

"Tell you what," Cameron said, turning to her. "We'll take you up on your offer and I'll make it up to you to-morrow night. Luther can get Flynn ready to go while we're driving."

"I really don't mind," Jonni said. There was safety in numbers. Cameron might come up with a way to send the others off in a cab and she'd be alone with him—and temptation.

"Thank you, Mrs. DeVries," Luther said. "I didn't want to get underfoot during the tea party, but I'm quite handy in the kitchen."

"Well, I'm not," Cosey said.

Jonni wondered where the girl had learned her manners. "Perhaps you'd like a lesson?"

Cosey shook her head. "Oh, no, I'm going to be an actress. Mr. Scott has promised to put me in his movie."

"Oh, he did?" P.J. looked quite interested. "Luther, you didn't tell me they were still casting."

"We're not," Cameron said. "Cosey, I didn't promise you this movie."

"Yes, you did." Her lips ballooned into a pout.

"No, I did not."

"When you snatched me away from Billy, you said you would get me a job."

Jonni considered the young girl, wondering whether she was eighteen or not. "How did you and Mr. Scott meet?"

Cameron groaned, a reaction that made Jonni want to know the answer even more than she had a moment earlier.

"Luther, pop open that makeup case and start turning Flynn into Mister Benjamin."

"Do we have to?"

"Was that a live grenade in that pit or what?" Cameron grinned as he asked the question.

Flynn flipped him the flying finger and said, "What a man doesn't do for his buddy."

"I'd do the same for you," Cameron said. He flicked the intercom button and told the driver to return to the original pickup site.

"So how was it you met?" Jonni asked, leaning forward toward the girl.

Cosey shrugged. "I don't mean to be ungrateful, because Mr. Scott did rescue me from a real creep."

"He did?" Jonni glanced over at Cameron, who shrugged as if to say, *No big deal.*

"It's true," Flynn said. "I forgot about that act of

mercy. Sometimes you do have blood pumping inside that muscle-bound cage you call a heart."

"Anybody else would have done the same," Cameron said.

"If that's so, why did everyone else walk on by?" Cosey was watching Luther. "Hey, you think you could teach me how to do that? I love makeup." As if to prove her point, she opened her purse and pulled out a lip liner and lipstick palette.

Luther stuck his nose in the air and kept working his magic on Flynn's face.

Jonni studied Cameron. She had known he wasn't as callous as he liked to pretend. She'd be willing to bet Cosey wasn't the only person he'd ever stepped in to rescue. From the looks of the girl and the tidbit of the story they'd told, she assumed Cosey had been in the clutches of a hustler, maybe even a pimp. And thanks to Cameron, she had a chance for a fresh start.

And it looked as if Flynn wanted to aid in that new beginning. Jonni was pleased to observe that Cameron regarded Cosey in almost a fatherly fashion.

"How about Creole omelets?" Jonni asked. "I've got some lovely huge shrimp—"

Cameron caught her hand to his side. "Minx," he said, his lips moving against her hair so that only she could hear.

Jonni giggled. She felt as young as Cosey, and even more carefree.

The car slowed and stopped. "Last one inside is a rotten egg," she said.

"Hey, I'm an old man," Flynn said.

"Deep voice," Cameron said. "And limp. You forgot your cane if anyone asks."

"And put these on," Luther said, handing him a pair of white gloves. "I skipped your hands."

"Yeah, yeah, yeah," Flynn said.

Cameron opened the car door. "I owe you big time and you know I won't forget it."

Jonni slid across the seat and took the hand he held out for her as she stepped from the stretch limo. The driver had gotten out of the car and was watching them, his face impassive, no sign of his earlier treachery showing.

"Go on inside," Cameron said. "I'll catch up with you." He turned toward the driver, his back to the rest of the group.

Curious as to what he was going to have to say to him, Jonni almost hung back. But she'd been better schooled than that. She was the hostess and these people were her guests, so she led them through the front gate and up the sidewalk to the house.

"Nice digs," P.J. said as they entered the foyer.

"Thank you," Jonni said. "We're going to be very informal, so let me show you to the breakfast room."

She led them to the back of the house. Luther promptly quit grumbling about working overtime and installed himself as chief chef. Jonni excused herself and ran up the back steps. Isolde and Erika hadn't been in the den so they were probably in Erika's playroom.

Her daughter, garbed in her Curious George pajamas, almost collided with her as she rounded the top of the stairs.

"Mommy, did you bring Mister Benjamin with you?"

Isolde appeared, moving at a more dignified pace. "You're back early. It wasn't another one of Those Dates, was it?"

Jonni touched the tip of her tongue to her lips. She could still taste Cameron. Blushing, and hoping the astute nanny didn't notice, she said, "Oh, no, but movie star fame does carry a price. There was a commotion at the restaurant so we're whipping up something here."

"I see," Isolde said, with a wink at Jonni. "Shall I keep Erika upstairs so the two of you can have your privacy?"

"No," Erika said.

"Shh," Jonni said. "Isolde was asking *me* that question, but the answer is of course not. We've got quite a crew with us. Including," she said, ruffling Erika's hair, "Mister Benjamin."

"Well, I hope so, Mommy!"

"This I've got to see," Isolde said.

"Come on down," Jonni said.

The scene in the kitchen was priceless. She paused in the doorway, surveying Luther, draped in one of her Williams-Sonoma aprons, directing Cosey in the art of chopping onions. P.J. was at the sink, cleaning shrimp. Mister Benjamin, as befitted his advanced years, sat at the breakfast table, folding napkins into clever shapes. The radio was tuned to her favorite oldies station and Cameron was handing an apron to, of all people, the limo driver.

"Aha," Cameron said. "Here they are, the latecomers. Never fear, there's a job for everyone. And this is Mike and he's joining us. Can't have him sitting out there in the dark without any dinner."

Jonni saw the same kind heart all over again. She smiled at Cameron and swayed to the rhythm of the ballad filling the room. Her kitchen had never been so full of life.

Erika giggled and launched herself not toward Mister Benjamin, as Jonni had expected, but straight at Cameron. Grabbing him around the knees, she looked up and said, "You brought Mister Benjamin. Just like you promised!"

Cameron looked down at the child, then over to her mother. Something sharp and fierce turned in his gut. The desire to protect them from harm rose within him. It was the way he felt about his younger sister. He nodded, not quite trusting himself to have the right words to say.

"Thank you," she said, and then turned to Mister Benjamin's side. "I thought you were the best," she said, watching him fold napkins, "but now I like Mr. Scott even better. Too bad he can't have his own TV show."

Flynn's face was a study. Cameron watched as his buddy struggled not to laugh. He finally managed to come out with, "True, true," in a fair imitation of the raspy voice Cameron had perfected. Maybe it was wrong of him to carry out the pretense, but if it made her happy he didn't see how it was any different than telling a kid their Christmas presents had been overnighted by Rudolph Express from the North Pole.

And the expression on Jonquil's face was worth the world to him. She remained close to the door, her hands clasped, the smile in her eyes making it pretty darn hard to resist crossing the room and taking her in his arms.

He made it through the rest of the impromptu dinner

party, though later, trying to fall asleep in his huge, empty bed, he didn't know how.

Without doing anything other than being her own gracious self, she'd teased and tantalized him, the body-hugging black dress and high heels even more enticing in the bright light of the kitchen. They exchanged no further words in private, even when they'd called it a night and everyone had climbed back into the limo for the trip to the hotel.

At least he'd told her he'd make up the dinner to her the next night. He'd find her during a break the next day and confirm a time. He'd learned his lesson. He'd take a cab to pick her up and make no reservations.

Cameron balled up yet another pillow and then tossed it off the bed. His arms ached to hold her, his hands itched to trace the curve of her breast, his mouth craved the taste of her sweet, hungry tongue.

His body wasn't going to let him sleep.

Neither was his mind.

In the Garden District, all was quiet. The occasional streetcar rumbled by on St. Charles, a long block away. The only other sound Jonni heard was the rhythmic tick-tock of her clock, reminding her with every beat that she'd yet to fall asleep.

She relived the evening, from the first kiss in the limousine to the companionable dinner they had all shared. Even Isolde and Cosey, discovering common ground in both being vegetarians, had made their peace.

And Cameron had asked her out again. She smiled, and nestled against the pillow.

Oh, no!

She sat straight up. She'd told what's-his-name she'd have dinner with him. She couldn't even remember his name. How could she cancel? Her mother would know. *Calm down. You said you'd go. Go. You know better than to fall for Cameron Scott.* Besides, being unavailable was smart dating. Her sister the Love Doctor had written more than one column based on that classic advice.

Jonni punched her pillow.

When it came to Cameron Scott, she didn't want to be unavailable.

The next evening, Jonni dressed for her dinner date with Stephen Propper with a true lack of interest. The only highlight of her day had been the look of loss in Cameron's eyes when he'd asked her what time he could pick her up and she'd answered that she had another date. It gave her hope that he sincerely wanted to spend time with her.

She pulled on the same cream linen suit she'd worn to the reception with Daffy, a pair of sensible heels, and a pearl bracelet and earrings. Facing herself in the mirror, she stuck a tongue out at the stuffy matron who stared back.

What had happened to last night's siren? Well, at least beneath the suit, she had donned silky, slinky underwear, bare scraps of satin and lace, not because of her hot date, but because it was her little secret that made her feel more like a devil than the boring angel she was. The kisses in the limo with Cameron had stoked fires she hadn't known burned within her, and she wanted to keep them going.

Until she saw Cameron again.

And who knew what would happen then?

She started humming under her breath, and went downstairs. Erika was waiting for her in the foyer, looking none too happy.

"What is it, sweetheart?"

"I never get to spend time with you anymore," she said.

"We spent the day together," Jonni said.

"That's different," Erika said.

"I have a meeting to attend," Jonni said. She bent down and kissed her daughter's cheek. "Be a good girl. I'll be home before bedtime."

She pulled her car keys out from her purse.

"Isn't Mr. Scott picking you up?"

"My meeting isn't with Mr. Scott," Jonni said.

Storm clouds appeared in Erika's eyes. Jonni sighed and said, "Don't worry about me. I'm coming home." She held her daughter to her, stroking her hair. Of course she worried. Her father had gone to a dinner meeting and never returned.

Isolde appeared just then, phone in hand. "Cosey wants to come over. Is that okay?"

Erika looked up. "She dresses funny," she said.

Grateful for the distraction and for the way the two young ladies had buried the hatchet the evening before, Jonni nodded, ignoring Erika's critical comment. Cosey cried out for a ticket from the fashion police. "Maybe the three of you can design a new wardrobe for her."

"What a great idea," Isolde said. "She lost all of her clothes when she had to leave her apartment and only has what Mr. Flynn and Mr. Scott bought for her."

"Look in my spare closet," Jonni said. "She looks like a six, and goodness knows I've got lots of those I'll never wear again."

Erika patted her tummy. "No more baby brother," she said, somewhat sadly.

Jonni kissed her once again, and dragging her feet, made her way to her car and drove the few blocks to Commander's Palace as slowly as the other traffic permitted.

Stephen Propper was truly everything that was proper. Gray suit, maroon tie, gold cuff links with a crest that matched the signet ring that crowned the pinky of his right hand. Excellent table manners, good knowledge of wine.

But no matter how hard Jonni tried to concentrate, her mind kept drifting to the evening before—when she and Cameron hadn't made it inside the doors of the landmark restaurant.

The waiter had just delivered their turtle soup. Her date decided against the dash of sherry the waiter offered. The buzz of conversation in the downstairs room was genteel, yet Jonni found it difficult to hear what her companion was saying.

Or perhaps she simply didn't want to be a part of the conversation.

"I've put in an offer on a house on Sixth and Coliseum," he said. "It needs a lot of work, but it's the least one can do to add to the tradition of the city."

"We'll be neighbors," she said, her tone polite.

He smiled at her, a rather possessive expression she didn't quite understand. And then she realized her mother must have been at work, no doubt plying this man with the idea that all Jonni needed was another up-wardly mobile husband of good family. Yes, she could hear her mother now, assuming Jonni would go along with a quick courtship, and fall easily back into the sub-servient role she'd fulfilled as Mrs. David DeVries.

"Unless I put my house on the market," she added, some imp in her brain activating her tongue.

He lifted his left hand from his lap and placed it lightly over hers. "Your mother didn't do justice to your beauty," he said.

Good for him he lifted his hand quickly. "You know how mothers are," she said. "I gather she'd forgotten to mention my own daughter to you."

"That she did," he said. "But I like children. I have two nephews in Houston. They both go to boarding school but are home for holidays."

"How nice for their parents," Jonni said, thinking how dreadful that sounded. She took a swallow of her soup. And another. And another. And another. Without realizing it, she scraped the bowl clean. She looked up to see he was staring at her. Horror-stricken was the only way she could describe his expression.

Jonni smothered a laugh and dabbed at her mouth with her napkin. "That was delicious," she said. "I think I'll have another cup."

"But your shrimp remoulade will be here any minute."

"So?"

"I've never seen anyone eat two soups. It just isn't done."

Echoes of her dead husband's maxims and preachy

advice ricocheted in her head. Jonni lay her hands against her temples. She had to get away from this man. He reminded her so strongly of the life she had lived for far too long, of the woman she'd never even questioned.

"I'm not feeling very well," she said.

"Eating too quickly will do that," he said, continuing his measured spooning of soup from bowl to mouth.

Jonni put her napkin on the table and picked up her purse. "Thank you for dinner," she said, "but I'm going now."

He lay his spoon across the soup plate. "No one leaves in the middle of dinner."

"Is that so?" Jonni slid from the booth. "It's really best this way," she said. "I don't think you'd want me to make a scene." She touched her forehead. "My mother didn't tell you about my migraines, did she?"

"Why, no, she didn't." He'd half risen but he sat back down.

Jonni sighed. "You know how moms are," she repeated. "Blind to their children's faults."

"Apparently so," he said, his voice almost bitter.

The waiter approached. "Is everything all right, sir?"

"The lady isn't feeling well," he said. "The soup is quite good, only I detect just a shade too much pepper."

That did it for Jonni. She turned and hightailed it to the door. The owner-hostess, who knew her well, came over and asked her if she was okay.

"Never better," Jonni said. She thanked her and stepped outside into the humid August air.

Never better, she repeated to herself, clutching her valet ticket and calculating the short distance between

Commander's Palace and the Windsor Court—and wondering whether the impulsive idea that had leaped into her mind would chase itself away before she arrived at Cameron's hotel.

Chapter Twenty-one

Inside Cameron's hotel
Later that evening

Cameron brushed off Flynn's suggestion they have dinner and try their luck at the craps table at the casino across the street from the hotel. His face itched from the heavy makeup, his head hurt from the stupid wig, and he couldn't keep his mind off the idea that Jonquil was having dinner with some guy who knew five-syllable words and belonged to her civilized world.

He escaped unnoticed in the bustling lobby and headed up the stairs to his suite. No wonder he was feeling less than his usual self. He hadn't worked out in several days. He should track down his trainers and have them fit in a session at a local gym. Cheered by that, he took the stairs two at a time, clicking off floor after floor without breaking a sweat.

His suite was quiet. Cameron shrugged off his shirt and dropped it on one of the couches in the sitting room. The floor-to-ceiling drapes were open and the last sun of the day was fading fast. Lights were on in nearby buildings. He crossed to the window, lifted one arm against the glass, and wondered what the people in those buildings did when their workday ended.

Did they go home to their families in the suburbs and throw a burger on the grill and watch the kids ride their bikes? And then watch TV and pop a few beers and fall into bed to rise to do it all again the next morning?

He scratched his chest and yawned. He'd always made fun of that sort of life, but right now, alone again in this elegant hotel suite, with two bedrooms and three bathrooms and only himself to fill it up with noise, he wasn't so sure who was the smart one.

'Course, normally he was never alone. He could always summon a chick of the moment to his side.

Cameron kicked off his shoes, unbuckled his pants, and shucked them onto the floor.

He could call someone.

He ran his hands around the elastic band of his bikini briefs. The image of Jonquil's dainty hand holding his cock through the fabric of his pants burned in his mind.

His body responded.

Cameron groaned and moved away from the window.

There was only one woman he wanted to call.

He flung himself to the floor and counted off thirty push-ups.

"Get a grip," he said, doing just that with his hand. He could taste her hot kisses just by running his tongue over his lips. But he wanted more. He wanted her breasts free of her dress, filling his hands, the sight of her naked and smiling and trembling and panting for him to take her.

Cameron groaned and jumped up from the floor.

Physical release alone wouldn't set him free. He was like a junkie who needed a fix, and the only woman who could answer that craving was out of his reach.

Not that he could win her. She'd responded to him in the limo, oh, yeah. But then it was like—or was that supposed to be "as if"—she'd catch herself and back away.

Jonquil DeVries was not some Hollywood hanger-on seeking a notch in her dick list.

Cameron caught sight of himself in the long mirror over one of the side tables. He had to laugh. He looked ready to play the lead in a XXX flick. He couldn't walk around like this during his time in New Orleans, his mind and body full of thoughts of Jonquil. He simply had to figure out a way to seduce the woman and get her out of his mind.

He paged Robby and Heather, met them for a quick, challenging workout, and returned to his room an hour later, as restless as ever.

Cameron decided to order room service and do some housekeeping on his body. His chest hairs could use a touch-up and his face, after hours and hours inside that heavy makeup, cried out for a facial.

Cameron had learned to take care of his body the way a hand model pampered her hands. He might be an action hero, but the day he quit looking good was the day he would have to get a real job. His personal care routines were another one of his closely guarded secrets, like the truth of how Flynn had saved his life. Macho guys weren't supposed to know the difference between granular-based exfoliants and fruit acid AHAs.

Cameron did, though, and used the knowledge to his

advantage. He grabbed a room service menu, and called in his dinner selection, smiling when he requested a double order of shrimp cocktail. Willing his ever-ready hard-on to "take five," he strolled into the luxurious bathroom and set to work. If he had to spend the evening without Jonquil, he'd make the most of it. Because tomorrow night, come hell or high water, the two of them were going to find themselves very, very close.

Jonni clung to the steering wheel of her Volvo as if she were holding on to a life preserver. She navigated the turn into the busy circular drive of the Windsor Court. The valet opened her door, and slowly she came to her senses and unwrapped her fingers from their leather support.

"Checking in, ma'am?"

"No," she said.

"Dining with us?"

She nodded, then shook her head, then nodded again, wondering what had possessed her to visit Cameron's hotel. Goodness only knew she wouldn't find him. He was probably out partying with at least five, no, a dozen starlets. This crazy idea must have been percolating in her subconscious since she'd overheard him telling Sunny how ironic it was that a good old boy like himself had been put up in the hotel's presidential suite.

"When you're ready, just leave your key in the ignition," he said, sounding professional but regarding her as if she were a less than satisfactory customer.

"Of course," she said, mustering her dignity. She fished a five-dollar bill from her purse and he perked up when she climbed from behind the wheel and handed him the tip.

She'd been to the Windsor Court many times. She and David had entertained clients at dinner at the Grill Room and she had enjoyed many high teas with friends. During an annual bar convention, David's firm had used the same suite Cameron had mentioned he was staying in.

Jonni walked up the steps past the shrubbery alive with twinkling white lights and into the spacious lobby. The massive arrangement of fresh roses reminded her of the entry areas of the Metropolitan Museum in New York. She never tired of the sight of flowers done as creatively as any work of art.

But right at this moment, it wasn't horticultural beauty that drew her onward.

She joined a well-dressed older couple in the elevator. They were conversing in French, and Jonni pretended not to understand their dismay at finding the local gambling not at all up to the standards of Monte Carlo.

She maintained a polite silence, not unfriendly, but properly so. Proper. Jonni always did the proper thing. She wrinkled her nose, remembering how repulsive she'd found Mr. Stephen Propper.

Watch out world, she thought, feeling the skittering of her pulse, Jonni was stepping out tonight!

She was about to throw herself shamelessly at Cameron Scott. Trading proper and prideful for one night of passion. She'd seen the handwriting on the wall during her interrupted date. Her mother, and her friends, would keep after her until she agreed to wed another acceptable husband such as David. They'd wear her down until she accepted the role they wanted her to play.

If she was destined to live her life as the docile wife of a socially acceptable husband, she'd live on the edge at least once.

Cameron no doubt had this happen to him all the time. Women flung themselves at his feet without any encouragement at all. And last night, those kisses—well, she hadn't made that up. He wanted her. She wanted him.

So that ought to be simple enough, she thought, nodding as the couple exited the elevator and she rode to the next floor.

Her destination.

Never mind that she'd never had sex with any man other than her husband. Not for her the playing around in high school, the experimentation in college. Her twin had been wild enough for both of them. Jonni had followed David's lead in all things, and he'd taken her virginity on their wedding night.

Not that there had been so much to fuss over about it all. Just the way she'd felt when Cameron kissed her had whipped up more passion than she'd ever known was possible.

Jonni wet her lips and watched the elevator doors slide open effortlessly.

And then slide closed.

She hit the Open button with the palm of her hand, surprised to find her skin slightly damp.

Well, heck, she'd gone this far. And Cameron would know what to do, how to react when he found her on his doorstep.

If—she stepped out and almost performed an about-face—he was in.

She should have called first. How stupid of her, really, to drive to the hotel in such a harum-scarum fashion. So unlike her.

Good.

She straightened her shoulders, put her chin up, and started down the hall.

If she'd called, he might have said no, or she might have changed her mind.

At the doors of the suite, she paused. Glancing around and seeing no one else, she pressed her ear to the door. Music blared from within. Recognizing an old Beatles tune, she smiled. Cameron liked the music of the sixties and early seventies as much as she did.

Raising her hand, she knocked on the door.

Cameron had given up whistling along with the radio when the clay masque he'd applied had begun to set and dry. Now he shrugged out of the hotel robe and dipped a comb into the hair dye solution he'd mixed in one of the room's ashtrays. For whatever reason, the tips of his chest hair tended to silver. Normally he had the touch-up done by his hairdresser, but what with Flynn hanging around his Bel Air house to make sure Cameron didn't escape prior to flying to New Orleans, Cameron had skipped his appointment.

Careful to dampen only the ends and not smear the mixture onto his skin, he combed the hair that covered his pecs and the center of his chest. If only the press could see him now, he thought, almost grinning and then remembering not to crack the mud masque.

Hell, if he drove a truck for a living, he'd make damn sure he changed the oil and rotated the tires on a regular schedule. In his line of business, this bodywork was no different from mechanical upkeep. And he hadn't always been rich and able to rely on others to scurry around at his every whim, anxious to advertise they serviced the body of Cameron Scott.

His stomach growled. Where was his dinner? In addition to the shrimp cocktail and his customary champagne, he'd ordered a secret indulgence, Elvis' favorite, peanut butter and banana sandwiches. If he was staying in for the evening, he was going to do it up right.

Just then he heard a knock. Shrugging back into the robe, careful not to let it touch his chest, he headed to the front of the suite. He'd unlatch the door, then pop into the powder room off the entrance till the waiter disappeared. He'd leave the tip on the check.

"Come in," he managed through his stiffened face, though it probably sounded more like cu-u-u-m-n. That made him think of Jonquil and more than his masque grew taut.

From behind the shield of the powder room door, he waited, estimating how long it would take the waiter to deliver the goods and retreat. Cameron had the music so loud he couldn't really hear much.

He thought he heard his name so he said, "Okay, leave it," but knew those words were pretty much indecipherable.

No doubt the waiter was cussing the ungrateful rich under his breath. Cameron counted to a hundred, and stepped out from behind the bathroom door, into the entryway, and smack into Jonquil DeVries.

She screamed.

Naturally. He looked like the creature from the spa lagoon, for Pete's sake.

He grabbed her by the shoulders. "Is okay," he croaked. "Me, Cameron."

She stopped screaming.

And started laughing. Pointing at him, she said, "I can't believe that's you under there!" He was still holding her shoulders and she was shaking with laughter. Tears started down her cheeks and she lifted one hand to wipe them away.

"Sorry," she said, then burst into giggles all over again.

There was only one thing he could do.

He pulled her close and kissed her.

She kissed him back, eager, hungry, giving him all he wanted and more. He groaned and crushed her to him, taking her mouth, sucking on her tongue, swift, then slow, swallowing all he could. He cupped her butt, massaging her cheeks with a greedy hand.

Knock. Knock. Knock.

His heart was beating so fast he could hear it in his head. Cameron very slowly freed his mouth from hers as the pounding sounded again.

"Room service," came a voice from the other side of the door.

Jonquil stepped back, her lips a beautifully gorgeous pout of desire. "Oh, my," she said.

"Oh, yeah," Cameron said, realizing his cock was about to break free of his bikini briefs.

He reached over and tenderly lifted several flecks of masque from her cheek. "Sorry," he said, able to move his face a bit more since the kissing had dislodged some of the masque. To the door, he said, "Just a minute."

He held out a hand to Jonquil and led her to the powder room. He grabbed a washcloth and cleaned the traces from her face and then swabbed it over his own, removing most of it. He tossed the cloth into the basin, and when he lifted his head, his eyes locked on the front of Jonquil's cream-colored linen suit.

"Hell's bells."

Her face fell. "What's wrong?"

Being caught in a facial was one thing. Confessing to dyeing his chest hairs was another. He shifted from one foot to the other, considering.

And then she glanced down.

And screamed again.

The knocking at the door grew louder.

Cameron tied the robe around him. He'd already ruined her suit. What was one more ruined bit of clothing?

He opened the door to the waiter, to find a curvaceous brunette eyeing him the way a shark might examine an unfortunate swimmer. Cameron was pretty sure she'd unbuttoned the top of her uniform an extra inch or so. Perfume competed with the aroma of his dinner.

"I've brought just what you ordered," she said, her voice low and promising.

"Great," he said. "Just put it in the room there."

"Whatever you say, Mr. Scott," she said.

From behind the bathroom door, Jonni listened to the exchange. She could picture the room service waiter. What a hussy, throwing herself at Cameron!

Then she caught sight of her kiss-swollen lips and the sparkle in her eyes and decided she shouldn't be quite so hypocritical. As a matter of fact, she probably ought to slip out the door and let the other woman finish what she'd started. Without Cameron's arms around her, Jonni was starting to lose her nerve.

Just then he leaned into the room. With a smile, he whispered, "Don't you dare run away."

Flattered, Jonni felt something oddly akin to a surge of power. She stretched her arms over her head, tingling all over. Her body was definitely more awake than it had been in a long, long time. Even the stains on her suit couldn't bother her.

She heard the door slam and Cameron swung back into the powder room. Taking her by the hand, he said, "I've ruined your suit."

Jonni stood on tiptoe and kissed him, very lightly, on the mouth. Then she unfastened the top button. "Does it matter?"

She watched him swallow. That crazy rush of feminine power shot through her and she undid the second button, then the third. "I can always slip into something else," she said, shrugging out of the linen jacket and letting it fall to the floor.

"I like the way you think," he said, his robe joining the jacket.

Chapter Twenty-two

❦

Cameron's hotel suite (cont'd)

"And I like the way you taste," he said, his voice low and soft against her hair.

Jonni sighed. "Me, too," she said.

"Oops," he said, pulling away. "I'm not thinking straight here. I've got to wash this stuff off."

"What is it?" She didn't really care; she just wanted him to keep kissing her.

"If I'm not careful you'll wangle all my secrets out of me," he said, grinning. "Hair dye."

"Oh," Jonni said. "I see."

He shrugged. "You've seen more than any other human being ever has of Cameron Scott."

"Mmm. I certainly like what I see." She couldn't help herself; even as she finished the sentence, her gaze settled on his bulging bikini briefs.

"Let me wash up," he said, "and you can look all night long."

She blushed. He kissed her, a hard, swift taking of her

lips, then said, "Make yourself comfy. I'll be back when I'm not dangerous."

He showed her into the living room of the suite then disappeared through one of the other doors.

Jonni thought of following him, but she figured it was a matter of male pride to be left alone to wash the dye from his chest. She glanced around the suite where she'd been before, the very proper Mrs. David DeVries, entertaining other lawyers and their spouses during the bar convention.

Liking the contrast very much, she kicked off her heels. She wanted to have the nerve to slip off her skirt, but she lacked it. True, Cameron was 99 percent naked, and no doubt that room service waiter would have been out of her uniform in a trice with just an inkling of invitation, but Jonni couldn't quite manage that daring of a gesture.

She did open the champagne, though, achieving a very satisfactory pop of the cork as Cameron reentered the room. He'd slipped into a pair of jeans and a white T-shirt, and when Jonni saw his change of clothing she blushed.

"Thinking naughty thoughts?" He took the bottle from her and filled two glasses, handing her one and plunking the bottle back in the ice bucket.

"Oh, nothing special," she said.

"Truth serum," he said.

"What's that?"

Cameron sat on one of the sofas and patted the space beside him. Jonni joined him.

"It's a tradition my sister and I have had for years. When either of us skirts the issue, we call out, 'Truth

serum,' and the other has to say what's really going on."
He tapped the top of her head.

"I like that," Jonni said.

"So what were you really thinking when I walked
back into the room?"

Jonni stared into the bubbles frothing at the top of
her flute and then met his gaze. She'd liked being able to
talk so openly with him. Funny, but she liked talking
with Cameron almost as much as she liked kissing him.
"When I saw you'd gotten dressed, I was glad I hadn't
ripped all my clothes off while you were in the other
room."

He slid one arm behind her. Toying with the ends of
her hair, he said, "And were you considering doing
that?"

"Truth serum?"

"Truth serum."

"Yes," she whispered.

"I'm glad you didn't," he said.

"You are?" Jonni couldn't keep the disappointment
from her voice.

"Uh-huh," he said, lifting her glass from her hand
and setting both drinks on the coffee table. "Because I'd
like to have that honor," he said.

"Oh," she said, a delicious shiver filling her body as
Cameron leaned over her, one hand skimming the line of
her camisole where it dipped into the vee between her
breasts.

"And I'm going to take my time," he said.

"You are?" Not that she was the model of experience,
but Jonni knew better than to think a man would go
slow when it came to sex. David had been as methodical

about lovemaking as he'd been about every other aspect of his life. He was considerate and polite but not at all racy.

Racy.

What a great word.

Jonni glanced downward, following the path of Cameron's hand, her breasts warming even though he hadn't yet touched the skin beneath her camisole.

"Nice and slow," he said, circling one nipple through the fabric.

Her body responded, puckering against his touch. Feeling she should do something for him, Jonni tipped her head up, kissing him lightly on the mouth.

His fingers kept skimming that same slow drumbeat to her senses over her breasts as he sucked her lower lip into his mouth, then plundered her tongue.

Jonni cried and pushed her body against his hand. She needed more. That feather touch was doing things to her she couldn't withstand.

"Please," she said, gasping as she broke free of his kiss. "Please."

Cameron grinned and forced himself to move his hand from her body. He didn't need to look at his crotch to understand that plea. He craved the same release she was begging him for.

But she wasn't ready for more.

Not by a long shot.

Cameron reached over and handed her champagne to her. Looking disappointed, she took the glass.

"Not the beverage you're thinking about, is it?" He loved the way she blushed and then nodded, her eyes all bright and sparkling and damn it, trusting.

Shit.

He hated to have a woman trust him.

Not that it happened often.

Maybe never?

He grabbed his own glass, holding on to it for safety. He ought to keep his hands off this innocent woman, but so help him, he didn't think he could.

"Hey, didn't you have a date tonight?"

She nodded and sipped her bubbly.

"Guess it didn't last long," he said, strangely relieved.

She shook her head and her hair caught the light. He wasn't given to romantic descriptions, but he sat there thinking "shimmered" fit the bill perfectly. Leaning over, he touched the flow of her hair as it covered her creamy white shoulder, bare except for the trace of a camisole strap and the weight of her hair.

Without thinking, he buried his face against her hair and breathed, inhaling her scent, her perfume, her quiet strength.

He felt her hand against his head, stroking the back of his neck, her breath on his hair as she bent her head to his. She was murmuring, sounds he couldn't make out at first. And then they formed words, but words that had no connection to him.

"Sweet, sweet Cameron," she was saying, the phrase keeping time with the leisurely strokes of her fingers against his scalp.

He wasn't sweet. He was randy and troublemaking and temperamental and selfish.

"Shit," he said, and lifted his head from her hair. Sloshing champagne, he put both of their glasses back on the table, back where they belonged so his hands could have free rein of her body.

Gently, but with a hunger he couldn't deny, he lowered her to the sofa, his mouth on hers, swallowing those words that didn't describe him. Never had, never would.

He had her skirt pushed around her waist in less time than it took to suck her tongue into a dance with his own that gave fair warning that he'd forgotten all about taking his time.

She wore stockings, not pantyhose. A scrap of satin bikini showed damp. He touched her and the heat shot through his hand.

He had to have her.

Now.

He had to get her out of his system, clear out this web she created in his mind that had him thinking crazy.

"Cameron."

He'd lifted his hands to his zipper. At the sound of her breathy voice, he paused and met her gaze.

And almost drowned in it. Her blue eyes were almost black, the pupils taking over. Her chest rose and fell and her nipples like crowns pushed against the silk of her skimpy top. One hand lay above her head, the other lay at her side, palm open, welcoming him. Her lips were parted slightly, and her thighs spread wide.

"Name whatever it is, Jonquil, and it's yours," he said. Shit, even if she said, "Turn your back, I've changed my mind," he'd do it. He'd do anything this woman said right at this moment.

But he needed to take her and get that nonsense out

of his head. How could a man function if he walked around thinking that stuff?

"Cameron," Jonni said, repeating his name, tasting the sound of it on her tongue. "What a nice name." And then she lifted her arms to him. "More."

"More, hmm?" He was half standing over her on the couch, still dressed. Surely he wouldn't play the gentleman and walk away.

He took her hands, turned them over, kissed each palm. She lay open and trembling and wanting. He kissed one wrist, then the other, then the insides of her elbows.

Jonni moaned. She felt as if her bones were no longer solid substances, but quivery flames running beneath the surface of her skin where his lips touched her flesh.

He brushed his lips over the curve of her shoulder, tucked an arm over her head, and nuzzled the skin of her armpit.

She giggled. "Tickles," she said, quite happily.

He smiled. One knee now on the couch, he bent forward and moved those sweet, torturing kisses to her breasts, edging the camisole down and taking first one nipple, then the other in his mouth.

Heat and need shot through her. Jonni clasped Cameron by the back of his neck and hung on for dear life. He slipped one hand to her thighs and circled his way up her leg, cupping his palm over the mound that throbbed and wanted more than a hand or finger could give.

Or so she thought.

As Cameron opened and explored and teased her

with his hand, he kept his mouth on her breasts, every so often lifting his head and brushing his mouth over her parted lips. Jonni was so lost to the sensations he was stoking inside her starved body she couldn't even focus on his face as he watched her, a half-smile and something dark and beautiful yet unreadable in his eyes.

She arched her back and cradled his fingers, pushing them deeper. "More," she said again, panting, begging.

He lifted his head from her breasts and his fingers from her hot, wet inner lips, and Jonni cried out. He couldn't stop now!

"Don't worry, fire angel," he said, "I'm only shifting position." He ripped his shirt from his chest and Jonni saw the white cotton T-shirt fly across the room.

She smiled, awed by the sense of feminine power she felt as she watched the way his erection bulged against his jeans. She ran her tongue over her lips, tasting Cameron, then shifted to raise herself against the end cushions of the sofa.

"Let me," she said, reaching for the zipper of his jeans.

He captured her hands and kissed her knuckles.

"If you start kissing me all over again like that, I may just die," Jonni said.

Cameron grinned. "You'd go happy, wouldn't you?"

She nodded, suddenly shy yet pleased to be exactly where she was.

"Tell you what," he said, "I promise to let you unfasten these jeans when I just can't stand to keep them on another second."

Puzzled, Jonni glanced at his crotch, unable to figure out what he was waiting for.

He obviously caught her expression. Kissing her hands again, he sat back down and said, "Your husband was a lousy lover, wasn't he?"

Jonni stared at him in amazement. "I didn't think guys talked about, you know, other guys."

He rested her hands on her breasts, circling a finger along the curve as he said, "Oh, yeah, we do. Just not the way chicks do."

"Really?" Jonni thought about that statement. "You know, I don't think I can ever remember discussing my sex life with anyone."

Cameron grinned. "Me, either."

"But you just said—"

He kissed her on the side of her neck. "Let me put it this way, Jonquil. If I were in a locker room right now, I'd say something like, 'Yeah, old Pistol what's-his-name, shot off every round early. And never did figure out how to lube the barrel.'"

Jonni wrinkled her brow as she translated his words. Her husband had always been in a hurry, careful to ask if she was "ready" without doing much to make that state a dazzling reality, the way Cameron had been doing so wonderfully well. "I think I understand," she said. "So now can we go back to the lube part?"

Cameron shouted a laugh. "You are precious," he said, then his face quickly sobered. "I can't believe I said that."

Jonni reached up and smoothed his forehead. "Why? I liked it."

"It's just not the sort of thing I usually say," he muttered.

"I think it's nice," Jonni said. "And so are you."

Cameron groaned. "Enough of words," he said, kneeling beside the couch and leaning over her thighs. He stroked the insides of her legs, tugged her panties from her, and tossed them over his shoulder. Then, shifting her slightly sideways, he spread her wider, cupped her cheeks in one strong, hot hand, and lowered his mouth to her already quivering center.

Jonni cried out, the sound a strangled blend of shock and pleasure so intense she did forget all about words. Her only reality became Cameron consuming her, ministering to her, teasing her, torturing her, his lips and tongue and breath unlocking a need so deep inside her she hadn't realized just how badly it needed to be set free.

Cameron fed her passion, rocking her, stroking, urging her upward. He'd known by her first reaction that she hadn't expected oral sex. Hell, the jerk she'd been shackled to probably had been one of those pussies who thought it was unmanly to suckle his wife. Jonni shuddered, caught her breath, and tensed slightly.

"Oh, yeah," he murmured, delivering with gentle fingers exactly what she needed. "God, you are beautiful," he said, his words drowning in the sweet dampness she was offering him.

She grabbed at his hair and arched against him. He glanced up and smiled at her as she cried out, her body trembling, shooting with exquisite pleasure.

Cameron smiled and lapped her heat, enjoying the pulsing motion of her satisfaction. If he didn't do some of the same himself soon, he wouldn't be walking for a week. But he'd wanted to take Jonquil to a place he knew she'd never been before. Oh, yeah, he'd bet she'd never felt this good.

One hand remained tangled in his hair. He lifted his face to watch her. The other hand cupped her breasts, and the smile on her face was that of an angel.

Her eyelids fluttered, and she smiled back at him. "I may never move again."

He grinned. "That's okay by me. You can lie here on my sofa and we'll have sex every"—he checked his watch—"quarter of an hour."

She blushed and started to sit up.

Cameron lay a hand on her shoulder. "I want you to feel good."

She kissed the back of his hand. That simple gesture sent a shiver of emotion, both good and scary, through him. Then she reached up and tapped on his leg. "We're not finished, are we?"

Cameron shifted her hand from his thigh to his hot cock. "What do you think?"

She tugged at the buttons of his jeans, and Cameron thought he'd explode if he didn't help her out. But he stood stock-still, reciting his seven-times tables as she edged the first metal button free of the heavy fabric.

"It's hard to do when you're . . ." She blushed again and Cameron laughed and forgot whether seven times seven was forty-nine or sixty-three.

"So hard?" he said, giving in to his need to hurry to feel her still-quivering, wet, hot warmth wrapped around his cock. "Let me help." He ran his hand down the other buttons, and they opened easily. He kicked his jeans and bikini briefs off and groaned, taking himself in his hand, happy to be free of that clothing.

"Oh, my," Jonquil said.

He looked at her wide eyes and then down at his

cock, and being the guy that he was, couldn't help but be pleased at her impressed reaction. He grinned and said, "See something you like?"

She smiled in that sweet, shy way of hers and reached out and touched him, one dainty hand cupping him.

Cameron lost his grin. Her touch shot through him and he almost lost his control. "Shit," he ground out.

"Don't you like that?" She sounded dismayed.

"I like it," he said. "Oh, yeah."

"Good," she said, sounding so satisfied he almost laughed. But he couldn't quite manage that. She was stroking him, in a rather exploratory fashion. He leaned over the couch, his hands on the back, his body above hers. He wondered whether she'd take him in her mouth, but dismissed the idea. As surprised as she'd been by his oral attentions, he would bet she was a stranger to that concept.

That was okay. He'd teach her that another time. Right now he wanted to bury himself inside her.

She'd taken him in both hands now, and tightened the pressure. Cameron groaned, pulled back, and reached out his hands. "Let's go in the other room," he said, not because he preferred the bed to the couch, but he needed a condom and he didn't want to leave her for even a minute.

"Mmm," she said, and lapped at the end of his cock with her tongue.

Cameron felt himself begin to lose control. "Sweetheart, let's do that next time," he said, and hauled her to her feet, across the room, and into the bedroom.

He unfastened her skirt, and she stepped free of it as he hunted in a half-opened suitcase for a pack of Trojans. Shit, where were they? Despite his reputation, he'd been celibate for a hell of a long time, but he knew he wouldn't have packed without them.

Just in case.

Just in case he felt like partying.

Jonquil was watching him, her eyes wide and dreamy, yet not quite as much at ease as she'd been on the couch.

Just in case he met a woman who mattered to him. Cameron quit fishing in his suitcase and sat on the bed, taking her hand and drawing her to him. She sat beside him, her thigh cozy against his.

"I'm looking for condoms," he said.

"Oh. I thought perhaps that was the case."

Cameron put his arm around her. "Got to do the right thing," he said.

She nodded, the gesture a tender up-and-down movement against his shoulder. Something about the way she'd gone quiet reminded him of something he'd wanted to ask her, but had been chased from his mind.

His body warred with his mind, but he had all night to satisfy his cock. He leaned them back on the bed, so they faced each other, and traced the line of her mouth with his thumb.

"You're too beautiful to cry," he said. "I heard you the other day. I'd snuck up the stairs looking for you. Something had made you awfully unhappy."

A look of hurt filled her eyes.

"Do you want to tell me about it?" Cameron didn't exactly recognize himself. First, he was talking during sex. And asking about a woman's tears.

Damn. He'd have to turn in his good old boy card if anyone ever found out.

Chapter Twenty-three

In bed together

Jonni hated that one little tear had snaked its way down the side of her nose. "You don't really want to hear about that," she said, hoping he hadn't seen that betraying moisture. The reminder of what she'd discovered about her husband was too painful even to think about.

He reached over and smoothed her hair over her shoulder. She liked the feel of his hand and the slide of her hair over her bare skin. "You make me forget the bad things," she said softly.

"Good," he said, kissing the tip of her nose.

They lay on their sides, facing each other. Jonni wore only her bra and camisole, and Cameron was completely naked. "Wouldn't you rather, you know . . ." she said, and trailed off.

"Are you avoiding telling me something awful?" He scowled, a mock-stern expression. "Like you were crying because you always boo-hoo when you break a fingernail? Now that I can't stand." He grinned and lightly kneaded the edge of her temple. "I'd like to get to know you."

Jonni couldn't believe her ears. She'd tracked him to his hotel room for a fling, for the night of passion he was delivering so beautifully. Yet he seemed to be offering more than a quickie. And then she thought of those letters and how deceitful David had been. She couldn't take anyone at face value.

"Oh, oh," Cameron said. "Bad thought alarm." He made a screeching noise and flapped one arm. "Evacuate the brain. Evacuate the brain!"

Jonni couldn't help herself. She had to laugh. "Where did you learn to be so silly?"

"Ma'am, I am a master of many skills. Besides, I've been hanging out with child actors. It's no doubt had an impact on me."

"Yes, Erika would say something like that," Jonni said. She wiggled a little closer on the bed, enough so that she could offer him a kiss on the lips.

He responded and the heat surged within. He reacted, too, and groaned. Against her mouth, he said, "Maybe we've talked enough. Want to tell me all about those tears later?"

She nodded, and reaching out, clung to him. He rolled them over so that she lay beneath him, and she cried out in delight and when he worked his way back down her body to the damp need between her thighs.

This time, though, he kissed her slowly, building the heat, and then when she knew she would peak and shudder again any second, he reached over and found the condom packet and ripped it open.

His breath heavy, his voice low, he said, "I want to feel you exploding around my cock."

Jonni swallowed and nodded. Cameron was everything she thought he'd be.

And more. So much more.

She watched through half-shuttered eyelids as he began to work the condom onto his erection. She didn't see how he could possibly stretch the rubber that far. Feeling brave and sensuous, she lifted her hands and said, "Let me help."

Sitting up, she leaned toward where he rested on his knees between her thighs. Funny, but she realized she'd forgotten all about feeling self-conscious about being overweight and pudgy around the tummy and thighs. With Cameron, she felt beautiful.

She sighed and pulled him to her, kissing his body where his rigid manhood rose from a thatch of black hair. Then she placed her hands around the condom and wiggled it upward.

He groaned and stroked the top of her head. Jonni smiled, feeling a rush of feminine power. "I like it when you make that sound," she said.

"You do, do you?" Cameron snatched her around the waist, and before she knew it, Jonni was lying above him, his strong arms holding her inches above his body.

She nodded.

He lowered her onto his chest, then reached around, worked her camisole off her, and unfastened her bra. Then he lifted her again, letting her bra fall free.

And fastened his mouth on her breasts.

Jonni lowered her legs, and slowly, her breath coming fast and the heat ripping from her nipples in waves down through her belly to the swollen inner lips he'd been kissing into an explosion of passion, she lowered herself onto his sheathed erection.

At the first touch, Cameron groaned. He let go of her waist where he'd been holding her up, lowered her, and cupped her derriere, nudging her up, then down, then up again as the size of him filled her ever so slowly, ever so beautifully.

Now it was Jonni who moaned, panting sounds she didn't recognize as her own, her need for him to completely take and fill her driving her on, driving her wild. Her hips danced and he danced with her, until the length of him had claimed her.

When he'd taken her so intimately in his mouth on the couch, she thought she'd expire from the exquisite pleasure. But now she knew that had been only a taste of what Cameron could do to her body, her mind, her heart.

He gazed up at her, eyes dark and wild and so alive. "Ride me, sweetheart," he said, his voice rough and seductive.

And Jonni did, with an abandon she didn't know she was capable of, whetting her own screaming, mounting need, swiveling and driving her hips, the heat and depth of his thick shaft finding and releasing every pent-up sensation.

"That's it," he murmured, guiding her, his hands supporting her even as his touch added to the sweet torture.

She was panting and sweating and unable to breathe. Waves of sensation mounted within her, each promising, then denying, the release she sought.

Cameron pulled her to him, stilling her hips against his body.

"Please," Jonni breathed, "I think I'm going to die."

He laughed, a low promise. "If you do, you'll have a smile on your face," he said.

"Oh, yes, thanks to you," Jonni said, wiggling her hips against his, loving the way their bodies were connected and how free she felt with him.

He rolled them over and lifted his upper body, his shaft still claiming full possession of her. He moved slowly, ever so slowly, his eyes fixed on her face.

She sighed and arched against him.

He lowered his mouth and circled one nipple with his tongue, flicking, sucking, lapping, as he continued stroking fast, then slow, finding even more sensitive points.

Jonni was losing herself again. Cameron was moving more quickly, his breath as ragged as her own. She forgot where she was, who she was, what day or month or year it was, as she clung to Cameron, riding the crest of sensation, and exploding within, bucking against him, crying out silly things she didn't even know were words.

And then Cameron found his own release and dropped to the bed beside her, his arms wrapping around her, clasping her to him.

Jonni snuggled close, holding the moment, savoring Cameron's body surrounding her, both inside and out. Soon she'd have to go, back to her daughter and her responsibilities. But for now, she sighed and nestled against him.

Cameron stroked her hair and let his heartbeat slow

down a bit. Damn, for someone in great shape, he'd almost been done in by this woman. It was his breathing being all messed up, of course, due to the way she managed to take it clean away from him.

"I knew you were a wild one under that proper surface," he said.

She tipped her head up from his chin and smiled demurely.

Cameron kissed her forehead, his body already stirring, wanting more. That had to be some sort of record.

She had to have felt him growing hard again, because she had that wide-eyed look on her face.

"Isn't this where you fall asleep?" she said.

"And waste a moment with you?" Cameron shifted, pulling away enough to dispose of the condom. He heard a plop and thought he might even have hit the wastebasket.

Jonquil was watching him, a funny little smile on her face.

"Penny for those thoughts," Cameron said, rolling back and wrapping his legs around hers, one hand idly stroking her breast.

"You're such a guy," she said.

"I sure as hell hope so." He tightened his legs, his cock nudging her thigh. "I wouldn't be much use to you if I wasn't."

There, she did it again, that sweet blush he found so irresistible. "You deserve to feel fantastic," he said. "And now that I think of it, I do, too."

"Don't you do this . . ." she trailed off, obviously embarrassed.

"Don't I do this sort of thing oh, let's say, four times

a day, each time with a different gorgeous babe like yourself?" Cameron ran a hand over his chest, wondering how many of the women he'd known would have taken his hair dyeing in stride without laughing themselves silly or running off to tattle to some gossip columnist.

"Well, maybe twice a day?"

Cameron shook his head. "It's that manager of mine, Flynn, spreading those rumors so I can make a lot of movies and a big stack of money. Action heroes have to be horny."

He felt her hand as she wrapped it around his cock. His body shot to attention.

"Very horny," she murmured.

"Mmm," he said, rocking against her hand. "Very." He maintained some semblance of mental control, even while enjoying the sensations she was stoking. "Tell me why you were crying and then we can have dessert."

"We haven't even had dinner."

Cameron lifted his head. "You are right!" Reluctantly, he eased her hand from his cock, kissed her fingertips, and said, "Come on, let's eat."

"I am hungry," she said, rolling onto her back and stretching her arms over her head.

"Do that one more time," Cameron said, devouring the sight of her naked and lush and so open, "and food'll be the last thing you eat."

"Oh," she said, not moving.

Cameron took her by the hand and pulled her from the bed. "All right, Miss Naughty, if you don't need food to keep up your strength, I do."

He crossed to the bathroom, pulled his silk robe off

the back of the door and dressed her in it, then found the hotel one for himself and shrugged into it.

"That robe looks better on you than it ever has on me," Cameron said, admiring the way the silk slipped off her left shoulder, leaving her breast open to his view.

Jonquil rearranged the fabric and it slid back almost at once. She gave up and left it that way, much to his satisfaction.

Back in the sitting room, Cameron carried the tray over to the coffee table. "I'd forgotten the radio was still on," he said, with a wink. He lowered the volume from its earlier blare and then lifted a cover from one of the plates and winked at her. "You drove everything out of my mind."

She smiled and peeked at the plate. "What's for dinner?"

"One of my favorite indulgences," he said, holding out the china plate. "Peanut butter, banana, and mayonnaise sandwiches."

The look on her face was priceless.

"Not what you were expecting?" He removed the covers from the two iced shrimp cocktails.

"I guess I figured you for a steak man," she said. "I've heard of these, but I've never had one."

"You don't know what you're missing," Cameron said. "You know it was Elvis's favorite, don't you?"

She nodded.

"I've been making these for myself since I was tall enough to reach the fruit bowl in my mother's kitchen," Cameron said, watching her lift a half from the plate. He handed her a napkin, put the plate back, helped himself to a sandwich, and sat on the couch beside her.

They sat there together, chewing in companionable silence. As soon as he could talk, Cameron said, "As much as I like these sandwiches, I've never shared one before."

"Really?"

He shook his head, and frowned.

"What's wrong?"

"Nothing," he said and took a big bite. Jonquil was definitely getting under his skin, getting in under his protective radar. It bothered him a little bit, but what concerned him even more was that he liked it. He chewed on his sandwich, mulling over that thought.

He reached over and poured champagne into the glasses they'd abandoned earlier. After taking a swallow, he said, "How about you tell me now why you were crying the other day?"

Jonni started, thankful the gooey sandwich made it impossible for her to have to answer immediately. He'd caught her off-guard by bringing up the topic again. She was surprised he still wanted to know, having assumed he was asking as part of the intimate play and exchanges leading up to sex.

Now that they'd done it, it didn't occur to her that he'd return to the topic.

Which just went to prove she kept underestimating the man. And that both embarrassed and frightened her. One night of passion was one thing; but liking the guy, well, she wasn't up for that emotional roller coaster.

Cameron had finished his sandwich. He licked his fingers, such a little-boy gesture from such a big tough guy.

"You're pretty good at hiding the real you, aren't you?" She spoke softly, wanting him to know she wasn't being critical.

He shrugged and reached for one of the crystal dishes of plump shrimp. "Know why I ordered this?"

She thought she knew the answer, but didn't want to be presumptuous.

"First answer that comes to your mind," Cameron said, lifting one large shrimp and holding it to his lips.

"Because of the way I described eating shrimp?"

"Yep," he said, smacking his lips. "Let me feed you one."

Without waiting for a response, he plucked another shrimp from the dish, dabbed it in the cocktail sauce, and held it out to her. She opened her mouth, and he slipped the juicy shrimp between her teeth and then pulled it back, sliding the taste over her lips and grinning quite wickedly as he did so.

The heat that had resettled in the core of her body leaped to life as he let her suck the shrimp from his fingers and into her mouth. She chewed it, swallowed, and then leaned over and licked the tips of his fingers.

He made one of those low growl sounds, and Jonni realized she'd succeeded in distracting him from why she'd been crying. Triumphant, she fed him a shrimp, teasing him as he'd teased her. Another few minutes of this play and she'd find herself panting beneath him again!

The silk wrapper fell off both her shoulders and Jonni wiggled and helped it fall to her waist. Cameron moved the dish and the glasses back to the tray and pulled her over on top of him, his mouth moving hungrily over her breasts.

Jonni sighed with pleasure. She could feel his erection through the thick cotton of the robe. Slipping a hand down, she shifted the fabric and took him in her hand.

Cameron lifted his mouth from her breasts and looked her square in the eyes. Jonni returned his look, knowing her need was as great as what she saw in his expression.

"You were faithful to your husband, weren't you?"

"What?" The question caught her by surprise. "Of course I was."

He nodded. "And the jerk didn't return the courtesy."

"How did you know that?"

He smoothed her hair over her shoulder. "Call it macho guy intuition."

She smiled at that. Exactly as he'd known she would, she was willing to bet. "But how did you know that's why I was crying?"

"Aha," he said, the picture of satisfaction. "I didn't, but it was a good guess, wasn't it?"

"You're smarter than I am," Jonni said, somewhat sadly. "All that time and I never knew until the other day. I suspected, but he was so good at being Mr. Perfect."

Cameron kept on stroking her hair. The gesture was so soothing and protective. "I found a file with letters in it. And they were so graphic." She felt herself getting mad. "He did things with her he never did with me."

"Little double standard there?"

"I guess."

"You were his wife, she was his mistress." Cameron smoothed her forehead with the back of his thumb. "I don't believe in walking both sides of the line, but then I've never cruised either one."

"You mean you've never had a serious girlfriend?" Jonni found that hard to believe.

"Don't you feel sorry for me?"

"I can if you want me to," she said. "Sometimes I feel sorry for me, for having been so gullible and trusting and stupid and—"

He cut off her tirade with a kiss. "He was the shit, not you," he said. "You're beautiful, and if he didn't know what he had, he was an idiot."

A tear was threatening to form. Jonni dropped against Cameron's chest and hugged him. "Thank you," she said. "I don't care what anyone says, you're a nice man and I like you."

Chapter Twenty-four

Inside Cameron's suite (cont'd)

Oh, no, she couldn't *like* him. Things had gotten way out of hand here. Cameron didn't know whether he should scare her off or take her again. He'd thought once would have slaked his thirst, but he was still so eager to taste her, plunder her, explode inside her tight heat, that he couldn't bring himself to drive her away yet.

Liking him was the first step to thinking she was in love with him. Cameron had been down that route before, and it was always a pain in the ass, convincing the chicks they didn't want him, persuading them they only enjoyed the magic he worked on their bodies.

Jonquil, what with her jerk of a husband and having been celibate for some time, was prime for getting his signals mixed. To give him time to think, he pulled her close to him and kissed her.

Besides, she was too innocent to play on his turf. The women he knocked around with knew the score. Cameron never played for keeps.

She returned his kiss, deepening it, then pushing him down on the arm of the sofa.

He gave himself up to her. He could think later.

She was all over him, kissing his mouth, then nibbling on his earlobe, and then moving down his chest. It felt so good to lie back and be pleasured, he relaxed his head, watching her through half-closed eyes. "Feels good," he said, his voice rougher and lower than even his Mister Benjamin tones.

She made some sort of sound that he couldn't make out, and kept on kissing her way down his chest. But when she touched his cock with her sweet mouth, Cameron thought he'd died and gone to heaven.

Then she lifted her head and said, "Would you like me to kiss you more?"

He was pretty sure he knew what she was asking, shy little devil-angel that she was. He nodded, and then thought to add, "If you'd like to."

She opened her mouth wide and tasted the head of his cock. Then she licked her lips and said, "You make me want to do things I've never done before."

Her husband had to have been a true idiot if he'd never let her suck him into that dainty mouth, Cameron thought, giving himself up completely to the feel of Jonquil's lips heating his already overheated cock. She slipped him deeper into her mouth, in a tentative way that drove him even wilder to push into her throat. He held back, letting her feel her way, moving in a slow then fast up-and-down motion that was whipping him into a frenzy of pounding blood and sex, dancing to the rhythm of her coaxing, tasting, teasing mouth.

He groaned and tangled his fingers in her hair. He

couldn't take much more of this without letting go. "Jonquil, Jonquil," he said, tugging at her hair, wanting her to go on forever, yet needing her to pull away.

Something she seemed to have no intention of doing. "I've definitely died and gone to heaven," he muttered.

Jonni couldn't help but smile. She was as worked up as Cameron, what with the rush of sensation and the taste and feel of him, an amazing montage of steel and silk and pulsing, heated sex in its most primal form.

He was thrusting against her curious and sweetly greedy caresses, and running his fingers through her hair. Suddenly, he dragged her head up and pulled her to his chest, then nudged her forward so that she practically sat on his face.

She grabbed the edge of the sofa and held on for dear life as he turned the tables on her and started kissing her again, the way he'd done before that had driven her so beautifully insane.

Which he did again, so quickly that she cried out almost at once and fell against him.

Cameron scooped her in his arms and moved both of them from the sofa to the bedroom in what Jonni figured had to be record time. He found their protection and once again rocked her body and her world.

That time they fell asleep, arm in arm.

Jonni wasn't sure what time it was or where she was when she felt Cameron stirring against her, his breathing deep and steady. She blinked and stared and all she could think was, *What have I done?*

She tried to move, but he only tightened his arms, stirred, and smiled in his sleep.

He looked so peaceful. For a long moment, she lay

still, marveling at how beautifully serene he seemed. The waking Cameron carried an edge of some raw, unfocused energy. Asleep, and maybe because of all their sexual activity, Cameron appeared at peace with himself.

Something Jonni wished she could be.

But she had to get up and go home. Her body craved the feel of Cameron, as sweetly sore as she already was from the unaccustomed activity. For a man like this, any woman in her right mind would stick around indefinitely.

But Jonni had come to Cameron's hotel room uninvited, and she'd gotten what she'd bargained for.

Another glance at his face and she acknowledged they had both received far more than an exchange of sexual satisfaction.

She'd made Cameron happy.

And he'd made her want more and more of him.

Which was another darn good reason for her to wiggle free of his oh-so-satisfying embrace, find her scattered clothing, and tiptoe out of the suite.

She lifted one arm and he stirred.

"Bathroom," she whispered, and he slackened his grasp. She slipped free and Cameron rolled over, his long legs stretching across the bed.

Jonni couldn't remember where her underwear was. She stepped on her skirt as she got off the bed. One piece down. Her jacket was in the sitting room, as were her shoes. The rest she'd have to abandon. It took only a minute or two to dress, sweep at her hair with her fingers, and tiptoe toward the door. Her purse was near there, inside the powder room.

One hand on the doorknob, she turned, surveying the

room behind her, part of her aching with loss. *Stay,* her body urged. *Go,* her brain commanded.

Her mind won the battle. It would be embarrassing enough to reclaim her car, but in the light of day, unthinkable. That photographer would have a field day if he saw her in this state. And she had to be home for Erika.

Chicken, she thought. *Those are excuses.* Jonni knew Isolde had things at home well under control. Administering a dose of truth serum to herself, Jonni admitted she was afraid to face Cameron in the light of morning, afraid he'd be thinking, *What are you still doing here?*

She closed the door quietly behind her and headed to the elevator.

Rat-a-tat-tat.

Cameron threw a pillow across the room. People were always knocking at his door.

"Leave me alone," he said, and pulled the covers over his head.

The pounding continued.

He heard Flynn's voice.

Cameron tossed the sheet back, and a shimmer of silk flew from the covers. "What the hell?"

It was a lady's stocking. And then he woke up all at once and every image from the evening before flooded his mind, even as the blood surged through his body.

Jonquil.

But where was she?

Holding the stocking, he padded across the room, peered in the bathroom, the living room, the other bedroom, the other bathroom, the entryway, the powder room. Circling back to the sofa, he grabbed the robe and shrugged into it as he headed to the foyer.

Flynn knocked again.

Cameron opened the door. "What do you want?"

"Good morning, how are you? Fine, thank you. And what a fine day it is," Flynn said, stepping into the room so quickly Cameron missed his chance to slam the door on his friend's far-too-chipper face.

He waved a sheaf of papers, then even his smile faded.

"Good buddy, you're not into cross-dressing, are you?"

"What the hell are you talking about?" Cameron crossed his arms and glared at his manager, then realized the effect was completely spoiled by the thigh-high stocking dangling from his hand. He laughed, despite his frustration at finding Jonquil gone. "Oh, this," he said, and stuffed it into the pocket of his robe.

Flynn had invited himself into the sitting room. "Wild night, I take it?"

Cameron shrugged.

"Tell me you haven't violated your morals clause again," Flynn said, sinking to the sofa.

Cameron shrugged.

"Who is she?" Flynn glanced around and said under his breath, "Is she still here?"

"Nope." He scowled.

His friend regarded him with a rather too-knowing look in his eyes. "Ran out on you, did she?"

"Don't be ridiculous," Cameron said, stubbing his toe against the thick carpet. "Nobody runs out on me."

"Maybe you've met your match," Flynn said. "Just so it's nobody involved with the production, I won't ask any more questions."

"Good," Cameron said, taking a seat on the end of the sofa where Jonquil had first sat last night. He took a deep breath and reached for the magnum of stale champagne. And then he realized it must be almost time to go to work, and he dumped it back into the ice turned to water. "Could use some coffee."

"It's on its way," Flynn said, shaking out the thick papers he carried.

"Nobody runs out on me," Cameron repeated, the stocking back in his hand.

Flynn raised his brows. "Okay, let me guess. No, wait, let me propose a wager."

"Whatever it is, I bet you have no idea who was here last night." Which was a pretty stupid thing to say, as Cameron didn't intend to tell even Flynn, his best friend, that it was Jonquil DeVries's stocking he was smoothing across his hand at that very moment. What had passed between Jonquil and him wasn't something he wanted to share with anyone.

Flynn pursed his lips, apparently deep in thought. "Why don't we skip that bet?"

"Really? I can't remember you ever saying that."

"Maybe we're older and wiser," Flynn said. "Because I am 99.99 percent sure you'd lose that and then you'd be sore at me and right now all I want you to be thinking about is this offer I'm holding in my hands."

"There is no way you know." Cameron sounded really stubborn, even to his own ears. Lucky for him, room service arrived. This time the waiter was a serious-faced older gentleman who carried in a continental breakfast and efficiently disposed of the mess from the night before.

While he worked, Cameron leaned back against the sofa, sensing Jonquil all around him. He breathed deeply and smiled just thinking of how much pleasure she'd experienced.

And how much she'd given him.

He groaned, ever so slightly, and turned to find Flynn watching him, his expression one of a man about to dial 911.

"You've got it bad," Flynn said, a smile breaking across his face. "Man, am I happy for you."

"I don't know what you're talking about," Cameron said, pouring coffee for himself and then remembering his manners and passing the first cup to Flynn.

"It doesn't take a genius," Flynn said. "I saw the two of you together the other night. The whole time we were making omelets you were making eyes at each other. I just hope Ms. DeVries isn't too much of a lady for you to handle."

"I'll have you know I can handle any woman I decide to," Cameron said, managing not to confirm Flynn's guess.

"Yep," Flynn said. "Whatever you say."

Cameron shrugged and took a long, satisfying swallow of hot coffee. "What's the deal you've got there?" It was funny, but he wanted to talk about Jonquil. He wanted to jump up to the roof of the hotel and shout out her name to the city below. Yet at the same time, he wanted the feelings she stirred within him to be their secret, and theirs alone. When the rest of the world got involved, things usually got all mixed up.

Like her running off during the night. Why had she gone and done that? No doubt because she was concerned about what others might think. But why not wake him up? Let him drive her home?

"You're not listening," Flynn said.

"Heard every word you said," Cameron muttered.

"Then you'll do the sequel."

"What sequel?"

"Aha!" Flynn said. "The sixth installment of Macho Force Man."

"They're not going to drag that piece of shit back into production, are they?"

"Do you know how much money that particle of feces has made for you?"

Cameron shrugged. "It's the same thing, every time."

"Are you feeling well?"

Cameron grunted.

"It's what you've always done. It's what you're famous for."

"Yeah, well, why did you trick me into doing this kiddie flick if you want me to keep on being Cameron Scott the macho action hero?"

"Quentin Grandy wanted you, and I think it's good to stretch your abilities."

"So go find me something else to work the kinks out of my abilities," Cameron said, almost not quite believing what he'd just told his manager.

Flynn folded the papers, stirred some sugar into his coffee, and sat back against the sofa. "Good buddy, you're growing up," he said.

*   *   *

The film crew had moved inside to her front parlor. Jonni remained upstairs, torn between aching for a glimpse of Cameron and her belief that he must have these one-night stands all the time. The last thing she wanted to do was act as if it had been anything more than that.

Isolde, finished with her summer class, had taken Erika to the park. Jonni had started to go with them, then had changed her mind at the last minute.

She wore her running clothes.

Yet she wasn't moving.

"Idiot," she muttered.

At least she wasn't downstairs shoveling the contents of the refrigerator into her mouth. She flopped back on her bed and closed her eyes, reliving the magic of the night before. The enormous bouquet he'd sent to the house the day before filled her room with their lush scent. Jonni breathed deeply, her mind and her body replete with thoughts of Cameron Scott.

How did he do it? How did he stir such need within her? Jonni had always envied her twin her flamboyance, her walks on the wild side, and assumed she knew all about pleasures Jonni only read about, especially after Daffy and Hunter had found each other. Anyone could tell just by looking at those two that they dwelled in their own secret universe, bonded by all things intimate and good.

And beautifully naughty.

The way she'd been with Cameron last night.

Jonni sighed and stretched one arm over her head,

aching to feel Cameron's mouth and lips on her body, touching her in his wild and greedy ways.

Not that that was going to happen.

"Now that's a picture that would bring tears to a blind man's eyes," Cameron said.

Jonni shot upright, her eyes wide open. Cameron, in the guise of Mister Benjamin, stood just inside the door of her bedroom.

She stared, glad that he'd sought her out, nervous that she'd betray what had been in her mind only moments before.

"Sunny said you were upstairs. May I come in?" His voice was more Mister Benjamin than Cameron Scott, the cadence more formal, the tone gentler.

Jonni wondered if he was aware of that. Scooting to the edge of the bed, she said, "Yes."

He walked slowly toward her, not saying a word. Jonni tried to think of something to say, something sophisticated and worldly-wise, but speech failed her.

Cameron stood before her, in his old-man makeup and gnarled hands, his butler's suit of black striped pants and morning coat over a starched white shirt.

One more step and his knees would brush against hers.

He halted, watching her. And Jonni realized then that he didn't know what to say, either. That thought shot through her, freeing her from her own self-imposed restrictions and expectations.

She reached up, touched him on his arm above the makeup. "It's good to see you," she said.

He smiled. "Yes, it is."

She patted the bed next to her. "Sit?"

Cameron sat. Their hips and thighs nestled into a comfortable resting together position. He nodded. "Please don't run away again."

Jonni glanced sideways at him. "I wasn't . . ." She trailed off. "Okay, I was. But it was just so awkward to stay and wake up and be in your way."

He put an arm around her shoulders and cradled her head against him. "Don't think if that's what you're going to come up with. Listen to your body."

"That's not very sensible," she said, but nuzzled his neck instead of pulling away and making a better argument.

"Not everything in life makes sense," Cameron said.

"I insist on order," Jonni said, rather more fiercely than she'd intended.

He patted the top of her hair. "Let go and let life happen."

"We're not very much alike, are we?" Even as she asked the question, Jonni wrapped her arm around his waist. He felt so good to hold on to.

Cameron shrugged. "Go figure. You know what they say—opposites—"

"—attract," Jonni finished with him.

He chuckled. "Ready for a bet?"

"Now?"

"Now."

"Okay," she said, holding on to these moments of connection, the marvelous sensation that Cameron actually liked her, as a person and not only as a chick to be bedded and abandoned.

"I bet I know what you were thinking when I walked into your room."

She blushed and stuck her tongue out. "Bet you don't."

He grinned and rose from the bed. "I have to get back to work, but since we both know I know, I'll be back to claim my winnings." He winked and just like that, he was gone.

Chapter Twenty-five
❦

Inside a production trailer
Later that day

He had to be nuts. Lounging in the makeup trailer while Luther freed him from the layers of wrinkles, Cameron read himself the riot act for giving in to the temptation to visit Jonquil in her bedroom.

He'd forced himself to remain somewhat in character. Otherwise, he would have taken Jonquil there on her own bed. The dreamy smile on her lips, her dainty hand cupped against her breast, the way her legs lay open and tilted upward and outward as if poised for his pleasure—hell, he'd known she was replaying the night before.

Something he wanted to do himself. For real.

He shook his head, and Luther frowned. "Hold still or this will get in your eyes," he said.

"Yeah, yeah," Cameron said, thinking Jonquil had already gotten under his skin.

Clear of the goo at last, he rose and glanced out the

small window just in time to see a florist delivery truck double-park in front of the house.

"Your hands, Mr. Scott," the makeup man said, one hand on his waist, the overtried patience of a school-teacher weary of dealing with rowdy kids showing on his face.

"Yeah, yeah," Cameron said, extending one, keeping an eye on the truck.

Was someone sending flowers to Jonquil?

Nah. He had no rivals.

She probably had arrangements delivered as a matter of routine.

The delivery man walked through the gate, holding a vase containing long-stemmed red roses. Cameron counted them as the man approached the front door.

Five.

Five! How cheap could a guy get. At least a single rose a woman would see as romantic; five marked a guy as too cheap to send a dozen, or even half a dozen.

Jonquil appeared in the doorway, smiling broadly when she spotted the roses. She took them and disappeared back into the house.

"Damn," Cameron said.

"Sorry," Luther said. "Other hand. We're almost done."

"Yeah, yeah," Cameron said, and to his surprise, the makeup man repeated his words with him.

"I'm a grouch today, is that what you're telling me?" Cameron turned away from the window.

"Well, I'm not sure I'd go that far," he said, "but something tells me we're not happy."

"I'm as happy as any other guy," Cameron said. "I just have a lot on my mind."

"We're having love troubles, aren't we?"

Cameron scowled. "You're not thinking of dishing out advice are you?"

The man toweled Cameron's hand free of the cold cream. "Only if we want some," he said, studying the hand for traces of makeup grime.

"Well, 'we' might need some, but 'we' don't want any," Cameron said.

"My, my, you are in a state."

"I've never needed anyone," Cameron said, as much to himself as to the other man.

"Mmm," Luther said.

"I've always been a free spirit. Getting tangled up, that's for other guys. Know what I mean?"

"No," Luther said. "I was with my partner from the day we met until the day he died last year. Man was not meant to face the world alone. You met P.J. the other night. I haven't known him long, but it's much better to be with someone else than it is to fly solo."

Cameron stared at him. "I'm sorry for your loss," he said, meaning it.

Luther nodded. "Thank you. You're all done."

"Right," Cameron said. "So it's okay to feel this way?" Even as he asked the question, he realized how stupid it sounded. He hadn't even discussed what was going on and there he stood acting as if Mr. Makeup could give him answers even some head shrink probably couldn't.

The other man patted him on the arm. "It's okay to want to be with someone else so much it aches when you're not with them, and you glance up every time a door opens a certain way because you can tell, even without seeing to the other side, when it's that special person. So, if that's what's troubling you, you really have no problems."

"I don't? I mean, no, I don't."

"Unless of course you fail to let the other person know just how special they are." He started cleaning up the makeup supplies.

"Yeah, yeah," Cameron said. "Thanks and I know I don't have to ask you to keep this—"

"I am a professional," the man said, his nose in the air. "I do not dish on anyone."

Cameron gave him a thumbs-up and headed out of the trailer. His mind back on the paltry floral offering, he decided his first mission was to order several dozen roses. He'd show Jonquil how a man spoiled a woman.

And whatever doofus had sent those other roses would learn he'd been bested by a master of the game.

"Thanks so much for letting me have my friends over, Mrs. J.," Isolde said, arranging cheese and crackers on a platter.

"You're welcome," Jonni said, somewhat distractedly. Cameron hadn't even stopped by after he finished filming. More than two hours had passed and he hadn't called, either.

Darn it. He'd gotten her hopes up. She'd known better than to let herself be taken in by a playboy. "I think it's wonderful that they are celebrating your anniversary with you."

"Me, too," Isolde said. "And it was very thoughtful

of them to send the roses. There's one for each year of my sobriety, plus one to grow on."

"You've turned out so well," Jonni said. "I'm lucky to have you as Erika's nanny."

"Thanks," Isolde said. "It's not always easy, but I like me so much better now than I used to. I asked Cosey to come over, too. I think she can use some friends here in town."

"That is nice of you," Jonni said.

Isolde shrugged. "I didn't like her at first, but she's not so bad under that silly surface."

"I think her life hasn't been too easy," Jonni said.

"She's an example of Benign Neglect. Middle-class, suburban, decent education, but no Love." The way Isolde pronounced "love" and clasped her hands over her heart, Jonni knew she was speaking in capitals.

"So she went looking for it in all the wrong places?" Jonni cracked open the refrigerator and stood there staring. She should fix dinner, but for once she had absolutely no appetite.

"Yep," Isolde said. "But she's beginning to understand my body parts theory and I think now she'll look for a man who isn't a Butt."

Jonni couldn't help but grin. "I hope I can learn that lesson," she said, the smile fading as she considered whether she'd been a fool to throw herself at Cameron.

"Mrs. J., you could never choose a Butt."

Jonni looked over her shoulder. "No? Well, what do you call a man who pretends to be a faithful and devoted husband and father and all the while is out screwing around?"

"Two-faced Bacterium," she said promptly. "Scum like that don't even rate a major body part."

The doorbell rang, the sound chiming through the house. Jonni slammed the refrigerator door shut and whirled around.

"Are you expecting company, too, Mrs. J.?"

"Who, me? Oh, no, no, I'm not. Why do you ask?"

Isolde looked at her, her expression far too knowing. "Shall I get the door?"

Jonni smoothed her hands on her skirt. "Sure. It's probably one of your friends."

"They're not coming for another hour," Isolde said, heading out of the room.

It had to be Cameron. No doubt he'd taken it for granted that she'd be available and had driven up in his chauffeured limo to sweep her off her feet again.

Which both impressed and annoyed her. She liked to plan things, not operate on impulse. Whatever he wanted to do, she'd say, *No, I'm sorry but I already have plans*. Of course, she could have won the title of Ms. Impulsive last night, knocking on Cameron's door the way she'd done.

"Idiot," she whispered, just as she heard Isolde calling her name.

"Mrs. J.! Come see!"

Maybe it wasn't Cameron. Jonni crossed the kitchen and made her way toward the front of the house, stepping carefully over the heavy cables that criss-crossed the long hallway.

An enormous vase of long-stemmed red roses crowned the entry table, with four others, in a range of hues from pink to coral to white, surrounding it on the floor. A delivery person was walking in, holding another huge display. "This is the last of it, then," he said, adding that dozen to the others on the floor. "Somebody sure likes them roses. We had to beg 'em off all the other florists in town."

Jonni stared at the mass of flowers. "Isolde, someone really likes you," she said.

The nanny handed her a small envelope. "These are for you," she said.

"Me?" Her voice actually squeaked. David had given her flowers once, on their first anniversary. After that, he never seemed to remember how much she enjoyed receiving flowers, especially roses.

She stared at the envelope, but all that was written on the outside was her name and address.

"I'll be going then," the delivery man said, but not making any move to leave.

"Oh, Isolde, would you run upstairs and get my purse?" The man wanted a tip.

"No need to tip me, missus," the man said, "I'm just dying to know who ordered all these flowers and said we had to get them over here right away. They wouldn't say at the shop, which kind of tells me they didn't know, and I sure would like to be the one to know who'd do such a crazy thing as this."

Jonni regarded the man. Well, he wasn't the only one. Only one possibility came to her mind, but why Cameron would do such a thing, she couldn't guess.

"Mrs. J., open it!" Isolde said.

Jonni did, her hands trembling slightly, to her annoyance. There was no signature, just one phrase neatly penned, no doubt by the order taker at the florist.

Poof! Shazashabam!

Jonni smiled and tucked the card back into the envelope.

"Well?" The delivery man and Isolde spoke in unison.

She thought of the photographer who had invaded their private kiss, and the way Cameron must have to guard his life. Matter-of-factly, she said, "Oh, these are for a scene the director added to the movie. They needed them here for filming first thing in the morning." There, she'd made that story up like a seasoned liar. What was coming over her? Jonni DeVries was bursting out of her cocoon.

"No romance?" Isolde sounded so disappointed.

The driver rubbed his chin. No doubt he wanted a tip now that he'd been denied any juicy scoop for his pals at the shop. Jonni went in search of her wallet, pulled out a five-dollar bill, and returned to the foyer. After giving him the cash, she closed the door firmly behind him.

Isolde was watching her. "You can tell me the truth," she said. "They're from Cameron Scott, aren't they?"

Jonni nodded. Just then Erika appeared at the top of the staircase. "I'm through playing Barbie," she announced.

"Come down and we'll make dinner," Jonni said.

"Look at the flowers," Erika said, hurrying down the stairs. "Pretty. Pretty."

"I think he's trying to Make an Impression," Isolde said. "Where shall we put them all?"

"Different rooms," Jonni said, still stunned by the

number of roses. The fragrance was filling the hall and permeating her senses. "I'll take the deep pink ones to my bedroom."

"Aw, you're sweet on him, aren't you?" Isolde paused, her arms around one of the large vases.

Jonni didn't answer. "Little vases carry big microphones," she said.

Isolde glanced over at Erika, who didn't appear to be paying any attention to her mother, busy as she was stroking the petals of several of the roses.

"These dwarf my little bouquet," Isolde said, tactfully changing the subject.

"What did you say?"

"A dozen is so much larger than five roses," she said.

Jonni snapped her fingers. "Hang on." Had Cameron seen her opening the door and accepting the delivery of Isolde's small vase? Had he then sent these in order to best some perceived competitor? "He would do that," she said. "What an annoying man."

"Who?" Isolde asked. "Do what?"

"Pretty," Erika said.

"Cameron Scott," Jonni said. "We're not keeping these flowers."

"You're not serious?" Isolde was clearly astonished.

"Oh, yes, I am. Shazashabam, my foot. It's more like Mabahsazahs. I'm taking these roses to Touro Hospital. The patients there will appreciate them, which is more than I can do."

"I don't understand, but whatever you say, Mrs. J."

What if she were wrong? Jonni stood there, torn between longing to keep and savor the roses as a sign that Cameron was this amazingly wonderful, incredible guy,

and wanting to haul them out of the house, as befit the
gift flaunted by a competitive macho jerk.

The logical thing was to check her facts before acting.
Wow, she'd been about to act purely on the impulse of
the moment. Jonni frowned, then smiled. For better or
for worse, Cameron was rubbing off on her.

"You want the role of a lifetime? Get your lazy self
down to the second-floor bar," Flynn said.

Cameron cradled the phone against his ear, busy
pulling on his socks. He'd given the florist plenty of time
to deliver the roses, and he intended to drop by to see
Jonquil's reaction. "I'm busy," he said.

"Busy? You're finished filming. You never bother
watching the rushes not that you can watch them now
anyway because Quentin Grandy is here in the bar at this
very moment, discussing a project I think you'll like."

"Don't tell me he's directing Macho Force Twenty
Nine Hundred and Forty-Two." Cameron stepped into
his shoes.

"Very funny. You said you wanted to branch out. See
you down here in five."

The phone clicked in Cameron's ear. He held it out
and stared at the plastic receiver. His manager had
started getting very, very bossy. But he'd also made
Cameron very, very wealthy.

He glanced at his watch. It was after eight. He could
spare a few minutes on his way back to the Garden District.

A few minutes morphed into several hours. Quentin
and his producer wife Mia had been joined by a writer
they introduced as Beetle and his wife, Amity, and Mr.

and Mrs. Marv Chessman, the retired ambassador-turned executive producer of *Mister Benjamin* and his artist wife, who turned out to be a pal of Amity's.

At first, he couldn't concentrate on the story they were discussing. Cameron felt like a man missing an arm and a leg as he watched the three couples, all of whom moved in sync and finished one another's sentences. He wished Jonquil was there with him. That would have left Flynn the odd man out, but his buddy had always been able to fend for himself.

They were discussing a screenplay for a romantic comedy Beetle had finished writing recently and Martin was thinking of pushing the studio to co-finance. Quentin and Mia were ready to get the project greenlighted by MegaFilms. They wanted a fresh face for the hero, a country-western megastar facing a meltdown in his personal life who finds redemption after disappearing from his own life and, while pretending to be a down-and-out truck driver, meets the woman of his dreams.

Flynn, naturally, had been pitching Cameron for the role. And by the time the eight of them left the bar, the deal had been made.

The hands on his watch stood at ten minutes till eleven.

"I don't believe it," Cameron said, alone with Flynn after the others had gotten off the elevator.

"Why not? It's a great deal. It'll open up a whole new audience to you."

"Not the deal, you dummy," Cameron said. "I wanted to see Jonquil tonight, and now it's too late to even call her without waking up her daughter."

"You're getting mighty thoughtful," Flynn said. "I can remember a time—as in last week—when that little courtesy never would have crossed your mind." He stuck his hands in his pockets. "Not that you would have dated a woman with a kid."

"I am not dating Jonquil," Cameron said.

"No?" Flynn whistled a bar or two, decidedly off-key. He'd had quite a few single malt scotches during their time in the bar. "Don't tell me you're selfishly schtupping her without remorse."

Cameron shook his head. "Come again?"

Flynn pushed him up against the wall of the elevator. "What I mean, good buddy, is I hope you are not taking advantage of that lady. And I'm not talking about your morals clause."

Cameron glared at his friend. "What kind of a guy do you think I am?"

"Just checking," Flynn said, patting Cameron on the shoulder and straightening his jacket. "She seems like a true lady, and when you find someone like that, well, you ought to treat her right."

"For your information, I am doing exactly that," Cameron said, in as dignified a voice as he could manage. He'd had his own share of Glen Fiddich.

"Good," Flynn said. "Remember that stupid pledge we made?"

"Which one?" Cameron asked the question even though he knew what Flynn was talking about.

"How we'd save each other from any woman who tried to drag us to the altar?"

Cameron nodded.

"Well, I was thinking," Flynn said, staring at the elevator doors as they slid open and punching the button to take them to their floors.

"Dangerous," Cameron said, leaning into the corner of the elevator car.

"Couldn't help but notice how happy that writer and his wife were, and Mia and Quentin, and the other couple, too."

Cameron nodded.

"Well, I just thought I should say if you were to find the same sort of thing, I wouldn't hold you to that vow." Flynn hiccupped, detracting somewhat from the dignity, but not the sentiment, of his statement.

Cameron grabbed his friend in a bear hug and kissed him on first one cheek, then the other.

The elevator doors swung open and a well-dressed middle-aged couple stepped inside the car.

They regarded Cameron and Flynn wrapped in their embrace and nodded, a polite recognition of creatures far different from themselves.

"Howdy-do," Cameron said. "Don't you just love New Orleans?"

The man and woman smiled, rather nervously, and Flynn slapped at Cameron's hand. "You are so bad," he said.

Cameron grinned. "If you don't tell Jonquil," he said, "I'll let you be best man at our wedding."

Chapter Twenty-six

Crepe Nanou
Lunchtime

"Stephen Propper was quite disappointed you couldn't stay for dinner," Jonni's mother, Marianne Landry, said, leaning forward in her chair and fixing her gaze on Jonni.

Glancing around the small restaurant for any diversion, Jonni murmured under her breath, hoping her mother would take that as appropriate apology on her part. Normally, Jonni was her mother's favored twin, Daffy having long ago exasperated their socially correct parent.

"One can't prevent a migraine," Daffy said.

Jonni flashed her a thankful look. This mother-daughter luncheon hadn't been the inspiration of either of the offspring.

"As a matter of fact," Marianne said, "one can do exactly that. It's all in the mind." She sighed and tore a small piece of roll and placed it daintily in her mouth.

"Ah, the Mind," Jonni said, speaking in capitals the way Isolde did.

"Anyway, dear, I asked for this luncheon not just to catch up with my girls, but to see what your plans are."

Daffy had taken a large bite of salad. That was just as well, as Daffy tended to be pretty outspoken in these family situations. Jonni studied her mother, her beautifully conserved face, the coifed hair, still as blond as her own, the size four frame draped in a designer suit. Who would have guessed this same woman had been caught in the act with another man in her house, by her teenage daughter?

Appearances, Jonni had learned early, covered all sins.

That made her think of Cameron, of his bad boy image that hid the sensitive and caring man.

"My plans?" Jonni realized she was the only one not eating. Even her salad sat untouched. "I am returning to college this fall to finish my degree in English."

"That's great," Daffy said. "You were always a better writer than I was."

"Not true," Jonni said.

"True," Daffy said.

Jonni smiled, thankful for the bond with her twin, and also because the exchange made her think of Cameron's expression "truth serum." But then, very little didn't remind her of Cameron.

"That's nice," Marianne said. "A woman should have her degree. And our family has always gone to Tulane."

"Daddy went to Loyola," Jonni said.

Marianne inclined her head.

Jonni wished she could ask her mother why she was such a snob. No wonder she'd doted on David. He'd been cut from exactly the same cloth. "If you're asking whether I intend to see Stephen Propper again," Jonni said, "the answer is no." *Not on your life.*

Her mother's finely penciled brows rose. "Stephen reminds me of your dear David."

"That he does," Jonni said, "but he lacks David's depth." There, that ought to end the discussion.

"Perhaps Brett Eustis is over that nasty divorce of his," Marianne said.

Daffy had finished her salad. She set down her fork. "Mother," she said, "why is it so important that Jonni be married?"

Marianne laid her fork carefully across her salad plate. She took a sip of water, and in a voice low enough to ensure the other diners didn't overhear, she said, "The two of you should understand that without me having to go into such a painful subject."

Jonni exchanged looks with Daffy. Neither one of them spoke, but Jonni knew Daffy was thinking the same thing. Their mother was afraid of her own sexuality, afraid her daughters were as wild as she'd been, fearful that unless there was some stronger force present in their lives, they'd act out as passionately as the younger Marianne Livaudais Landry had done.

Jonni helped herself to a drink of her iced tea, feeling a flush of heat across her breasts as she reflected on just how unrestrained she'd been with Cameron. Was there something that ran in their blood? Was that why she'd been drawn unconsciously to such a steady and controlling husband, a man who ensured she'd never stray down the path of earthly, sensual delights the way her mother had?

But what was wrong with passion that crowded out all perception of time and place and consumed one's sight and hearing and taste and touch?

"I do understand," Jonni said. Her lips curved in a smile. "And that's exactly why I don't plan to get married again."

"That answer is not acceptable," Marianne said.

Jonni, always the good twin, removed her napkin from her lap, set it beside her salad plate, and said, "It is to me, Mother." She pushed her chair away from the table, leaned over, and kissed her mother on the cheek. "I've got to go. Don't worry about me. I'll be fine."

Daffy mouthed, "Call me."

Jonni nodded and picked her way around the tables toward the door, feeling both brave and foolish.

She felt even more foolish after she raced back to her house, only to discover, through discreet questioning, that although other scenes were under way there, Cameron was shooting at another location that afternoon.

So she invested several hours in transporting all but one dozen of the roses to the nearby hospital and distributing them to nurses' stations. While she was at the hospital, she watched the medical professionals, wondering why she'd never settled on a career.

Definitely she had to get her act together. She could be a doctor, a lawyer, an astronaut. Her mother was right about life being under the control of one's mind.

Finished with that task, she flew home again, anxious to see if Cameron had called.

When Sunny answered in the negative, Jonni's shoulders slumped. Her housekeeper made that all-too-knowing sound she did with her tongue against the top of her mouth, and Jonni grinned.

"You know me too well," she said, plopping down on a chair in the kitchen.

"Yes, I expect I do," Sunny said.

"What shall I do with my life?"

The housekeeper turned from where she was unloading plates from the dishwasher. "Now what kind of question is that?"

Jonni shrugged. "I had lunch with my mother, and she wanted to know my 'plans.' "

"Oh, I see," Sunny said. "Sometimes we have plans and sometimes we don't. Life can happen to us or we can happen to it."

"Hmm."

Sunny nodded. "Life happened to me. So far it's happened to you, too, for all that I can see. But maybe it's time for you to take what it is you want by the horns."

Jonni smiled, picturing the horns she wanted to take hold of. "That's good advice," she said, "but I still don't know what to do with me."

The stack of plates on the counter grew with a light clattering sound as Sunny continued shifting them out of the dishwasher. "I sure wish I had your problems, Miz Jonni."

Jonni had the grace to feel guilty, sitting there doing nothing and complaining while her hardworking housekeeper stood on her feet that had walked many a more difficult mile than Jonni had ever known. She jumped up, and said, "I do sound like a spoiled brat!"

Sunny shook her head. "You could never be a brat.

It's been hard on you having to adjust to not being Mrs. David." She leaned against the counter and folded her arms over her chest. "But I haven't raised a family, not to mention taking care of my own little brothers and sisters, and not learned a thing or two. And Lord forgive me for saying so, but your life is a sight better now than it was with Mr. David on this earth."

Jonni walked over and hugged the older woman. "I don't know about the Lord, but I forgive you. And thank you, too."

"You'll find yourself a good man, wait and see," Sunny said, handing the plates into the cupboard.

Jonni clamped her lips shut. Why did happiness have to be channeled through a man?

And then the way Cameron made her feel floated through her mind, claiming her body's physical memory, and she couldn't help but smile. But because he turned her libido on overdrive and her bones to Jell-O didn't mean she had to marry him, for Pete's sake.

The phone rang and Jonni jumped.

Sunny made that umm-huh sound of hers.

"I'll get it," Jonni said, ever so casually.

Sunny snorted.

"Hello," Jonni said, her voice businesslike.

"Hello, angel," Cameron said, his greeting deep and inviting.

Jonni swallowed. She'd been waiting all day to hear him speak, and now she had no idea what to say. Before she could answer, the back door slammed twice, and Isolde and Erika bounded into the room.

"Mommy!" Erika flung herself against Jonni, wrapping her arms around her hips. "We had such fun. We saw the monkeys, and Isolde says I used to be a monkey."

Jonni laughed and hugged her daughter.

"I can't wait to see you again," Cameron said.

"I feel the same," Jonni said.

"You do?" Erika wrinkled her nose. "But I'm a girl, not a monkey."

"That wasn't meant for you, pumpkin," Jonni said. To Cameron she said, rather reluctantly, "I'd better go now."

"Have dinner with me?"

"Can we have pizza tonight?" Erika said, gazing up at Jonni with one of her most endearing expressions.

"Not tonight," Jonni said.

"But pizza is good," Erika said. "Isolde says it has all the food groups, only she eats the ones with vegetables."

"I like pizza," Cameron said. "Tell you what, invite me over and I'll deliver."

Jonni picked up on the double entendre in Cameron's words. She smiled, yet felt rather frustrated, caught between dueling desires. She'd gone out the last two nights. Her daughter had commented on that as she'd been leaving for the dinner with Stephen Propper. And Erika had a sleepover at Pepper's house the next evening; Jonni could very well wait twenty-four hours to see Cameron Scott.

"I'll even do the dishes," Cameron said.

"Now that I'd like to see," Jonni said, unable to believe the star so many women went ga-ga over was practically begging to spend time with her and her five-year-old.

"Madam, your wish is granted. What time shall I appear?"

Jonni glanced at the kitchen clock. "Six," she said. That would give her two hours to decide what to wear. "And I'll order the pizza."

"Does that mean I just got out of cleanup?"

"Mommy!" Erika was patting Jonni's leg. "Who are you talking to?"

"Mr. Scott," Jonni said. "But he's hanging up now."

"Bye," she said, and Erika waved a hand at the phone.

Jonni replaced the phone in the cradle. "Mr. Scott's coming to dinner," she said, to no one in particular.

Isolde, munching on a handful of the cereal she liked so well, smiled.

"Now ain't that something," Sunny said.

"He's nice," Erika said. "Was he a monkey, too?"

It wasn't the type of romantic date Cameron had in mind when he came up with the novel idea of asking Jonni to marry him. He figured she'd want the full swept-off-her-feet treatment, and he hadn't even thought to look for a ring.

Hell, he'd never done this sort of thing before.

Lucky for him they'd finished the day's filming early or he'd never have made it to the house by six. He figured with as many roses as he'd sent the day before, he shouldn't show up with flowers, and since Jonni was handling the pizza, there was no need for him to bring a food offering. He decided against champagne, too, as this was clearly a child-oriented occasion. Still, he felt some urge to appear with a gift in hand, almost as if his mere presence wasn't enough to entitle him to enjoy the evening.

And was that a funny feeling for Cameron Scott.

But when Jonni opened the front door and greeted him with a smile in her eyes, all was right with the world. She wore candy-pink capris and a matching sleeveless top that clung to her curves.

"Hey there," he said, his voice as casual as ever, though he could swear his heart was beating the way it did when he and Robby played a couple of games of pickup basketball.

"Hey yourself," she said softly, holding out a hand to him. "Come on in."

He took her hand, anticipating the jolt of desire her touch sent through his body. "Seven times seven," he said.

"Excuse me?"

Erika bounded up. Jonni let go of his hand, and Cameron was spared the explanation of why he found it necessary to repeat his times tables in Jonni's presence.

"Mr. Scott, I thought you were the pizza man," Erika said.

"I hope I don't disappoint," he said.

She giggled.

"We're in the den," Jonni said. "It's picnic night."

Cameron followed Jonni and Erika along the wide hall, admiring Jonni's gliding walk and the way the capris outlined the curves of her cheeks. She glanced back and caught him staring at her. She blushed softly, the way he adored, and said, "How was work today, Cameron?"

The ordinary question threw him off. "Work was work."

"You weren't filming here at the house?"

Ah, so she'd noticed. And missed him, too.

"We had a scene to do at the Museum of Art. We have one more day there, and then I'll be back here."

Erika stopped in the doorway, her hands on her hips. "What do you mean?"

Cameron realized he'd just blurred the lines between Mr. Scott and Mister Benjamin. He glanced toward Jonni, seeking guidance. Was this the time to explain that he was both actor and character?

"Mr. Scott works on the *Mister Benjamin* movie," Jonni said.

So this wasn't the time.

"Tell Mister Benjamin I said hi," Erika said, seemingly unconcerned with pursuing the topic, and skipping ahead.

Cameron let out his breath. A guy could use lessons when it came to dealing with children. Jeez, how did anyone ever get smart enough to become a parent?

And then it hit him, the enormity of what he was considering. By asking Jonni to marry him, he was asking Erika to accept him as a stepfather.

He almost walked into the doorframe.

"Careful, Cameron," Jonni said, touching his shoulder. "Are you okay?"

"Sure, sure," he mumbled. Glancing into the room, he saw Erika helping Isolde spread out a blanket in the center of the floor. The coffee table had been moved to the side of the room. "Never better."

"Hi, Mr. Scott," Isolde said.

He greeted her.

"Do you have picnic night?" Erika asked him as she arranged paper plates on the blanket.

Cameron shook his head.

"We didn't use to, either," Erika said. "Mommy started it."

After the stuffy husband had the good grace to take himself off, no doubt, Cameron thought. He took the napkins Erika handed him, knelt on the floor beside the blanket, and put one on top of each plate.

Jonni hung back. She leaned against the arm of the sofa, watching the group on the floor. Cameron caught her eyes and smiled. She wondered what he was thinking, the movie star pressed into service by the adorably bossy five-year-old.

She knew what she was thinking.

How much she wished the two of them could be alone right that very minute.

Ever since she'd left the lunch with her mother and sister, and had reflected on how there was a side of her she'd repressed for so very long, Jonni had been extra aware of the sensations, the hunger, the needs Cameron had awakened within her body.

When she thought of him kissing her, her breasts tingled and she grew moist and aching deep inside her body. When she watched him kneeling beside the impromptu picnic blanket, she pictured herself spread wide on that very blanket, open to his every greedy touch and kiss and possessive demand.

"Mommy, why aren't you helping?"

"What?" Jonni jerked back to reality, embarrassed by her flight of fantasy.

"Your mother's thinking," Cameron said, then winked at Jonni. "And I'd pay a cool grand for those thoughts."

"It's supposed to be a penny," Erika said.

"Some are worth more," Isolde said, also with a wink.

Gosh, was she that transparent? Jonni rose and said, "I think I hear the pizza man. I'll go check." As she rushed from the room, she could swear she heard Cameron chuckle.

She heard the back doorbell chime. Jonni had given Sunny the rest of the day off, whether to assuage her own guilty feelings for complaining about her lot in life, or because she didn't need another set of eyes watching her salivate over Cameron Scott, Jonni wasn't sure.

Jonni paid the driver, carried the two large vegetarian pizzas into the kitchen, and searched in a utensil drawer for a pizza cutter and serving spatula.

"Can I help?" Cameron appeared in the kitchen, as Jonni had hoped he would.

She turned toward him, a tool in each hand. He filled the room with his presence. She caught her breath as he covered the space between them in three swift steps.

And then she was in his arms, her mouth crushed to his, her heart beating in tempo with his.

He pulled away, only slightly, and said in the playful voice she liked so well, "Told you I'm good in the kitchen."

She smiled and, feeling brave, said, "I bet you're good in every room."

He laughed and kissed her again. "Just you wait, Jonquil," he said. "Every room, every city, every continent."

Darn it. There he went again, talking as if some future lay ahead of them. Jonni clung to him for another moment, then pried free. "Good thing I didn't poke you with these," she said, waving the kitchen implements still in her hands.

"It's hard to hurt me," he said, his smile a little on the crooked side.

"Tough guy," she teased, determined to keep things light. Another embrace like that one and she'd be tempted to forget her responsibilities. "Grab those pizza boxes."

"Whatever you say," Cameron said, stealing one more kiss from her before he followed instructions.

An hour later, Cameron lay back on the floor against a stack of cushions, his stomach full, his heart happy, a rather pleasant sentiment for him to be experiencing. Jonni was attempting to explain the theory of evolution to Erika, who was having none of it.

"Monkeys live in the zoo," she said. "Therefore, I am not a monkey."

"Not all monkeys do," Cameron said. "Lots and lots of them live in their own houses."

Erika swung around to face him. "Really?"

He nodded. He saw Jonni looking at him as if he'd lost his mind. "Really. I've seen them in Africa and South America. They only live in zoos in cities where we don't have big enough jungles. Because everyone knows monkeys prefer jungles, the way some people are country folk and others are city slickers."

"You have a very quick mind, Mr. Scott," Isolde said, glancing up from her homework. "Maybe we can do that interview tonight."

"And are you country or city?" That was Jonni. "You weren't born in L.A., were you?"

Cameron shook his head. "Very few people are. I'm

from southeast Missouri originally. I don't get back there much."

"Your family must miss you," Jonni said.

He shrugged. "I think I told you most people don't like me too well once they get to know me."

She bristled. "And that's an old line you think fits you, but I believe you've outgrown that like a shoe."

"Ooh, Mrs. J., that is so Deep," Isolde said.

"Not particularly," Jonni said. "We all have those messages we think are us and then one day we realize the tune doesn't carry truth anymore. I've been learning about that in my own life."

"Do monkeys whistle?" Erika asked.

The grown-ups all looked at one another. Cameron said, "I bet they do."

Erika nodded, satisfied. "Then I don't mind if I'm a monkey."

"Would you like to run up and take your bath?" Jonni said.

Erika shook her head. "Monkeys don't bathe."

Cameron grinned, wondering how Jonni would get around that objection.

"Oh, yes, they do," Jonni said. "Just ask Mr. Scott."

"What's that?" Cameron sat up straighter.

Jonni faced him, laughter brimming in her eyes. "You know, in those monkey houses you were describing from Africa and South America. Didn't they have bathing facilities?"

"They're like a campground," Cameron said, spouting the first thing that came to his mind. "You know when you go to a KOA campground and everyone shares the community bathhouse? Well, that's what monkeys do. They go down to the lake or the river and use the bathhouse there."

"What's a KOA campground?" Erika had veered from monkeys. Having grown up sleeping in tents on various fishing and hunting vacations, Cameron was startled to realize Erika was completely unfamiliar with the reference.

Jonni was looking at him, also, apparently waiting for an explanation. "You mean you all don't go camping?"

They shook their heads.

"No sleeping under the stars and making a fire and roasting marshmallows and tubing down a river?" Cameron heard the longing in his voice. Damn, he'd forgotten how much he enjoyed the simple pleasures. He probably hadn't done any of those long-ago treats in the past decade.

"It sounds interesting," Erika offered.

"Would you like to go sometime?"

"Is Mommy going?"

Cameron glanced over at Jonni. "Would she?"

Jonni wrinkled her dainty little nose. "Promise me there won't be any snakes or frogs or ants?"

"If there are, I'll save you from them," he said.

"Okay, Erika, Mommy will go, too."

Jonni went along with the invitation, but she found it next to impossible to credit that Cameron Scott would recall ever asking such a thing. Once he was back in his world, he'd no more stretch out under a canvas roof than Jonni would snuggle up to a snake.

She'd have to enjoy the time they had together and store it up to treasure after he had left, taking with him a little bit of the sparkle she now found in every day.

Chapter Twenty-seven

Jonni's house
That same evening

Cameron hung around as long as he could, weighing his five A.M. call time the next day against the chance to speak to Jonni alone again. A voice in his head told him to chill, but he ignored it. As impulsive as he was, he couldn't wait another day to ask Jonni to marry him, to gaze at her beautiful face as she smiled and flung her arms around him, and drowned him in one of those deep, soul-rocking kisses.

Man, what had gotten into him? He was thinking the way soap opera writers wrote.

Jeez.

Jonni reappeared, with a freshly scrubbed Erika in her pajamas and robe.

"These are Curious George," Erika told him, pointing to the pictures of the monkey on her nightwear.

"They still have those books?" Cameron was surprised.

"Did you read them when you were a little boy?"

Cameron nodded. "Yeah, I related real well to the little scamp." And then he reckoned he shouldn't give Erika any inspiration to follow in his troublemaking footsteps. "They're good for reading practice," he added, sounding stuffy even to his ears.

"Would you like to read Erika her bedtime story?" Jonni had crossed the room and was standing beside her daughter, close enough that he could reach out and take her hand.

But of course he didn't do that.

"I can read," Erika said, "but I like a story before I go to sleep. It's a tradition." She stumbled just a touch on the last word.

Cameron smiled at her and her mother. "That's a nice tradition," he said. "I'd be honored to read your story tonight."

"Good," she said. "I won't have one tomorrow night because I'll be at Pepper's house."

Cameron's ears perked up at that news. "Sleepover?"

"It's for her birthday."

"So you spend all night at her house?" Cameron knew Jonni was angling for his line of sight, but he kept his attention squarely on the daughter.

"Yep."

"I have a sleepover, too," Isolde said, glancing up from a thick book she was reading.

"You do?" That was Jonni. "Oh, that's right, it's your night off."

"I'm going to visit Meg and the kids. Parker had to go to New York on a business trip."

Cameron practically licked his lips. He'd have Jonquil

to himself, all night long. Their eyes met over Erika's head, and he grinned.

The hunger in her expression was unmistakable. And he couldn't wait to have her crying out and pulsing the hot heat of her sex beneath him, begging for more.

"Bedtime," Jonquil said.

Cameron grinned even more broadly.

The two of them walked upstairs with Erika. She located her favorite Curious George story, handed it to him, and hopped under the covers. Jonni tucked her in, and watching her kiss her daughter on the forehead, Cameron felt a tenderness he'd rarely if ever known.

He had to clear his throat before he could begin to read the adventures of the curious monkey. He acted out the story as he read, to Erika's delighted applause.

When he finished, she demanded another one. He looked over at Jonquil, who said, "Well, one more."

So he treated her to the next one she selected, wondering how he'd gotten to be thirty-six years old and never experienced the joy of reading to a child.

When he and Jonquil were walking down the upstairs hall, she said, "That was marvelous! Have you ever read for *Between the Lions*?"

"Uh, no," he said, having no idea what she referred to.

"Don't tell me," she said slowly, "you've never heard of that show?"

"Got me on that one," he said, flashing his famous grin.

"Well, that is a shame," she said. "But I guess you're not around children much . . ."

He didn't want her to start thinking about his tabloid-fodder lifestyle. "What is it?"

"It's a reading show on public television. Lots of movie stars participate in it."

"I'll have to see if I can get involved," he said, meaning it, and not saying it only to score with Jonquil.

They were at the top of the stairs. Conscious of Erika and that any minute she might decide to slip out of bed and follow them, Cameron was on his best behavior. But as they walked down the front stairs, he realized the evening had come naturally to an end.

Jonquil paused beside him in the entryway. "I'm glad you came over," she said.

"Me, too," Cameron said. "Look, can I help you clean up? I promised I'd do the dishes."

She laughed. "We used paper plates."

"The trash, then. Let me run those pizza boxes out to your trash."

She looked a little puzzled. "You really don't have to help, but I appreciate the offer. I'm not used to men pitching in."

Cameron stepped closer and said in a low voice, "I told you I'm not like other guys."

She moistened her lips with the tip of her tongue. "You showed me that, too," she whispered.

He groaned. This woman made him want her constantly. "Let's go in the kitchen and get that trash," he said.

Once there, they moved as one into each other's arms. After their first frantic, hungry kiss, Jonni nestled her head against his chest. "You feel so good," she said. "I hate to toss you out along with those pizza boxes."

"Mmm," he said, and before common sense could click in, he said, "Marry me?"

He could swear she stopped breathing. After a long moment, she lifted her head. Instead of jumping with joy, she stepped back from his embrace and said, "What did you just say?"

"Marry me."

Jonni clasped her hands over her ears, then dropped her arms, unable to believe Cameron Scott had said those words to her. "That's what I thought."

"I take it you're not exactly overwhelmed?" His voice was rather edgy, and Jonni realized she had hurt his feelings.

"Cameron, I'm sorry," she said, pressing a hand against his heart, then snatching it away before the feel of him overcame her common sense. "I appreciate the sentiment, but you know you don't mean it."

He looked even more wounded. "I've never asked a woman to marry me. You're the first." He straightened and looked her in the eye. "The first, the last, and the only."

Jonni shivered, both in delight and in sorrow. But she couldn't accept that he meant what he said. Why, he was a playboy, a playboy with a generous sensitive heart, to be sure, but no way was he going to settle into marriage with a wife and child.

"You wouldn't know what to do with me if you caught me," she said, lightly, deciding it was best to pretend his words couldn't be taken seriously.

"I'm a fast learner," he said, reaching out and tracing the line of her throat with the tip of one finger. "And so are you."

She trembled. She might dismiss his words, but she couldn't discount the effect his touch had on her. "I think we are both too horny to think straight," she said, proud of herself for not blushing when she used the "H" word. She reached for the empty pizza boxes and handed them to him.

He accepted them. "I guess I know when I'm being kicked out," he said, but with good grace and humor in his voice.

She smiled. "Thanks for understanding."

He moved toward the back door. One hand on the knob, the other on the trash, he said, "Don't thank me for that, because I don't. But I'm smart enough to let it go." He swung open the door, and Jonni heard him cross the porch and whistle his way down the steps and across the flagstone driveway to her outside trash container.

In a few quick minutes he was in the kitchen again, far too near for comfort. She wanted him to stay. She needed him to go. She needed to be alone to think.

Why had he asked her to marry him?

And why did she refuse to believe he meant it?

Cameron tipped her chin up and kissed her lightly on the mouth. He stroked her forehead with the back of his thumb. "Still on for our sleepover?"

"I'd like that," she said.

"Your place or mine?"

She thought about it, picturing him in her big, wide, empty bed. She'd like to be able to remember him there once he was gone. "Here," she said.

"I'll bring the picnic this time," he said. "Sleep well tonight, because if I remember from my childhood, you never sleep during a sleepover." He winked and headed toward the front door, pausing by the den to say good night to Isolde.

When Jonni shut the door behind him, the silence of the big house settled around her.

Funny, but she never noticed it when Cameron was with her.

Cameron wasn't about to make the same mistake twice. He'd known he shouldn't toss out "marry me" the way he did "catch a movie?" yet he'd done it anyway.

During a break in the next day's filming, he casually asked Quentin how he'd proposed to his wife. Of course, he had to endure the director's too-knowing look in order to do so.

"What's the matter?" Quentin said in his cheerful voice. "She already turn you down once?"

Cameron, decked out as Mister Benjamin, responded with a stately shrug.

"Great," Quentin said, "I'm on my way to winning that bet we made."

Cameron smiled. "I may as well pay you now," he said. "She's bound to say yes and there's no way I want to wait a year."

"Oh, yeah, you've got it bad. I'll take a check, by the way." Quentin pushed his glasses up on his nose and grinned. "Do you realize how few women there are in this world who would turn down an offer of marriage from Cameron Scott?"

Cameron had considered that question many times the night before. And he had to say he respected Jonquil even more for not jumping at the opportunity. Though it was possible she saw it as no opportunity at all, but rather a potential emotional nightmare.

He had, after all, made a point to tell her that no one

liked him once they got to know him. Darn his big mouth!

"Anyway," Quentin said, "the way I proposed to Mia won't work for you."

"Why's that?"

"We were both in the hospital. We'd been in the same accident and were just coming out of a coma. There's nothing like a brush with death to open a man's eyes to true love. As soon as I could move, I rushed into her room and asked her to marry me."

"And she said yes right away?" He couldn't help but feel somewhat competitive.

Quentin nodded and then clapped an arm around Cameron's shoulders. "She'd been after me for ages, but I was too blind to see it. Not your situation at all."

Cameron took heart from that comment.

During the next break he rustled up Cosey and assigned her the task of finding the items he wanted to have in place for that evening. Her big eyes grew even wider as she took notes on a clipboard she carried.

Watching her, he noticed her clothing had toned down considerably. She wore jeans, a cotton blouse, and a pair of cute leather slides. "Are you enjoying your job?"

"Oh, yes, Mr. Scott," she said, her hair bobbing with the intensity of her nod. "I like working on a set almost as much as I do acting. And I think Flynn was right when he said it would help me in my knowledge of the business. He says I can audition for your next film."

"He does, does he?" Cameron realized he'd been saddled with Cosey, for better or for worse. "And when will that be?"

"Early fall."

Cameron couldn't remember if he'd committed to another action flick or not. The prospect of doing the script Beetle had pitched the other night had driven other projects from his mind.

A mind pretty much filled with thoughts of Jonquil.

"What are you going to do until then?"

"I thought I might stay in New Orleans. Isolde says she'll fix me up with some friends who can use another roommate. I might even go to school. She says I can go part time to her college, get a job during the day, and audition in some of the local theater productions."

"That sounds great," Cameron said. "Does that mean we're returning to New Orleans for the auditions or are you coming to L.A.?"

"Flynn says that's up to Mr. Grandy."

"Ah," Cameron said, wondering where he and Jonquil would live. No doubt she'd want Erika to grow up in New Orleans with her friends and family. Well, he could commute. They could keep his place in Bel Air for summers and for him to use when he was doing business on the West Coast.

"So you want me to have these ready and in your limo by the end of the day?" Cosey was chewing on the end of her pencil and studying the list Cameron had dictated.

"Yep," he said.

"Okay, and good luck to you. Mrs. Jonni is a very nice person. Isolde says she's a wonderful boss, too."

"Thank you, Cosey," Cameron said, slightly flustered. "Look, let's keep this a secret, okay?"

"Certainly," she said, in the most dignified voice he'd yet to hear her use. "I am a professional."

* * *

Jonni was as nervous as a cat in a lightning storm. After dropping Erika at Pepper's house, she prowled the floor. Isolde had gone over to visit with Meg, so she had no audience for her what-shall-I-wear? fashion show.

That didn't stop her, of course. Wearing only a short silk robe and bikini panties, she'd pulled at least ten outfits from her closet and dumped two dresser drawers on the bed, in search of the lacy black bra she was sure she'd bought three years earlier.

Ironically, that had been one of the times she'd been convinced David was seeing someone else, an intern in his office, and she'd thought a trip to Victoria's Secret would solve the situation.

Ah, there it was. Jonni tugged the scrap of a bra from the pile. The price tag dangled from the strap. She clipped it with a pair of nail scissors, dropped her robe on the top of the mass of clothing, and leaned forward, adjusting the bra. She had to fasten it in the last hook, but thankfully she could fit into it.

She studied the effect in her cheval mirror. The lace of the cups was practically sheer except for a rose petal effect that swirled around each nipple. Definitely naughty. Jonni fluffed her hair and pictured Cameron standing behind her, holding her close, his hands coming around to cup her breasts.

A shiver of anticipation built within her body. Of course, that delicious feeling didn't answer the question of which outfit to wear when she greeted Cameron at her front door. Sensibly, she turned from the mirror.

The doorbell chimed.

She whirled from the bed. "Oh, no, he can't be here already!" She hadn't even done her makeup.

The chimes sounded again. Jonni shoved one leg, then the other into a pair of jeans, tugged a black T-shirt over her sexy bra, and headed downstairs, barefooted.

She peeked through the glass portion of the door. Sure enough, Cameron stood there, graceful and commanding as always, dark glasses covering his eyes despite the setting sun. He wore khakis and a striped cotton dress shirt. He carried a huge picnic hamper in one hand.

He lifted his free hand and knocked.

Jonni swung the door open. He perched the glasses atop his head as he stepped inside.

"You look great," he said.

"Oh, no, I don't," Jonni said, closing the door. "But you certainly do."

Cameron set the basket down. "Now let me see," he said, "is this our first disagreement?"

She laughed. "Cameron, I just stepped out of the shower. I haven't done my makeup or dressed. Those are just facts."

"Mmm," he said, smiling. "If you only knew how refreshing you are, you might become quite impossible."

"Highly improbable," she said, a thought striking her. Was her appeal to Cameron simply that she wasn't one of his usual crowd? Well, it didn't matter, did it? She knew he was only dabbling, no matter what he'd said the night before.

Cameron sighed.

"What's wrong?" she asked.

"Come here," he said, opening his arms.

Of course she obeyed, snuggling into the shelter of his arms and chest. He tipped her chin up and kissed her, lightly at first, then with greater urgency. He rocked his lower body against hers, and she responded by deepening their kiss.

After several long, delicious moments, Cameron lifted his mouth from hers and said, "Remember not to think too hard. Life is fairly simple unless we screw up and make it more complicated than it is."

She nodded, still pressed against him. "What's in the basket?"

"I hope it's okay if we have picnic night two evenings in a row," he said, "because that's what I've done."

"Fun," Jonni said. "Where shall we picnic?"

Cameron stroked the back of her neck. "How about your bedroom?"

"Perfect," she said, though even the question made her nervous, as did the nonchalant tone with which she answered, implying that such an event was not out of the ordinary. "And very naughty," she added. How had he managed to transform her into a shameless wanton?

"That's one of my attractions, isn't it?" Cameron pulled back, studying her. "Tell me. Do you like the man or the bad boy?" He said it lightly, but Jonni heard the true question. *Me or the image?*

Why, Cameron Scott was as insecure as she was! She reached for his free hand and lifted it to her lips. Kissing the tip of his pinky finger, she said, "I like the man who cares enough to rescue girls from evil pimps." She'd gotten Cosey's full story from Isolde.

He shrugged. "That was nothing. Anyone would have done the same."

She shook her head and kissed the tip of his ring finger. "I like the man who obviously loves his baby sister." She did the same with his middle finger, grinning, as she said, "I like the bad boy, too, the one who's so competitive he has to send more roses than the other guy."

Cameron glanced around. "Hey, what happened to all of them?"

"Did you or did you not see that small vase delivered?" She wanted to know.

"Okay, so maybe I did. I mean, what schmuck would send five roses to a woman?"

Jonni tapped his index finger against her chin. "I like the man who's determined not to be outdone by an imaginary rival." She felt an improper surge of satisfaction at realizing he had been trying to outdo someone else, even if she had been annoyed at his high-handed competitiveness at the time. "The five roses were for Isolde, to celebrate her sobriety."

"Oh," Cameron said. "Jeez, what an idiot I am!"

Jonni smiled. "The roses were very pretty. I took most of them over to the hospital to share with the patients."

"What a nice thing to do," he said.

"You're not offended?"

He kissed her on the mouth and then wiggled his thumb.

"Ah," Jonni said, pressing the thumb to the side of her neck where her pulse was already beating double time. "I like the man who melts my inhibitions and turns my insides to liquid heat."

"Mmm," Cameron said. "Now I'm glad I asked that question."

And he was, too. Cameron had blurted it out, wishing the minute the words had crossed his lips he'd kept his vulnerability locked in that deep internal pit where it damn well belonged. "Funny," he said, "but I've never cared about being an acceptable human being before."

Jonquil shook her head. "You pretended not to care, I think, and spent a lot of energy persuading everyone that was the true state of affairs."

He furrowed his brow, wondering if she was right. But wrong or right, he had other matters pressing on his mind and body at the moment. "Picnic?"

She nodded and led them across the hall toward the broad front staircase.

He halted, one foot on the bottom step. Looking around, he said, "There's something wrong with this scene."

A slightly anxious expression appeared on Jonquil's face. He'd have to work on reassuring her, he realized. "I know," Cameron said. "You need to be properly swept off your feet." He set the basket down and scooped up a surprised Jonquil in his arms, then hefted the basket and started up the stairs.

She giggled. "I feel just like Scarlett in *Gone With the Wind*," she said.

"Just you wait. You're going to have a smile on your face that will leave Vivien Leigh in the dust."

She sighed and wrapped her arms around his neck.

The trusting gesture really got to Cameron. He tightened his hold and swore to himself he wouldn't hurt this gentle lady. Damn, but he was getting as sentimental as a soap actor. "Left? Right?" he said. He'd come up the back stairs on his other two visits to the upper story.

"Down the hall on the right," she said. "I must be awfully heavy to carry."

He snorted. "A mere feather."

"Now that's romantic," she said.

"Don't go getting pencil thin on me," he said.

"Fat chance," Jonquil said, making a face.

Cameron paused on the threshold of her bedroom. He surveyed the clothing strewn all over the elegant four-poster bed. "Going on a trip?"

Jonquil turned and glanced over her shoulder and shrieked. "I forgot about the mess! I was uh, um, deciding what to wear."

He set her down and left the hamper on the floor. He noted one massive vase of deep pink roses on a table in front of the window. So she hadn't given all his flowers away. That realization made him happier than it should have had the power to do. "I can teach you a technique that's a lot more effective," he said.

"You can?"

"Oh, yeah," he said, slipping a finger inside the waist of her jeans. "It's a no-brainer," he said, his lips close to her hair, his fingers unworking the button and zipper of her jeans. His hands inside the denim, he cupped her cheeks, and then wiggled the fabric down her legs.

She kicked the pants away from her ankles.

"That's it," Cameron said. "You're catching on real quick." He lifted the hem of her T-shirt, tugged it over her head, and let it fly toward the bed.

"You see, you don't need to worry about what to wear." She was smiling at him with those big trusting eyes, and it was all Cameron could do to keep from taking her in his arms and just holding on to her. He'd never felt such a need to be so damn close to a woman. Touching her hands, her mouth, her breasts, wasn't enough. It was as if he wanted to enter not just her body, but her whole self.

He had to get a grip.

"Now that's a nice bra," he said, tracing the pattern of the rose with the back of one thumb. "What you have on right now," he said, "is the perfect outfit."

She grinned and snapped the elastic of her skimpy bikini panty. "I'm not wearing too much?"

"No, but I am," Cameron said, shucking his own clothing in record time.

He stood before her, naked and needing her, and for the first time in his life, he sought a connection that was greater than the mere joining of flesh. It confused him, this strange emotion, and worried him.

And then she held out her arms to him and he swept her up, and the two of them fell on the bed, on top of her whole darn wardrobe, and Cameron forgot about worrying.

He also forgot about all the props he'd had Cosey assemble and pack for him—the massage lotion, the Kama Sutra oils, the silky feather brush, the champagne and strawberries and caviar.

He had everything the two of them needed right there in his arms.

Jonni blinked as the bright sunlight chased across her eyelids. Her body felt sensational, mellow and liquid and so very well loved. And she'd been dreaming of strong, gentle hands massaging her back and arms and legs.

She lifted her head from her pillow and, detecting a sensual scent of lavender and patchouli, glanced around at the tangled bedcovers. Cameron wasn't lying beside her, but, as she came more fully awake, she realized she hadn't dreamed up those clever hands.

He knelt over her legs, bent forward, caressing her lower back, working the scented lotion into her skin.

"Good morning," she said. "What a beautiful way to wake up."

He grinned. "One of my two favorite ways."

She blushed, knowing well what the other one was. They'd made love at the first light of dawn and then fallen asleep again. Cameron had been as exciting as the first time, taking her to places she'd never known existed. At the same time, he'd been—well, she couldn't quite define the difference. But it was as if he'd been sweeter and more tender.

As if he cared about Jonni the woman, Jonni the person. She wasn't just his playmate for the night.

But then, she'd appeared without warning at his hotel room, offering her body, and he'd performed on demand. In the short time in between, something had shifted.

Had he really meant it when he proposed marriage? But if he had, wouldn't he have referred to the subject again? And despite the intimacy of their night and morning, he'd said not a word on the topic.

He moved his strong strokes upward to her shoulders, where he worked his fingers under her shoulder blades.

"Mmm," Jonni said, "how did you know that's my favorite spot?"

He kissed the back of her neck. "Just listening to your body."

"You do that very well," she said.

"It's because you have such a beautiful body," he said.

Jonni sighed into her pillow. "When I'm with you," she said slowly, "I feel as if I've died and gone to heaven."

His fingers slowed. "You don't have to kick the bucket to find happiness."

"I like the way you talk," she said. "It makes me smile."

"Good," Cameron said, "You deserve more of that." He slipped down beside her on the bed, his head on the same pillow. And that's when it happened. One minute he was in control of his tongue; the next, it had mutinied on him. "Please marry me, Jonni."

The words lay there.

For a long moment she said nothing, but her smile faded. She didn't look upset, just somber. "I wish you wouldn't ask that of me," she said, her voice low, yet somewhat wistful.

That note gave him a glimmer of hope. "Does the idea scare you? Or is it me?" He slapped his forehead. "Truth serum."

She smiled then. "Truth serum. It's not you." She touched the side of his cheek. "I got lost inside the whole marriage institution. Right now I'm finding me—for the first time in my life. Getting married again simply isn't in my life plans."

"Oh," Cameron said, relieved. Of course she needed

time to recover from being married to a jerk. And plans could be changed. "Funny how now that I finally bite the dust it does me no good."

She grinned and trailed one finger down his chest. "I'd say you're getting some good out of the situation. I know I am."

He wrapped his legs around hers, entwining their bodies. Patience had never been in his repertoire, but he was enjoying all the new emotions he was experiencing with Jonni. Heck, he might as well add patience to that list.

Within the warm shield of his embrace, Jonni reflected on how amazed she was that Cameron had asked her a second time to marry him.

Many more moments like this, arm in arm after a magical night together, and she'd be tempted to overcome her fear of hurt and betrayal and say yes.

But she had her daughter's well-being to consider, too. How would Erika react to a stepfather? And would Cameron be a good influence? She snuggled closer, picturing him reading Curious George to Erika and pretending to morph so she wouldn't worry about Mister Benjamin's welfare.

It wasn't Erika she was protecting by rejecting Cameron's proposal—it was her own vulnerable heart.

Chapter Twenty-eight

On Location
Outside Jonni's house

Cameron kicked himself for his lack of self-control that morning in bed with Jonquil when he'd blurted out those fatal words, "Marry me," a second time.

Jonquil wasn't a woman to be impressed by the impetuous or the impulsive. How the heck had Quentin Grandy known she'd turn him down? Normally he hated to lose a bet, but he'd do it gladly if it meant Jonquil would finally accept him.

He stayed in his trailer during the filming breaks that day, assuming his absence would drive her as crazy as his forcing himself to avoid her did him. When the long day had come to an end, after having his makeup removed, he stopped in wardrobe.

His heart stuck somewhere between his throat and his gut when he spotted the back of that beautiful blond hair.

"Jonquil," he said, pleased she was visiting his territory.

She turned, and Cameron realized it wasn't Jonquil, but her twin, something he would have realized at once if he hadn't had his entire mind filled with thoughts of Jonquil.

Her sister smiled and held out her hand. "Daffodil, but please call me Daffy."

Queenie Gilmore flashed her customary gimlet-eyed look at Cameron and said, "Set yourself down. Miz Daffy is interviewing me."

That wasn't exactly the way the Hollywood pecking order worked, but Cameron, curious to know more about Jonquil's sister, nodded and settled in a director's chair that had the name "Queenie" spelled out in sequins on the canvas back.

It was strange to see how similar Jonni and Daffy looked physically and yet note the personality differences. Cameron watched as Daffy charmed Queenie's history from her, drawing out what her ramshackle life in the Ozark hills had been like, and how Quentin Grandy had discovered her, helped her into alcohol rehab, and hired her as wardrobe mistress on all subsequent films.

Daffy was lively and engaging and could jaw with the best of them, Cameron noted. Where Jonquil would have approached the interview in a quieter way, she would have gotten the same information, if not more, he concluded.

Daffy finished taking notes, thanked Queenie, but didn't head for the door.

"So," she said, as the wardrobe mistress fussed over a

tear Cameron had managed to put in his Mister Benjamin jacket, "how's my twin?"

"Fine," Cameron said, then unable to help himself, broke into a wide smile. "Very fine."

Daffy nodded. "Are you going to hurt my sister?"

Queenie glanced from Cameron to Daffy, eyes sharp and obviously interested. She had a couple of pins sticking out of her mouth. Cameron glared at her and said, "Repeat one word of this conversation—"

The pins spit from her mouth, landing every which way. "Nothing said in this room gets out of the cracks, ya hear? I am a professional."

"Thank you," he said. Turning to Daffy, he responded, "I realize my reputation deserves that kind of question, but the answer is no and no and no. I don't know what's gotten into me, but for the first time in my life, I've met a woman I want to put my arms around and protect."

Daffy was looking at him, her head cocked to one side, a knowing look on her face, a look that almost said, *You poor bugger.*

"What?" She was making Cameron nervous. "Don't you believe me?"

"I do," Daffy said. "I was just thinking I should introduce you to my husband, Hunter."

The name rang a bell in Cameron's head. She'd introduced herself as Mrs. James the other evening. "Hunter James, the high-tech whiz?"

"One and the same, but that's not the reason you should meet him."

No doubt Flynn wouldn't mind a few tips from the savvy entrepreneur. "Why's that?"

"He's the one guy who might be able to help you out with a bit of advice on how to win a woman determined to run as far and as fast as she can from the best man she's ever met."

"Ah," Cameron said. "This trait runs in the family?"

"Yep," Daffy said. "I wish you luck. You'll need an extra dose with Jonni. She was married to a jerk, and she's not likely to be won over easily. But if you've fallen as hard as it sounds as if you have, you might just be the one."

"Now ain't that romantic," Queenie said.

"More like desperate," Cameron said.

Queenie slapped him on the back. "What comes easy ain't worth winning."

With that sage advice in mind, Cameron laid his plans carefully. For the first time he could remember, he worked out a strategy for achieving a goal. He had two weeks left on location in New Orleans, and he made the best of every moment he had with Jonquil.

He took her and Erika to the aquarium and laughed along with mother and daughter as Erika clapped in delight at the penguins playing in their icy home.

He asked Jonquil what was one thing she'd always wanted to do and never done in her hometown. When she answered, "Take the ferry at night across the river," he made it happen. Standing next to her on the upper deck, riding across the currents from one bank to the other, he watched the look of joy on her face as she admired the lights on the river bridge and those in the high-rises of downtown. The full moon added to the mood and once again, Cameron had to battle himself to keep things light and entertaining.

He accepted Daffy's invitation to dinner, and naturally she invited her sister and niece, too.

Sitting around after dinner in the Hunter's comfortable living room, in an old fire station Daffy and her husband had renovated, Cameron realized he hadn't felt so at home since he'd left Missouri for the army, so many years ago.

"So what's your next project?" That was Daffy, asking the question as she passed around cups of tea.

Cameron glanced at Jonquil, seated beside him on one of the two loveseats that faced each other across a cypress plank coffee table. He winked. "Do you mean my next movie?"

"*Mister Benjamin Comes Back*," Erika piped up, from her play spot on the floor.

"Studio executives are getting younger every year," Cameron said.

"What's an executive?" Erika rose and stood beside Jonquil.

"A business person who leads a company," her mother answered.

Erika cocked her head to the side and repeated the word. "So Uncle Hunter is an executive?"

Jonquil nodded.

Erika turned to Cameron. "What's Mr. Scott?"

"Ouch," Cameron said. "I'm a lowly actor."

Erika wrinkled her nose. "But Mommy likes you."

"Sweetheart, why don't you keep playing Barbie?" Jonquil smoothed her hair back from her face.

"Okay. Grown-ups are so confusing."

Cameron grinned, as did the other confused souls. He accepted the cup of tea from Daffy, thanked her, and realized he was feeling much clearer-headed as he'd been relying less and less on his customary champagne for entertainment. Hanging out with Jonquil was good not only for his heart, but for his health.

"You'd be a great teacher," he said, the thought popping out of his mouth.

"Yes, she would," Daffy said. "Don't you think so, Hunter?"

Her husband nodded. He didn't talk a lot, but it was clear to Cameron from the way he and his wife interacted that they communicated on a plane where words weren't necessary. They sat close together, and seemed to move and think as one.

So it shouldn't have come as any surprise to him when Hunter invited him to shoot a game of pool and leave the ladies to their "girl talk." And sure enough, they hadn't more than racked the balls when Hunter launched into the advisory Cameron was sure Daffy had asked him to deliver.

As soon as the guys had left the room, Daffy said, "So how are things?" She stressed the last word.

Conscious of Erika's precocious ears, Jonni said, "Fine. School starts in two days. I'm looking forward to it."

"Of course you are," Daffy said, making a face and pointing toward the doorway. "But you know what I mean."

Jonni sighed. "Have you ever wondered whether the things you plan are the things you really want to have happen?"

"What do you mean?" Her twin tucked her feet under her on the loveseat and propped her chin on one hand.

"I'm quite determined to pursue the path I've charted for my life, to put it back together again and earn my degree and find a career. I'm as determined about this plan as I was about making David the perfect wife. But sometimes . . ."

Daffy nodded and tapped her chest with one slender finger so like Jonni's own. "Sometimes you want to forget about your head and listen to your heart, right?"

Jonni nodded.

"But you're afraid to?"

She nodded a second time.

"Don't be afraid, Mommy," Erika said. "You always say the bogeyman can't get me."

Jonni smiled. "Thank you, sweetie. I'm not scared afraid."

"Just happy afraid?" Daffy said.

"That's probably a good way to describe it," Jonni said, thinking wistfully that if Cameron did ask her again to marry him, she still didn't know that she could bring herself to say yes. Between her plans and her fear of being hurt, it was much safer to stay her course.

Not, of course, that he showed any signs of repeating his impetuous request a third time.

Not that night, or the next day, which, Jonni learned to her shock, was the last day Cameron would be filming at her house.

She was in the breakfast room, along with Isolde, Sunny, and Erika, comparing the stacks of textbooks they'd purchased that afternoon at the campus bookstore, when Boswell, garbed in his requisite solid black, knocked on the door and then strolled on in.

"Mrs. DeVries," he said, "I wanted to let you know we're finishing ahead of schedule. We will, of course, honor our contract for the length of time specified. The director has been extremely pleased with our efforts, and we're moving on to some second unit locations."

Moving on? Jonni wasn't sure she was ready to hear those words, and especially not from Boswell. Where was Cameron? Why hadn't he told her? Why hadn't it occurred to her to ask him how much longer he'd be in town? Why did it matter so much to her?

"I hope you're not displeased," Boswell said. "I thought you'd be happy to have your home back to normal. The cleanup crew will move in after we finish a few retakes tomorrow."

Jonni felt everyone else in the room staring at her. "Thank you, Boswell," she said. "It's been a very pleasant experience."

"I'll send one of my assistants around to check with you after the cleaning has been completed. We do pride ourselves on a job well done."

And with that, he headed back from where he'd come. Funny, Jonni thought, standing there next to her stack of textbooks and assigned novels, but the day he and his black-draped assistants had knocked on her front door seemed like a lifetime ago, rather than a matter of weeks.

"Did you know they were leaving?" Isolde asked the

question, and Jonni interpreted "they" as meaning "Cameron."

Jonni shook her head. "This book looks fascinating," she said, pointing to a treatise on literary criticism whose title had blurred slightly.

Darn it, the last thing Jonquil Landry DeVries would do was shed a tear just because she was disappointed. She'd been through worse, far worse.

"Mine is more fun," Erika said, holding up a copy of *Green Eggs and Ham*.

"Would you like me to take Erika for a walk?" Isolde asked the question softly.

Jonni was grateful for her nanny's sensitivity, but the last thing she wanted was time alone with her feelings. Was Cameron even going to come say good-bye to her? Or was it as she had feared from the start—she was his distraction, his casual amusement while he was in town for the film.

She dabbed the back of her hand at her eyes. "I think I've got some mascara in my eye."

Sunny folded her hands across her chest and shook her head and sighed. "That man's gone and broke your heart, hasn't he, Miz Jonni?"

"Don't be silly," Jonni said, realizing as she protested that she had indeed lost her heart over Cameron Scott. She'd thrown herself at him, wanting one night of passion, and, boy, had she gotten more than she bargained for!

The doorbell chimed.

Jonni dropped the heavy treatise, just missing her foot.

"Careful, Mommy," Erika said. "Books have feelings, too."

Despite her muddle of emotions, Jonni had to smile. "You're precious." She hugged her close, not realizing Sunny had headed toward the front of the house to answer the door.

Cameron found her like that, her arms around her daughter, with Isolde watching them from across the large breakfast table, concern on her face.

He shouldn't have come. He had made up his mind to leave right away, and seeing Jonquil again was only going to make it harder to stick to his guns and follow Hunter's advice. He sure hoped Hunter knew what he was talking about, advising him that the best way to win Jonni was to return to L.A., ensuring that she would miss him terribly. Meanwhile he'd prove his loyalty and devotion, and then return to sweep her off her feet. Hunter had assured him that absence made the heart grow fonder, and that's the ploy he'd used to finally convince his wife to trust her heart to him.

Hesitating in the doorway, he turned, thinking he'd just back out of the room. Given two minutes alone with her, he'd hand her his heart on a saucer and not leave until she agreed to marry him.

He reckoned without Sunny, coming up behind him and nudging him onward.

"Look who's here," the housekeeper announced.

Jonquil turned around and took a step in his direction. Then she stopped, leaned over, and picked up a thick book from the floor.

"Homework already?" he said.

"I like to be prepared," Jonquil said.

Damn, but Hunter was right. Jonquil wasn't going to run off into the sunset with him. Managing a grin, he said, "So I guess you wouldn't want to spend a few days in L.A. this week?"

Something he could only think of as a shadow flitted across her precious face, and Cameron knew as sure as he knew his own name that he'd said the wrong thing.

Jonni didn't know what she'd expected, Cameron down on one knee in front of her daughter, nanny, and housekeeper, proposing marriage? Still, the almost off-hand invitation struck her as very off-key. "School is going to be very hectic," she said, sounding every bit as prim as she had the night they'd met at the reception. "The dean's office is letting me carry extra hours so I can fit in all my requirements before next May's commencement."

"That's great," he said. "Maybe you can visit then."

"Road trip," Isolde said.

Erika giggled. "Road trip," she repeated, looking up from the pages of her Dr. Suess book to wave a hand at Cameron.

"I'm headed to the airport now," Cameron said.

Jonni caught her breath. She was strangling, trying so hard to be so nonchalant. "I guess you're in a hurry to get home and back to normal."

He shook his head. His eyes were dark and almost pleading. "We're shooting the rest of the scenes on the MegaFilms lot. Duty calls."

"Of course," Jonni said. "Let me walk you to the door. Erika, say good-bye to Mr. Scott."

Erika waved again, marking her place in the book with one finger. "Bye, Mr. Scott. Next time you visit, will you read this book to me?"

He walked over, bent, and kissed the top of her head. "I promise," he said.

Erika smiled.

Jonni tried finding breath in her lungs. She couldn't let his leaving matter so much to her. If she did, she was likely to embarrass them both by flinging herself at him. Her mother had raised a lady, and a lady waited to be asked for her hand in marriage.

"Flynn's out front," Cameron said, shaking hands with Isolde and then Sunny.

Jonni headed for the kitchen door, Cameron so close by her side yet so distant.

Neither one of them spoke until they reached the front door. He reached out and put his hand on the knob, and she remembered kissing each of his fingers, telling him how and why she liked him. Meeting his eyes, she said, "Let us know how you're doing."

He nodded and handed her a business card. "It's my home number," he said, "and Flynn's office. If you need anything, call."

"Sure," she said, knowing she wouldn't.

"Jonquil," he said, and then stopped.

"Yes?" Her heart leaped. She knew he wanted to say more.

A horn honked out front.

"I'll be back," he said, and bent and kissed her mouth quickly. And then he was gone.

Jonni stood there for a long time, her fingers pressed against her lips. When she could manage a semblance of self-control, she returned to the breakfast room, just in time to hear Sunny telling Isolde that they hadn't seen the last of Mr. Scott.

Jonni paused just outside the door. Isolde was saying, "I agree. It's funny and kind of sad, too, but there goes a guy we thought was going to be a Butt and he turns out to be a Heart."

Two months later Jonni had made it successfully through her midterm exams. She was lounging in the den, getting ready to watch the reading show on public television with Erika. She'd been so busy she'd almost learned not to miss Cameron.

Though he didn't make it easy. Every time she'd assume he'd forgotten about her, she'd open the mailbox to find a scrawled postcard, usually a scene from southern California, but last week's had been postmarked in Calgary. And yesterday, to Erika's delight, the UPS driver had delivered a huge box, addressed to Miss E. DeVries.

She'd torn it open to find a four-foot-tall Curious George doll.

Erika was sitting beside the monkey now, evidently preparing to teach the stuffed animal how to read. Jonni smothered a smile. Sure, of course, right, she mocked herself. Of course she'd learned not to miss Cameron.

He never called and evidently he didn't believe in email. Jonni sighed and switched the television on.

The show was under way. She returned to her thoughts.

"Mommy, look, it's Mr. Scott!" Erika called out, delight in her voice.

Jonni swiveled her head, expecting to see him walking into the room.

"On the TV," Erika said, pointing.

Sure enough, there he was, the guest star reader of the day.

Jonni's jaw dropped.

He'd done it for her, because she'd mentioned the show to him.

And suddenly she couldn't stand it anymore, this being apart from him. She didn't care about being ladylike or restrained or about wearing her heart on her sleeve. If she went to him, and he brushed her aside, well, she'd think of something to do to break through his protective defenses.

Sweet Cameron. He was no doubt as afraid of being hurt as she was. Watching him on the screen, hearing his voice, and soaking up that gleam in his eyes she knew so well, Jonni knew she couldn't sit back and wait.

It was impulsive. Impetuous. But she wasn't taking time to think things through. She was going to L.A.

Jonni was on the phone with her mother the minute the show ended, arranging for Erika to spend the weekend with her grandparents. She'd already told Isolde she could have two days off, to recover from her own midterm crunch.

Before she could change her mind, Jonni booked a flight to LAX, threw some clothes in an overnight bag, and headed first to her parents' home across the lake, and then to the airport.

She was airborne before she considered a fact that underscored the value of advance planning. She didn't have Cameron's address. The card he'd given her had his phone and Flynn's office phone.

Well, that was enough. She'd call Flynn first so she could surprise Cameron at home.

She took a deep breath and tried to watch the movie, one of Julia Roberts's romantic comedies. The happily-ever-after story left Jonni nervously shot through with anticipation, and by the time she landed, collected a rental car, and made her way through the plugs of traffic heading into the center of the city, she was doubting her own sanity.

Flynn was taking a meeting, his assistant reported when Jonni rang his office on her cell phone. So Jonni asked for the address and directions, hoping she could remember the string of freeway numbers the woman recited.

Eventually, she found her way to Flynn's plush yet understated suite of offices on Sunset Boulevard. The woman at the reception desk could have doubled for any of Boswell's black-clad wraiths.

Smoothing her unruly hair and rumpled linen suit, Jonni agreed that she could wait for Mr. Lawrence.

The receptionist offered her bottled water and a crystal glass. Jonni accepted it gratefully, and after half an hour, was wondering whether she could wangle Cameron's address out of the woman instead of waiting for Flynn.

Just then, Flynn came out from behind the mahogany doors, a welcoming, if curious, smile on his face.

"What a nice surprise," he said.

Jonni rose and he kissed her on both cheeks. "Hello," she said. "I hope I'm not imposing. I just need a few minutes of your time."

"Of course. Come on into my office." At the reception desk, he paused and said, "Hold my calls."

Inside his spacious office, Jonni accepted the seat he indicated, a broad leather chair across from one of the most luxurious black leather couches she'd ever seen.

Flynn evidently knew something about making money. But money was the last thing on her mind. Jonni sat forward and said, "I've come to see Cameron, only I don't know his address, and I'm hoping you can give it to me."

"Oh, dear," Flynn said.

Jonni gripped her purse. "Does he not want to see me?" She heard the wistful tone in her voice.

Flynn leaned forward from where he'd perched on the edge of the sofa. "If you don't mind me saying so, you're the best thing that's happened to Cameron Scott since the two of us became buddies."

Jonni smiled at him. "That's a rare compliment."

"Well, I mean it. You should see him, since he's been back from New Orleans. The guy's taking acting lessons, for Pete's sake. He's doing theater, off-Melrose, actually learning to be a real actor, something he never had to do. Something he still doesn't have to do, but he wants to now. He says he wants to make something of himself." Flynn was shaking his head. "And I couldn't be prouder."

"Oh, that's wonderful," Jonni said. No wonder he hadn't called or visited. He had been as busy as she was. "May I have his address?"

"I'll give it to you," Flynn said, "but it won't do you any good right now."

Had he taken up with someone else? Carefully, Jonni said, "Why not?"

"He's in New Orleans, reshooting one of the street location scenes for *Mister Benjamin*." Flynn looked worried. "I thought for sure he would have told you he was coming."

"Oh," Jonni said. "Has he been there long?"

"Probably arrived while you were taking off," Flynn said, after glancing at his watch. "And he's coming back the day after tomorrow."

"Why, this is terrible!" Jonni leaped up. "I've got to go." She grabbed Flynn by the shoulders and kissed him on both cheeks. "Thank you," she said, already on her way out the door.

Two o'clock in the morning and still no one home. Cameron slumped behind the wheel of his rental car, staring at the dark windows of Jonquil's house. He'd been by several times, with no results. No one answered the phone or the bell at either the front or side gates.

He leaned forward and beat his head against the steering wheel. Dammit, he'd stayed away as long as he could. From the moment he'd stepped from the plane and onto the sidewalk, his time with Jonquil had flooded his mind, his senses. Even if she sent him packing afterward, he was going to drop to his knees and beg her to marry him. He had no pride left.

Being his wife didn't mean she had to drop out of school. As a matter of fact, he would insist she finish, the same way he planned to pursue the new interests he'd taken up since realizing life held so much more than being everyone's favorite bad boy.

Cameron lifted his head from the steering wheel. He'd leave a note on the gate and ask to see her tomorrow. He had to be up for filming along the river at six. As it was, he'd barely get any sleep.

He scrawled his name and hotel number on the back of his flight confirmation, got out of the car, and tested the gate again, hoping illogically he'd find it unlocked this time. Just as he reached for the mailbox set inside the bars of the fence, bright lights flooded on from behind him and Cameron heard a menacing voice shout, "Freeze! Police!"

"Aw, shit," he said, turning around.

He heard the click of a revolver and realized his mistake. Lifting his hands quickly over his head, he said, "I'm harmless. I can explain."

"Yeah, yeah," the policeman said. "That's what they all say."

"But it's true," Cameron said. "Look, nothing personal, but I do not want to visit your city's finest hotel again."

"Repeat offender, eh?" The officer unclasped a pair of handcuffs from his leather belt. "I've been watching you case this house for two hours now."

A lone car drove slowly up the street in their direction.

"That better not be an accomplice," the officer said.

"That would be impossible," Cameron said, "as I'm no criminal."

"Yeah, yeah," the man repeated. "Turn around and put your hands behind your back." He snapped the cuffs on.

The car stopped, right in the middle of the street. The driver's door flew open.

"Cameron? Cameron, is that you?"

Jonquil ran toward him, her arms outstretched.

"Halt," called the officer.

"Stop!" Cameron shouted, afraid that the policeman might misinterpret Jonquil's rush in his direction.

She froze. And then slowly, she started to laugh. And she laughed even harder, tears running down her cheeks as she walked toward them. "It's okay, Officer," she said. "This is my house and this man is my—"

She paused, and cocked her head to one side. "My fiancé?"

Cameron dropped to his knees, his hands cuffed behind him. "You mean you will marry me?"

"Nothing would make me happier," she said, and running forward, threw her arms around him.

The officer holstered his gun and looked from Jonquil back to Cameron. "I've heard of shotgun weddings," he said, "but this here's a new one on me."

Epilogue

Protected by a canopy from the sun reflecting off the
swimming pool, Jonni marked her place in the manu-
script of *The Adventures of Sniggle and Snaggle*, her first
children's story, and glanced over at Cameron. He, too,
was reading, engrossed in the script for the Quentin
Grandy film slated to start production next week. She
couldn't help but smile as she studied his face, lost in
concentration. They'd been married three months now,
since the day after her graduation from Tulane. Sometimes she had to pinch herself to make sure she was Jonquil Livaudais Landry DeVries Scott, and not some
fairy-tale princess.

Certainly her surroundings, Cameron's Bel Air estate,
were that of a dream. They were spending the summer
there, and this was their last week before Jonni and
Erika headed back to New Orleans and Cameron flew to
Alaska to begin the new film. Jonni would join him there
for a week after Isolde returned from her vacation and
Erika had started first grade.

Cameron lowered his script, and Jonni knew despite

the dark glasses he wore that his gaze was fixed on her. A smile hovered on her lips, as she remembered how he'd kissed her awake earlier that day.

Cameron grinned.

Jonni couldn't help but blush. "You read my mind so well," she said.

He stretched out a hand, and she slipped hers into it.

From the pool, Erika called, "Look what I can do!" She clambered out, took a few steps away, covered her nose with her fingers, and jumped in feet first. Droplets of pool water spritzed their feet.

Cameron let go of her hand and applauded. Paddling to the edge and hopping out, Erika dashed water from her face and grinned. "Thank you. Thank you," she said, bowing, before repeating her performance.

"She's growing up so fast," Cameron said. "At the beginning of summer she couldn't even tread water."

"Watch me again, Pere," Erika called.

"I love it when she calls you that," Jonni said. The French name for father had been Jonni's mother's suggestion for what Erika should call Cameron, as Erika was starting to study the language of the Livaudais branch of the family.

"I do, too," Cameron said, taking her hand again. "You and Erika have turned this hunk of a house into a home, and I treasure that more than I can find ways to say."

Jonni squeezed his hand and decided there was no better opening for the news she'd been waiting to share with him.

"You know how you've taught me that Hollywood loves a sequel?"

"Yep." His eyes narrowed. "You're not thinking of becoming a producer, are you?"

"Not exactly." She couldn't help but giggle. "Not movies, anyway." She laid a hand across her tummy, gently mounding once more.

"If not movies, then what? You're already writing a book." A funny look, something between awe and sea-sickness, danced across his face. Suddenly, Cameron shot upward. His script hit the deck. "Are you telling me that you're—that we're—?" He pointed to her tummy.

Jonni nodded.

Unable to speak, Cameron moved over and sat beside her on her lounge chair, cradling her in his arms.

"I hope that's okay," Jonni said quietly.

"Okay?" Cameron knew he was grinning from ear to ear. He kissed her on her precious mouth and said, "I was going to ask you tonight if it would be okay if we started planning a baby brother or sister for Erika, but I was worried you would want to wait."

Jonni held him even more tightly. "And here I was afraid that *you* might feel it was too soon after our wedding. I mean, I'll be waddling around and—"

"And there won't be a more beautiful sight in all of Hollywood," Cameron said. "Or New Orleans."

"What are you two talking about?" Erika had climbed out of the pool and stood in front of them, wrapping a towel around her shoulders.

Cameron and Jonni exchanged glances, and then smiles. "Your mother and I have something to tell you." Jonni patted the lounge, inviting Erika to join them.

Cameron lifted her up onto his lap, and the three of them sat there, a family together.

Jonni began, "Remember last year when you asked me if you were going to have a baby brother or sister . . ."

COMING IN JULY—
SUMMER'S HOTTEST HEROES!

STEALING THE BRIDE by Elizabeth Boyle
An Avon Romantic Treasure
The Marquis of Templeton has faced every sort of danger in his work for the King, but chasing after a wayward spinster who's run off with the wrong man hardly seems worthy of his considerable talents. But the tempestuous Lady Diana Fordham is about to turn Temple's life upside down . . .

WITH HER LAST BREATH by Cait London
An Avon Contemporary Romance
Nick Alessandro didn't think he would ever recover from a shattering tragedy, until he meets Maggie Chantel. But just when they are starting to find love together, someone waiting in the shadows is determined that Maggie love *no one* ever again. Now Nick has to find the killer—before the killer gets to Maggie.

SOARING EAGLE'S EMBRACE by Karen Kay
An Avon Romance
The Blackfeet brave trusts no white man—or woman—but the spirits have spoken, wedding him in a powerful night vision to a golden-red haired enchantress. Kali Wallace is spellbound by the proud warrior but will their fiery love be a dream come true . . . or doomed for heartbreak?

THE PRINCESS AND HER PIRATE
by Lois Greiman
An Avon Romance
Not since his adventurous days on the high seas has Cairn MacTavish, the Pirate Lord, felt the sort of excitement gorgeous hellion Megs inspires. Though she claims not to be the notorious thief, he knows she is hiding something—and each claim of innocence that comes from her lush, inviting lips only inflames his desires.

REL 0603